Praise for *Do No Harm*

"Gripping and unflinching, *Do No Harm* explores the ferocity of a mother's love—and shows, in heartbreaking detail, how she'll risk everything to save her child."

—Sarah Pekkanen, *New York Times* bestselling author of *The Wife Between Us* and *You Are Not Alone*

"*Do No Harm* is a pulse-pounding deep dive into the dark heart of addiction. The stakes couldn't be higher in this smart, breathlessly paced, and emotional novel about love, family, and how far we'll go when our child's life hangs in the balance. Riveting, ripped from the headlines, and not to be missed."

—Lisa Unger, *New York Times* bestselling author of *Confessions on the 7:45*

"Christina McDonald has a real talent for bringing suburban domestic suspense to life and showcases it to great effect in *Do No Harm*. Tense, taut, and absolutely unmissable, you'll find yourself wondering how far YOU would go to save your child's life."

—J. T. Ellison, *New York Times* bestselling author of *Lie to Me*

"McDonald takes the heart-wrenching premise that has become her trademark and ratchets it up a notch in *Do No Harm*, blurring the lines between good and evil in a doctor desperate to save her sick child. A gripping, emotional roller coaster with a sting in the tail."

—Kimberly Belle, internationally bestselling author of *The Marriage Lie*

"Gripping and timely."

—*Book Riot*

"*Do No Harm* takes on the air of a cat-and-mouse thriller, with each character trying to outwit the other and come out on top. Drawing upon the searingly timely topic of the opioid crisis and adding some much-needed context to the severity, classism, and racism of the issue, McDonald pens a suspenseful thrill ride that is as socially aware as it is meticulously plotted . . . Instantly gripping and full of gasp-worthy twists, the book is clever, tense, and utterly addictive. You won't stop until you've turned the last page."

—Bookreporter

"Grace Fraser and *Do No Harm*'s Emma have a lot more in common than what meets the eye . . . From the outside, selling opioids sounds like a horrible and irresponsible idea, but readers will quickly become fans of Emma, Christina McDonald's protagonist . . ."

—PopSugar

"*Do No Harm* is a cross between *Breaking Bad* and Kohlberg's theory of moral development."

—CrimeReads

"[A] complex medical thriller that will have the reader asking themselves what they would do if they were in Emma's position . . . McDonald explores the many perspectives of the opioid crisis with insight and compassion . . . Readers looking for a fast-paced and emotional story will enjoy *Do No Harm* and be thinking about it long after the last page is read."

—*Seattle Book Review*

"This raw, emotional story echoes fear that would result when denied necessary available health treatment due to lack of funds. And it brings into question how far a parent can morally go to save their child."

—*Authorlink*

"A deftly woven blend of suspense, family life, amateur sleuthing, and an opioid epidemic, *Do No Harm* is an inherently fascinating and engaging novel by Christina McDonald that examines whether the ends ever justify the means—even for a desperate mother."

—Midwest Book Review

"In her suspenseful new thriller *Do No Harm*, Christina McDonald brings a controversial topic right out of the real-world headlines and displays a fantastic ability to truly examine it from all sides . . . *Do No Harm* is an absolute page-turner! McDonald has once again perfectly balanced little twists that the reader can feel clever for figuring out with big, sudden, gasp-out-loud moments. Fans of the author's previous books, *Behind Every Lie* and *The Night Olivia Fell*, should be ready to jump right into this intense new thriller!"

—The Nerd Daily

"*Do No Harm* poses morally gray questions . . . McDonald's novel doesn't just tell a story of a doctor trying to use the opioid crisis as a quick payday, she examines different angles of the crisis and how it plays out for different people, exploring who benefits, who suffers, and who is left behind."

—*Fairfield Citizen*

Praise for *Behind Every Lie*

"*Behind Every Lie* is a deep, suspenseful novel packed with family secrets. Christina McDonald has a true gift for creating characters that are so well developed, it feels like you know them. An outstanding achievement!"

—Samantha Downing, author of the #1 international bestseller *My Lovely Wife*

"In *Behind Every Lie*, Christina McDonald brilliantly intertwines page-turning suspense with jaw-dropping family secrets. An emotionally charged domestic thriller that is sure to please!"

—Wendy Walker, national bestselling author of *The Night Before*

"A riveting collision of motherhood and memory—where a sinister and inescapable past haunts those struggling to make sense of their lives and protect their children. What's *Behind Every Lie* is a shocking truth—and for readers, a jaw-dropping, page-turning whirlwind of a thriller. Instantly captivating and endlessly surprising! Christina McDonald is a star."

—Hank Phillippi Ryan, *USA Today* bestselling author of *The Murder List*

"A clever, tense, and absorbing novel—this tale of family secrets had me racing toward the final pages."

—Emma Rous, bestselling author of *The Au Pair*

"Christina McDonald follows up her smashing debut *The Night Olivia Fell* with another winner. McDonald starts with a bang, then builds the action steadily, a gradual unfolding of secrets and lies that will have you constantly switching alliances. Read it like I did, in one sitting and straight through to the end, because you won't want to put this one down."

—Kimberly Belle, international bestselling author of *Dear Wife*

"Christina McDonald's *Behind Every Lie* is a layered, gut-wrenching domestic thriller that explores the complexities of mothers and daughters and the secrets families keep. Smart and intense, and with more than enough twists to give you whiplash, McDonald's beautiful, emotional storytelling will leave you breathless. I don't think I exhaled until the end."

—Jennifer Hillier, author of *Jar of Hearts*,
ITW Award winner for Best Novel

"Christina McDonald's *Behind Every Lie* is a cleverly plotted and emotionally charged page-turner about memory, trusting yourself, grieving, and letting go. Family secrets run deep in this compelling exploration of how far a mother will go to protect her child. Full of twists and turns, this is domestic suspense at its best!"

—Karen Katchur, bestselling author of *River Bodies*

"In *Behind Every Lie*, a lightning-strike survivor discovers that memories are fallible, identities are fungible, and she can't trust anyone—including herself. With nuanced and dubiously trustworthy characters, dual timelines revealing decades of secrets, and a tension-packed plot, Christina McDonald has crafted an engrossing and utterly addictive thriller. I couldn't turn the pages fast enough!"

—Kathleen Barber, author of *Truth Be Told*

"Addictive and emotionally resonant, *Behind Every Lie* is a twisty, fast-paced thriller with secrets nestled inside secrets. Nothing is as it seems in this story exploring the sorrow and strength of brokenness, and with complex characters and a relentlessly compelling plot, you'll be unable to stop reading it—or forget it once you do."

—Megan Collins, author of *The Winter Sister*

"[An] intriguing suspense novel . . . McDonald weaves together Eva and Kat's narratives, which span past and present, to create a compulsively readable and fast-paced yarn that explores the lingering effects of trauma and abuse as well as the complex bonds between mothers and daughters. Readers who enjoy character-driven thrillers will be pleased."

—*Publishers Weekly*

"Told in alternating narratives from Eva's traumatic life and her mother's mysterious past, the story twists and turns with one shocking revelation after another until it threatens to careen out of control. But behind every lie there is always a reason, and there is a satisfying ending once everyone's hand is played out."

—*Booklist*

"*Behind Every Lie* is a page-turner and an entertaining read. Many readers will enjoy Eva's breathless race of discovery and journey of survival."

—Bookreporter

Praise for *The Night Olivia Fell*

"*The Night Olivia Fell* by Christina McDonald is a stunning thriller that instantly grabbed me by the throat and wouldn't let go until the final, poignant sentence. McDonald artfully brings to the page the emotionally fraught, complex relationship between mother and daughter in this atmospheric, absorbing page-turner. *The Night Olivia Fell* cracked my heart into a million pieces and then slowly pieced it back together again."

—Heather Gudenkauf, *New York Times* bestselling author of *The Weight of Silence* and *Not a Sound*

"In Christina McDonald's *The Night Olivia Fell*, Abi gets the call every mother fears: her daughter has fallen from a bridge and is brain-dead . . . but was it an accident or a crime? McDonald reveals the answer in steady, page-turning increments, a gradual unfolding of truths and long-held secrets that culminates in a heart-wrenching resolution. A suspenseful debut that packs an emotional punch."

—Kimberly Belle, international bestselling author of
Three Days Missing and *The Marriage Lie*

"I was absolutely hooked; it was such an emotional read that I was broken by the end. Heartbreaking and thrilling at the same time."

—Jenny Blackhurst, bestselling author of *How I Lost You*

"Beautifully written and moving, with characters I felt I knew, *The Night Olivia Fell* is a stunning debut that kept me guessing right until the final, heartbreaking twist."

—Claire Douglas, bestselling author of *The Sisters*, *Local Girl Missing*,
and *Last Seen Alive*

"Christina McDonald's *The Night Olivia Fell* takes a mother's worst nightmare to a whole new level. This is an intense, twisting, heartbreaking thriller that explores in painful detail the consequences of family secrets. The reader will be riveted until the final page . . . and may even feel a bit of hope when all is said and done. Don't miss this one!"

—David Bell, bestselling author of *Somebody's Daughter*

"Christina McDonald has crafted an emotionally charged mystery that will leave readers equally gut-wrenched and gripped. *The Night Olivia Fell* welcomes a talented new addition to the world of domestic suspense."

—Mary Kubica, *New York Times* bestselling author of *The Good Girl*
and *When the Lights Go Out*

"[A] complex, emotionally intense first novel . . . Fans of twisty domestic suspense novels will be rewarded."

—*Publishers Weekly*

"McDonald ratchets up the suspense with every chapter, including plenty of gasp-worthy twists and turns as Abi and Olivia's story pushes toward its devastating conclusion. The suspense is supplemented by relationships of surprising depth and tenderness, providing balance and nuance to the story. A worthy debut from an up-and-coming domestic-suspense author; readers who enjoy mother-daughter stories in the genre should line up for this one."

—*Booklist* (starred review)

"This book is a tearjerker, so have tissues at hand. A well-structured story of how lying corrupts from the start that will keep pages turning."

—*Library Journal*

"A thrilling page-turner you have to read."

—PopSugar

THESE
STILL BLACK
WATERS

OTHER TITLES BY
CHRISTINA McDONALD

Do No Harm
Behind Every Lie
The Night Olivia Fell

THESE STILL BLACK WATERS

A JESS LAMBERT THRILLER

CHRISTINA McDONALD

THOMAS & MERCER

Published by Thomas & Mercer, Seattle

www.apub.com

Amazon, the Amazon logo, and Thomas & Mercer are trademarks of Amazon.com, Inc., or its affiliates.

ISBN-13: 9781662511615 (paperback)
ISBN-13: 9781662511622 (digital)

Cover design by Sarah Congdon
Cover image: © Naoki Kim, Ethan Daniels, kosmos111 / Shutterstock; © Rialto Images/Stocksy United; © Velvetfish / Getty Images

Printed in the United States of America

For my sons,
Adam and Aidan.
I thank the stars and moon above
For all your sweet and perfect love.

Chapter 1

The body cooled quickly on the ground beside me.

The night was deep, the woods thick enough that the moon did not interrupt my work. I'd always equated darkness with unknowing. The unconscious, I believed, was unknown until something crossed into the light of awareness. A wood at night, as an example. What was ahead was obscured until you moved close enough for it to be illuminated. But tonight, although I worked in darkness, I knew exactly why I was here.

I'd made my choices.

That's all life was: a series of choices. That was what it all came down to in the end. It didn't just happen. We made our choices. The good. The bad. The mundane. Free will.

We made choices every day, both knowingly and unknowingly. From simple ones like what to eat for dinner to bigger ones like whether to take that promotion we knew would move us across the country. Some choices we regret. Some we are proud of. Losses. Gains. Successes. Failures. Friends. Enemies. We have the power of choice. The only inescapable thing is the inevitability of choice.

In other words, the past may be dead, but it is our choice if we bury it.

I sat on the cold dirt floor next to the body and extracted an item from my pocket. I turned it over in my hand. The colors were dull, the edges covered with dirt. It was small. Too small to carry such destruction. Wasn't it funny how the smallest things could carry the greatest weight?

I closed my eyes and let the past play over the screen of my eyelids. Somewhere far away, I heard the sharp whoop of a police siren. Whoop, whoop. And the wind rustling in the trees, like the hissing of a snake.

I needed to leave, but I didn't. Not yet. I listened, the sounds a melody, a rhythm, a poem, and I let myself be carried away until they swelled too big, like the surf, louder and louder, a cacophony of noise. I clapped my hands over my ears, trying to focus on the image of her face. It was the only thing that gave me peace.

If—when—people find out what I've done, I hope they understand that, at least. Why I made these choices. Why I had to do it.

It was all for her.

Later, people might say that I snapped. I lost my mind. Blew up, broke down, went crazy. All the mundane adjectives people use when they don't know the inside of a person.

But that wasn't true. I'd made my choices with a clear mind in the cold light of day. I knew exactly what I did and why I did it.

I often thought of life as an echo. Stand on the edge of any abyss and shout into the dark, your echo will return. What you send out comes back. You could choose to do what was right or you could choose to do what was wrong, but when you chose wrong, rest assured, those ghosts would come back to haunt you.

Choices have consequences.

They chose wrong.

Chapter 2

NEVE

We don't take much with us when we leave. There doesn't seem to be a point.

What nobody tells you about being the victim of a home invasion is you never know when they're coming back. And so we left.

That's why Ash and I stand almost empty-handed in front of the creaking old Victorian house of my childhood summers.

I say "almost" because I'm holding a glossy-leafed plant Eli got me for our ten-year anniversary. Ash named the plant Priscilla years ago, when she was still a cute kid and not an angsty teenager. Priss the pinstripe calathea.

I set Priss on the gravel drive, and we stare up at the house. It looks like something out of a Brontë novel looming above us, a brooding presence with shiny pale bricks and washed-out, jutting attic dormers and dark, spiky turrets. The roof is steep and gabled, the windows long and narrow. The front porch is almost hidden beneath a sweep of ivy that stretches over the brick.

Above the front door in elegant script: *Dullahan House*.

It is different and yet the same. The house. The driveway. The rustling trees. Standing in the harsh, hot sunlight, staring up at it, I feel the strangest thing. A bizarre disturbance in the air. A restlessness. Like when your skin knows a storm is coming, or the prickly waves of something electric wash over you.

"So this is it." Ash looks underwhelmed. "How long since you've been here?"

"Over twenty years. We came every summer when I was a kid. It's been in my family for years."

I have my reasons for not returning after that last summer, but some things are better forgotten than spoken of. Life goes on whether you dwell on the past or not.

"It's nice, right?" I say.

Ash's lips twist, a hand on one hip. "Whatever. I don't have the same disease you do, Mom."

"What's that supposed to mean?"

"You legit have denialitis. Like, *look* at this place! It's totally falling apart."

I look again at Dullahan House. "Maybe it's a little . . . shabby, but . . ."

My voice trails off as I take a second look. The pale green trim is cracked and peeling. Some of the brickwork is crumbling. The wooden porch is listing to the side, the shrubbery a little wilder than it should be. I suppose I see what she means. It has a sort of . . . deserted air about it.

It's the windows. There are too many of them. As if the house is staring at me. Something about it is uninviting, a little stark. A shiver rakes over me despite the midday sun beating down on my arms. Because I of all people know that appearances can be deceiving.

"It's fine," I say, because it is. It's still perfectly pleasing. The front lawn has recently been mowed by the property management company, even if the grass is getting a bit scorched. The gravel driveway has been weeded. "It's just not been used much lately."

We've had it available as a vacation rental since my mother went into a care home, but since the pandemic hit, it's just sat there empty.

Ash rolls her eyes. "Whatever."

My body tenses. I wish Eli were here to provide a buffer between us. But now it's just Ash and me and this house, the only place I could escape to after everything that's happened. All we have is what's ahead of us. A new start. A new home. A new life.

"Hey, would you rather have a mullet or no toothpaste for the rest of your life?" I ask as a way of lightening the mood. Would You Rather is something we've played since Ash was little. I like it because, like life, it's a game of choice, and theoretical choices are a lot more fun than real ones.

Ash thinks about this. "A mullet. I could just put it in a ponytail."

I laugh. Down the road, an ornate black gate creaks open, the shrill, metallic shriek carrying fast under the still, hot sun. The gate encloses this lakeside community of six houses, all made with the same grand old Victorian architecture: three, including mine, sitting directly on the lake and three across the street on a slope.

A BMW rolls through the gates and parks in a driveway across from us. The house is smaller than mine but still beautiful with leaded windows and classic Victorian features.

A woman gets out. She is middle-aged and shaped like a carrot, with scowling, argumentative eyes. Her dark hair is scraped into a high, round bun, and she's wearing full workout gear, like she's been to the gym.

A small dog hops out of the car, some sort of Maltese mix with cropped white fur. He catches sight of us and darts across the road as the woman gathers groceries from her trunk. I kneel, my hand extended so he can sniff it. He licks my fingertips and wags his tail.

"Hey, sweetie!" I croon.

I think of my dog back home, Molly, her silky black-and-white fur, her trusting brown eyes, and all the animals at the vet where I worked, and I feel an ache for everything I've lost.

"Toby, come!" the woman snaps, her eyes skittering over us. Toby obediently trots back to her, and a second later, they disappear inside.

Ash turns away from me, her blue-black hair ruffling as a hot gust of wind kicks up. She cut it a few weeks before, a short punk-rock bob with a funky little line shaved into the side. I could tell at the time that Eli secretly hated it, but I liked that Ash was confident enough to pull off something so bold. I think it's brave. *She* is brave. Brave and courageous. The bravest person I've ever known.

An eerie quietness descends. I don't like it. It reminds me that bad things have happened here. At one point in my life, I swore I would never come back, and yet here I am. I wonder, not for the first time, if returning was the right choice.

"You're going to love it here." I sound too bright, shiny as a pearl in the sunlight. "The lake is out back, and there's a beach and a dock and kayaks. Plus, there's all the woods to explore. And there's an old boathouse down by the lake. We can get outside more. Go hiking or swimming. Whatever you want."

This is wishful thinking. Ever since the home invasion, Ash mostly stays locked in her room, where she feels safe. I'm hoping being here can bring a semblance of normality back to our lives.

Ash's green eyes pin me with a hard glare, forcing me to see the angry red scar the bullet scorched along her hairline near her temple. "Whatever I want except see Dad."

I want to be honest with her, but what's the point when I'm not even honest about the things I've done? I've held my secrets close for so long, they've become like a second skin. But secrets turn into lies when they're spoken out loud, so I measure my reply carefully before giving it.

"It won't be forever, Ash."

So often in parenting, love and guilt are intermingled, nearly impossible to separate. I should do this; I shouldn't do that. It's never clear until you look back. Hindsight is twenty-twenty, as they say.

"The lady from the property management company will be here in about half an hour." I set Priss in the shade of the porch and grab Ash's hand. "Come on. I'll show you the lake."

We push through a path running along the side of the house. Ash's black combat boots, too hot for this weather, crunch over the gravel. We emerge into the backyard, and there it is, Black Lake. The water is lower than I've ever seen it, climate change and successive droughts taking their toll, but it's still there, glistening hypnotically in the sun. A wooden dock juts out into the water, shared between my neighbor's house and mine. Kissing the dark waters is a narrow sand beach that runs for miles in either direction. In the distance, wooded islands dot the lake, towering white pines fringing the shore.

It's exactly as I remember it: beautiful even though so much ugliness happened here.

"Gee, you can really see why they named it Black Lake." Ash's voice is tight and sullen.

"It's the tannin from the trees. It's safe, though, I promise." I point at a path that disappears into the trees fringing the lake. "Let's go for a walk. There are trails back there."

I see her hesitate. She's eager to get inside, to hide away playing *Fortnite* or reading a book or zoning out while listening to grunge music. Before she has a chance to argue, I head for the wooded path. With no other choice, she follows.

We wander the trail, our shoes crunching over dried twigs and pine cones and packed earth. We follow the shoreline and soon come to the boathouse. It's ghostly, derelict, crouched among the reeds. The door is locked, so we carry on, following the narrow ribbon of dirt as it cuts through weeds and bushes.

All around us, the trees are thick and tall, the air clean and fresh, practically humming with birds singing and insects buzzing. The heat on my skin and the beads of sweat sliding between my breasts make me feel alive.

I find peace in the quiet stillness and exhale in one massive breath, the way I used to each summer when we'd finally arrive. Those days when I could take my shoes off and run into the water, slurp on half-melted Otter Pops, and marathon Nick at Nite with my summer friends were the best.

Until they weren't.

We walk for about twenty minutes until we reach a small beach with a felled tree jutting into the lake. Ash unlaces her boots, pushes up her leggings, and walks into the water, one hand pressed against the tree for balance.

The water hits her knees, and there's a small smile on her face. It warms my heart, and I begin to think maybe, *maybe* we'll be okay here.

Ash dives into the water. After a minute, she comes up gasping and laughing, water streaming from her hair. Sometimes the child in her still emerges, the quiet, gentle girl I know. The world is so hard on soft things, I find. On sensitive, bookish introverts like my girl.

"Come in, Mom!"

"Absolutely not!"

She smacks the surface with her palm, sending an arc of water toward me. I jump out of the way, laughing. God, it feels good to laugh!

"All right, all right!" I slip my sundress off and wade in wearing just my bra and underwear.

The water is frigid, and I gasp as the chill bites my skin. "You'll get used to it!" Ash calls.

The bottom falls away steeply, and soon I am underwater. It steals the breath from my lungs, but Ash is right. It is invigorating.

I swim out to Ash, and gradually our muscles warm as we race each other into deeper water and back. We lose track of time, our fingertips wrinkling as we splash in the shallows and float on our backs.

I'm treading water and laughing, Ash bobbing up and down in the water a little way from me, when I start to feel dizzy. It's as if the whole world is tilting, a mudslide that I'm caught in. In front of me, Ash shimmers, a mirage in the bright sunlight.

And then, abruptly, she disappears.

I swim in a circle, stunned and confused.

"Ash?" My voice is shrill with panic.

There's no reply. Adrenaline kicks in my veins.

"Ashley Rose, come out now!"

But she doesn't.

The lake in front of me has righted. It is flat and calm. My body stills, my eyes darting, my mind forensically flashing through each possibility, the way I do when an animal is sick at the vet, running down the list of likely outcomes.

There are days in the late summer when the air is so thick with heat that time seems to slow down until it feels as if it has stopped altogether. That's how it feels now—as if time has stopped.

I dive under the water. I can't see much of anything. It's just a hazy mud color. I scoop my hands back and forth, feeling for Ash's hair, an arm, a leg. But there's nothing. My lungs are burning. My heart feels like it's about to explode. She was *just here*! What's happening?

I bob to the surface, gasping, blinking water out of my eyes.

"Mom!"

I spin, and there's Ash, and then I'm crying so hard that my body is shuddering, and Ash is wrapping cold, slippery arms around me.

"Where were you?" My fingers dig into Ash's upper arms. I shake her, just a bit but hard. Too hard. I push away and tread water. "Where'd you go?"

Ash looks confused and a little scared. "I was . . . under the water."

"You can't do that!"

"I'm sorry!"

We stagger out of the water, climbing onto a tree log and letting the warm air dry our skin and hair and clothes. I take deep breaths to calm myself. This is not like me at all. I am cool in a crisis. It's what makes me a good vet.

Next to me, Ash wraps her arms around herself, rubbing at goose bumps that have popped up despite the heat.

"I'm sorry," she says again.

I shake my head. "You were just messing around. This is my own thing, Ash. I was scared, and it got the best of me."

She gets it, I can tell. We're both haunted by the things that happened.

I close my eyes, but I can't get the image of her disappearing out of my head. Because it wasn't like she dipped beneath the water's surface. This was more like a mirage, the light reflecting off the surface of the water turning her into an optical illusion: there one moment and gone the next.

I have the strangest feeling that I'm coming undone, that my head has opened and the contents are spilling out, swirling into the frigid water. I stare across the lake wondering, not for the first time, what coming back here will do to me. If Dullahan House will be the fresh start I hoped for or the death knell I fear.

Chapter 3

NEVE

"Come on." I reach for my clothes. "We need to hurry or we might miss the lady with our keys."

The sun is high and merciless, my bra and underwear nearly dry, so I step into my dress and slip my watch back on. There is a flash of something caught in the edge—rust or dirt. I scrub at it with my fingernail. The watch isn't expensive, just a simple minimalist Nordic style. But Eli bought it for me, and even now, maybe especially now, that means something.

It's almost old-fashioned to have a watch like this, but in my profession, they're a necessity. As a vet, I monitor heart rates and respiration rates. Check for appointment times and break times. All day, we make choices. About life and death, blood analyses and X-rays, medicine and palliative care. Good choices. Bad choices. Much of my care is time sensitive.

It was a sweet gift. But Eli was always romantic like that. He knew I was nervous after so much time away. I'd realized one day watching twelve-year-old Ash walk toward her friends at school, not even a backward glance at me, that it was time for me to rejoin the land of grown-ups.

Fortunately, my old clinic was looking for another vet, and two weeks later, I was back at work. Once I'd returned, I realized I'd missed it. Motherhood was satisfying but hard, often grueling and exhausting and thankless. I never regretted taking the time off to raise my daughter, but I loved being back in the clinic. The calming daily routine, the reassuring presence of animals, so much better than people. Animals have no pretenses; they don't hold grudges or know how to hate. They are the only part of my life that is uncomplicated. Of course, there were parts of the clinic that were complicated, but I'd rather not think about those. Sometimes to see the future clearly, it's best to wipe the residue of our past clean.

We stroll back to the house, but there are no new cars parked out front.

"She should've been here with our keys by now," I say, worried.

A flash of something catches my eye from one of the upstairs windows. I turn, expecting to see someone, but there's nothing there. Still, a prickle of unease crawls over my skin.

I climb the steps and peer inside the glass windows, but it's too dark to see very well.

"What about that?" Ash points at an electronic keypad on the front door.

"It's for the property management company."

"Do you know the code?"

"Yeah, but we're meant to get a set of keys, too."

Ash motions at the door impatiently. *Come on, then!*

I shrug, tapping the code, and the door clicks open. I step inside, darkness swirling in my wake. There is a slight smell, heavy and damp, like it's been empty for a long time. But overlaid on top of that is something else: bleach and something floral. Perfume? It's a strange contradiction, although I'm glad the place was cleaned thoroughly before we arrived, even if the property manager hasn't shown up yet.

The entry is dimly lit, with gray mosaic tiling. A sweeping wooden staircase rises in front of us, an ornate chandelier hanging above. I flick on a light while Ash yanks back heavy, tasseled drapes in the living room, revealing a large picture window.

The furniture is covered in thick dust sheets, and yet there's no dust anywhere. The place is immaculately clean. The property management company has done a good job of maintaining the inside, at least. Ash and I pull the dust sheets off one by one, exposing matching overstuffed couches and dark wood end tables. There are antique lamps with flamingos carved into their wooden bases, blue velvet wingback chairs, an ornate cast-iron fireplace with an intricately carved mantel.

The decor is dated but in good shape. Blue on white with Victorian touches. There are hardwood floors, gilded wainscoting, high ceilings, and deep archways. Mounted over the fireplace is a widescreen television, and to either side are floor-to-ceiling bookshelves stocked with thrillers, memoirs, slim books of poetry.

"Nice." Ash surveys the room, hand on jutted hip. "A super-old vacation rental in a dead tourist town."

She doesn't yet realize that sometimes words are like weapons; they cut to the bone. She's become an expert at wielding them lately, while I have never mastered the art of shielding myself. Perhaps on some level, I feel I deserve it.

I force my voice to stay neutral. "It's good enough to pay for Grandma's care."

I tuck the dust sheets away in a drawer and open the kitchen blinds to let in more light. Large windows and glass double doors open to a wraparound deck that overlooks the glistening silver-black lake.

We explore the rooms, and as we do, I am taken back in time. Nostalgia is a heavy drug pulling me back into memories of pizza parties in the basement, movie marathons with bowls of popcorn, days exploring the woods outside, posing in my swimsuit with my friends on the beach.

I grab Ash's hand. It is cold, clammy. Her face is pale. But I feel hopeful. We can make a life for ourselves here. "I want to show you something."

I pull her up the twisty staircase inside the turret. At the top, we step inside a bright, circular bedroom decorated in soft shades of yellow. We pull off the dust sheets to reveal matching furniture.

Ash crosses to four tall, arched windows and gazes outside. Her eyes widen as she takes in the stunning vista of water and islands, pine trees and sky.

"This was my room," I say, feeling something close to pride. "Yours now. If you want it."

"It's hard to imagine you spending your summers here when you were my age."

I try to laugh, but it gets stuck somewhere in my throat. "Everybody has a past."

I realize I sound a little harsh when she darts a surprised look at me. I force a smile. I meant nothing by it. We all carry our injuries, our dirty little secrets, burying them inside boxes we hide in the deepest, darkest parts of ourselves. We work to forget the bad things we've done so we don't have to believe what we don't want to believe.

Sometimes I wish I could go back in time and use an eraser to smudge out the things I did, the bad I carry inside me. But unfortunately, life doesn't come with a gift receipt. You can't just exchange it for a better one and carry on as if nothing has happened.

Back in the kitchen, I make ham sandwiches for dinner. I'm pouring us each a tall glass of orange juice when I hear Ash twisting a door handle. I spin around.

"Ash, stop!" My voice comes out shrill.

Ash freezes. "Why?"

I muster a smile, my throat clutching a cry. "That's the basement. We can't go down there."

"Why?"

"It's locked. I don't know where the key is."

My body feels hot, flushed. I haven't been down there in over twenty years, and I don't plan to go now.

Fortunately, Ash shrugs and grabs her sandwich. My heartbeat settles, and we take our food and orange juice to the living room and sit in front of the TV. There's no Netflix or Prime Video, but there's an old movie playing, black and white and unrecognizable.

Outside, the sun sets abruptly, turning the air sweet and the sky a melancholy bluish lavender as it sinks on the horizon. The air lifts and cools, and I feel myself relaxing, the sweat drying on my skin.

My eyes are gritty, and I'm exhausted. I haven't slept well in what feels like forever because of Ash's nightmares. Most nights, I wake to her screams. My heart pounds as I launch myself to her, scooping her into my arms, her body stiff and unyielding, until she realizes where she is, that she's safe, and she lets herself be held.

I check and double-check every lock in the house. The front and back doors, the deck door, the windows. Fortunately, they are new and modern, double-glazed, with thick euro cylinders and sensors that attach to the alarm on the front door.

I glance at Ash. How will I be able to leave her alone all day when I start my new job?

The veterinarian clinic is close, within walking distance, and will provide a new challenge. My previous job was working with smaller animals, performing regular checkups, administering vaccines, treating broken bones. This new vet is more rural, so I'll see large animals and do farm visits, too. It's only two days a week, but I won't lie. I'm a little worried.

"When are we going home?" Ash asks.

I stare at her. Ash didn't want to come. But there was an awful lot more to consider than just her fear of leaving, and so I dragged her here with me. It's safe, and right now, that's what we need.

"Let's see how the rest of the summer goes," I say vaguely. "We'll figure out next steps then."

Ash gives me a look of such disdain, I feel my insides shrivel. Sometimes being a mother is like death by a thousand cuts. But still, I want to reach out to her, the way I would have *before*.

Before is all a little hazy still. It's a common symptom of posttraumatic stress disorder. The trauma of the home invasion has played havoc on me. Sometimes my memories are a little jumbled; I have flashbacks and fall asleep abruptly. I am plagued by a strange sense of disorientation, like everything is just a little wrong.

The worst thing is, I can't even remember Ash being shot. I don't remember holding her, although I must have done it.

I clench my teeth as vague images skuttle past.

Black sky. Air on bare skin. Hissing breath. A scream. Then blood.

But not Ash; I don't remember the shot.

I'm too scared to ask Ash what happened. I worry that I froze, that I stood unmoving as the bullet streaked toward her. That I didn't try to save her. And what kind of mother doesn't fight for her child?

Is this the reason she's so distant with me? I wish I'd been able to protect her the way I should have. That I could've stopped the attack.

There's so much I don't know. What I *do* know, though, is the intruder escaped into the greenbelt at the back of our house. He's still out there. Somewhere. Another reason we had to leave.

Fatigue pulls at me, settling like an ache in my eyelids. I am drifting, floating, my head thick and gauzy. All I want is to sleep, but Ash's voice pulls me back from the dark.

"You're sure we're safe here?"

And I say the only thing I know to say. "I'll protect you, Ash. Nothing's going to happen to us here."

Chapter 4

NEVE

I fall asleep on the couch while Ash watches TV, diving into the strange heavy sleep I've been having lately. Like I'm drugged, even though I haven't taken a thing. Ash's screams wake me at 2:00 a.m. I shake her gently, crooning, "Mom's here; you're safe" over and over.

I guide her to an upstairs bedroom and tuck her into bed, climbing in next to her. Her skin is cool, damp with sweat. I brush her hair off her forehead, careful not to touch the scar at her temple, and hold her until her breathing returns to normal.

I can't get back to sleep, so I go downstairs to make myself a cup of tea. I've always had trouble sleeping, and even when I do, I'm susceptible to sleepwalking. My parents would find me doing all sorts of strange things in the night. Once I decided my cat was stuck in the closet, so I emptied out all my clothes and shoes, shouting her name. My mom came in and told me I was dreaming and to get back into bed, but it was so real to me. It was like looking at myself, but myself superimposed over another me, like changing dimensions. That's how I've felt ever since the home invasion, unsettled and uncertain. Here, but not really.

I root around in the kitchen cupboards and find a mug and a jar of black tea. There is a book of poetry by Robert Frost sitting on the island next to a small bowl of sugar. I crack the hardened glaze on the sugar and scoop a spoonful into my tea, taking it and the book to the dining table, where I listen for any sound from Ash.

Sometimes I get caught in my own world of worry. *Catastrophizing.* I know the worry and anxiety exist only in my head, but the truth is that sometimes fear screams an awful lot louder than logic.

I rub my thumb over the smooth skin where my wedding ring used to be. There's the slightest ridge there, an indentation from years of wearing something that's now missing. I wonder how long it will take to feel normal. I think, briefly, that I should call my mother and ask how long it took for her to feel normal. If she ever got used to being alone after my dad left.

I know myself that you can still feel lonely even when you've chosen to be alone. There are different types of alone. There's the isolated type, where you have no one around you and you feel lost and uncertain, but there's also being alone when you're surrounded by people you don't, or can't, connect to. Perhaps my mother and I have more in common than I ever realized.

But time, loneliness, these are things my mother no longer comprehends. Alzheimer's stole time from her, stole memories from her. In the end, it stole her from me.

When I was a kid and was upset about something, I remember my mom coming into my room and sitting next to me, lacing her fingers through mine. She wouldn't say a word; she'd just be there, the warmth of her hand heating mine. Later, she'd say, "Do you still feel my hand in yours, Neve?" And I'd smile and say yes, because I knew that was what she wanted me to say. And then, when I left and went off to college, I'd call home, unbearably lonely, and she'd say, "Do you feel my hand in yours, Neve? It's always there, even when it's not."

I never appreciated my mother's hands until now, when she can no longer hold mine.

Sometimes I say those words to Ash. "Do you feel my hand in yours?" But just like when I was younger, she doesn't get it. Not yet.

No, I can't call my mom. She doesn't understand who I am on the phone. I need to visit, to see her in person, but it's hard. I suppose I'm the type of person who prefers forgetting to talking. Everybody thinks knowledge is power, but I've always sided more with Sophocles: "Not knowing anything is the sweetest life." It's easier to keep things as they were, letting my memories stay mired in the past.

I fold my legs under me and open the poetry book. The volume is thin, a quick read, and as I near the back, I feel something thicker wedged between two of the pages. A poem—Robert Frost's "The Road Not Taken"—has been bookmarked with a folded piece of paper. I unfold it. There, jotted in red ink, is a message: *I know what you did. Did you ever stop to consider the consequences? Because there will be consequences. There always are. And yours are coming soon enough.*

Something slithers over me, sticky and black. A memory? A dream? It's like I've seen this before, but I'm certain I haven't. Letters shimmy across the backs of my eyelids, but before I can read them, *poof,* they're gone.

I set my mug on the table and stand, paranoia and fear crawling up me like a spider. Who is this from? Who's it for? I try to remember if the book was on the kitchen island yesterday when we arrived, but my mind is blank. If it was there, I didn't notice.

It must've been left by one of the vacation renters, I tell myself.

I check the front door, but the alarm is still armed, the reassuring red light blinking every few seconds, so I return to the kitchen table and sink into a chair. I sip my tea, which has gone lukewarm. The air inside the house is thick and humid, sweat prickling the skin under my arms.

I take my tea to the sink and dump it out. As I do, something outside on the deck catches my eye. I cross to the sliding glass door to get a better look. Something moves in my peripheral vision. I scream.

Because on the other side of the sliding glass door is a face. Someone is there, staring at me.

"Bee?" I gasp, shocked relief filtering in.

Bee used to live next door to Dullahan House when I was a kid. She was my best summer friend. From the moment I arrived every June, we were inseparable, our friendship formed by the heat and the laughter of those sweet summer months.

Now Bee is soaking wet, her long dark hair hanging in wet strands around her ice-white face. Her feet are bare, a small puddle expanding around her. Her mouth is smeared with something red, her eyes so dark, they almost look like holes in her face. I flick the light switch up, but the motion-activated floodlight doesn't turn on. The bulb appears to be blown.

"Are you okay?" I ask Bee through the glass. I fumble with the lock but remember the alarm is on. "Hold on, I have to turn the alarm off."

I turn to go to the alarm panel, which is by the front door, but Bee's voice stops me.

"She knows," she says.

"What?" I'm not sure I heard her right. "Hold on two seconds."

I hurry down the hallway and tap in the alarm code. It beeps, telling me it's disarmed, and I jog back to the kitchen to let Bee in.

But she isn't there.

I unlatch the glass door and slide it open, the metal rails making a toe-curling shriek. I peer over the railing, look down the stairs, gaze out across the water, the graphite outline of the forest.

"Bee?" I call.

There's no answer.

In the distance, a shrill sound cuts the black night, the squeak of a bat, perhaps, or a hawk diving for its prey. A cat yowls, and a frog belches nearby. To my right, my neighbor's house huddles in the dark, eerily illuminated by a pale slip of a moon. The lights are out, not a soul awake at this time.

I step into the place I'd seen Bee standing. A pool of cool air washes over me. It feels like fog, clinging to my bare legs like water. I look down at my feet and see the small puddle of water near the sliding glass door where Bee had stood. I kneel to touch it.

My fingers come away damp.

I step back inside, shivering, my arms prickling with sudden goose bumps despite the warm night. I don't know where she's gone, but she isn't here anymore.

I slide the glass shut and lock it, then reset the alarm. I move around the house one more time, rechecking all the locks, the windows, the doors. Then I climb back into bed next to Ash and wait for sleep to find me.

Chapter 5

NEVE

I wake at dawn to birdsong, heart thundering in my ears. There was a sound, I think. A click, like a door shutting. I listen, trying to sift whatever it was from the birds chirping. But there is nothing.

I focus on Ash's sleeping noises: a little click at the back of her throat, an occasional snuffling. I roll onto my side and watch her. She looks younger in sleep, and I remember when she was a baby, smelling of milk and powder. Nothing about that time went the way they tell you in books and movies.

I had a difficult pregnancy, a difficult labor. I lost so much blood that I needed a blood transfusion. I was so exhausted, I left Ash's care to Eli, who was infuriatingly capable from the start. Then when I'd recovered and was desperate to take over, she screamed for Eli, seeming to resent my touch.

I felt like I'd been rejected. That she knew every one of my flaws and had found me unworthy. But she was my daughter, and I was determined to win her over. I let her sleep on my chest for hours, stroking her soft head and singing to her. I walked her up and down the hallway and told her every story I knew. And during these moments, I fell in love with her, this little miracle I'd grown in my body. I vowed I would do whatever it took to protect her, to keep her safe. She was a part of me.

The good part.

I feel a swell of love for her now, followed quickly by a pang of missing. She's getting older, separating from me in a way I know is completely natural. When she was small, we'd spend hours building forts or painting our fingernails or having a duvet day, huddled under the blankets watching movies. When Eli was around, it was all activity, all go, go, go. Constant movement, constant bustle. He's always been a good father like that, determined to be more than his own absent father was. He made time to play after work and wiped the counters after dinner, his knuckles shiny with soap, making plans for the next day, the weekend, the holidays. When it was just Ash and me, it was more restful, more relaxed, like we were the only two people in the world.

"Mo-om, stop staring at me." Ash's voice is rusty, and she yanks her pillow over her head, blocking me out.

I smile and slip out of bed. I wonder if all kids feel the shimmering weight of their mother's adoring gaze.

I step into the bathroom. Golden light is streaming through the windows. I contemplate going for a run, but even this early, the sun is beating down, the air oppressive. Outside, the ground is scorched, the bladelike grass yellow and stiff. The trees hang with wilted leaves, the sun a fiery ball in a hot blue sky.

I catch sight of my face in the mirror. I've lost weight. Tall and willowy to start, my cheeks are now hollow, my collarbones like sharpened arrows. Flat dark hair with caramel highlights that needed updating a good three months ago. Dark circles under my eyes. I look tired. The kind of weariness that no amount of sleep can help. My skin is waxy and pale. That's what fear will do to you. What wandering the halls of a hospital will do.

I'm drying my hands when I notice the drops of blood to the left of the sink. They're small, almost imperceptible. More like flecks, really.

My stomach goes hot, and my mouth twists in disgust. A shaving cut, perhaps? But I thought no one had been here for years. It must be old, I decide. I dampen two squares of toilet paper. The blood wipes easily away, a smear of crimson against the snow-white tissue. I make a mental note to mention it to the property management company. Not a speck of dust but flecks of blood. Gross.

Downstairs, I put the kettle on for tea. I hear Ash stirring upstairs. The toilet flushes and the taps turn on, a low clunking coming from the belly of the old house. She comes downstairs, entering the living room while rubbing her eyes.

"Morning, sunshine," I call.

She grunts a reply. Ash used to be cheerful in the mornings, but since hitting her teens, her mood swings give me whiplash.

"I've got a good one," I say. "Would you rather get your butt cheeks pierced or your face cheeks pierced?"

Ash looks like she's holding in a laugh, and I count it as a win. But before she can answer, a wail splits the air. I think for a second it's the kettle, but the sound is coming from outside. I follow Ash up the twisty turret stairs to get a bird's-eye view.

I fling open the curtains, and we peer into the bright morning. An ambulance is bumping over the grass, cutting down the lawn toward the dock between my house and my neighbor's. There's a small army of police officers and people in forensic suits standing by the water.

The beach extends in one undivided sweep along the lake. There are no fences here, and from the height of my house, its position on a slight incline, I can clearly see when the ambulance parks and two paramedics get out. They speak to an officer who is erecting a white tent; nearby, another is stringing yellow police tape.

A little way from the dock, I see my neighbor, the carrot-shaped, anxious-looking woman from across the street. She's wearing bright-pink-and-turquoise running gear and holding her dog to her chest like a shield.

A detective is speaking to her. He is soft-bodied and prematurely balding with round black glasses and pink skin. He reminds me a little of Daddy Pig from that kids' show *Peppa Pig*. He seems a little too jolly for this job.

I'm a bit of an expert at being a detective, I imagine him saying.

"What happened?" Ash asks, eyes wide.

Children always seem to think their parents have all the answers, like we are omniscient or something. But I don't know what's happened, and I tell her so.

Something moves in the water near the dock, the hooded head of a diver in a slick black suit. He's pointing at something tangled in the reeds. My heart beats faster, and I press against the window, my eyes frantically scanning the water.

"Mom, what are they doing?" Ash's voice is high and panicky.

"I don't know," I breathe.

"Is that a body?"

But this time, I don't answer, because I think she's right. And I know from experience that sometimes not knowing is better than knowing.

"Stay here," I say. She opens her mouth to argue, but I use my firmest voice. "Seriously, Ash. Stay here."

I should've protected her better last time, but I won't make that mistake again. I won't fail my daughter again.

Outside, the morning is already thick with heat. A handful of wispy clouds brings a new humidity to the air. I hustle down the path toward the lake, stopping in front of a retaining wall that holds brightly colored flowers. My neighbor releases her dog, and he scuttles to the dock, his nails scraping against the wood. He sniffs around anxiously until she calls him back.

Another vehicle pulls up, a white van, MEDICAL EXAMINER emblazoned on the side. I draw in a sharp breath. They don't need the ambulance after all.

Two men get out, pulling out a body bag that glistens in the sun, shiny and black as a beetle. They carry it down to the white tent that's been erected. I edge closer.

Just then, the roar of an engine cuts the air. A motorcycle brakes hard, lights flashing, as it pulls up next to the ME van. The woman riding it takes what looks to be a cane out of her backpack. She unfolds it and uses it to lean on as she dismounts; then she unsnaps her helmet and surveys the scene with something like contempt on her face, eyes squinting, one side of her lip pulled back slightly. Ash would call it *resting bitch face*.

She has a badge snapped to her hip. Another detective. She's in her midthirties with dark hair tied into a tight ponytail, a pair of aviator sunglasses shielding her eyes. Her cheekbones are high and sharp.

She moves gingerly down the hill, leaning on her cane. She and Daddy Pig exchange a few words.

I have a thousand questions. Was it an accident? Did somebody drown? Or is it something darker? Like murder. They wouldn't be here for a drowning, would they?

I creep closer so I can hear what they're saying. Nobody pays any attention to me, carrying on with their business as if I'm not even there.

"Thanks so much for chatting with us, Vivienne." The male detective is speaking to my neighbor, the woman with the dog.

Vivienne's eyes are dull, her skin shiny with sweat. She's in shock.

"That's hers." She points to the house next to mine. Whoever's in the water was my neighbor. "She bought it from her parents when they moved to Florida."

Something dances in my peripheral vision. I look up at Dullahan House, a cold feeling sliding down my spine. But it's just Ash. I want her to move away from the window. They'll think we're voyeuristic, that we're meddlesome and coldhearted.

A shout comes from the water. The diver emerges from the reeds. He waves an arm as he pushes something toward the shore. It's a body, a woman's, floating facedown amid the reeds, long black hair fanning out like velvet on the cold water.

I step back. Again and again, until the backs of my legs smack against the sharp stones of the retaining wall. Pain shoots up my calves, and I gasp. The detective with the cane turns, her eyes meeting mine for a brief second, before she returns her gaze to the other detective.

The diver hefts the woman into his arms and carries her out of the water. Her hair trails over her face, wrapping around her throat like a noose. Water streams onto the summer-scorched grass. Her skin glistens, waxy and water-bleached against the diver's black wet suit.

The urge to vomit hits me hard. With the bright summer sun beating against my eyelids, my daughter watching from the turret bedroom, it feels like I'm in a dream. Like I'm standing outside my body. It's impossible to look away.

The diver is speaking to a paramedic: ". . . in the water a few days."

My eyes dart again to Dullahan House. According to my mother, the house was named by one of our ancestors after the Dullahan, the mythological headless horseman from Irish folklore who was a harbinger of death, representing a past that never dies and haunting the living wherever he roamed. The Dullahan, the story goes, rode past shortly before his child was found mysteriously drowned in the lake.

I turn to look at the small crowd of people gathered by the water's edge, studying their faces in turn. With news like this, it's hard not to think the worst of everyone. It's hard not to feel like our fresh start is already slipping out of my grasp.

A woman died here, maybe was murdered here, practically in my own backyard. I came back hoping for a fresh start, hoping we'd be safe. But can we be safe in a house that holds such terrible secrets?

Chapter 6

JESS

I pick my way carefully down the hill toward my partner, leaning harder on my cane than I'd like. My leg is throbbing, like most days, but I'll be damned if I let the other cops see how much it's bothering me. It's hard enough being the only female detective in this town.

Will catches sight of me and waves from the white tent that's been erected by the lake. Even in the white-hot sun, the water looks black, the surface glistening like oil.

Sweat prickles my armpits, sticking my shirt to my back. Summer's been hot before, but not like this. Sticky, record-breaking heat. The sun is already beating down, the scorching morning stifling, airless. A small crowd has started to form. Neighbors and locals watch as CSIs in white forensic suits float like ghosts, sifting through the lake and its sandy shore.

Near the tent, speaking to a uniformed cop, is a middle-aged woman with dark hair scraped into a tight bun. She's wearing full work-out gear, and she's clutching a small white dog. She's shaking like a leaf. It doesn't take a detective to know she found the body.

Inside the tent, the air is thick and oppressive. A crime scene photographer is taking pictures, documenting evidence.

I force myself to look down at the body, a steady beat of trepidation thudding in my belly. Water droplets cling to the woman, her skin partly blackened and loosened from the water. Her dark hair is long, slicked back, her eyes open in a murky death stare. Her cheekbones are high, dangly silver earrings in her ears. Her mouth is hinged just slightly open, something drawing me closer to the hidden space between her blue lips. I kneel awkwardly, my eyes on her mouth, feeling like I'm under some sort of spell. My hand reaches out, unplanned, unbidden.

"Jess?" Will's voice snaps me back.

He's standing over me, a bewildered look on his face. Touching the body before the pathologist examines it is a massive no-no. I'm not sure what came over me.

I try to shake off this cloud of disorientation. "Sorry."

Will does things by the book, the way a good cop should. He still treats the job like he's just out of the academy, fresh and enthusiastic about every detail. I've seen plenty of bodies and worked plenty of cases, but a lot has changed since I started in homicide. *I've* changed.

"The deceased is Bailey Nelson. She lives there." Will jerks his chin in the direction of the big Victorian behind us. "Her neighbor, Vivienne Jones, found her while out walking her dog."

"Anybody find her phone?" I ask.

"Nah. Probably still in the house. It's locked. Her neighbor says her husband's outta town. We'll get his permission to go in. But that's not what I wanted you to see."

I return my gaze to the body. The woman is wearing a silk blouse and black pencil skirt. Her feet are bare, her toenails painted bloodred. Her hands . . .

Something's wrong. I bend closer, my mouth popping open as I realize what I'm seeing.

"She was restrained," I say with some surprise. Silver duct tape circles the woman's wrists, holding them in place behind her back.

Will nods, mouth pressed into a grim line.

My leg won't support me on my knees anymore. I lean on my cane and get to my feet. Nobody binds their own hands behind their back.

I look again at the woman on the ground and then at Will.

"This wasn't an accident," I say. "This woman was murdered."

◆ ◆ ◆

Once the pathologist arrives, Will and I clear out to give him space. Will offers to speak to the woman who found the body, and I tell him I'll chat with the neighbors congregating around the lake.

I scan the crowd and notice a woman walking up the hill, away from the crowd, away from the lake. There's something about her; maybe it's the way she walks, very still, very controlled, as if she's trying not to be seen. So of course, she's exactly who I want to talk to.

I head after her, digging my cane into the hard, brittle ground.

"Excuse me?" I call, waving to get her attention.

The woman is tall, willowy, with long dark hair and very pale skin. She has unusual green eyes, the color of spring grass. One of her front teeth is just slightly crooked.

"I'm Detective Jess Lambert," I say. "That's my partner down there, Detective Will Casey."

Her expression remains blank when I introduce myself, her body calm and still. People react in all sorts of ways to death, but generally, they show at least a little surprise when introduced to a detective at the scene where a body's been found. Everything about this woman, however, screams self-restraint. She's the type who never has that second drink, who goes for a run instead of eating cheesecake, who never eats with her hands and turns the TV off in time to get a good night's sleep. Basically, the opposite of me.

I stick a hand out, and she shakes it. "Neve," she says. "Neve Maguire."

"Can I help you?" I say. "I saw you down by the lake."

"I . . . I . . . just wanted to find out what was going on."

"Do you live here?"

"Yes. We only arrived yesterday, though."

"We?"

"My daughter and me."

There's something about the way she says it, the words heavy and weighted. And then she tells me she and her husband are separated.

"I'm sorry to hear that," I say, because what else can you say? "Do you mind if I ask you a few questions?"

"I'm not sure how much I can help. Like I said, we just arrived yesterday."

I take a notebook out of my pocket and flip up the top. "That's okay—anything you remember is good."

"I saw the ME's van. Did someone die?"

"We're still trying to establish all the details, but yes, unfortunately your neighbor has died. Bailey Nelson. Can you tell us anything about her?"

"Bailey Nelson." Shock ripples across her face. "She was my neighbor?"

"You knew her?"

"She was supposed to meet me yesterday to give me the keys, but she never showed up."

Bailey Nelson, it turns out, was not only Neve Maguire's neighbor, but she also worked for the property management company that managed her house. Sparks Property, Neve says they're called.

I make a note to check in with them soon.

I ask Neve a few more questions, but she doesn't appear to have seen anything. After arriving yesterday in the early afternoon, she and her daughter had gone for a swim in the lake, then returned to the house and went to bed early. They hadn't seen anyone at all, according to Neve.

"Where'd you say you moved from?" I ask.

"Boston. The suburbs."

I ask her why she moved here, and she hesitates. In that hesitation, I sense she's holding something back.

"I used to visit when I was a kid," she finally says.

Down by the lake, the ambulance door slams shut, and she jumps, a flare of panic crossing her face. It's the first crack in her armor I've seen. A hand comes up to her forehead, as if she's dizzy. Her body sways. She looks like she's going to faint.

"Hey. Are you okay?" I touch her arm, concerned, and she swings wild eyes to mine.

"I'm . . . I'm fine."

Compassion spasms in me. Something has happened to this woman. Something terrible. I want to help, so I tell her about the local grocery, The Jumbo, that took over for the Whole Foods a few years back. I tell her about Sammy's, the best bar in town, and the market in the library parking lot on Tuesdays.

"I'd guess a lot has changed from when you were a kid," I say.

"That's really kind of you, thank you."

"It's no problem. Just real quick before you go." I pull out my phone to show her Bailey Nelson's Facebook profile picture. "Could you take a look at this photo of Mrs. Nelson? You said you visited when you were younger. Maybe you knew her."

I hold out my phone, but as I do, something shifts in the air. I blink, trying to reorient myself. I'm aware of a weird feeling, a strange disorientation combined with a pressure building in my ears.

I clear my throat. "I . . . did you know her?"

A buzz has started around the edges of my brain. Blood rushes violently in my ears.

Neve says something, but her words drift like silent balloons into the air. Because there, standing at the top of the hill just over her shoulder, is a girl, her blonde hair lifting as a small breath of wind stirs it. If I wanted, I could go over and touch her.

I try to drag my gaze back to Neve. My eyes settle, bizarrely, on her fingers, which seem frozen in midair. Her nails are perfectly done, like she's just had a manicure, the polish the soft pink of a ballet slipper, the nails smooth, glossy ovals. My own nails are tattered claws, ragged from months of gnawing them.

Sweat collects in my armpits. I struggle to concentrate, to find my next question.

It isn't real, I tell myself. *What you're seeing isn't real.*

My phone rings. The lieutenant.

"I gotta . . . gotta . . ." My breath comes in great ragged chunks as I back away from Neve.

What you're seeing isn't real.

I don't bother saying goodbye; I simply turn and make my way back to the lake, fumbling to answer my phone. I want desperately to distract myself, distance myself.

Anything but confront what—or rather, who—I thought I saw standing just over Neve's shoulder.

"Hello?" I answer the phone.

"Jess." Lieutenant Luis Rivero's voice is strong, authoritative. "You're at the scene?"

"Yes."

"I want you to lead on this one. You ready?"

I swallow hard, butterflies swarming in my belly. Not nerves, no. Anticipation. This is exactly what I need.

I keep my gaze fixed on the lake, the white tent down there, refusing to look again at the girl I just saw.

"I'm ready," I tell him.

Chapter 7

NEVE

I wanted to know what had happened, but everybody seemed too busy, and I didn't want to get in the way, so I left.

Sometimes I feel like this, like people don't really see me, like I'm living in a different realm. I'm just beneath the surface while the rest of the world hovers above it. Mirror images, but not quite on the same plane. I know it's just my own insecurity showing, but I can't help it.

I'm almost at the top of the sloping lawn when I hear a woman's voice behind me.

"Excuse me?"

The detective with the cane waves, shuffling determinedly up the hill toward me. I stop and wait for her. She's wearing all black: black trousers, a sleeveless black blouse, black ankle boots. I wait, wiping my hand over my forehead. The sun is climbing higher, chasing away the wispy clouds.

Eli would love it, but I struggle with the heat, preferring the chill of fall, while he luxuriates in the heat of summer. Another way we are opposites. I'm not the easiest person to live with, while he is laid-back and carefree. I am deliberate and sensible while he is impulsive and creative. He would leave *I love you* notes on my laptop while I'd get distracted and forget to say goodbye in the morning. He'd whisk me away for a spontaneous river-rafting trip or some other unanticipated adventure. Eli always loves to surprise, loves to be surprised, the type to live in the moment. That unrestrained passion for life is what drew me to him in the first place.

"I'm Detective Jess Lambert, and that's my partner down there." She waves toward Daddy Pig. "Detective Will Casey."

"Neve." I shake her hand, catching the faintest scent of stale booze on her breath. I hesitate, then decide to give my maiden name. "Neve Maguire."

"Can I help you?" The detective lifts her sunglasses onto her head. She's a little out of breath, a sheen of sweat glistening on her forehead. "I saw you down by the lake."

"I . . . I . . . ," I stutter like a child caught doing something naughty, but I catch myself and fix a concerned look on my face. If there's one thing I'm good at, it's keeping up appearances. "I just wanted to find out what was going on."

"Do you live here?" She's all business, straight-backed, serious-faced.

I glance up at Dullahan House and find myself thinking, briefly, of that last summer here, the things that happened and the consequences that rippled out. I wish I could undo my mistakes, but finding atonement is like finding Atlantis, nebulous, futile.

"Yes," I say. "We only arrived yesterday, though."

"We?"

"My daughter and me."

I hear the emptiness there, the weight of Eli's name in its absence, and I feel more alone than ever. I wrap my arms around myself. Being alone is my way of life now.

"My husband and I are separated," I explain, even though she hasn't asked and surely doesn't need to know.

I'm the one who asked for a divorce, and I asked for a divorce because of the affair. But the distance was there. It just took me a while to acknowledge it. Sometimes, I've learned, the only way to accept the truth is to destroy it along the way, like how firefighters start little fires to stop the big one. I know well the haunt of memories, the way they burn. This time, I can't let it destroy me.

"We can work through this," Eli had pleaded. "I don't want to lose you."

But some mistakes, I know, aren't so easily forgiven.

It wasn't even two weeks after this conversation when the home invasion happened. By that stage, the tension between Eli and me had become unbearable. We were sitting down to tell Ash about our decision—my decision—to separate that very night.

I knew we could never go back to the way things were. Undoing damage like that is like trying to unscramble an egg. And anyway, I figured there was nothing left to save. So I left Eli the house, the cat, the dog. I quit my job. I just needed to get out of there.

The detective's gaze dips to my left hand, where my wedding ring no longer resides, and says she'd like to ask me a few questions.

I'm not sure if I can help much, since we only arrived yesterday, and I tell her so. She says anything I can remember is good and pulls a small coil-bound notebook from an inner pocket. She tells me my neighbor, Bailey Nelson, has died and asks if I know anything about her.

A current of shock zips through me. "Bailey Nelson. She was my neighbor?"

"You knew her?"

"She was supposed to meet me yesterday to give me the keys, but she never showed up."

Because she was dead. Her body tangled in the reeds. We went *swimming* in that water yesterday. We stood *right here* by the water's edge yesterday and I hadn't seen a thing.

I feel sick, cold leaching into my stomach.

I explain that Bailey Nelson worked for the property management company that manages Dullahan House. I didn't realize she was my neighbor, too.

"What company is that?" the detective asks.

"Umm . . ." I sift through the information my mom gave me when she moved into the care home. It wasn't like she was very cognizant by that time. "Sparks Property."

"And what time was she supposed to meet you?"

"Three. But we arrived around two. She wasn't here, so we went for a walk."

I tell her about going swimming, how I thought we'd missed our chance to get the keys. Detective Lambert watches me as I talk, occasionally jotting down notes. Her eyes are a pale golden brown, the color of aged whiskey. They are lined, the whites webbed with red. After a few minutes of babbling, I start to get the sense she is becoming a little impatient. She wants the facts, that's all. She is a practical woman, no-nonsense.

"When we got back, I just used the code to enter," I finish weakly. "I figured she'd bring the keys another time."

"Did you see anything . . . unusual when you were out for this walk?"

"Unusual?"

"Perhaps someone hanging around one of the houses or maybe out on the trail. Someone who didn't belong? Anything suspicious."

I press my hand to my throat. "Do you think she was murdered?"

"It's too early to say that. I'm just trying to establish a timeline. Find out what you might've seen."

"No, I didn't see anyone suspicious. In fact, I didn't see anyone else at all. It seemed very quiet. Very peaceful. I remember thinking I was glad about that."

The detective smiles tightly, tapping her fingers against her cane. She does that a lot, always moving, fidgeting. The type who can't sit still, who has too much energy, like a pent-up child who's been kept inside for too long.

"That's what people always love about it here," she says. "The peace."

I don't return her smile. It isn't the peace that attracted me. It's the safety, the sense of security, the chance for a fresh start. But if my neighbor's been murdered . . . have I made a horrible mistake?

The detective shifts her weight, leaning a little heavier on her cane. I wonder what happened to her leg, if it was an accident on the job or something at birth. The adapted motorcycle, the job choice, the sharp glint in her eye show someone who's haunted but doesn't allow it to keep her down.

"Where'd you say you moved from?" she asks.

I didn't say, but I tell her anyway. "Boston. The suburbs."

Her eyebrows lift. "Suburban-rush to country-quiet. Black Lake's pretty different from Boston."

"Different isn't so bad sometimes."

"Is that why you moved here? You wanted a change?"

She seems curious rather than accusatory, but I don't know how to reply. I don't want to tell her about the home invasion, and it seems too personal to tell her about Eli. And anything about my summers spent here as a teenager are out of the question.

I finally settle for: "I used to visit when I was a kid."

A loud crash down by the lake makes me jump, and for a second I'm spinning, tumbling back to that night. *Boom. A horrific sound from the front of the house. The front door splintering, cracking.*

And again, boom.

And then a person is there, clad in black head to toe. There's shouting and I'm running. I'm screaming for Ash, and then there's a gun . . .

I drag my gaze away from the ambulance. The back doors have just slammed shut. It's nothing. But my heart is still thudding, like I've been attacked or something. I put my hand to my forehead, feeling, not for the first time, that strange, dizzy sensation, like vertigo, like I'm sleepwalking and nothing is quite real.

Detective Lambert touches my arm, her face creased with concern. "Hey. Are you okay?"

"I'm . . . I'm fine."

The other detective is staring in our direction, a strange look on his face. Worry, or perhaps suspicion. I step away from Detective Lambert, needing to be inside, somewhere safe. Alone.

"Hold on a sec." A soft breeze ruffles her hair, and I catch that smell again. Stale booze. "The local grocery is called The Jumbo. It took over the old Whole Foods a few years ago. Next to it is Sammy's. It's the best bar in town now. There's a church across the street, and on Tuesdays there's a market in the library's parking lot. I'd guess a lot has changed from when you were a kid."

"That's really kind of you, thank you."

"It's no problem." Her eyes have softened from the flint that was there earlier. Compassion? Or pity? Maybe she feels bad for me. Or maybe, like me, she recognizes a lost soul when she sees one.

"Just real quick before you go," she says. "Could you take a look at this photo of Mrs. Nelson? You said you visited when you were younger. Maybe you knew her."

She holds out her phone, the screen zoomed in on a Facebook profile picture. I reach for it, but my hand freezes in midair. My body stills, my mouth instantly going dry. I try to inhale, but it feels like my lungs are made of stone.

I don't understand. It isn't possible.

But before I can reply, the detective retracts her phone. A strange look crosses her face as her eyes dart to something over my shoulder. Fear?

I turn to see what she's looking at, but there's nothing there.

"I . . ." She looks flustered. "Did you know her?"

I shake my head and take another step back, needing more distance between us. "No, sorry. I don't."

It's the truth, just not all of it.

Chapter 8

NEVE

I head up the hill as fast as I can without looking suspicious. Already I'm regretting the lie, and yet there's no way to undo it. Words are like bullets, I find; once fired, they can't be taken back.

Anyway, it's sort of the truth; I *don't* know her. At least not anymore.

Inside, I lean against the door. The house is cool and silent. Ash must've gone back to bed. I slide to the floor, my butt hot against the cool tile, and think of the picture the detective showed me of a woman I used to know. She had changed; it had been more than twenty years, after all. But I still recognized her.

Back then, I knew her as Bee. Bee Naldoni. My summertime best friend.

I didn't know Bee now called herself Bailey Nelson, or that she owned a property management company, or even that she still lived next door to Dullahan House. I suppose it makes sense my mother hired Bee's company to manage our property. What doesn't make sense is the diver saying that Bee had been dead *a few days*.

Because I saw Bee last night. And she was very much alive.

I don't know why I lied to the detective. I suppose I was in shock, a little, finding out Bee was supposedly my dead neighbor. Besides, everything that happened was so long ago; it doesn't matter anymore. And to be honest, I don't want to remember.

Have you ever done something so terrible that you push it to the back of your mind? You remember it, but it isn't there unless something triggers that memory. And then it's more like a dream than a memory, something you watched but didn't partake in. That's how it was to me.

I just can't believe she's dead. Not three days ago, and not now. There must be some mistake.

I think about those long, halcyon summer days together. Best friends, no phone, just whole days stretching in front of us. Hot sun, burned shoulders, the coconut smell of suntan oil as we waggled watermelon-sticky fingers at boys passing by. Bonfires and lightning bugs and my first sip of a strawberry wine cooler.

But that was all before I learned what people are capable of. What *I* am capable of.

You are more than the worst thing you've done, I remind myself.

They are my mother's words from when I was a child. I'd stepped on an ant and killed it. Worse, I did it on purpose, just to see what would happen. When I realized it was dead, I burst into tears.

"That was a bad choice, Neve," my mother had said. "But you aren't a bad person. You can choose to do good next time. You are more than the worst things you do."

My head is thudding, a headache pulsing at the base of my skull. My hands are shaking, and I feel the sudden urge to find a bottle of wine and guzzle the whole thing. I gave up drinking years ago, when we had Ash. I wanted to give my girl the best start possible, and while I may be a lot of things, bad things, I am a good mother. I love Ash with a love I never knew could exist. She is the only redemption I've ever needed.

Anyway, I soon found other vices to replace alcohol. We all have our addictions. Drugs. Drinking. Gambling. Sex. Sometimes self-destructive behavior is like a boil festering under the skin, something that needs to be lanced to release the poison.

But there is nothing now to help, so I grab a romance novel from the bookshelf and take it outside to the deck. I've always been a bookworm. When I was a kid, I used to beg my mother to drive me to the library. It was, and is, my favorite place to be. In fact, the library is where I first met Eli.

It was a summer's day much like today, bright and blistering hot, when I parked next to a car that still had keys hanging in the driver's side door. I took the keys to the information desk, and he happened to be arriving in a panic right then. When he saw his keys in my hands, his entire face lit up. He said his name was Elias, or just Eli. He asked me out for coffee "to thank me." Within six weeks, we were engaged. It was an overwhelmingly happy time for me, one long throb of happiness that I knew I didn't deserve. Everyone said whirlwind romances never last, and normally I'd agree. But can you blame me for grabbing that happiness with both hands? Hoping for a clean slate wiped free of the remnants of my past mistakes?

Eli had a capacity for joy I'd never experienced before. As quiet and contained as I am, he is impulsive and unburdened. He introduced me to skinny-dipping in the ocean and all-night dance clubs and sex on Ecstasy. His ability to love life intoxicated me. My father was overly religious, a zealot, I suppose they'd call him now, and after his many rants about death and atonement, Eli's capacity to live life in the moment felt like being reborn.

The sound of voices jolts me back to the present. I creep to the edge of the deck and peer over. I can just make out the tops of the two detectives' heads, Detectives Lambert and Casey, as they walk up the path separating my house from Bee's.

". . . to the media. This is a murder, Jess," Detective Casey says.

The words slide down my skull, digging into the back of my neck like talons. I take a step away, my hand flying up to cover my mouth.

Bee was *murdered*.

They move away so I hear only fragments of what they're saying.

". . . statement," Detective Lambert says. "We won't . . . mouth . . . Got it?"

And then they're too far away, and I can't hear anything. I lean against the house as images flash, hot and bright. The trace of something, vague and undefined, nags at the edge of my consciousness.

I bury the images, as I always do, pressing them into the dark, secret corners of my mind. I am shivering despite the heat, a sharp knot of fear tightening in my chest. I'm unable to shake the sight of Bee's lifeless body in the diver's arms.

I can't help but imagine what her last moments were like. If she was scared. If she knew her killer or if she ran from a stranger. Perhaps someone broke in, chased her through the house. She ran outside, into the dark night, down the hill . . .

I am breathing hard, dark spots speckling my vision. I feel the desire to turn and run, to scoop Ash up and return to our past. But are we any safer there?

The police never caught the person who invaded our house. Will they catch Bee's killer? The statistics on unsolved murders are terrifying. At any time, there are hundreds of thousands of murders that remain unsolved, which means murderers are walking around every day, free to murder again.

And what if someone broke into Bee's house? I can't just dismiss the possibility, not after what Ash and I have been through. What if they come back? Statistically speaking, you're more likely to be a burglary victim after being a victim once. Burglars return to the same scene again and again and again.

My eyes fly to the neighbors gathered down by the lake, roving over their faces, committing them to memory in case I need to recall them. They're all potential suspects now. How do I know the killer isn't here, right now, watching us?

My heart throbs, and I move quickly inside, pulling the sliding glass door shut, twisting the lock into place. I brought Ash here so we could feel safe, yet now I feel more vulnerable than ever. I wish I could turn this feeling off as easily as snapping off a light switch.

Suddenly, I feel a desperate urge to check on Ash. I'm terrified she won't be here any longer. That I haven't been able to keep her safe.

That she's disappeared.

I hurry up the turret stairs and push open the door, and there she is, burrowed under the covers. I breathe a silent sigh of relief. She is curled up like a bean facing away from me, her hands fisted under her chin. It's how she's always slept, even as a baby.

My hand hovers over her forehead. I want to touch her, but I don't. The scar on her temple is a vivid, bright pink. Tears well in my eyes. I blame myself, of course. I wasn't able to protect her. That's all I want, all any mother would want, to be the life jacket protecting her child from every crashing wave of the sea. And I failed.

A soft scratching comes from outside. I push the curtains aside and peer out. The limbs of a giant oak tree are pressed against the house. Could someone climb it and get in? I check the window to make sure it's locked.

From up here, I can clearly see the houses to my left and my right. I press my hand to the glass window. My reflection stares back at me, a haunting silhouette sketched against the burning haze washing over the landscape. The air is stifling. It sticks in my throat.

A sudden movement catches my attention. It's my neighbor with the dog, Vivienne. She's crossing the road and heading for Bailey Nelson's front door. She's scowling, her mouth bowed and sour. She's angry, or maybe stressed. The type to get a spurt of pleasure when seeing someone get a parking ticket.

Vivienne climbs the stairs to Bailey's door. She throws a glance over her shoulder and drops to her knee behind the railings. When she stands, she's holding a ceramic flowerpot painted to look like a tuxedo cat. It's a dead ringer for a cat I used to have. She died a few years back, and every time I see a tuxedo cat, I think of her.

Vivienne pushes open a false bottom, extracting a key. She slips the key into the lock and, a second later, Vivienne has disappeared inside.

She's gone only a few minutes, exiting with a small white paper bag in one hand and a green folder under her arm. She replaces the key in the flowerpot and slinks back across the road, disappearing into her own house.

It could be something simple. Maybe they were good friends. Maybe they always let themselves into each other's homes with the spare key.

But someone was murdered next door to me. I don't think it's irrational to be suspicious right now. There's no one to protect Ash but me.

The sun is a scorching ball in the late-morning sky, a spotlight searing my corneas. I feel exposed under that light. Vulnerable.

I hurry downstairs and pull the blinds shut, draw the curtains, trying to shut out the relentless daylight, to feel less exposed. I circle the house three times, checking all the locks, the windows, the front and back doors. There's been a murder just outside my house. I can't help but wonder if we are safe.

The headache finally gets the best of me, and even though it isn't yet 10:00 a.m., I climb under the blankets in my room and fall asleep. When I wake, it is slowly, awareness coming in chunks. I know instantly that something is wrong.

Some primal instinct in me is horribly certain that someone is there, in my room, standing at the foot of my bed. I am paralyzed with fear. I don't dare move. My heart whips in my chest, my breathing serrated against my ribs.

I flash back to that moment when I knew someone had broken into my house, invaded the innermost privacy a person can have. How terrified I'd felt.

I feel that now.

I imagine this person moving to the side of my bed, wrapping their hands around my throat. Squeezing.

"No!" I leap out of bed, ready to fight.

But there's no one there.

I slump onto the sweat-dampened sheets, my legs shaking violently, my heart thudding. Sweat beads on my brow. I inhale deeply, the breathing exercise I'd learned to calm a panic attack.

Outside, the light has shifted. The digital clock on the bedside table blinks 2:00 p.m. I've been sleeping for hours.

My phone is on the bedside table, and I grab it, thinking I'll call Eli. But I stop myself just in time. Nothing has changed between us. And I know that sleep paralysis, which often involves intruder hallucinations in those moments between wakefulness and sleep, is common for those with PTSD. The mind buries feelings when they aren't spoken allowed, and I haven't spoken about my experience to anybody. I tried talking to Eli at first, but he refused to speak about it. Ash was the one who was injured, so I understood why his thoughts were primarily consumed with her, but it felt like he'd shut me out.

Or was keeping secrets.

A home invasion, it turns out, is more about losing your sense of safety than about losing your stuff. You feel violated, unsafe in your own home. I couldn't stay in a place where I didn't feel safe. Where memories stung and guilt lingered.

I won't call Eli after all, I decide. Instead I go downstairs. I check the windows and the doors in the kitchen and living room, but when I move to the front door, where the alarm is, I see that the red light isn't blinking.

I stare at the red light, my brain trying frantically to remember if I'd set it when I came inside earlier. The locks, the windows and doors, yes. The alarm? I'm not sure.

I run to the kitchen and grab a serrated knife from the knife block. I carefully twist the door handle to the basement, but it is still locked. I move slowly, carefully through the downstairs, my heartbeat ratcheting up with every step. There's no broken glass. No signs of forced entry.

I work my way through the house, through each bedroom and bathroom. Nothing. I climb the stairs to the turret room, but like the other rooms, it's empty.

The curtains are open, the window thrown wide. A soft, warm breeze drifts through, smelling hot and verdant. I stand there, my arms limp at my sides. There's a presence here, something I can't really explain. It isn't physical; it's more like the wind, intangible. I feel it, but I can't see it.

"Ash?" I whisper.

A scratching sound comes from downstairs. I descend slowly, the knife in front of me. My heart is galloping. At the bottom, I sense something in my peripheral vision darting into the kitchen. A swish of fabric. Blonde hair.

I steel myself and burst into the kitchen.

Someone screams.

"Mom! What the hell?" Ash has both hands up, her eyes wide.

I stare at my daughter, speechless. The knife slips from my numb fingers, clattering against the tiled floor. "I'm sorry. I thought . . . someone."

Ash's face softens. She scoops the knife up and sets it on the counter. "It's okay, Mom. There's nobody here but me. We're safe."

"I'm sorry. I think I . . . overreacted a little."

"Let's go home." Ash's voice is wheedling, like she's trying to get a piece of candy out of me. "Please, Mom. I want to see Dad."

A flash of black. Air on bare skin. Blood that gleams like oil.

Panic ties itself into an ugly knot in my chest. We can't go back. Not yet.

I force a smile and change the subject. "Why don't we go kayaking? I'll show you some of the little islands out on the lake."

Ash hesitates but eventually agrees. "Sure. That sounds nice."

We leave the kitchen, her arm around my waist, mine around her shoulders. I throw a quick glance over my shoulder. But there's no one there. There never was.

It's just the murder at the back of my house making me on edge.

Chapter 9

I heard the thud of something hit my window the moment I walked into my bedroom. I was tired. Work had been grueling. My job could be demanding, often physical, my patients difficult. I couldn't tell you how many times I'd been bitten. All I wanted was a shower and bed.

I opened my curtains, but it was too dark to see, so I grabbed a flashlight and went outside. The shrubs were overgrown, the grass long due for a cut.

I swept the flashlight beam over the ground and heard something small rustling in the bushes. When I drew back the leaves, a small bird was staring up at me with panicked, beady eyes, his wing bent at an odd angle. The poor thing was terrified and tried to fly away but crashed back to the ground.

"Come here, baby," I crooned.

I gently scooped the bird into my hands and took him upstairs. I set him in an old cat carrier I found in the storage eaves and placed it next to a glossy-leafed plant standing in the corner of my room while I gathered some first aid equipment. His wing was broken, so I used bandaging tape to set it, then slid a bowl of fresh water into the cat carrier. I would need to buy some bird food soon, if he was to survive.

And I wanted him to survive.

Unlike her.

I'd had a lot of time to think about her. Obsess about her. Every waking moment was consumed with thoughts of her. I guess you could say she haunted me, long after she should have.

I followed her for a long time first. Following people was one of my greatest skills. There was a certain craft to it, a patience that most didn't have. The more you watched, I'd learned, the more you saw how hard someone worked to hide their darkest secrets.

Sure, most people never imagined they would be followed, or they were distracted by their phones or by the inner turmoil of their own lives. But you could learn so much just by sitting in the shadows and watching a person, the way they used their hands, their body language, the subtle movements of their mouth. In the shadows, you could see what others had missed.

I was very good at blending. I'd spent my life blending, always blending, people thinking I was one thing, when really I was another altogether.

I have secrets. Doesn't everybody? Perhaps mine were darker than others, but beneath everything, I was still human. I bled, I hurt, I had passions and hopes and fears.

I loved.

Love was what brought me here, after all.

In the kitchen, I poured orange juice over my bowl of Rice Krispies and took it to my bedroom to read the news while Tweety chirped in the background. Most people prefer milk, but I am not most people. It's a treat I allow myself each morning.

A cough came from downstairs. I had about five minutes before my name was called. I ate my cereal first, in great bites, then sipped the orange juice from the bowl as I opened the news on my phone. The top story was about a woman who'd killed her child, buried him, then reported him missing, as if nobody would ever find out the truth.

I shook my head. Some people didn't deserve the good they got in life. They hid their secrets, hoping they would never see the light of day. That the dark shadow in them would never be exposed. And then, when it was, they were surprised. They denied it. Because nobody wanted to believe the worst about themselves.

That was what I learned the first time I followed her.

I kept my eye on her car as she drove into the night. I knew more about her than anybody else I knew. What pastries she liked, where she went for yoga, the color she dyed her hair, and the intimate secrets of her marriage.

She surprised me that night when she pulled onto a secluded dirt road. I followed, my headlights off, bumping along the path until I saw that she'd stopped, her car wedged up against a bush. Another car was already there, parked a few feet away. I watched as she climbed into the passenger's seat of the other car.

She stayed fully clothed when she climbed on top of him, hitching her skirt up to allow him to slide inside her while she rode him. She grabbed his hands and slapped them against her breasts, dragging them through her hair and tearing it from the roots. The moon bounced off her skin, creamy and pale as she tilted her chin to the sky.

Perhaps she didn't think she was doing anything wrong. You'd be surprised how quickly some turn to excuses. If you tell yourself a lie for long enough, it becomes polished with the sheen of truth.

Her eyes stayed open the whole time, her hair tangled in his fists, only closing them at the end, as if blocking out what she'd done. Further proof she deserved what was coming to her.

Because there were always consequences.

Chapter 10

JESS

Wind ripples over my skin. Buffets me with hot summer air.

The shiny chrome-and-black machine roars a comforting melody as I take each curve, my body coiling tight. The road opens beneath a hot blue sky, a hazy black ribbon of asphalt unspooling like a bat's wings in front of me.

I lean to the left, rounding another curve. Just me and the road, the speed, the wind. The world diminishes around me. The pain in my leg, the Bailey Nelson case, the first the lieutenant has asked me to lead since I've been back. Even the person I thought I saw at the crime scene earlier today.

Everything melts away like ice cream in the sun. Damn, if it isn't the best feeling in the world.

I come out of the curve and hit the throttle. The machine leaps at my touch. It was specially adapted for my disability after the accident—clutch-less gear shift, thumb throttle, modified foot plates, hand-operated side stand. It's ironic that I can't get back in a car, but on a motorcycle I feel completely in control. Not just in control, *powerful*.

I slow as the lake sweeps into view. Slow again when I pass the town sign and hit the sharp, nearly ninety-degree curve, fittingly named

Widow's Bend by the locals. This curve has made more than one drunk driver's spouse a widow.

Now the town's erected a steel barrier so people who miss the curve won't go careening over the ledge into the lake. I'm not really sure it's any better smashing into a steel wall, but you know, tomayto, tomahto.

The lake flashes silver to my right as I hug the bend and head into town, past the café, the post office, the church with its white steeple, an arrow pointing up at the hot white sun. Black Lake is still charming in a faded, vintage sort of way, but there's an aura of the forgotten about it these days. It's still cute, with its old-fashioned gazebo in the park, its playground with the rusted swing set. But the municipal library is now tired and dingy. The lake with its wide, sandy beach no longer has lifeguards or hot-dog carts or ice cream vans.

The light's fading when I turn in to the local bar. Sometimes I get here earlier, sometimes later. But I always get here.

I park at the back, where Sammy keeps a spot open for me. Sammy's a gentleman like that. I flip open the compartment for the hand-operated side stand and yank the lever. It pops open near my right heel. I kill the throttle and dismount clumsily. I still haven't totally gotten the hang of it.

I unstrap my helmet and pull the cane from my backpack, twisting my knuckles into my aching thigh. All I want is to get that first drink into me.

Sammy's is bustling. Thank goodness. I hate the dull thud my cane makes against the hardwood floor. The bar is old, with cracked black vinyl booths and stained wooden tables, mismatched barstools and wood-paneled walls. The stale scents of cigarette smoke and old beer seep from the pores of the place, but nobody seems to mind. Not the cops who regularly visit, nor the locals or out-of-towners or blow-ins.

Sammy's behind the bar wiping down glasses with a white cloth. He's a hunched older man, something of an aging hippie, with a wild salt-and-pepper beard, a full head of gray hair, and the eyes of a wizard, lined and all-knowing. He nods at me when I limp in, trying, as always, not to be obvious about dragging my left leg.

A few people stop drinking as I pass, heading for the bar. I feel their eyes on me. Eight months since the accident and people still stop talking when I enter a room. I hate it.

"They pity you," I tell myself silently as I grab a drink and make my way to my usual booth at the back.

At least, I think I've said it inside my head. I've caught myself speaking out loud lately. I've seen people staring. They think the grief has driven me out of my mind.

Maybe they're right.

The first whiskey goes down like silk, cool and smooth. I wave at Mei, the waitress, for another. Mei brings my whiskey, then hurries away. She's busy, moving among tables, refilling drinks, dropping off the occasional greasy burger or bowl of soggy nachos. She's young, a college kid home for the summer but desperate to get away. Everyone's desperate to get away from here.

Once upon a time, Black Lake was a bustling tourist town. But then the pandemic came, and the shops closed and the tourists stopped coming. The young left; the old died. That's how it is here.

I'm neither young nor old. I'm right smack in the middle, but I can't leave; I know that.

Not now.

I think about calling Mac, my ex. He's the only one who understands my pain. But I can't bring myself to do it. I know he blames me.

Just not as much as I blame myself.

I'm working on my second drink when Will hefts his bulk into the booth across from me, a drink in his meaty hand.

"Hey, old girl," he says with a grin.

I try not to let him see how annoyed I am. All I want is to drink in peace until it's time to go home, fall into bed, and sleep without dreaming. Alcohol is the only thing that quiets the nightmares.

"Hey." I don't look up. I hope if I don't engage, he'll go away.

I am mentally and physically exhausted. My afternoon consisted mostly of dealing with the media, with false leads and subpoenas and interviews with Bailey Nelson's neighbors. And then the worst part of my job: telling the victim's loved ones.

All I want now is a little quiet before it all begins again tomorrow.

"Fancy joining us?" Will asks, jabbing a thumb in the direction of the table of cops he's sitting with. I see Robert and Sean, as well as Sean's fiancée, Charlotte.

"I'm good, thanks."

When I was a kid, my mom liked to call me "Mary, Mary." "Because you're a little scrap of contrary," she'd say. My middle sister was the daydreamer, the peacemaker, my littlest sister the fun-loving free spirit. But me, I was a fighter, all fists and claws and passion, like a stray cat. If she could see me now, I wonder what my mother would say. Now that I've lost that passion. All I feel these days is a restless, anxious energy.

"Found out a few things from that witness," Will says.

"Which one?"

He gives me a funny look. "The one you asked me to talk to. Vivienne Jones. Bailey Nelson was dog sitting for her while Vivienne was on vacation. She said when she got back, Bailey didn't answer her phone. She went over and found the dog alone in the house. She took him home, thinking Bailey would show up, but she never did. The next day, she was out for a run when the dog started barking at something in the water."

I try to tamp down a buzz of irritation. I'd forgotten I asked him to speak to her. Worse, I hadn't gotten a chance to talk to him about it. After I'd spoken to Neve, I'd been distracted, preoccupied, which is never what you want at the start of a new case. Especially when you're the lead and you have an awful lot to prove.

I swallow, wipe my mouth, and inhale deeply.

"Right. Yeah, thanks for that. I was following a few footprints one of the CSIs found in the side yard."

"They take imprints?"

"Yep." I massage my aching leg with my knuckles. "I got a statement from the other neighbor, too." I tell him about my conversation with Neve. "I made a few calls. Turns out it's her mother's house, Holly Maguire. She's in a care home now. Alzheimer's."

"I'll look into it." Will opens a notebook.

"I also located Bailey Nelson's husband, Angus Nelson. He's on his way from New York. He'll be in for an interview tomorrow. Her parents are flying up from Florida tomorrow. Why don't you try to track down Bailey Nelson's phone? If we don't find it, we'll need to subpoena the call log."

"Got it." Will's quickly jotting notes in his notepad.

"Tomorrow I'll speak to Angus Nelson and get official ID. Why don't you get the ball rolling on a warrant to search her house?"

We continue discussing the case, speaking quickly and efficiently, the way those who work well together do, and eventually I settle into it. The conversation. The companionship. Will isn't a bad guy, and maybe I spend too much time alone these days.

I twist my glass of whiskey, watching the light bounce off the amber liquid. My hand is shaking just slightly.

"You sure you're okay to be on this case?" Will crosses his arms over his large stomach and leans back against the booth, eyeing me.

I take a long gulp of whiskey and eye him right back. It's been a while since we've had a homicide in Black Lake—not since the case I was working before the accident. But that isn't why he's asking.

"It's my job. 'Course I'm okay."

I down my drink, the ice clicking against my teeth. Will keeps waiting, like he's expecting me to pour my heart out. He'll be waiting an awful long time.

Will lowers his voice. "I'm worried about you."

My hand stiffens on the glass, which has started vibrating just slightly.

"If you don't pull it together, you're gonna get sent to a desk somewhere." Will finishes his drink and stands, throwing a pointed look at my glass, empty already. "Lay off the sauce. At some point, you gotta choose to join the living."

He turns to go but, at the last second, faces me and says, "Come over for dinner sometime this week. Shelby would love to see you."

"Sure. I'll try."

It's bullshit and he knows it. Worse, I know it. "Jess, you know if you need anything . . ."

"I know." I don't need a fucking heart-to-heart right now. I hate that people still act like I'm some tragic head case.

Will says goodbye, returning to the table of cops on the other side of the bar.

I lift a hand for another drink and sit quietly, getting just drunk enough to not care about my too-quiet, too-dark house haunted by things I want to forget. Then I stagger the three blocks home, leaning heavily on my cane, and let myself inside. The pain in my leg is mostly gone now, numbed by the weightless sensation of alcohol winding through my bloodstream.

I climb into bed fully clothed, hoping for sleep to come quickly. Sometimes alcohol does the trick; sometimes it doesn't.

I'm just drifting off, grateful that tonight I've been set free, when something in the air shifts. Ice trickles down my spine, my breath fogging in front of me despite the warmth of the evening. My teeth clatter, and my ears start ringing, the thick, uncomfortable pressure you get on an airplane. Blood rushes violently in my ears.

I draw the blankets to my chin, squeezing my eyes tightly shut as the bed beside me dips under someone's weight.

"Mommy?" My daughter's voice reaches me from very far away. And then the pressure of her small hand on my shoulder. "Mama, are you awake?"

I feel like I can't process the words. Exhaustion and alcohol jostle for position in my brain, making me feel dizzy and disoriented. Everything feels unreal, like I'm living in a bad dream.

Screaming pierces my brain, a flash of red, of tearing flesh, shattering glass, and then a horrible, horrible silence.

I shove the images away.

"Not tonight, Isla," I slur. "Please. I can't talk tonight."

I keep my eyes squeezed tightly shut. After a minute, the weight on the bed shifts. My ears pop. I burrow farther under the blanket until my teeth stop chattering.

When I open my eyes, there's nothing there. Just the soft darkness of night, the faint glow from the bathroom light down the hall, the outline of my dresser across the room. I exhale, both sad and relieved at the same time.

It isn't real, I tell myself for the second time today. *It isn't real.*

Ever since the accident, I've become very good at denial. I've found choosing to believe what I want to can be very seductive. It becomes a slippery slope I can tumble down, no rope to pull me back up.

The problem is, denying the truth has never been good enough to change the facts.

Chapter 11

JESS

Monday morning, I'm up early, heading to the morgue located in the belly of the hospital. We'd briefly talked to Angus Nelson yesterday, gotten official ID on Bailey Nelson, and today is the autopsy.

I park my motorcycle at the back of the hospital, yanking the side stand handle a little too hard. Another restless night has left me feeling off, a weird, anxious energy buzzing inside me.

I extract my cane from my backpack just as my cell phone vibrates in my pocket.

"Hello, Jess, it's Dr. Overton returning your call. Is everything all right?"

I lean against a crumbling brick wall to take a little pressure off my leg. "Thanks for calling me back, Doc."

"Of course." Dr. Pamela Overton's voice is smooth as honey, a comforting southern drawl that invites you to spill all your secrets. And I do. I've spilled my secrets every Tuesday night for the last six months like a good little patient. Not that it helps.

"You sounded upset in your message. How can I help?"

"I . . ."

I massage my leg. I want to take something to dull the pain. But I won't. I'll wait until the sweet bliss of that first cold sip of whiskey. One addiction is enough, thanks very much.

The sound of screaming pierces my brain. The sense of weightlessness. Shattering glass. The punch of the airbag. And then the horrible, horrible sound of silence.

It's all my fault.

Guilt is one of those emotions that doesn't have an off switch. It rears up now and hits me like a blow to the face.

"Jess?" Dr. Overton cuts into my thoughts.

"Sorry. I'm . . ." I gnaw on a ragged thumbnail, the sharp taste of blood filling my mouth. I'm going to sound crazy; I *do* sound crazy. "I keep . . . seeing her. Isla."

The shrink stays silent, waiting for me to continue.

"I was interviewing this woman at a crime scene, and I saw Isla. And then Saturday night, she was in my bedroom. She sat on my bed. The bed dipped, actually *dipped* from her weight."

I'm a pragmatist. My father was a cop, my mother a science teacher. I grew up on facts and science and data. I know how to change a tire, fix a faucet, write a crime report. My feet are firmly planted on the ground. One, in fact, is planted far more firmly than the other. But I can't explain what I've been seeing.

"It was so real." My hands are damp with sweat.

"Remember we talked about the effect grief can have on our psyche," Dr. Overton says. "What you're seeing isn't real. Auditory and visual grief hallucinations are a normal reaction to bereavement, especially when you're suffering with acute grief. They play an important part in the mourning process."

"You said they'd go away."

"Do you want them to go away?"

Tears fill my eyes. I don't know how to answer that, so I don't.

"Everybody processes grief differently," Dr. Overton says gently. "I know this doesn't help now, but losing a child, especially in such a traumatic way, as you did, is like losing a part of yourself. Bereavement causes a sudden hole in one's life, and these visions are filling that hole. I would urge you not to fight them and instead let them be a positive and comforting presence until your mind is able to return to a place where you no longer need them."

I inhale slowly, letting the warm air fill my lungs.

"I know this is difficult, but I believe there's nothing wrong with you, Jess. However, if it would make you feel better, I'm happy to refer you for an MRI, just to make sure there's nothing else going on."

Just then, I spot Will getting out of his cruiser across the parking lot. He adjusts his stomach over his belt and slips his blazer over his white shirt. I wipe quickly at my eyes, my mouth pressing into a tight, grim line. I can't let him see me like this.

"Sure, Doc, a referral would be great," I say. "Look, I gotta go. Thanks for calling."

I smooth my ponytail, fixing a smile onto my face as Will approaches. I'm an old pro at pretending, folding each piece of myself into separate, neat little boxes.

Will hands me a coffee. "Hey, old girl," he says gently.

I ignore the pity in his eyes and take the coffee. "You're a gift from the gods. Thanks, Will."

I slug back a mouthful of coffee but choke and almost gag. I stare at the cup in horror. "What the hell is this?"

"Skinny latte, two sugars, right?"

"Don't bullshit me, Will. This isn't a skinny latte. What is it?"

Will smirks. "It's almond milk. Shelby's on this health kick." He pats his bulging stomach.

"And you figured you'd take me down with you? Shit, I thought we were partners!"

Will laughs and takes the cup, throws it in the nearest trash can. "All right, I owe you."

We cross the parking lot and step inside the arched entrance of the hospital. When we reach the elevators, Will jabs the "Down" button to the morgue. "You ready for this?"

"Ready to do my job, you mean?" I say snippily.

The elevator dings, and the doors slide open. I brush past him and step inside. I wish everyone would stop treating me like I'll break.

We ride down together in silence. I can't stop fidgeting, smoothing my hair, grinding my teeth, nibbling my nails. I blow out a long, impatient breath. Will wordlessly pulls out a pack of gum. I flush and take a piece, wondering if he can smell last night's booze on my breath.

"Sorry, Will. I'm not sleeping so great."

Will smiles, his shiny pink face creasing. "No need to apologize. This part's always the hardest."

He's right. Attending autopsies *is* the worst part of our job, but this time it's worse than normal. I haven't been here since it was my own daughter lying on that slab.

Still, I feel like I owe it to not only the dead, but also their families. Losing someone you love is like having your heart ripped out. Observing, taking notes, claiming evidence, it's a small gift I can offer to the brokenhearted.

Too bad it feels like it's taking a chunk of my soul, too.

I wipe my damp hands on my trousers. I just need to get through this. But what I really *want* is a drink.

We pull slip-on booties over our shoes and plastic gloves onto our hands, completing the ensemble with a paper gown. The room is thick with the reek of formaldehyde and disinfectant.

We exchange pleasantries with the medical examiner, a black-haired man with the face of a crow: tiny, beady eyes; a sharp, hooked nose; flat, thin lips. Like me, Dr. George Arquette is a transplant to Black Lake. I arrived with my husband, Mac, who grew up in Black Lake, nearly ten years ago, both of us looking for a quieter life, a more peaceful life. The type of life we thought a small town could give us in order to raise a family. It's ironic, really, considering Mac is the one who left after our daughter died, left his mother, his father, neither of whom speak to me anymore, and returned to his job as a criminal defense lawyer in New York.

Dr. Arquette looks rushed, a little harried. He explains he's running behind. Black Lake is located in a small county, with only one medical examiner and one assistant. Unfortunately, the assistant's kid has COVID, so he's with her, leaving Dr. Arquette with a truckload of work to do on his own.

He shows us to the slab where Bailey Nelson lies. She's still wearing the silk blouse and pencil skirt she was found in. Her head is supported by a stand, but I can clearly see where her skull was hit.

Dr. Arquette begins his examination, narrating into a recording device that sits on the slab above Bailey's head. "No needle marks. No signs of drug use. Her general appearance suggests a healthy, well-nourished forty-year-old female. Her body is intact, but the skin on her hands and feet has just started loosening, blackening from the water. I would estimate she died five to six days ago."

"Can you be more specific?" Will asks.

"Tuesday. But I couldn't definitively say an exact time based solely on body decomposition."

Will turns to me. "Her neighbor Vivienne Jones said Bailey watched her dog while she was out of town. On Tuesday, the dog ate some green algae, and Bailey took him to the vet."

"That could be the last place she was seen," I say. "Let's speak to the vet."

Dr. Arquette carefully snips the duct tape around her wrists. "She's wearing some sort of bracelet on her left wrist."

He peels a rainbow-colored bracelet from the duct tape and drops it into an evidence bag. The bracelet is braided into a fancy diamond pattern with an adjustable clasp.

"A friendship bracelet," I say. "My friends and I used to make these when we were kids."

"A little childish for a woman like this to be wearing," Will notes.

"Definitely."

Dr. Arquette bends low over Bailey's body. "No sign of sexual assault, but she definitely had sex prior to death. I'll take samples of the semen."

I frown. We'd spoken briefly to Angus Nelson yesterday, after he'd returned to Black Lake, and he'd said he hadn't been home since last week. "Her husband was at a medical conference last week and stayed in New York after that. I called and checked. He was definitely there."

"If he was really there, that wouldn't be his sperm," Will says. "Maybe she was having an affair. That's motive right there."

"Maybe he left and came back. Let's set up another interview with Mr. Nelson. At his hotel, somewhere he's comfortable. We need to find out where he really was last Tuesday and why he didn't report her missing. And let's check with the property management company she worked for. It should've raised some flags if she didn't show up to work."

Dr. Arquette continues with his examination, explaining his findings as he goes. But I'm no longer listening. The pressure in the morgue has changed, a high-pitched buzzing sound vibrating in my ears. The fine hairs on the backs of my arms are standing on end.

Two slabs down from Bailey sits an eight-year-old girl. She has a high forehead, a heart-shaped face, bright blue eyes. A pretty girl with a quiet sweetness about her. She's wearing a blue-and-white dress with a Peter Pan collar, her long blonde hair braided on either side of her head, the pink Hello Kitty satin bow headband I bought for her last birthday perched atop her head.

"Please, Mama!" Isla had pleaded. "Louise and Elorie have Hello Kitty headbands. I'm the only one who doesn't, and I really, really want one!"

I tried not to laugh, tried to take the injustice as seriously as Isla clearly did. I knelt in front of my daughter and gently tugged one of the braids she always begged me to put her hair into. "It's almost your birthday. How about we call it an early birthday present?"

Isla looks exactly the same now.

Her blue eyes still sparkle cheerfully. The gap where her two front teeth fell out is still there. She lost them late, at seven and a half, and then both at the same time. But nearly a year since Isla died and no new teeth have grown in that space. That in itself tells me everything I need to know.

It isn't real, I chant. *It isn't real. What you're seeing isn't real.*

I'm a detective, for God's sake. And I sure as hell don't believe in ghosts. I know better than most that people see what they want to see. Clearly, I'm just seeing the person my heart most desires.

"Isla." Her name comes out of my mouth before I can stop it, ripping apart the silence of the morgue.

Both men turn to stare at me. Will's eyes are pinched with pity.

I try to remember what my shrink said. Grief hallucinations are a normal reaction to bereavement, my brain's way of comforting me during difficult times. And being back in the same morgue my daughter was in just under a year ago could definitely be classed as difficult.

The grief is just as sharp now as it was after the accident when Mac told me about Isla. Every morning since then, I've woken missing my daughter, wishing, in fact, that I hadn't woken at all.

I'm consumed with grief, but that's not all. I'm consumed with guilt.

Isla waves and makes a silly face. I don't wave back. I rub my eyes, squeezing them tightly shut.

Sleep. I really need sleep. And a drink. I'm glad I topped up my flask this morning. The vodka is waiting patiently in the saddlebag on my motorcycle. I just have to make it through this.

When I finally peel my eyes open, Isla is gone. And Will is looking at me, a strange expression on his face.

"Sorry," I croak.

My hands are shaking, a thick, foggy headache pressing on my brain.

"You want me to take over?" Will asks.

I can't speak; my throat is bone-dry. I need to pull it together. If word ever gets back to my lieutenant that I'm talking to my dead daughter, he'll put me on desk duty. Or worse, extended leave. He won't let me do my job, and the job is the only thing keeping me going right now. It's the only thing getting me out of bed these days. If I can't do this, I'll have lost everything.

"Detective Lambert?" The patience in Dr. Arquette's voice is waning.

"Sorry." I drag my attention back to the autopsy. "Please go on."

Dr. Arquette continues his examination, and my eyes settle on Bailey Nelson's mouth. My gaze sharpens, and I bend closer, thinking I see something hidden in the dark space there. I feel that strange hypnotic pull, like I did that day by the lake. There's something there, between her lips.

"Her mouth . . ." I cut Dr. Arquette off midsentence. The doctor blinks, a little stunned. He obviously isn't used to being interrupted, nor does he look like he appreciates it. "There's something inside her mouth . . ."

I pull the light hanging from the ceiling closer and angle it directly at her mouth as Dr. Arquette gently eases Bailey Nelson's jaw open. I bend over her, so close that I feel the cold seeping from her body.

"What's that on her tongue?"

Dr. Arquette pulls out a pair of long tweezers and grabs the tongue, extracting it from Bailey Nelson's mouth.

"Oh!" He gives a little gasp of surprise. "Well, we don't see this every day."

I tilt my head, trying to understand what I'm seeing. Carved vertically into the puckered purple flesh of Bailey Nelson's tongue is what looks to be a letter and some numbers.

"M1237," I read out loud.

I look at Will, who's turned a little green. "Looks like our killer was sending a message."

Chapter 12

NEVE

Bee is dead.

I hear it on the local news the next day. There is no question about it now. The detective makes a statement to a local reporter, confirming the body was that of local real-estate-company owner Bailey Nelson and that she'd been killed on Tuesday, three days before I thought I'd seen her. Detective Lambert won't be drawn into speculating on a motive or naming a suspect but simply requests anyone with information to contact the police as soon as possible.

I change the channel, wanting to block out the news. An oily presenter preens at a camera like a self-obsessed peacock, ranting about end times and the state of the world. He makes me think of my father, the self-righteous glint in his eye, the twist of his mouth as he thundered about the wickedness of man. He used to thump his fists so hard against the table, the glasses would jump. My mother was the opposite, soft and sweet, always ready with a hug and a kind word. But the effects of my father's tirades lingered long into adulthood.

I turn off the TV. A black nausea worms in my solar plexus. Silence settles over the living room. Sun streams in from the windows, a glare settling on the blank TV screen.

I must've dreamed seeing Bee. Being back in this place, surrounded by my past, it's gotten in my head. And it makes a bizarre sort of sense. I've been sleepwalking again, having strange dreams, and waking in unexpected places. I just need some time. Soon the detectives will catch whoever did this, and Ash and I will settle into our new life.

We spend the next week trying to pretend like everything is normal. We go swimming and take the kayaks out to explore the wooded islands. Anything to keep our minds off the crime that has occurred right in our backyard.

And I mostly succeed, although I probably enjoy our time together more than Ash does. She has grown up too fast. I try not to let it bother me that at fifteen, she is already more woman than girl. I can feel her pulling away, chafing at my inquiries, my attention. I know it's normal, but I would be lying if I said it was easy. To be honest, I think I'm having a harder time letting go than I really like admitting.

But by Monday evening, neither of us can ignore the elephant in the room any longer.

"Do you have to go to work tomorrow?" Ash is standing in the kitchen, anxiously peering out the window that overlooks crime scene tape fluttering in the breeze.

"I'm afraid so."

"You could stay if you really wanted to." She's using that bratty voice that makes me want to take a cheese grater to my eardrums.

A tight wire of tension squeezes deep in my gut. Guilt. It's my fault she's scared. Maybe I shouldn't leave her. But I have to work; there's no getting around it.

I set my book down and go to her, wrapping my arms around her. "This was a really bad way to start out here, but we're safe, I promise. The detective said they're looking at her husband as a suspect."

This isn't exactly true, but I'll say anything to reassure Ash right now. Some lies heal instead of hurt. Besides, for all I know, it *was* Bailey's husband who killed her. It's always the husband, right?

But Ash doesn't believe me. She pushes away, muttering, "Whatever," and then she is gone, leaving me alone in the kitchen with the things that haunt me, the voices in my head. And a few seconds later, I hear the slam of her bedroom door.

That night, I lie awake for a long time, thinking, the lonely night ebbing and flowing around me. I consider calling my friend Megan, who I trained with at veterinary school. She's always been a compassionate listener, someone who can be strikingly wise. But she's also kind of a gossip. She tends to extract more information than I want to give, and that's the last thing I need right now, after the things I've done, the remorse and guilt I carry.

I finally get out of bed and check the windows and doors. Downstairs, I check the red alarm light is still blinking reassuringly. I fill a glass with water for Priss and pour it over her dry soil. She's looking a bit wilted, her leaves dull, the pink stripes a little faded, even though I just watered her yesterday.

I unlock the door and step out onto the deck. I wasn't able to find a bulb for the floodlight, so the deck remains shrouded in black.

I watch a star bleed from the sky, but I don't bother to make a wish. I feel lonely. Empty. Haunted. The way I used to when Ash was a baby and I would get up to feed her, sitting in the rocking chair and feeling like I was the only person in the world. Looking out at the black night now, I feel like a ghost moving through the night, marooned from the rest of the world.

I've never believed in ghosts per se, but I do think we can all be haunted. Sometimes by loneliness. Sometimes by grief. Sometimes by regret because we just can't let go. Of the past. Of our memories. Of the things we can't change and things we can.

Memories I've locked away are stirring, clawing at me with sharp, pointed nails. I think of Bee and wish I'd just been honest back then. Or better yet, I wish I hadn't met her or that I'd stayed away from her that last summer, the summer we were seventeen. Something was different about her; I knew it the day I'd arrived.

Usually Bee came running over as soon as we pulled up to Dullahan House, all toothy grin and messy hair and that glint in her eye. Bee was so *fun*. I was eight the first time we met, small with pigtails and crooked teeth.

I was a shy and anxious child, terrified daily by my father's vivid images of the rapture and end times, of being left behind and getting my head chopped off or worse, committing unforgivable sins and being sent straight to Hell. He thought *A Thief in the Night* was a perfect Sunday school movie.

But Bee had the easy confidence that came with not having a lot of parental input. She invented our games, and I followed along. We climbed trees and built forts, caught fireflies, roasted marshmallows, went kayaking, and swung on rope swings into the lake.

But that day, when we arrived, there was no Bee. After a while, I made my way over to her house. Her mom answered the door, looking gaunt and grim, her cheekbones jutting like straight arrows. She gave me a one-armed hug. She was already half-drunk, her eyes glassy, even though it wasn't yet lunchtime. She had a giant insulated thermos in one hand, and the reek of whiskey came off her in waves.

"Good to see you, doll!" she exclaimed, too loud. "Bee's up in her room."

When Bee opened her bedroom door, I gasped.

"Bee, wow, you look . . . amazing!" She was all angles and sharp lines. And her boobs were huge, or was her bra padded? Her pink crop top and short shorts left little to the imagination.

"Neve! I didn't know you were back!" She threw her arms around me, then twirled dramatically. "It's my new diet, doll."

There was something about her mother to this new Bee—the sharp cheekbones, the padded bra, the airy use of the word *doll*. I didn't like it.

"Where's Sandra?" I asked.

Sandra Baker had become the third part of our friendship triangle in the last few years. She'd moved to town when her dad got the youth pastor job at our local church. Bee had become her advocate of sorts.

Sandra was shy and awkward, all arms and legs, with ill-fitting clothes and tangled blonde hair. But Bee had treated her with kindness. She'd taken her shopping and did her hair and introduced her to her friends. Bee always liked a good project, and eventually, Sandra sort of bloomed. We usually met her and Zac, Bee's boyfriend for the last two years, the day I arrived.

"Sandra's probably with her new boyfriend," Bee said. The way she spit the word—*boyfriend*—told me something was up. "I don't think we'll be seeing much of her this summer."

It turned out she was right. But not for the reason I was thinking.

I'd pushed all of that to the back of my mind for so long. Some people are so good at filing bad things away in little folders. I wonder if when we die, part of getting through those pearly gates will include rifling through that filing cabinet, our own personal string of sins, white tabs with all our dirty secrets. The things we hid in the darkest parts of ourselves.

I saw Bee quite recently, actually. She called me out of the blue a few weeks ago and insisted we meet. Said it was urgent. She named a swanky restaurant in Back Bay and hung up, confident, as always, that I would do her bidding.

And just like before, I did.

Chapter 13

NEVE

When I arrived downtown to meet Bee, I was running late. I'd had a Labrador with an emergency intestinal obstruction, the X-ray showing a wine cork in his stomach. I could've sent the dog and his owner to the emergency clinic so close to closing time, but I stayed and did the surgery myself. The out-of-hours clinics were expensive, and I wanted to make sure the dog got the care he needed.

When I finally arrived, the sidewalks of Back Bay were packed. Every neighborhood in Boston had its own personality, but this one, with its moneyed Victorian and Edwardian homes, its affluent residents and its artfully curated shops, had always seemed more distinct than the others.

The restaurant was busy. It was one of those upscale places with minimalist decor and dimmed lighting hanging like twinkling stars from the ceiling, where the women wore stilettos and the men had bleached teeth and artificially formed muscles. It was new, difficult to get a reservation unless you booked months in advance, but Bee always had her ways.

I recognized Bee immediately. She was still gorgeous, even more so now at forty. Her cheekbones were sharp as cut glass, her porcelain skin flawless, her dark hair spilling in glossy waves down her back. She was curvy in all the right places, wearing a figure-hugging red dress with a deep-cut back and a cowl-neck paired with impossibly high Louboutins. She drew stares from both men and women.

I couldn't help comparing my plain white blouse, high-waisted black trousers, and sensible flat loafers. At least I'd had my fingernails done yesterday, my nails painted the ballet-slipper pink I loved. It was a silly bit of self-indulgence, especially considering my job, but it was one thing that made me feel sexy, feminine.

Bee wiggled her fingers at me while whispering a few words to the hostess. The hostess nodded and grabbed two menus.

In life, there are the Debtors and the Collectors. The Debtors are those who are constantly in debt for something. A friend buys them a bracelet and they accept it, but a balance is added to their column. And then there are the Collectors. The people who *want* others to owe them. They will do things for you, buy you gifts, and do little favors. They keep your secrets and do your dirty deeds. But it's only so you owe them. So they *own* you. They saddle you with obligations you never accepted in the first place.

Bee was a Collector. She had so many in her pocket. So many were obligated to her. The hostess at a fully booked restaurant. The cop who never ticketed her. The PE teacher who gave her an A even though she never participated. Bee was manipulative, bold, generous. Powerful. Her own little one-woman mafia.

I had somewhere else I wanted to be, so I ordered a side salad, along with a dry martini with a twist, which is exactly what she'd ordered. The waiter exchanged a lingering look with Bee before leaving. I spotted the wedding ring on her left hand but looked quickly away. She could probably have any man she wanted any time she wanted. Sometimes people hooked up when they were married. It wasn't like I was naive to that.

"Nice to see you, Bee," I said after the waiter had left. But Bee wasn't interested in pleasantries. She was never one to mince words.

"I've received three of these in the mail the last few weeks." Bee pulled a manila envelope out of her Gucci purse and set it on the table. "Are you sending them?"

I lifted the envelope flap and pulled out three photos. They were all the same: a picture of Bee, Sandra, and me the last time I was in Black Lake. The light was low, the sun sinking. Our arms were flung around each other, spaghetti straps falling off our shoulders, cheeks creased, grins wide. A bonfire crackled, slightly blurred just off-center.

"I don't understand. Why would I send you three of the exact same picture?"

Bee sipped her water, her dark eyes assessing me. "So you didn't send them?"

"No."

"My bracelet's gone, too."

"Which one?"

She tapped her wrist in the picture. "My friendship bracelet. I . . ."

Something shifted in her demeanor, her composure slipping slightly, and for a second I saw the old Bee. Genuine. Sweet. A little uncertain.

"I lost it. That night. Remember, the clasp kept coming undone? But I had an extra one. They came in a pack, and I never got rid of the other one. But it's disappeared. After I got the first picture, I looked for it. It isn't there."

"It's been more than twenty years, Bee." I waved a hand and sipped my water. "Maybe you lost it."

She paused as the waiter set down our salads and drinks. "Do you know where yours is?"

I shoved a bite of lettuce in my mouth. "No."

It was a lie. I'd packed my bracelet into a shoebox with a bunch of mementos the day I left. My mom had called, telling me she'd put all my old boxes into storage in the boathouse before she moved into the care home.

"Have you told anybody?" she asked.

"Of course not!"

She drained her martini, watching me, tapping her nails on the varnished black table. My phone buzzed on the table where I'd set it. A text from Eli. I'd told him I was meeting an old friend and, trusting as he was, he hadn't questioned it. The text told me he'd taken Ash to driver's ed, that she was doing fine, excelling like she did at most things.

I quickly replied, then went into my phone's settings and turned tracking off. Not that he'd look, but I couldn't risk it. Later.

"I suppose you must like your life," Bee said, her eyes flinty. "Your little family. Your daughter in that fancy private school. Your sweet husband, so naive. So ignorant." She laughed, a harsh, brittle sound. "Is that him texting you now? He doesn't know what you're doing, does he?"

A chill moved through me.

"I could ruin all of that with one phone call," she continued. "I've kept your secrets. The ones from the past *and* the present. *You owe me.*"

As an adult, I got that Bee had been a kid who was definitely neglected, possibly abused. It had turned her steely, given her a desire to never let any weakness show. She needed to feel like she was on top, in control. But the malevolence in her gaze burned away any compassion I might have once felt for her.

I thought then how I'd loved her, the deep, boundless love of first friends. It's funny how love can be so beautiful. Or so, so ugly.

"*I* owe *you?*" I laughed, even though my hands had started to tremble. "I think you'll find it's the other way around."

"You think I didn't keep the tape?" Her lips twisted into a smirk. "You know that isn't my style. I always have leverage."

My throat felt as if Bee had wrapped her hands around it. She must've made a copy. Or I destroyed the wrong tape.

I'd been so stupid. I wondered how many lives she'd ruined with her recordings, how many people she'd exploited.

I stood so fast, my chair almost tipped over. I fumbled to right it, my cheeks burning.

"Release it," I said defiantly. "I dare you. You'll go to prison, too."

"How do you think Eli and Ash will feel about you when you're in prison? You think they'll just wait around?"

I stared at Bee in disbelief. "Don't you care at all? Don't you regret . . . *anything?*"

She threw her head back and laughed, exposing the creamy skin on her throat. "Of course not! I got to live my life. I don't regret a single thing."

Only liars and sociopaths have no regrets. I had a pretty good idea which she was.

"How do you live with yourself?" My voice was pinched, like it had become twisted somewhere between my belly and my tongue.

She crossed one slim leg over the other. "Don't be so naive. Life goes on. That's your punishment and mine."

"At least I care."

"Does it matter? Either way, you're just as bad as me."

We stared at each other for a long moment. The space between us stretched, the throbbing music surrounding us. Finally, I looked away. "Just do me a favor, Bee. Never fucking contact me again."

I hurried outside to my car, but I didn't go home. I sat in the driver's seat, my hands shaking. Sometimes you search inside yourself for good, even just a sliver of it. But all you find is the emptiness of darkness.

I fumbled through the zippered compartment in my purse and pulled out a phone hidden there.

I looked at myself in the rearview mirror. I wanted to feel bad about what I was going to do, but I didn't. The feeling wouldn't come. Instead, what I saw was blood. I saw blonde hair and a girl with a gentle smile and a midnight road with a sky full of regrets.

I unlocked the phone, and I texted him.

Chapter 14

NEVE

I think of that friendship bracelet now as I stand on the deck, looking out into the velvet-black night. I feel a pressing urge to find it.

In the kitchen, I rifle through cupboards and drawers until I find a flashlight. Miraculously, it turns on. I grab the spare key from the silverware drawer and lock the back door behind me.

The air is warm, stroking my bare arms like fingers. My skin feels damp, sticky with sweat. The moon is full and sweet, creamy light finding me even amid the trees.

I move silently, briskly through the forest. I didn't put my shoes on, I realize, and yet the dried twigs and leaves that litter the path don't hurt at all. I'm not typically scared of the dark, but the woods in the dark is another matter altogether. I feel something unsettling and dangerous about it as I move deeper into the trees, letting them swallow me, until I burst out of the tree line, and there it is. The boathouse.

It rises above the black lake like a hulking skeleton. The boathouse is balanced on concrete slabs that are suspended over the water. There's a small boat dock below, and above is a living room area that has been turned into a storage room.

I press my feet along the edges of the slabs, clutching the timbers as I carefully skirt the side and move out over the water to the front.

Our old boat is long gone, but the top of the ledge holds a key my mother hid many years ago. I stand on tiptoe, wedging my hip against the steel post for balance, and feel along the ledge until the cool metal slides into my hands.

I drop the key into my pocket and carefully sidle back to solid ground. I climb the narrow wooden stairs, rotting and cracking with age, and jiggle the key into the lock. It is rusted and damaged, but it opens with a groan. Something rushes at my face, and I stagger back, hooked claws clutching at my hair. I scream and duck as wings bat the air.

As the sound of rushing wings diminishes, it is replaced with a strange, girlish chattering. The sound, soft and sweet, is coming from inside the boathouse. I sweep my flashlight around the room, but there is no one there.

I try the light switch. *Click. Click.* It doesn't work. I take in the A-frame timber beams damaged from nesting birds, the peeling once-white paint, the dark couch, the cushions now dirty and molding. The shelves that line the room are splattered with bird poop. At the back, a tarp covers a hulking mound.

The soft chattering swells, but still I can't see anyone. I have that strange, disoriented feeling, like I've just woken and still carry the lingering edges of sleep with me. I move closer to the tarp, my flashlight making it look huge, monstrous. Shadows bounce around the room.

"Hello?" I turn in a full circle, the beam of my flashlight raking across the boathouse walls, the black of the lake beyond. "Hello?"

"Do you see?" I catch sight of blonde hair, messy braids.

The girl reminds me of Sandra as a girl. But I must be dreaming. Sandra is forty years old. She lives with her sister in a small town just outside Black Lake.

The outline of the girl's body stutters in the weak light, like a glitch, a defect in a game. Without saying another word, she steps back, through the closed glass, until she is on the other side. And then she melts into the night, blackness swallowing her whole.

"Sandra?" My voice is a hoarse whisper, and I realize I'm shivering, my arms prickling with goose bumps.

It's a nightmare. A hallucination, I tell myself.

There is a whooshing, and shadows writhe and shift in my peripheral vision. My whole body is shaking. My pulse drills into the soft skin at my throat, making me viscerally aware of how vulnerable I am here. Alone. With nothing to defend myself.

Something cold moves across me. Like a breath or an exhale gusting over me. Icy fingers of fear trickle down my back, tapping along the vertebrae. There's a smell, too. It's not altogether unpleasant; it's just so sweet, like rotting gardenias. Something—a memory—fires in my mind, an image that is there and then not.

And then whatever it is disappears, like evaporating mist. The chattering stops. And I'm alone in the hot, sticky summer night, holding my flashlight and wondering if I've just experienced some sort of awake nightmare. Like I've fallen asleep standing up and am again experiencing sleep paralysis.

I grip my cell phone, thinking I'll call Eli. But if I do, I'll never hear the end of it. If he knows I'm scared, he'll want to drive out here, take over, make sure we're safe. And then we'll be right back where we started. But I'm so scared right now, I don't even care. I unlock my phone and tap into my messages. What I see there makes me freeze.

Because the most recent message on my phone isn't from Eli. It's from an unknown number.

I know what you did. But what goes around comes around. There will be consequences.

I scroll up and see more.

You won't get away with it.

You're going to rot in Hell, Neve.

I've never replied to any of them, not in the months since they first started arriving.

My heartbeat swells in my ears. The boathouse, already small, feels oppressive, the walls closing around me. Those words, "there will be consequences," they're similar to the letter I found in that book of poetry in the kitchen.

The malicious texts unspooling on my screen bring it all back. Everything I've pushed away. I wiped them out of my mind the way the sea sweeps away the sand. But I remember now.

At first, I thought they were a wrong number. Then I thought they were meant for someone else. And then whoever it was had used my name. I didn't want to worry Eli, so I ignored them.

Denialitis. I hear Ash's voice in my mind.

For a second, I think I'll return to the house. But the texts make me more determined to find what I'm looking for.

I throw the tarp back, revealing about a dozen plastic storage boxes. I place the flashlight faceup on the floor. The thin beam of light is weak, a pathetic little circle directed at the ceiling.

Time contracts and stretches in strange ways as I search the boxes. There are knickknacks from family trips. Cracked, aging homemade pottery. Ratty old sports equipment. A jersey from the summer I joined a soccer team. My mother's golden statue for winning the Best Chili Competition. An assortment of framed family photos.

I finally find the box with my things in it. Inside is an old leather-bound diary that I only rarely wrote in. A purple bottle of Extra Hold Aqua Net. I accidentally hit the nozzle, and the hair spray sprays a viscous stream into my hand. The smell hits me, bringing memories with it. I wipe my hands on my shorts, wishing I could wipe the memories away just as easily. But they keep coming, seeping up through the floorboards and walls.

I lift the lid off the shoebox. Inside is an assortment of mementos: a VHS of *Beaches*, a package of Lip Smacker ChapStick I never opened, a handful of gel pens, a battered copy of *The Dollhouse Murders*.

There's also a picture. The same one Bailey had of Sandra, her, and me. It's a little creased, a little faded, with that vague blur that lets you know it was taken in the nineties. We're wearing tank tops and cutoff shorts. Our faces are lit from the bonfire, flames shooting sparks into the darkening sky. Our golden arms are tangled around each other. I'm in the middle with my arms around Sandra's waist. She has a soft smile on her face, her head tilted just so. Bailey is to my right, one arm thrown around my shoulder, the other tossed up in the air, à la *Beverly Hills, 90210.*

I smile at the image, our laughing, bright eyes, the promise of our youth shimmering and glowing around us. But my smile quickly dissipates. Because by later that night, everything had changed.

I set the photo down and return my attention to the shoebox. I turn it over in my hands. It looks like the lid has been broken, like someone stepped on it. It could be that my mom broke it while packing everything up, but as I look inside the shoebox again, I realize that everything has been swept around a little, as if a busy hand has tossed everything carelessly about.

I am suddenly certain that someone has been here. Someone has rifled through my things.

I take every item out, setting them on the floor next to me one by one in order to make sure.

But my friendship bracelet is gone.

My insides clench, and somewhere in the distance, I swear I hear the faint sound of laughter.

I don't know if there's something wrong with me or if this is a trick someone is pulling. All I know is someone I used to know, someone I share a past with, has been murdered *here.*

For my safety, and the safety of my daughter, I need to know who killed Bee. And I need to know why.

Chapter 15

NEVE

It's an hour past midday, the hottest part of the day. The heat rises off the pavement in waves, the sky a hazy blue as I ride with Dr. Lou Carter, the vet I'm working with for my first day of my new job.

"Goddamn shame," he mutters as he spins the steering wheel and guides the veterinary practice's old Ford truck onto another scorched stretch of road. I'm glad he's driving. I would've gotten lost out here in about two seconds, all these cloned roads and water towers and rusted scaffolds and ancient farms. "Goddamn crying shame."

He's muttering to himself, so I don't reply. He's one of those crusty old-timer types who seems to talk to himself a lot, about the injustices of life and the hot weather and his sick wife and the clinic, which he reckons he'll sell or close down in order to retire next summer. He's very tall, muscled, with dark skin and a shock of thick white hair and lines etched so deep, you know they hide stories in there. He's been doing this job a long time, and it shows in the world-weary hunch of his shoulders, the jaded glitter in his eyes.

"Got no business having dogs near horses." He shakes his head. "No business a'tall."

We've been out doing herd health rounds all morning. We've visited dairy farms, performed pregnancy checks on cows, and checked on calves. The emergency call for Champ, a horse with a possible broken leg, has only just come in. It's never good news if a horse has a break.

"I'm sure it was an accident," I say. But he just grits his teeth and keeps on driving.

We pass farms and tractors, barns and pony paddocks. The county fairground flies by, where kids gather at the end of the summer for carnival rides, arcade games, and 4-H shows.

The farm appears at the end of a dirt road like it's been painted there with delicate strokes, dust making it hazy in the distance. The house is brick red with white trim and has a wide porch with a swing. A dusty barn sits a couple hundred yards away, the paint falling off in great chunks, exposing the ancient timbers beneath.

Lou slows and turns, passing a fence that has been propped open. He parks next to a large, weather-beaten old jeep, and we step out of the cool truck into air that is still and thick with heat. We walk toward the paddock, the hot sun beating down on our scalps. The dirt is as dry as the air, our steps leaving little clouds of dust that hover and settle.

A bead of sweat stings my eye. I wipe at it impatiently with the crook of my arm.

The farmer meets us by the gate. She is a giant onion of a woman with a tiny head and flushed red cheeks atop a large, round body. She has a fuzz of pale hair and nicotine-stained fingers and she's dressed in a red button-down shirt and ratty jean shorts, from which oddly skinny white legs poke out.

"Heya, Doc," she says, sounding a little out of breath. She motions us to follow her into the paddock. "I'm Gretchen King. Sorry to call you out last minute like this. The dog got into the paddock. It was an accident, mind you, but the horse didn't take too kindly . . ."

Over on the other side of the fence, I see a girl, maybe twelve or thirteen, is holding some kind of collie who strains at her leash. The girl is crying, and I feel bad for her. Nobody wants to be responsible for an animal's injury, especially a kid.

Champ is lying on his side in the dirt. He's in obvious distress, his eyes rolling wildly as he tosses his head, whinnying miserably. I can smell the fear rolling off him, a bitter, desperate scent.

The leg is badly broken, bone piercing the skin. It's a complicated break, likely shattered in places, which is almost impossible to surgically reconstruct. Horses have a distinct lack of muscle and other tissue in their legs, and even with a cast, a broken leg has little to support it. This makes the chance of reinjury high. I see the truth on Lou's face—the horse will have to be euthanized.

I stand back while Lou readies a sedative to help Champ relax. His face is serious, his mouth set in a grim line. His hair dances around his lined face in the hot breeze as he jabs the shot into Champ's right flank.

Within seconds, Champ begins to calm. He lays his head on the grass and looks up at me. His eyes beg me to help. I often wonder in these situations if they are begging to stay or begging to be released.

I kneel next to his head, the dry grass like bristle against my palms. I stroke his soft muzzle, and he huffs out a soft breath. His eyes hold mine, huge and trusting. He relaxes at my touch, the weight of his head heavy on my hand. He is a chestnut Arabian with a white star on his forehead and a long, arched neck. Even in death, he is a beautiful, majestic animal.

"It's okay," I murmur. "You're going to be okay."

It is a lie, but I've learned sometimes a lie comes out smoother than the truth, especially when the prick of the truth is sharpened by guilt.

Lou stands and brushes dead grass off his jeans, then moves aside to chat with the farmer. He tells her that Champ won't survive the break, that he'll need to be euthanized. While the farmer likely knows the risks, he gently explains that complications such as static laminitis make it difficult for a horse to recover without ongoing severe pain and that the broken bone is impossible to repair. I see now what a good vet he is, the compassion he has for the animals he cares for.

Gretchen looks miserable. Tears glitter in her eyes as she glances at the girl holding the dog. She nods at Lou, and he hands her the necessary paperwork. She fills it out while he readies the sodium pentobarbital.

This is the worst part of the job. No matter how many times I've had to do it, euthanizing an animal feels horrible.

I hold Champ's head while Lou injects him. It takes only a few minutes. His body relaxes. His eyes blink heavily. They stay on mine as I stroke his neck, murmuring to him the whole time. His eyes close. And then they don't open. And he is gone.

◆ ◆ ◆

Back in town, Lou pulls into a small square of shade in the corner of the veterinary clinic's parking lot. He hasn't said a word the entire ride back. I suppose we're both lost in the bleakness of our thoughts.

"I'll go to Sammy's," he says decisively as he pulls the parking brake.

I'm not sure if he's simply talking out loud or inviting me along.

"I'm going to get home to my daughter," I reply awkwardly.

Lou looks suddenly so sad, I can't resist reaching a hand out to touch his forearm, where it still sits on the steering wheel.

"You did everything you could," I say. "He had a good death."

Lou looks at my hand on his forearm. His eyebrows furrow, and he inhales heavily; then he throws himself out of the truck, striding quickly toward the clinic.

I call out a quick goodbye to his retreating back, tell him I'll see him on Thursday. He tosses a goodbye wave in my direction just as I hear the roaring of an engine behind me. I turn to see Detective Lambert waving as she lifts her helmet off her head. I'm not sure if she's waving at Lou or me, so I stay where I am.

She does an awkward little shuffle, leaning on her cane to get off the motorcycle. I can't tell if I'm impressed or horrified. I'm afraid she'll fall.

But she doesn't, and soon she's limping steadily toward me.

"Hiya, Neve."

She is again dressed head to toe in black—black trousers, black blouse, black boots—despite the heat wave still crushing the region. It makes me hot just looking at her. Her dark hair is pulled into a tight, smooth ponytail. She looks remarkably put together, which makes me acutely aware of the sweat staining my shirt, my jeans dirty from kneeling next to Champ, my face shiny and flushed.

"How are you, Detective Lambert?" I say.

"Good, good. Do you have a pet here?" She nods at the clinic, curious.

"No, I work here. I just started today, actually. A few days a week."

"I didn't know Lou hired an assistant."

"Not an assistant. I'm a vet also."

She smiles, one hand unconsciously massaging her left leg. "I wanted to be a vet when I was a kid. You must love it."

"Most days," I say. Not days like today. "What about you? What made you become a detective?"

"I used to be a paramedic. There weren't any jobs for that when I moved here, so I trained to be a cop, then made detective a few years later."

"That's a big switch," I say.

She shrugs. "My ex says I'm better at hunting people than fixing them."

That makes me laugh.

"I'm glad I caught you, actually," she says. "I wanted to ask you a few more questions about your neighbor Bailey Nelson."

I look down at my grimy clothes, wanting nothing more than to go home, check up on Ash, and have a shower. "Can it wait until later?"

"It won't take too long."

"Okay." I push my damp, sweaty hair out of my eyes. "What can I help you with?"

"I spoke with Sparks Property. Mrs. Nelson managed Dullahan House for nearly ten years. You're sure you never met her in all that time?"

"Not that I'm aware of. I haven't been back here in much longer than ten years."

The detective eyeballs me. "The house isn't in your name."

It's a statement, not a question, and I'm a little annoyed that she's checked. She's interrogating me, I realize.

"No, it's still in my mother's name. She inherited it from her parents; it's where she grew up."

"But you never lived there?"

"No, we only came back for summer vacations. My mom moved back after my parents divorced in '07, but she's moved into a care home now. Advanced Alzheimer's."

"I'm sorry to hear that."

"She hired Sparks to manage the house before she moved into the care home."

I see Detective Lambert adding this detail to the invisible file she's keeping on me in her head, as if I'm a suspect, as if I could be responsible for killing someone.

"I guess it makes sense, since Mrs. Nelson was her neighbor as well."

I don't reply, because there's nothing to say.

The detective waits a beat and then asks: "You're certain you never met Bailey Nelson?"

I think carefully about my response. Lying once could be shrugged off, but a second time will seem suspicious. But before I get a chance to answer, the detective's expression shifts, her eyes tightening. She flinches, as if someone has touched her, and steps away from me, pulling her phone from her pocket. Her hands, I notice, are shaking.

"I gotta . . . gotta get back to the station," she says, not looking at me.

And then she's gone, her motorcycle engine a roar in the throbbing summer heat. I watch her retreating back, wondering what she saw, why she got spooked, and remind myself to be careful what I say around her.

Things are never as straightforward as they appear when you're dealing with people like her.

Chapter 16

JESS

I speed away from the vet, only slowing when I reach a turnoff by the lake. I yank the motorcycle onto the dirt road and bump along until I reach the water's edge, pulse punching, head knocking.

I get off the motorcycle too fast, hop around a bit on my good leg, and almost fall on my ass. Next to me, the motorcycle tumbles, in slow motion, to the ground.

"Goddammit!" I curse, extricating my cane from my backpack. "Gotta work on your dismount, Jess."

My voice bounces around the trees. I really need to stop talking to myself. People will think I'm crazy. And I'm a lot of things, but I'm not crazy. Even if I do sometimes think I see my dead daughter.

But that's grief, not psychosis.

Still, that's the second time I've been interviewing someone and Isla has shown up—plus the morgue. I don't know what my brain's trying to do to me, but I need to get a grip. The strange looks from the other cops, my lieutenant's casual chat yesterday morning, "How are *you*?" That long lean on the *you*, insinuating maybe I'm not okay.

People are starting to notice.

If I can just pull myself together and solve this case, I'll be able to prove to them all that I'm fine. And I *am* fine. I just need a drink to get myself back on track. It's what allows me to compartmentalize the way I do. A little something to numb the pain.

I pull the silver flask from my saddlebag and hobble over to a fallen log. I sit, dig my knuckles into my cramping thigh, and unscrew the lid. The vodka burns as it goes down, but it's a good burn. I swallow again. And again.

I stare at the lake spread like black velvet in front of me. Even today, the sun high and hot, the surface remains opaque and impenetrable. I feel, as always, that restless energy buzzing in my veins, the wild hysteria that catches in my throat.

And then the images are there. Shattering glass. The punch of an airbag. The sound of screaming. Sometimes I want to give in to it, deliriously melt into it. The relentless drumbeat of grief. The sweet clemency of release. But I don't. I can't. Instead, I push them away.

I yank my hair out of its ponytail, dark strands catching in the elastic and floating into the hot air. I smooth my hair, retie the elastic. I can't sit still. I get up and pace, taking deep swigs from the flask as I do. The sweltering heat has seeped into my skin, wet circles popping up in weird places: behind my knees, under my chin. I'm soaked in heat and dread and panic. It crackles, hot and fast, the way a fire roars in your ears, up and down my legs and arms. I want more than anything to strip off my clothes and jump into the lake, diving deep into the cool water at the bottom.

In ten minutes, I'm calm again. It never takes long for me to get control of myself. I've trained my grief. Wrestled it into its box and tucked it away.

For the most part.

I exhale heavily and sink onto the log, capping the flask. I don't feel better, but I don't feel worse, and that's something. At least the pain in my leg has dimmed a little, a gnawing ache rather than serrated fangs. Plus, I am finally alone.

That's what I want, right?

"No." I answer myself out loud. It comes out half word, half sob.

I fumble with my phone and dial a long-familiar number, tears pricking in my eyes.

"Hello?" Mac's voice on the other line is both comforting and agonizing.

I don't say anything. Just listen to him breathing.

"Jess?" His voice is so soft, it hurts. "Is that you?"

Still, I say nothing.

"I'm here," Mac whispers. "I'm here when you're ready to come home to me."

Tears fill my eyes, catch in my lower lashes. I thought our home was here, in Black Lake. It was where we moved to have a family. Where we built a new life together, where I built a new career, where we had our daughter.

Where we lost her.

But things weren't as easy or as peaceful as we'd hoped. The job was hard. Getting pregnant turned out to be hard. And then, once Isla arrived, raising a child when we both had full-time jobs was hard. Mac and I barely saw each other. We were ships in the night, blowing a quick kiss as one arrived and the other left.

I became increasingly preoccupied with work, a case I barely remember now. A mess of conflicting statements and alibis and evidence that is now, as far as I know, inactive. The days and weeks before and after the accident have been almost entirely wiped from my mind.

Isla had deserved better than me. A better mother than I was. Going back to Mac isn't an option I deserve, and so I hang up, tears tracking rivers down my cheeks.

I unscrew the flask and take another swig of vodka. I watch the water ripple in the slight breeze, raking at memories I've buried deep. That night comes back to me, sharp and barbed, and this time I don't even try to push it away.

What I remember is the crack of my truck hitting something in the road—a deer, I later learned. The weightless feel of the tires skidding on the road, missing the curve, and careening into the air. I remember

Isla's long, jagged shriek from the back seat. And the dizzying feel of the truck flipping, although I can't remember how many times. Then the dark face of the sky and the sound of water, hungry and urgent, as it slowly filled the cab.

Pain was a volcano that would melt me or wash me away, and there was no telling which would happen first. I roamed the mists between consciousness and oblivion, walking jagged plains of ice as the breath of winter cascaded over my neck.

When I next woke, I was facedown, lying half-in, half-out of the overturned truck, water lapping at my cheeks. The overflowing river was rising rapidly as rain pelted the ground. My leg was stuck fast in the mangled window.

"Mommy, you gotta get up." Isla's sweet voice was like ice on a burn, cool and soothing. She was okay. That was all I cared about.

"I can't," I murmured. Blood dripped down my cheeks like tears. "My leg . . . it's stuck."

"The river's getting too high." And then Isla's thin arms were tugging at me, ice-cold but solid and reassuring. I screamed as pain ripped through me, threatening to take me under.

The water tickled at my cheeks; I could taste mud mixed with blood.

Isla's voice became more urgent. "Mama, *please*!"

I tried to move but couldn't. The pain in my leg was overwhelming. A black fog was descending, and all I wanted was to burrow under it.

"Mommy!"

The crack of my daughter's hand across my wet cheek brought me back. I stared into Isla's eyes, those blue, blue eyes, the same shade as Mac's. Isla was scared, and that fear propelled me. I had to get both of us out of this mess.

I reached my hands down to pull my mangled leg free. Isla tugged under my arms as I used my good leg to kick myself out of the truck. An inch. Then another. Until we had moved away from the riverbank, a few feet from the truck. Then we lay gasping and sobbing together on the muddy ground, Isla's wet cheek pressed against mine, until finally, mercifully, blackness descended again.

I don't remember dragging myself up to the road or the elderly man who found us later that night, but the sound of Isla's scream—"Mommy!"—her warning that the river was rising, the feel of her arms as she half dragged me out of the truck, away from the riverbank, and her cheek pressed against mine before I blacked out, those things I remember.

Which is impossible, I later learned, because Isla had died on impact.

My phone rings, jolting me from the memory. It's Dr. Arquette calling to tell me he's finished Bailey Nelson's autopsy report. While he's running down the main points, my phone beeps, notifying me there's another call on the line. I ignore it and ask Dr. Arquette to email me the full report.

"One last thing," he says before he goes. "Preliminary tox screen came back showing chlorpromazine in her system."

"What's that?"

"It's a sedative typically used to ease agitation in those with psychotic disorders."

I make a mental note to check if Bailey Nelson has a prescription with that name, then say thanks and hang up. The report lands in my phone with a beep. I open the email and read it, then read it again before calling Will.

"Hey, old girl," he says.

"Dr. Arquette just sent through Bailey Nelson's autopsy report."

"Yeah? What's it say?"

"She would've died from the head wound at some point, but she was definitely alive when she went into the water. Drowning is the official cause of death, but the report says she had chlorpromazine in her system, which is some sort of sedative, likely delivered by an injection, although it's difficult to tell exactly where, due to the damage to the skin from her time in the water."

Will blows out a long breath. "Jesus. Smashed in the head, injected with a sedative, drowned. Sounds like overkill to me."

"Someone really wanted to make sure she died."

"I'll check her house for that drug. What do you make of the message carved into her tongue?"

"The autopsy report says it was done prior to death. The killer used a sharp, small instrument. Likely a scalpel."

"Medical professional?"

I make a noncommittal noise at the back of my throat. It isn't hard to get your hands on a scalpel. "Maybe. But what's it mean? It must be a message, but what?"

"Could be a million things. A code to a briefcase. Password to a safe. Passage from a poem or some sort of book."

I massage my leg thoughtfully. "True. But why the tongue? That must mean something."

"Hard to know for sure."

"Let's get some guys looking into it at the station."

"What'd you find at Sparks Property this morning?" he asks.

"Dead end. Turns out Bailey Nelson was the owner. They sell and manage properties in the area. She was on a week's vacation leave, which is why they never reported her missing."

"Damn. Well, I might have a lead."

"Yeah?"

"One of the CSIs called me. He said he tried calling you, but you didn't answer. He thought it was important so called me. He found a manila envelope with something interesting inside. It was torn into pieces and stuffed into the bottom of the downstairs bathroom's wastebasket."

"What was it?"

"Might be better if I show you."

I close my eyes, steeling myself. *Take two,* I think.

"I'm heading to the vet," I tell Will. "I need to talk to Lou. Meet me there?"

"Sure. See you in a few."

My hands are trembling as I press "End."

Just take it one step at a time, Jess.

It's what my dad always says. My dad's an ex-marine, ex-alcoholic, ex-cop, who put it all aside to build birdhouses around the time I married Mac. I call him every week, and that's the one bit of fatherly advice he keeps repeating. I always laugh and make some wisecrack about my leg and not taking steps too fast these days, but he just repeats it.

"Life is all about balance, and you know I'm not talking about physically. Take it one step at a time, Jess."

I lean on my cane and check my sobriety, standing on one leg for thirty seconds. I don't hop or sway, so I climb back on my motorcycle and return to town.

Dr. Lou Carter is just locking up the veterinary clinic when I roar into the parking lot. The sun is lowering on the horizon, burnishing his skin a warm mahogany, highlighting every white hair, every craggy line. He looks tired. Bone tired.

He waits as I awkwardly get off the motorcycle and limp toward him.

"Heya, Detective," he calls. "Back so soon?"

I know Lou well from the bar. His wife, Dorothy, is almost completely bedbound with advanced Parkinson's, so once the night nurse arrives, he heads to the bar for his dinner and enough alcohol to blur the emotional pain. The life of a functioning alcoholic.

"Heya, Lou. Yeah, I got a question for you." I tuck my cane under my armpit and pull out my phone, open Facebook, and type in Bailey's name. "This woman, do you recognize her?"

Lou pulls a pair of glasses from his breast pocket, slides them on, and peers at the picture. "Sure. She came in, let's see, Tuesday before last. Had a Maltese mix called Toby she said had gotten into some green algae. She was demanding to be seen right away. Cussed out my new receptionist, almost had her in tears."

Lou folds his glasses back into his pocket.

"What time was that?"

"Right before closing, so say seven o'clock."

That would've put Bailey Nelson home by about 8:00 p.m.

Lou shakes his head, still staring at the picture. "Insufferable, manipulative woman."

"Doesn't sound like you liked her much."

"I don't like most people. You know that."

I smile because it's true.

"What'd she do?" Lou asks.

"She's dead."

Lou's bushy white eyebrows shoot up, and he swallows hard. "Shit. I'm sorry to hear it."

A slight flush has started creeping up Lou's cheeks. I look at him an extra beat. "You never met her, say, outside the clinic?"

"Met her? No," Lou says, but this time, he doesn't quite meet my eyes. "You, uh, you find her cell phone? Maybe you'd get some info from that."

"We're looking." I'm intentionally vague.

Truth is, we haven't found Bailey's phone. It's either been turned off or the battery is dead, and getting a warrant for the records will take some time. Same with getting records from the security cameras we saw at the Nelson house. Everything takes time. Time I don't have if I want to prove myself to the lieutenant.

"She didn't pay," Lou admits. "Said Vivienne Jones would sort it out when she got home. She was real hoity-toity about it. Joyce, my new receptionist, was awful upset."

I'm impressed he's hired a new receptionist and vet. Some of us thought he'd go under after his daughter left the practice.

He peers again at the picture. "Hmm, maybe . . ." He looks like he's debating something. "You know, maybe I do recognize her. Couldn't swear to it, but I think I saw her at the charity auction the Wednesday before last raising funds for Parkinson's research. She was outside in the parking lot on the phone shouting at somebody. I saw her when I went outside for a cigarette break. I don't like to speak ill of the dead, but she didn't seem too nice to me."

"What'd she say?"

"Dunno. Just heard her shouting, angry-like."

Just then, Will's cruiser turns in to the parking lot. Lou says goodbye and gets into his car. I wait for Will, leaning on my cane in a slice of shade. Will crosses the parking lot and pulls a manila envelope out of his inner pocket. Inside is a 3x5 glossy picture that has been ripped into four pieces. An enterprising CSI has taped it back together.

The picture is of three girls, a much younger Bailey, maybe sixteen or seventeen, one long, tanned arm thrown up to the sky, and two girls I don't recognize. But the girl in the middle has her face scratched out. The black pen has scribbled so furiously, it's ripped the photo in places. Most interesting to me, though, is that all three girls are wearing rainbow-colored friendship bracelets.

Exactly like the bracelet found on Bailey Nelson's body.

Chapter 17

A bead of sweat rolled down my face, dripping slowly from my forehead to my nose. It tickled, but I ignored it. I could see her inside the office building's small communal kitchen window. I didn't need my binoculars, but I used them anyway. They gave a clarity my eyes didn't give anymore, and clarity, precision, was important to me.

I'd been watching her more frequently lately. The more I watched, the more I saw. She was a liar. She lied to her husband, to her colleagues, to her friends. To everyone. But they would soon find out exactly what she was.

I'd found the things I needed hidden in her office. Did she know? She'd certainly gone about her life as if everything was normal.

I watched as she dumped a mug of old coffee into the sink, her purse slung over her shoulder. She was wearing a long, cream linen dress. Sandals. Her hair tied in a loose bun, dark tendrils escaping around her face.

She looked . . . perfect. The perfect woman. But all of it was an illusion. A fairy tale with a pretty cover hiding a rotten story inside.

I knew the truth. The reality, not the illusion she presented or the narrative she told. People were rarely as straightforward as we liked to think they were.

She felt safe inside the little world she'd constructed. Secure. I could see it on her face. The entitlement. The privilege. She thought she deserved it. She thought she was protected from the terrible things she'd done.

I dropped my hand to the envelope of photos in my pocket. My fingers grazed the item I now kept in my pocket. I clutched it so hard, I felt my nails slicing into the soft skin of my palm, digging into my metacarpals. I remembered first finding it, how my heart had ached. Back then, I didn't know the importance it held. I put it away without understanding, my focus instead on her.

On how much I loved her. How I would do anything for her.

I still would.

That's when I started planning.

Rage blossomed in my belly, fierce and hot and dangerous. As if sensing my glare, she turned. A miniscule flash of emotion darted across her face, an almost imperceptible tightening of her jaw, a furrow of brows. A sound came from somewhere behind her, and she jumped, a flare of panic widening her eyes. She was tense. The woman in the window felt someone watching her.

I smiled. It was working.

She hitched her purse higher on her shoulder, preparing to leave. My body tensed, ready to follow.

I slipped my binoculars into my backpack and stood, throwing another glance at the woman in the window. Someone else had come into the kitchen, just out of my sight. The woman's face softened as she spoke. She laughed at something they'd said.

For a second, the briefest flash, I felt a little uncertain. But I reminded myself she was a wolf in sheep's clothing. And do you know what happened to the wolf in sheep's clothing?

When the shepherd wanted a sheep for his dinner, he took his knife out and he killed the wolf.

Chapter 18

NEVE

I walk along the road heading toward Dullahan House, dust kicking in bursts of hot summer air. I tap the code into the electronic gate and cross the street. Crime scene tape still flutters around Bee's house. A new car, an expensive-looking silver Jaguar, is parked outside.

I wonder how long it will take the CSIs to process everything.

"Ash?" I call when I let myself inside. The entrance is cool, a welcome respite from the beating heat outside.

There's no reply. I wonder if she's home: she's taken to kayaking around the islands in the lake out back. I'm not sure I'm happy about it—especially if there's a murderer on the loose—but she tells me I'm being annoying and to "just let go, for God's sake."

So I bite my tongue. Again. I've bitten it so frequently lately, I'm surprised I have a tongue left to bite. Instead, I tell her to make sure to wear sunscreen. Ash inherited my willowy height and dark hair but Eli's Nordic coloring, her skin so pale that it looks like it could be brushed with moonlight. Ever since a bad sunburn when she was a toddler, I've slathered her with sunscreen to avoid cancerous-looking freckles from appearing.

"Ash?" I call again, louder.

Ash comes in from the deck. Her blue-black hair is tousled, as if she's been in bed half the day, and she's wearing Adidas shorts and a belly-skimming tank top.

"Did you see him?" she asks.

She leads me out to the deck and points at a man down by the lake speaking to Detective Casey. He is very short, about five-six, with a receding hairline, a fluff of gray hair at the back, a heavy brow, and thick lips. There's a suitcase at his feet, as if he's been let into the crime scene to pack up some belongings.

This must be Bee's husband. He's older than I would've expected. Shorter too. As a teenager, Bee was always attracted to tall guys. "Tall, dark, and handsome," she used to say. But the guy's wearing a flashy Rolex, and that's right up her alley, too.

He and Detective Casey speak, his expression stony. He doesn't look sad at all, which makes me wonder about him, about their relationship. Was it a happy one? Did he treat her well? I wonder if he's a suspect, if they've questioned him.

"I bet he killed her." Ash's eyes gleam in an annoying way. She's far too interested in this, like we're watching TV rather than talking about a real person's life. "You said they were interviewing him, right? Maybe he hired a hit man to get rid of her."

"This isn't a movie, Ash," I snap. "I'm sure nobody hired any hit men."

Ash's face flashes with surprise, but I ignore it and head inside. Ash follows me into the living room.

"There'll be a memorial," she says. "Should we go?"

"No!" I reply, horrified.

I can think of nothing worse. What if someone recognizes me? The last thing I need is to be tied to Bee right now. I don't want Ash knowing I knew her, and honestly, I'm not sure I could grieve the way people would expect.

Words I don't even want to acknowledge glimmer in my mind: *Maybe she deserved it.*

"Why would you even think that?" I ask.

"Well, duh, she's our neighbor."

"We are *not* going to any memorial," I say emphatically. "It would be rude to just show up without an invitation."

I turn away from her and unlace my tennis shoes, kick them off. They land with a dull thump against the wall. My feet are damp with sweat, and I'm desperate for a shower. A headache presses on my temples, throbbing in time with my heartbeat. All I want is to be alone.

And then, as if I've said it out loud, Ash turns her back on me and heads upstairs, melting into the gloomy shadows draped across the landing. I stare at the place she stood, wondering if we can ever be happy here or if bad choices will haunt me no matter where I go.

Ash stays in her room all evening. Eventually I go to bed, too, but despite my exhaustion, I'm unable to sleep. My stomach is empty, and my mind is full. I regret snapping at my daughter. I regret not telling the truth about knowing Bee.

I wasn't always this way, my memories making a liar out of me. But aren't we all haunted by our pasts, by our regrets? We hide from them, presenting new versions of ourselves, the ones we want others to see, but they're still there, lingering like ghosts. I flop onto my other side as more regrets unspool in my head.

It's too hot for this time of night. Why did my mother never get air-conditioning installed? I toss and turn, my mind a dizzying merry-go-round, jumping from Bee's murder to Eli to Ash to Champ.

I shudder as I think of Champ's eyes as they met mine, and this leads me down a rabbit hole to the last time I had to euthanize an animal.

Euthanizing ill animals is part of being a vet, but it's never easy. I chose my profession because I wanted to help animals. I learned at a young age that people will let you down, but animals are a blank canvas for all the good we want in our world.

But that day, the last day I had to euthanize an animal, it was also the end of my life as I knew it.

I left the clinic early and drove somewhere I hadn't been in a long time. Saw someone I hadn't seen in a long time. I was shaking. With sadness and fear and anger. It felt as if everything was falling apart. I stayed there late into the afternoon, and then I twisted my key in the engine and drove back home.

I was just stepping out of the shower when Eli's knuckles rapped on the bathroom door.

"Neve?" Eli called. "You in there? Dinner's almost ready."

"Be right there!" I called.

I dried and dressed, ran a brush quickly through my hair. The mirror showed a middle-aged woman with blotchy skin and thumbprint-size shadows stamped under her eyes. I barely recognized myself those days.

After Eli's footsteps had receded, I opened the bathroom door, trying to focus on the task ahead. We were telling Ash we planned to separate. Not a divorce. Not yet. Just . . . time to figure some things out.

I could hear Eli and Ash talking, the occasional clatter of silverware, the grate of a pan sliding across the stove. I walked down the stairs slowly, passing family photos that lined the walls. A baby picture of Ash that she'd begged me to take down. Eli and me on our wedding day: beaming and radiant under the Hawaiian sun. I thought of that day, my feet bare on the white sand beach, thinking: *My lovely husband. Until death do us part.*

In the dining room, Eli and Ash were talking about *Fortnite*.

"I don't get it." Eli was frowning. "Why do you have to thank the bus driver?"

Ash rolled her eyes at him, her clueless father. "God, Dad, I already *told* you! It's to teach, like, manners."

She'd been so grumpy lately. I figured it was stress from the rigorous exams schedule her private school had set. Or maybe she was just annoyed to be home. She'd planned to go to her friend Angie's house to study, but Eli had texted our family WhatsApp group, saying he'd be home early and asking if we'd both be home for dinner.

I slipped into my spot across from Ash at the round glass dining table. My father was one of those old-fashioned guys who always insisted he sit at the "head" of the table. When Eli and I married, I'd bought a round table so there was equality in our marriage.

The table had been set with platters of carne asada, Mexican rice, and black beans. Tortilla chips with homemade guacamole and salsa. Molly, our rescue dog, a mix of collie, retriever, and maybe a little spaniel, stood to greet me, her tail wagging happily. She had been brought into the clinic eight years ago with a broken hip, and her owner didn't want to pay to get it fixed. She'd freely admitted she regretted getting her. I'd met Molly's trusting brown eyes and fallen in love.

"Hi!" Eli said, his tone overly bright.

"Welcome home. Your meeting go okay?"

"Yes, thank you. Good to be home."

We were speaking too formally. Ash's head bobbed between us, like a spectator watching a tennis match.

"You were only gone two days," I replied lightly.

"You know I don't like sleeping away from my own bed," he replied, equally light.

He threw a conspiratorial wink at Ash. Eli was that type of guy, the one you always felt like you were collaborating with on some big secret. Like the world was just a joke that the two of you were in on. As an architect, he created new things every day. He was excited by life, completely at ease with himself. Unlike me.

Something flashed through my mind. Sharp and brutal. Dark hair. Smooth skin. The sound of skin slapping against skin.

"You okay?" Eli's voice reached me from what felt like a great distance.

I stared across the table at him. "What?"

"You okay?" he repeated. He and Ash were both looking at me.

"I'm fine." My voice was coated with the shiny shell of sunny enthusiasm. I'd always been this way, calm, even when a volcano was stewing below. I buried things, hid them until the surface cracked. Then the explosions could be epic.

"It's work. I had to euthanize a chocolate Lab today. Wendy. She's been at the practice forever . . ."

My voice trailed off, because nobody wanted to talk about a dying dog at the dinner table. But then Ash surprised me.

"This is why I'm a Buddhist."

"You are?" I said, feeling as if I were at sea within myself.

"Totally. Reincarnation is, like, immortality," Ash said. "You can never really die; you just find a new life."

Eli's phone rang then, and he excused himself to answer it.

No more stalling, I told myself. Once he returned, we would tell Ash we were separating.

I opened my mouth to speak, but just then, a horrific boom came from the front of the house, the sound of the front door splintering, cracking.

I half stood. Froze. Part of me wanted to run, but the cool, rational side of my brain told me to stay. Fight. Protect my daughter.

And again, boom.

And then someone was there. All black. Shiny metal glinted in the light.

I turned to Ash.

"Run!" I screamed at her.

◆　◆　◆

I jerk my head, a small shake, trying to dislodge the memory. I don't want it there. I jump out of bed. Sweat makes my armpits slippery. I pad across the cool hardwood floor and climb the turret to check on Ash.

She is snoring softly, curled up like a potato bug on her left side. No nightmares. No screaming. Just the steady, rhythmic sound of her peaceful breathing. She's settling in well here, I think. Coming here was the right decision.

I go downstairs to the kitchen. The lights are off, a velvet blackness surrounding me. I stand in front of the basement door, my hand hovering over the doorknob.

Neve.

My name comes at me from somewhere over my shoulder. I whirl around, heart pounding. But I see nothing. Blackness presses on me from every side, feeling weighted somehow, thick and oily. I picture someone moving toward me in the dark, and then there are hands closing around my throat, squeezing. Has the person who invaded our home found us? Have they come for me?

Neve.

"No!" I try to scream, but it comes out a strangled rasp. I feel them, those hands around my throat.

I fumble in the darkness, and my shaking fingers finally find the light switch. Light floods the kitchen, and I see that I'm alone. There is nobody here, nobody trying to strangle me.

I think it's really that moment, as I stand there with my sweaty hands pressed to my throat, that I know. My choices are coming back to haunt me.

Life is just a game of choice, after all. Every one of us has the potential for great good and great wrong, but those who make the wrong choices usually pay somewhere down the line.

Because sooner or later, the past always comes for you.

Chapter 19

NEVE

Trinity Manor is the name of the memory care home where my mother lives. It's set within a hospital's specialist dementia wing, and it's been designed to look like a small town from the fifties. They say it helps the residents feel calm and reduces aggression and wandering.

Inside, there are courtyards and corridors. The tiny houses have faux fronts so they look as if they are separate buildings. They each have a front porch with a table and rocking chair overlooking an Astroturfed avenue, and all sit under a fiber-optic ceiling that mimics daylight and starry skies.

The facility is well staffed with specially trained nurses, occupational therapists, psychotherapists, physical and speech therapists. My mother, like most Alzheimer's patients, does well in her controlled environment, but the disease is definitely getting worse. The last time I visited, she'd lost most of her speech. I don't know what she will have lost this time, and guilt floods through me as I step inside the cool reception area, out of the gaze of the burning blue midday sky. It's been far too long since I've visited.

Sweat cools almost instantly on my skin. The air conditioner hums peacefully. In the center of the room, a three-tiered water fountain is bubbling away.

The receptionist, Doreen, is busy on the phone and doesn't acknowledge me when I approach. I try to remember the names of the people who work with my mother, even though I'm terrible at names. But I always remember Doreen because she has seven children at home. Seven! I struggled organizing my life around one.

I sign in and head through the double doors, then down the Astroturfed avenue. I pass a series of front porches, some with residents out front: a nurse helping an elderly woman swallow her medicine, an occupational therapist doing a puzzle with an old man, a speech therapist holding up speech cards.

I'd asked Ash to come with me for this visit, but she refused. Sometimes we can't see even when our eyes are open. Like the invisible gorilla test, which had people counting the number of throws and passes of a basketball, and yet found they didn't see when the gorilla walked right past the screen.

Intentionally or not, we focus only on what we can focus on. We fit what we want into our existing mental framework, allowing our brains to fill in the blanks to everything else. That's what Ash is doing with her grandmother.

Part of me wants to force her to acknowledge what's happening. There's more to the real world than only the things you can see. Just because you haven't observed something doesn't mean you should disregard it. But I myself am a big fan of that old adage from Thomas Gray's famous poem: ignorance is bliss. Because there is a double perspective here: if ignorance is bliss, knowledge must be misery. And the last thing I want is my daughter to be miserable.

My mother is sitting outside on her little porch, rocking slowly in her white rocking chair. Her expression is blank, her eyes fixed on nothing. She's changed so much in the months since I've seen her. She appears shrunken, her long gray hair thin and scraggly, her cheeks pale. *A crone,* that's what I think of when I see her.

A woman who's more dead than alive.

She's wearing sweatpants and a green sweater, as well as an old dove-gray cashmere scarf I bought her when I got my first veterinarian job and started making real money. She looks sad. Is this fake town with its fake porch and its fake ceiling really the best thing for her? It's a lie, after all. A facade.

But my mother was once happy here. Perhaps it's just the illness eating at her. I'm hoping today will be a good day, that I can get a few words out of her and find out if she remembers what happened to the bracelet. If she packed it or threw it away.

As I'm watching, a nurse approaches my mom. Ruby? Rita? Ruth? I always forget her name. She's one of those people you'd easily forget, boxy, homely, plain as a bowl of boiled rice. I vaguely remember her mentioning a disabled sister she cares for. Everything else about her fades to the background.

She bends close to say something to my mom. Mom's mouth hinges slightly, but she doesn't reply. The nurse drops a hand onto my mom's arm and squeezes before leaving.

"Mom?"

She smells slightly medicinal and unwashed, the faint whiff of urine. It's funny how when you're a kid, you see only your parents' strengths, but when you're an adult, you see only their weaknesses. How strict they were when you were a teenager. How lenient they are when they're a grandparent. How sick they are when they're elderly.

She doesn't answer, so I drop down to one knee and touch her hand. It is warm, the skin a little leathery. It's so small. When did that happen?

"Mom?" I say her name again, a little louder. "It's me. Neve."

She flinches a little, her eyes blinking rapidly. I pull over the foot-stool and sit on the opposite side of the table. I long to rest my aching head on my mother's lap, to smell the faint fragrance of lemons I remember from childhood. To feel her hand gently stroking my hair. My mother's touch was always magic, and now I can't even hug her.

So instead, I sit and talk. I tell her about Ash, the sense that she's moving away from me and how difficult I'm finding it. And I tell her about my decision to go back to Dullahan House.

"Why didn't you tell me you hired Bee to manage Dullahan House?" I ask. "Or that she got married?"

I don't expect her to answer, and she doesn't. She just stares ahead with dull, watery eyes, her shoulders slumped as if she's been defeated by the weight of the world. That sadness she's carrying, it breaks my heart. I wish I could hold her, the way she always held me when I was sad.

I reach for her cashmere scarf and pull it a little higher. She shivers, a tremor that reaches her chin. I lace my fingers through hers and tell her I love her, that I miss her.

"I still feel your hand in mine, Mom," I say, tears burning my eyes. "I hope you feel mine, too."

How much longer do I have with her? When I was about ten, I learned that my own grandmother, my mom's mom, had died of a stroke when Mom was a girl. That knowledge had built this giant fear inside me that one day, I would lose her and I'd be by myself. That same fear grips me now.

Of course, I would've had my dad, but it wasn't the same. He was barely around, always away at work, doing his own thing. Even when he was around, he was a little terrifying to a shy, introverted girl. He was a good provider, but not a great dad, and there's a big difference. My mom, though, nurtured me. Provided for me. Loved me. After they divorced and he moved on with someone new, she was all I had.

The thought of losing her is devastating, even now as an adult. I'm not ready for it.

"I'm here," I say, stroking my mom's hand. "I know I haven't been great at visiting, but I'm here now."

Mom doesn't reply. She's staring at her feet now, her expression blank. And so I sit back and continue talking, telling her about my separation from Eli.

"I haven't exactly told Ash the truth about everything, you know, with Eli and me," I admit. "The thing is, Mom, I had to leave him." My throat is already filling with tears. "I wish I could tell you it was his fault. That he cheated on me, but the truth is . . ."

A tear slides down my cheek, splatters onto my knee. "The truth is, *I* cheated on *him*."

I look across the Astroturfed street. An older woman is pacing back and forth in her room. Her hands are waving and gesturing, like she's having some sort of internal conversation.

"I know you used to say we're all more than our worst acts, but . . . I'm a terrible person. Eli doesn't deserve that. He's a good man. He's funny and kind and such a great dad. I guess I wanted someone to treat me the way I *deserved* to be treated. I wanted someone to see me for what I really am. I wanted . . ."

I stopped. What did I want? I knew sleeping with my boss would ruin my life or my career, and either way, I wouldn't come back from it unscathed. But sex with Stephen, a guy I cared little for, was a form of escapism. A release. Someone to rip at my flesh, to slash at my bones until my darkest secrets burst out, all of them, the ones I kept from others and the ones I kept from myself. Someone to tear at the mask I'd been wearing, to peer underneath and see my secrets, to see me for who I really was.

Secrets are just unspoken lies, after all. Underneath everything, I'm just another liar.

Maybe I *wanted* to ruin it all. My life, my career, my marriage. Set it all on fire because that's what I deserved.

All these TV shows and movies and self-help books these days tell us *don't worry about what others think* and *just be your best self* and *don't give any fucks*. But the truth is, if we all walked around being our truest selves, our most authentic, genuine selves, people would hate us. So I'd hidden myself because nobody really wants to see who another *truly* is. Scratch the surface and we're all petty, selfish beings with the capacity for terrible things. We don't show that to others, of course. We prefer pretty pictures to reality. And so we pull on a cloak of civility and we hide behind the versions of ourselves we want the world to see.

". . . I wanted to be someone else," I finish lamely.

Stephen was in a similar downward cycle: a looming custody battle, an ex-wife addicted to painkillers, a stressful tax audit. We were nothing to each other but a few months of assuaging the raw, physical ache inside, raking at each other's skin, drawing blood and washing ourselves clean.

It ended abruptly a few weeks ago when Eli presented me with a damning set of photos he said had been left on the windshield of his car. The photos showed a man and a woman walking into an old-fashioned motel with doors that entered from outside. The blinds were still partially open, enough to show them reenacting some sort of grotesque porno.

The woman was bent over the bed. Her crimson G-string was tangled around her ankles, her black skirt hitched over her waist. Her long dark hair draped over her face like a curtain. She was facing away from the camera so you got a good view of her pale ass but couldn't see her face. The man was behind her, fucking her doggy-style. It wasn't until the last picture that the woman's face turned to the camera. Her neck was thrown back, her throat exposed. Her green eyes were wide open, and you could clearly see that the woman in the picture was me.

They were pictures from after I'd left Bailey at the restaurant in Back Bay. I'd texted Stephen and driven directly to meet him at the motel.

I figured Bailey had taken them, intent on letting me know who was really in control.

Eli laid the photos on our bed one by one. A fury I'd never known consumed me, hot and dangerous. That bitch was going to pay.

But then I looked at Eli, and the tears in his eyes nearly broke me. Bad choices stick like honey, I find, and I had no way of untangling myself now. Eli loved me so much, but I wasn't worthy of that love, had never been worthy of it.

"Look at me," Eli said softly.

But I couldn't. It hurt too much to see his pain. Pain that I'd caused. *Me.* Because we hurt the people we love far more than we ever hurt those we hate.

That's when I knew. Nothing would ever be the same between us again. And it was all Bee's fault. I was going to fucking kill her. Bad people deserve bad things. *Bee* deserved bad things.

I told him I wanted some time apart. That's why he went away, not the work meeting we told Ash about. He needed to sort out his head as much as I needed to sort out mine. He called me a few days later to say he wanted to work through this.

"Stop pushing away the people who love you, Neve," Eli had said. "I don't understand why, but you're punishing yourself for something. You've always done this, and maybe someday you'll tell me why. But we can figure it out. Together."

What I couldn't tell him then was that maybe I wanted to punish myself.

We agreed to a trial separation. The day we sat down to tell Ash, the home invasion happened, tearing apart everything that could've been.

"I know some mistakes there's just no coming back from," I tell my mother now, "but I do love him."

A nurse walks toward us carrying a small pitcher of water and one cup. She sets it on the table between us. I'm not sure if it's for my mom or me, but before I can ask, she's gone, moving on to other patients.

"Anyway." I leave the water sweating on the table. "Ash and I moved into Dullahan House. I mean, we can't stay there forever, and eventually Ash will need to go back to school, but for now, it's where we need to be. Which reminds me, do you remember Bee? From next door to Dullahan House? The police are saying she was murdered. They found her in the lake."

Mom blinks several times and slowly lifts her eyes, her gaze moving from our joined hands up to my face. Her brow furrows, and I get the sense that she's listening. That she understands what I'm saying.

"She gave me a friendship bracelet when we were kids. Do you remember?" I speak quickly, before I lose her again. "I tried to find it. I went out to the boathouse looking through those storage boxes you told me about."

I lean in closer. There's that scent again, unwashed skin and the bitter smell of medicine. "It wasn't there. Do you know where it went?"

Confusion and something else—fear?—wash over her features. Her eyes finally land on mine.

And that's when she starts screaming.

Chapter 20

JESS

I've been mainlining coffee at my desk for the last three hours, but it isn't working. After another insomnia-filled night, I rolled out of bed right as the sun rose and made my way into work. A throbbing hangover nags at my head. My eyes are gritty, my brain fuzzy. So far I have nothing to show for coming in early.

I do a quick DMV check on Neve Maguire's name. Something about the look on her face when I'd asked if she was certain she'd never met Bailey Nelson is bugging me. I wonder if she did know her as a child. Or knew something about her. Of course, then I saw Isla and didn't get a full answer. But I don't find any records in the Boston area that roughly match the time period I would guess she was born.

I stare at my coffee, my mind ticking over. Neve said she was separated. Was Maguire maybe her maiden name?

"Why don't you ask it out?" Will says as he approaches my desk.

"Huh?"

"That cup of coffee you're staring at. Take it out to dinner. Propose. Make a few babies. Or . . ." He whips a tall Styrofoam cup from Java Jane, the best coffee shop in town, from behind his back. "Cheat on it and get yourself a hot new buzz."

"Oh my God, Will, you're my hero." I grab the cup with both hands. "Seriously."

"Skinny latte, two sugars."

I go for my first gulp but then pause, eyeing the coffee suspiciously.

Will laughs. "It's regular milk, not almond. I promised I'd make it up to you."

"Thanks, Will."

"Did the skin and blood scraped from her fingernails come back with a match yet?" Will hitches one large butt cheek onto the corner of my desk.

"Nope. The private lab we sent it to is rushing it, but it could be a few days yet. Have you heard from any of the canvassers? We have a meeting later today to see if they've found anything, but so far I've heard nothing."

Will shakes his head. "This killer was very careful."

"I agree. The tech team said they can't re-create the other girl's face because it's too damaged. Someone did a damn good job of scratching it out. But this girl here"—I tap the blonde girl's face—"might know. The only problem is the facial recognition software isn't pulling up anything, so that's a dead end. She's too young, and it's too long ago."

"There has to be a reason Bailey was wearing the same bracelet when she died that these girls are in this picture."

"But what?" I say, frustrated. I take another slug of coffee.

"We have that interview with Angus Nelson in a few minutes," Will says. "Maybe we'll get something out of him."

"Damn," I groan, looking down at the notes I needed to go over before talking to Angus Nelson but so far hadn't gotten to. "What about you?"

"I do have one thing that might cheer you up." Will drops an iPad onto my desk with a flourish.

I gape at the screen. "You're kidding."

"You may proceed with your hero praise," he says with a grin.

"Hail the conquering hero." I wave my hands like I'm bowing. "But yeah, maybe lead with that next time."

Will chuckles. "Most of the homes in the neighborhood have security cameras out front, but the only one that captured the exterior of the house was the neighbor across the street. Unfortunately, somebody moved the camera so it was pointing at the ground. *But* the Nelsons installed security cameras inside as well, thanks to a break-in at their property a couple of months back. It records for twenty-four hours, uploads to an app, then wipes after a week of no activity."

Will taps the screen, and a low-res color video of Bailey Nelson's living room begins loading. While we wait, Will says, "Look, I was thinking, maybe I should put the case into HTS."

The Homicide Tracking System collects and analyzes the main details of all murders throughout the state.

"Why?" I ask. "The system's voluntary. Tracking similar homicides is hit or miss."

"Can't hurt, right? I mean, the tongue carving is pretty specific. Could be a signature."

I shrug. "Sure, if you want to take ownership of that, go ahead. But the main focus has to be this case."

"Yeah, of course."

I press "Play" on the iPad. The camera is positioned in a corner at the front of the house, showing an open-plan living room, dining area, and kitchen. There's no sound, but the quality is good. We can see everything except the front door.

The dining room is dominated by a large glass table and hardwood floors. It faces a sunken living room with an expensive-looking couch and a vast white sheepskin rug. A statement leather chair faces the wall-mounted TV. On the opposite end of the house is a kitchen. Modern stainless-steel appliances. White cupboards. A three-seater island. The colors are muted, tasteful, with thick gray carpeting and clean, sophisticated lines. Bailey had good taste.

Will takes a noisy sip of coffee and points at the date and time stamp at the bottom of the screen. "It's six a.m. Bailey's just gotten back from a run with the dog."

Bailey is washing up a plate in the kitchen, her back to the door, when we see a corner of the door swing into view. I go to take a gulp of coffee and then pause, the coffee midway to my lips. It's Angus Nelson, her husband, letting himself in through the front door.

"He lied to us," I say. "Fucker."

"Blows away his claim that he wasn't there that day," Will says.

"And where's he been since?"

I nibble the raw edge of a hangnail and watch as Angus's mouth moves on the screen. Bailey whirls around. Surprise turns quickly to anger as Angus approaches. She lashes out, striking him across the cheek. Angus staggers back but recovers and launches himself at her.

He's so much shorter than Bailey that it's almost funny, except the rage on his face is anything but. He grabs her around the throat with both hands and shakes. Bailey's body flails about for a second until she recovers and karate chops him in the neck.

I laugh. "Good girl."

For a second, they eye each other like wild animals. And then Bailey leaps at him, claws out. But this time she wraps her arms around him, pressing her mouth against his in a furious, almost angry kiss. Angus lifts her up onto his waist, her running shorts hitching up, exposing the insides of her thighs.

They kiss violently, manically, their hands tearing at each other's clothes until they're naked. Bailey rakes her hands down Angus's back. Blood bubbles to the surface, dripping down his pale skin as they continue ravaging each other in angry, deliberate movements.

After a minute, Angus sets her down and pushes her away. Bailey glares at him, her eyes angry slits. She says something, her mouth contorting. Angus slaps her across the face.

Bailey's head lurches back, hair flying, hand coming up to cup her cheek. And again they're in each other's arms, kissing, scratching, biting. And then they disappear down the hall.

"Damn, that's messed up," I say.

Nothing happens on the screen for a while. I increase the viewing speed. After a few minutes, they both come out of the bedroom, Bailey now dressed in the white blouse and pencil skirt we found her in, and leave. Nothing else happens for hours. I again increase the viewing speed.

Finally, at 6:50 p.m., Bailey returns home. I slow the viewing speed down. She promptly takes the dog out for a walk. She doesn't get home this time until 8:00 p.m. When she does, she has a white paper bag in her hand.

"Must be the prescription for the dog she got from the vet," Will says.

We watch as Bailey makes what looks to be an egg white omelet for dinner, her back facing the front door. She holds a slim book in one hand—I can't make out the title—while the other beats the eggs with brisk, efficient strokes. Her head bobs in time to a rhythm, as if she's listening to music.

I catch sight of a sudden movement at the bottom right hand of the screen. A shadowy figure dressed in formless black clothes comes into view, creeping closer to Bailey, who remains blissfully unaware.

"Oh, shit," I whisper, leaning in.

It's the perfect disguise. Black trousers, chunky black sweater, black balaclava. It gives nothing away.

Nausea spirals through me. I feel sick knowing what's going to happen and not being able to do anything about it.

Run! I want to scream. *Move! Turn around!*

But there's nothing I can do except watch the scene play out.

The figure inches closer, dropping behind the leather chair. The dog comes over, sniffs at the figure, who holds out a hand. The dog wags his tail and returns to his bed.

"The dog knows the killer," I murmur.

The figure creeps closer to Bailey. At the last second, as if she finally senses another presence, Bailey turns. But the figure has ducked down again, hidden by the island.

I'm watching the screen so intently, my eyes have started watering. I blink, trying to clear my vision.

Bailey pauses, as if considering something. She turns off the flame on the stove and opens a small cupboard next to the back door. Inside is a neat row of keys. Still holding the book, she plucks a key from the row and shuts the cupboard door. She rifles through her purse sitting on the countertop, palms something, and heads out the back door.

"She got something from her purse," Will says.

I'd almost forgotten he was even here. "Did we find anything on her body, anything small that would fit in her hand?"

"Just the bracelet."

"She isn't wearing it here. Confirms the killer put it on her."

We watch as the figure follows Bailey outside. And then there's nothing else. Bailey doesn't come back.

I whirl to Will, excitement pounding in my chest. "You know what this means?"

"This isn't the primary crime scene," Will says.

"Exactly. Bailey must've been killed somewhere else. Maybe that's why the CSIs haven't been able to find anything. We should have the techs look at the other cameras in the neighborhood. And we need to find out what the canvassers learned."

Will nods. "Do you think the body type . . ." he begins.

"Looked an awful lot like Angus Nelson's?" I finish, standing and grabbing the file. "Sure do. Let's go have a chat with him."

Chapter 21

It was midday when I arrived, the roads quiet, empty. I parked a couple of blocks away, somewhere that wasn't covered by neighborhood security cameras, and slid a medium-size box from my front seat. I was wearing post-office blues and a blue baseball cap.

At a quick glance, I looked like any other delivery person.

I did my homework. It wasn't like this was my first time here. I wasn't one of those killers who wanted to get caught. I had planned every detail to ensure I remained free. Those who got caught were lazy or arrogant, or possibly both. Their own stupidity or guilty conscience landed them in peril. They confessed to a loved one or, worse, bragged to the wrong person. They wanted fame, notoriety, recognition for their deeds.

I didn't want any of that. My goal wasn't to #cancel anybody or #ruin-herlife. I wanted those responsible to be punished.

I wanted justice. My brand of justice.

Perhaps I was an unconventional hero, someone whose unruly passions and inconvenient thinking clashed with societal norms. I was careful to play the role people expected of me. At work I was diligent, at home I was dutiful, and in my spare time, I read or had the occasional drink with friends. Nobody would ever guess the things inside my heart. I had so many masks, sometimes I wasn't even sure who I really was.

The truth was, it was easy to be what others wanted you to be. People were entirely predictable, however hard they tried to hide their true nature.

All you had to do was find out what they wanted. Maybe we all cast our desires onto those around us.

I threw a last glance at myself in the car's window, ensuring my blond wig and prescription-less glasses were properly in place. I knocked on her front door, even though I knew nobody was home; then I took the box to her neighbor's house. She was a nosy old biddy, staring at the large block writing on the box with a look of disgusted delight twisting her wrinkled face.

I handed her the box, barely able to contain the thrill of pleasure I felt at what I knew was to come. Oh, how I wished I could be there when she opened it! To see the look on her face, to feel the terror seeping from her body! I truly hoped she understood the symbolism. No matter. It would sink in. And then she would feel sick with fear and anxiety.

That was why I sent the texts, after all. The letters. The photographs. This box. For months, I have been carefully unwrapping each phase of my plan. I wanted her to know what was coming first. Vengeance is far more satisfying when properly planned and executed. Served cold, as they say. What goes around comes around, after all.

I was already anxious to get home to Tweety. His wing was healing nicely now, and I truly enjoyed coming home to his sweet little chirps. Call me crazy, but I was pretty sure he was happy to see me, too. Everyone needed a bit of company now and then.

I forced myself to walk back to my car slowly, just another delivery person dropping off a parcel. I needed to be careful. Patient.

But I had always been a patient person.

Chapter 22

NEVE

"Mom?"

I jolt awake, my face still damp with tears. I haven't been able to stop crying since I ran out of the care home. I can't help it. The version of my mother I saw today is wiping out all the real memories I have of her, and it's unbearable.

"Mom?"

I blink.

Ash's face is a strange blur, in focus, then not. She's standing over me, her eyebrows furrowed. I'm lying on the floor under the window in her bedroom. My old room.

The outline of a thought hits me, unformed, its edges fuzzy. But before I can grasp it, it's gone, flitting off into the nighttime shadows.

"What are you doing down there?" Ash's face is creased with concern, a hand on one hip.

I sit up, disoriented, my head thick and swampy. I've been sleeping that strange, drugged sleep again. I turn my head to look at the window. It's dark outside. My body is stiff, my head throbbing.

I don't remember coming up here. I shake my head, a short jolt, but it makes my brain swim even more. I blink, trying to orient myself, and wipe at my damp face with the inside of my forearm. Frustration moves through me. What is happening to me?

Ash is looking at me expectantly. I wonder if she's been talking, and I spaced out. Have I been asleep up here all afternoon? I can't seem to corral my thoughts into any sort of coherent, intelligent order.

"Sorry, sweetie. I was . . . tired." My voice is rusty when I speak. I rub my eyes, ignoring the funny look she's giving me, and clear my throat.

"You sure you're okay?"

"Yes, of course."

"Okay." She grasps my hands and helps me stand. "Here's one. Would you rather be covered in scales for the rest of your life or watch an episode of *Keeping Up with the Kardashians* every day?"

I laugh, shaking first my left, then my right leg to ease the stiffness. I know what she's trying to do, and I appreciate it. I could use a little distraction right now. I can't figure out why I fell asleep on the floor when there's a perfectly good bed right here. Visiting my mom this morning must've rattled me more than I thought.

"Um, Kardashians. I could probably tune it out, I think!" I roll my shoulders. "So, where have you been all day?"

I vaguely remember looking for her earlier and not finding her in the house. Perhaps that's when I'd come up here and gone to sleep?

"I've been . . ." Ash looks toward the window. "Around. I took a kayak out to one of the islands and went for a hike."

I blink at her. "On your own?"

She laughs. "Yeah. I'm almost sixteen, Mom. I can do things on my own."

"I know, sweetie." Kids never realize how astounding it is for their parents to watch this person, who not too long ago couldn't even go to the bathroom on their own, suddenly turn into a grown-up capable of cooking and driving and spending the day entirely on their own. "I'm so proud of you."

I pull her in for a tight hug, using it as an excuse to sweep my gaze over her fair skin. There are no blisters, no signs of a sunburn. Moms gotta mom, after all.

She leans against me for a second, and I feel everything inside me melt. Ash has been so prickly lately. I've missed this. I want more than anything to freeze this moment, but soon she is wiggling out of the scorching heat of my embrace, filled with too much love.

"Mo-om. I know what you're doing. Stop checking me over. I told you I don't need sunscreen."

I stare at her milk-white skin. It's the kind of pale that almost has a bluish hue to it. There is no sign of the sun on it, no freckles marring the fresh cream. If she was out in the sun all day without sunscreen, she would've burned terribly. An appalling thought occurs to me. Is she lying about the sunscreen or lying about the kayak? Or both?

"Well, I'm glad you're settling in here." I keep my tone pleasant.

Ash scowls, like I've said something wrong.

"Are you for real? I'm *not* settling in here. I miss Dad. I miss my friends. I miss my pillow. And I know you like it here, but it's creepy. Sometimes I . . ."

Ash crosses to the window and pulls the curtains open, but not before I see her eyes brimming with tears. She stares out at the dark night sky.

"Sometimes what?" I press.

When she speaks, there's an odd note in her voice. "Have you ever thought something's wrong, something about someone you love? And it changes . . . everything. Everything you thought you knew about them."

"What do you know, Ash?" I wish she would turn and look at me. I don't like that I can't see her eyes. I don't know what she's thinking.

"Ash?"

"Nothing. I just . . . I don't want to stay here. I feel weird. Like, I keep losing track of time or something. I feel like I'm a balloon, like I'm gonna drift away any second. I don't like it." She finally faces me, her green eyes hollow, like staring into an abyss. "Please can we go home?"

"I'll find you a counselor here. I know it's been tough, and maybe talking to someone will help. We always knew PTSD could surface anytime."

I reach out to hold her, but she yanks herself away, her expression angry.

"I don't need a shrink; I need to go home!"

The blood pounds in my ears, a roar that fills my head. She's pulling away from me. Blaming me. I feel a sharp pang of guilt. It's my fault we're here. My fault she can't see Eli. I've failed to protect her, and now I'm failing to hold on to her.

The worst thing is, I could take steps to fix this. It's in my power to take her home. But I can't.

I'm not ready.

Something inside me is stuck, like a knotted kite string that's tangled in a tree. It feels like everything is on hold until I know who killed Bailey. Because I don't believe it was a random murder. I'm afraid someone came for me, and Ash became collateral damage.

Until I know we're safe, that Ash is safe, I can't let go.

"I want to go home." Ash's expression is fierce. Narrow eyes. Curled lip.

"Ash . . ." Fear spools through me, tying itself into knots in my throat.

"As soon as we can! Right now!" Ash's cheeks are blotchy. She begins feverishly picking up the clothes that are lying on her floor, tossing them into a pile on her bed.

"But you're doing so well here. You're getting out of the house and exploring and your nightmares . . . you've barely had any lately!"

Ash ignores me and grabs a backpack from the closet, stuffing the clothes, unfolded, into the unzipped compartment.

"Just give me two weeks," I plead with her.

"I don't have two weeks!" she shouts, whirling to face me. Her nose flares, hot coils of anger emanating off her.

I freeze. "What do you mean?"

Ash swallows, visibly trying to control herself. An uncomfortable silence fills the room as I wait for her to explain herself. But she doesn't.

"Ash, what do you mean you don't have two weeks?" I repeat in my sternest voice. "Two weeks is nothing. Two weeks and we can get you home in time for school to start, if that's what you want."

"Nothing," she says, sullen now.

My mouth moves, starts to form words, but nothing comes out. There's a strange feeling in my throat. My neck starts to burn, a prickly, panicky flush climbing the skin.

"Nothing," she says again, firmer now. "I just don't want to wait two weeks. I want to go home *now*."

"We can't leave yet."

She whirls to face me fully, pinning me with an acid glare. In the overhead light, her scar gleams, a puckered white knot. "We can't? Or you won't."

Her next words cause ice to trickle down my spine.

"Why are we *really* here, Mom?"

I've always been good at running away, and so I go for a run. Thanks to the heat, I haven't been able to since we arrived, but I figure now's as good a time as any. Back home, I ran every day in the strip of woods behind our house, and I've missed it. The temperature is still warm but bearable, the night suppressing the worst of the scorching air.

My tennis shoes pound against the pavement as I dive into the starry night, heading out the front gates to the main road beyond. I pass Vivienne and her husband out walking their dog, but other than them, the road is empty. I wave, but both are too wrapped up in their conversation to notice.

The sky is clear, a perfect midnight velvet, stars shining brilliantly, like pinpricks of light bursting through the carpet of black. The moon is a glowing white orb as I pump my arms, working desperately to turn emotional pain into miles run.

The road is flat, my shoes kicking up dust as I run along the shoulder toward the town's lights. I can't see the lake, but I know it's there, off to my right. I usually run in the morning, but I like this, I think, running at night. There's something invigorating about the black, feeling invincible, like I'm the only person in the world. There is an unexpected sense of nirvana, my skin shimmering in the moonlight.

I feel the oxygen hissing in and out of my lungs, the warm air brushing almost tenderly against my bare skin. The ground beneath my feet disappears, the black ribbon of road propelling me forward. I am flying, the sky and horizon merging, an awe-inspiring sweep of black and sparkling white.

The sound of my feet, the rhythmic *thud, thud*, triggers something. A memory. I stop running so fast that I almost trip, my body still moving forward, my feet rooted beneath me. I bend at the waist, eyes stinging, and grab my knees as I gulp in giant breaths of air, trying to push it away. And yet there it is, surging up in me like bubbles rising to the surface.

Black sky. Air on bare skin. Hissing breath. A scream. Then blood.

Boom. The sound of the front door splintering, wood cracking. *Boom.*

And then a figure in black appearing in the dining room doorway.

I turned to Ash and screamed, "Run!"

I snatched a steak knife from the table. Wooden handled. Sharp, serrated teeth. The blade sliced through skin and tendon with surprisingly little resistance. A shrill cry of pain and the person crumpled to the ground. Blood gushed in messy swirls onto the hardwood floor.

I didn't wait to see anything else. I dropped the knife and ran, only vaguely aware of Eli's shouts from upstairs.

The only thing on my mind was Ash. I had to protect her.

I burst into the garage just off the kitchen and followed behind her. The garage door was closing with a rattle and shriek. I stumbled toward it, slipping under before it slammed into the concrete.

I knew exactly where she'd gone, but I hesitated, instinct telling me to run to my neighbor's house. To get help. But the other part of me, the mother part, told me to find my girl. Keep her safe. And so I followed Ash, running along the paved path at the side of the house to the backyard. I burst past the neatly trimmed rhododendrons and rounded the corner, arriving just as Ash's feet disappeared beneath a loose plank under the deck. I dropped to my stomach and shimmied in behind her, my breath scraping in and out of my lungs like hot metal forks.

Ash was sobbing loudly. I wrapped my arms around her, her body shivering against mine.

"Shhh," I whispered. "He'll hear you."

I closed my eyes, counting my breaths and hoping that Eli was okay. That he'd called the police. We were sitting ducks here under the porch.

But what if he wasn't okay? What if Eli was dead? What if that's what the second boom had been?

And then it was too late. The back door slammed, boots stomping overhead. I dropped back to the floor, panic swirling through me.

Dust shook loose from the stairs, sprinkling onto our heads. Ash almost cried out, but I clapped a hand over her mouth. Footsteps clumped over us, thumping against the patio's wooden planks. The person moved in a slow, agonizing circle before heading toward the stairs.

The cold from the dirt under my butt seeped into my body, and I began to shake, my teeth clattering together like old bones. I clenched my jaw to stop, but it was no use.

The figure was at the bottom of the stairs now. We were trapped, just like I'd feared.

But then I heard it. The distant wail of a siren. Eli had called the police. Help was on the way.

Relief flooded me. I pulled Ash tighter against me, just as the creak of the loose panel slapped my ears. With a searing screech, someone wrenched the panel off, and we were exposed.

And then the figure bent, eye level with us, and raised a gun.

◆ ◆ ◆

I am on my knees by the side of the road, sobbing, retching, the terror of that night washing over me. I'd forced the home invasion to the back of my mind, but the memory has been there, a blood clot waiting to burst.

The next thing I knew, Ash was in the hospital. At first, nobody knew if she would wake up. Everything then became a blur until we came here, back to Dullahan House, where I thought we'd be safe.

But are we safe?

I have to protect Ash. I failed her last time, but I *will* keep her safe now. She doesn't know the full extent of everything that happened, and I won't tell her. Not until her brain is sufficiently healed enough for her to remember on her own. If I can protect her even in this tiny way, I will do that, even if she resents me, even if she hates me. Even if I don't fully understand everything myself.

My daughter's words crash into me, slippery as soap on my skin. "Why are we *really* here, Mom?"

I stand, trying to shake off the images. They're already fading, dissolving in the night like smoke caught by the wind. Something vital trickles through me, an unformed thought. And somewhere in the distance, an engine grows closer.

I have a gift for burying unpleasant things so they disappear, and I do this now. For a second, I can hear the shouting of my own faraway voice. But I shake my legs and pump my arms, running in place, and it grows fainter, until all I hear is the song of the nighttime insects.

The single headlight of a motorcycle sweeps past me, rumbling as it reaches a curve and slows, then accelerates. I watch as its taillight disappears in the murky orange light of the town, leaving me, once again, alone.

But seeing the motorcycle has given me an idea.

Chapter 23
JESS

My phone rings as I'm climbing off my motorcycle, which I've parked in front of Angus Nelson's hotel. It's my therapist calling to tell me she's referred me for an MRI. I jot down the clinic number to call later, then hurry inside after Will.

The hotel isn't located in Black Lake. All we have there are tiny B and Bs and one old motel. This hotel is set in a fancy Tudor-style house about ten miles away. It's upscale, sophisticated, all brick and climbing ivy, the kind of place that hosts weddings and has a spa downstairs.

As this was our second chat with Angus Nelson, we were aware we didn't want to scare him or risk having to deal with a lawyer. So we decided to chat at his hotel, informally, instead of bringing him in.

We find Angus in the bar waiting for us. He's already a little drunk. His shoulders are rounded forward, his head drooping. The bar smells of stale booze and bacon. My stomach rumbles. I haven't eaten since a slice of peanut butter toast this morning, and the smell of bacon makes my stomach growl.

Angus looks up as we approach. He's been crying, the redness and swollen eyes speaking of a long night behind him, a longer one ahead. The smell of his bourbon on the rocks makes my mouth water. My hands begin to tremble, and for a second, the longing for a drink is so strong that I forget why we're here.

Will reintroduces us while I take stock of Angus. He's older, late fifties, with a receding hairline and a half-moon of gray hair. But he's fit, compact, the type of guy who used to work out a lot to make himself feel sexy but now works out a lot to make himself feel young. The suave has melted off him like wax, and the dim bar lighting isn't doing anything for his coloring. He looks like he's going to be sick. Grief or guilt. With some people, it's hard to tell the difference between the two.

"Is my house free now, Detectives?" he slurs. He's been staying here while the CSIs process the house.

"Not exactly, bud," Will says with a big, sympathetic smile. "Just a few more things we thought you could clear up."

Good Cop is where Will really shines. He's the jolly guy who's their best friend—gets people to confide in him. Me, with my icy demeanor and skeptical questions and resting bitch face—yeah, I've heard people say it behind my back—I just get under their skin, make them defensive.

Will drops the iPad onto the bar in front of Angus. He presses "Play," and we watch as Angus lets himself into the house. Bailey turns, surprised. They argue. Angus slaps her.

"Maybe my notes are wrong," Will says, all guileless, a little self-deprecating. "I'm terrible at taking notes, to be fair. But I'm sure you said you weren't home the day of the murder."

Angus's eyes dart between Will and me. His hands are bunched together on his lap, his fingers twisting around each other as color rises up his cheeks.

"I d-did . . . ," he stutters. "I mean, I . . ."

"The truth would be a good place to start right now," I say, my voice cold. "Because from where we're standing, you're looking awful guilty."

Panic spasms across Angus's face. "No. I swear, I didn't hurt her. I mean, sometimes we fought like that. We hit each other." He gives a wry little laugh. "Trust me, Bailey gave as good as she got."

He looks away, his eyes glinting. "The truth is, Bailey and I had a . . . difficult marriage."

"How long were you married?" Will asks.

"Almost ten years."

"And why was it difficult?"

"I knew from the beginning that Bailey only married me for my money. I mean, look at me." Angus gestures at himself. "And look at her. She's gorgeous. She started having affairs right away, but at least they were discreet. And at first, I thought I could deal with it."

"What changed?" I ask.

"I wanted kids. I'm getting older; I want to pass down what I've built to my son or daughter. Before, the affairs were this thing we both knew but didn't talk about, but that all changed. I asked her to stop, but Bailey's like a cat. You can't tie her down, not really. She got attention wherever she went, and she liked it. She wasn't interested in kids. But when I didn't let up, she got pissed. A few weeks ago, she told me she wanted a divorce."

I find it extraordinary that Angus married a woman like Bailey, knowing full well what she was like. But then, most people go through life with their eyes shut. They want what they want without bothering to see reality. And love is the biggest blindfold there is.

"Why didn't you tell us this before?" I ask.

"I knew it would look bad. And it had nothing to do with what happened. Besides, she was stressed out before she even asked for a divorce."

"Why's that?"

"She'd started getting these pictures in the mail. The same picture over and over."

Will and I exchange a glance. "What was the picture of?"

"Just her and two of her friends when she was a teenager in front of a bonfire."

I flip open Bailey's file and find the picture.

"This one?"

Angus pulls a pair of glasses from his breast pocket, his brows knitting together. "Yes. Only, Bailey never showed me this one. The others were just this picture, no faces scratched out."

"Did you recognize the other two in the picture?"

"No."

"Do you still have any of those pictures?"

"I think Bailey threw them away. To be honest, I thought she was overreacting. The pictures seemed pretty innocent to me. I didn't understand why they upset her. She was on edge all the time. And then somebody broke into the house. That's why we had the security camera installed."

"Was anything taken?"

"That's the thing. Nothing that we could really tell. In fact, I wasn't certain anybody had even broken in except she insisted somebody had. She said things had been moved around, the bed was messed up, there was mud on the stairs. Weird stuff like that."

I adjust my cane, lean against the counter. "Why don't you tell us where you were the day Bailey was killed. We can see in the video you were home with Bailey that morning."

Angus's eyes widen. "No, no, no. I didn't kill her; you guys have to believe me. Yes, I came home to try to sort things out with her—"

"Did you have sex with her?" I cut him off.

"Well . . . yes. But that's it. We had sex, and I tried to get her to delay the divorce. Give me another shot. I said we didn't need to have kids." He gives a brittle laugh. "She said no, so I left. I went back to New York, to my conference. I was on a panel later that day, so I had to get back anyway."

"Where'd you go after the conference?" I ask.

"I stayed in New York. You can check with my doorman."

"What kind of doctor are you?"

"Thoracic surgeon. Here." He fumbles in his back pocket for his wallet. Pulls out a rumpled receipt and hands it to me. "My taxi receipt from Grand Central back to my apartment in the city."

I read the little piece of paper. There's the time and date stamp right there.

It's possible this is someone else's receipt. That Angus Nelson picked it up off the floor or took it from someone. He's still our prime suspect, but my gut tells me he's telling the truth.

He wasn't in Black Lake when Bailey was murdered.

Chapter 24

Bailey wasn't the first person I killed.

But she was the first one I've enjoyed killing. Last time, I wasn't prepared enough. I made mistakes, found myself on the back foot a few times. It was too rushed. Things happened I couldn't control.

This time, I planned it better, and the execution was perfect.

Bailey struggled a bit, which was to be expected. You can't always account for adrenaline, I've learned. Fortunately, I was prepared with the syringe I'd swiped from work. Her body stilled quite quickly after that, her muscles going flaccid and limp.

After I'd thrown both her cell phones into the lake, I snapped the bracelet onto her wrist and tied her hands with duct tape. You can never be too careful.

And then the icing on the cake: I used a craft knife to carve my message onto her tongue.

It's surprising how much a tongue bleeds, sheets and sheets of it. By the time I'd finished, the blood had formed a little pool at the back of her throat, and her neck and cheeks were streaked with crimson.

Imagine my surprise when she opened her eyes. She tried to move, but of course she was bound, and the drug had essentially paralyzed her. Weakness comes in many forms, and I could see it in her gaze. She wanted me to show her mercy. Absolution. Her eyes screamed at me. Why? *they asked.* Why are you doing this?

The world is full of extraordinarily selfish, manipulative people. Humans are capable of terrible things. Genocide, rape, slavery, murder. But just because we are capable of something doesn't mean we should do it. We all have our choices. No matter your religion, we are all given free will.

Should we really allow these people to be out walking around, engaging with normal society like they weren't a tumor, a cyst that needed to be excised? They wouldn't change. That was just a simple fact. They would always be a weeping, pus-filled abscess.

What a shame that humans were not more like penguins, who began their relationship with a pebble, the smoothest one they could find. Such a simple gesture to symbolize their lifelong fidelity. Of course, some penguins traded sex for pebbles, so perhaps the real takeaway was that nobody, neither human nor bird, could be trusted.

Bailey taught me that. Not to trust. She was selfish. Cruel. Capricious and conniving. As I did my research—I told you I was prepared—I learned more about her. I slipped into her office and rooted through her files. I broke into her home and excised every detail of her personal life. I followed her and discovered exactly who she was.

Bailey's hobby was seducing wealthy men. She ruined so many families, too many to count. Men with wives and children, men who were easily swayed by a pretty face. Men are so susceptible to beauty. They think with their penises, and it revokes all logical thought. It is most definitely a design flaw.

Once upon a time, I loved Bailey. Until I learned the truth. I knew who she really was. I knew what she did.

And so I told her.

She deserved what she got.

Believe me, I did the world a favor.

Chapter 25

NEVE

I walk into town, passing the veterinary clinic with its blue-and-yellow sign, the summer-crispened shrubs framing the front door. Next to it is the strip mall with the Cash Advance, a nail salon, a dollar store, a Subway. They'd all obviously shuttered during the pandemic, and only the Subway had reopened.

It looks like a ghost town, not a soul in sight.

A few blocks down is Black Lake's historic downtown, which is really just the main road with a handful of shops and cafés and bars separated by two stoplights that stay on red for far too long. At the other end is Sammy's, pressed between dying stores and dying trees, and opposite an old clapboard church and a dead-end street that leads to a sandy beach.

Noise floats out from the two-story wooden structure. The sign flutters neon, but the Y is going out, so it declares Samm 's or Sammy's, depending on how long you watch it. I cross the unpaved parking lot, passing clusters of people standing outside, smoking and laughing.

A blast of icy-cold air conditioning greets me as I enter, the stale scent of cigarettes and booze thick on its heels. The place is busy, cracked vinyl booths and mismatched stools and chairs filled with people in various stages of drunkenness. Behind the bar is a grizzled older man with wild gray hair and a full-on wizard beard.

I scan the room and spot Detective Jess Lambert. She's hunched over a drink, sitting alone in a booth at the back. A barely touched cheeseburger and a handful of fries sit in a congealing puddle of grease in front of her. It was an educated guess that she'd be here, considering she'd reeked of booze when I met her and this is the bar she'd recommended.

I cross the room, noticing her colleague, Detective Casey, laughing with a couple other cops in a booth on my left. I wonder why they aren't sitting together. If, like me, the good detective prefers to be alone.

"Detective?" I say when I approach her table.

She looks up with bleary, red-stained eyes.

"Neve," she says, but it comes out *Nnnnnvvvv*. I glance at the drink in front of her. Whiskey, by the smell of it. She's already had a few, by the looks of it.

She's still dressed in her detective clothes: black trousers, a dark blouse. A black leather jacket is draped over the seat next to a backpack and her folded cane.

"Sit. Sit." She gestures at the spot across from her.

I do as she says and slide in. The booth is a little sticky against the backs of my bare legs. I make a face.

"Gosh, it's so cold in here compared to outside, right?" She rubs her chilled arms and drapes her jacket over her shoulders. "How are you settling in?"

"Yeah, good. How are you?" The question is loaded, but she doesn't seem to notice.

"Good. I'm all good." She smiles like a sleep-drunk toddler, toothy and wide. Sitting this close, I see she has a constellation of freckles on her nose and cheeks and a thin scar above her full lips.

"I, uh . . . I saw your motorcycle and thought I'd stop by. Check on the investigation into the . . ." I choke on the word—*murder*—unable to get it out. "Into what happened to my neighbor."

The police still haven't arrested a suspect in Bailey's murder or said if they're close to solving the case.

She begins with the *we can't disclose any information* nonsense, which I expected, but this is why I've approached her at the bar. People's defenses lower when they've been drinking. I figure I can get more information—more *honest* information—out of her now.

"I understand," I say, "but I have a teenage daughter who's frightened by what happened, and I need to be able to reassure her. The husband, I saw him at my neighbor's house. Is he a suspect? *Shouldn't* he be a suspect?"

The detective's eyes narrow, struggling a little to focus on me. "Why would you think he's a suspect?"

"Don't most people who're killed know their killer? And in these sorts of cases, it's always the husband. Domestic abuse is a serious problem, and half of women murdered die at the hands of their abuser."

"Mr. Nelson has an alibi. He was out of the state at the time of Mrs. Nelson's murder. Besides, men don't kill this way in domestic violence cases."

"What way is that?"

She looks down at her hands. "Men fight with their fists. They beat their victims to death. They don't carve—" She cuts herself off; takes another long swig of her drink.

"Carve what?" I prompt her.

She glares accusingly at her empty glass, absentmindedly knuckling her left thigh. But when she lifts her eyes to mine, she has plastered a smile on her lips. "Look, I understand your concern, but I assure you, we are working very hard on this case."

Despite her inebriated state, I can tell I won't get any more information out of her. So I tell her what I came here for. "I saw my neighbor across the road—Vivienne?—break into Bailey's house."

The detective sits up a little straighter. "When'd you see that?"

"It was shortly after I spoke to you on Saturday. I was upstairs in my daughter's bedroom, and when I looked out, I saw her crossing the road and going right up to the porch. There's a ceramic flowerpot there that's painted like a cat, and it has a false bottom. She got a key out of it."

"Did she take anything?"

"Yes. She left with a white paper bag. Smallish, you know, like you'd get from the pharmacy. Oh! And a folder, I think. She'd rolled it up, so I could be wrong about that. I mean, maybe it's completely innocent. Maybe Vivienne was watering Bailey's plants? I just thought I should tell you. Just in case."

"I'll look into it. Thanks."

"No problem. If there's anything I can do to help . . ." Why would a detective want my help? What a stupid thing to say.

But she surprises me by saying, "Maybe you can help. Hold on. You wanna drink? I wannanother drink." She slurs the words together. *Wannanother.*

"Oh, no thanks, none for me," I say.

The detective waves at a waitress passing by with a tray of dirty glasses. The girl has glossy dark hair pulled into a messy bun, heavy mascara, red lips. She's wearing a short skirt that accentuates long, slim legs. She's working her tips in this male-dominated room. I did my fair share of waitressing to put myself through college. It's never easy for women in this industry.

"I wannanother, please, Mei," she slurs at the waitress. "And one for my friend here." She taps the table in front of me. "Double whiskey on the rocks."

The waitress looks between us, biting her lower lip. Her expression is a comical mix of uncertainty and concern. Jess is really drunk, and I wonder what the legal threshold for serving is. When I was a waitress, I always worried about serving too much. I had a bartender friend get sued by somebody who'd been in an accident after leaving the bar.

The waitress returns to the bar. She addresses the bartender, but I can't hear what she's saying over the chatter of drunken voices. After a minute, she returns, setting our drinks in the middle of the table.

The detective grabs hers and takes a long swig, then reaches into the inner pocket of her jacket and extracts something. "You mentioned you used to visit Black Lake when you were a kid. Do you recognize these girls?"

She holds out what looks to be a 3x5 photo. I don't take it. The photo flutters to the table. She straightens it, and I peer down at the photo. I feel my body tense, and I go perfectly still.

It's the same picture that Bailey showed me at the restaurant of her, Sandra, and me that last summer. Our arms are wound around each other, the bonfire in the background, the lake stretching behind us. Except in this picture, my face is scratched out, so hard that there isn't hair or a head or even shoulders. Just my body standing in the middle.

I rub a finger over Bailey's smiling face. "It's Bee."

"Excuse me?"

"Bee Naldoni. That's how I always knew her. I'm sorry, I didn't make the connection until now," I lie.

I worry that connection will come out anyway. I've decided it's best to get ahead of it now.

"So you knew her?"

"I knew her during the summers. She was my next-door neighbor back then, and we were friends. We played together, and then when we got older, we'd go to the Fourth of July parade and slumber parties and the end-of-summer bonfire."

"You didn't stay in touch?"

She's leaning toward me, both elbows on the table, her entire body tense, and suddenly I realize that even as drunk as she is, she knows exactly what she's doing. She's interrogating me.

I smile, cool and calm. "Once I went off to college, I didn't come back here for summers with my parents anymore. I guess we just drifted apart. Summer friends aren't real friends."

"You're sure you don't know who this girl is?" She taps the girl with the scratched-out face with one finger.

I swallow hard, my throat dry. "No, I don't know who it is."

"Do you think it could be you?"

I inhale sharply. "Me? Why would you think that?"

"Just brainstorming. It looks like the picture was taken in your backyard—the firepit, see?" She taps the picture. "It's still there."

"It could be someone else's firepit."

She shrugs. "Maybe. Take a good look. You're sure you don't remember this picture being taken?"

I stare at the picture, frowning. "Maybe vaguely? You have to understand, it was a long time ago. Back then, we were always posing for pictures. I don't remember each one."

"Want to explain why you lied about knowing Bailey Nelson?"

"Like I said, I never knew her as Bailey Nelson, only Bee Naldoni. I haven't seen her since we were teenagers, so I didn't recognize her when you showed me her Facebook profile picture."

It's a lie, but who can tell anymore? I've told so many, I sometimes don't even know what the truth is.

"I asked you yesterday if you knew her."

"You didn't exactly give me a chance to reply," I point out. "You left in quite a hurry after you got that phone call, remember?"

Detective Lambert flushes and looks away.

I throw my hands up. "Look, yes, I knew Bee when we were kids, but I haven't spoken to her since my last summer here in Black Lake."

I'm lying, of course. Again.

Because I spoke to her just the other day. I called her after Eli got those photos of me at the hotel with Stephen. She was at a charity auction raising funds for Parkinson's research, a ludicrously dishonest representation of the person I knew she really was. The words we spoke were fierce, threatening.

And then later, the day before the home invasion, I drove down to Black Lake to see her. I parked in front of her real-estate office and waited for her to leave. And then I followed.

I don't think any of this will convince the detective I wasn't the one who killed her.

Chapter 26

NEVE

"Am I in danger?" I ask the detective.

"Why would you be?"

"You just insinuated I'm in an old photo that possibly has my face scratched out. Surely I have a right to feel a little freaked out!"

And I am. Freaked out. I know all of us reach an age where we question if our choices in life were the right ones. We look back and wonder if the things we did, the decisions we made, were good or bad, right or wrong. The difference with me is, I know I was wrong. What I don't know is who else knows.

Bee tried to warn me, but I wouldn't listen. It's what we fought about the night she was at the charity event. I called her on her work cell, the only number I had, furious at how low she'd stooped.

"You left my husband pictures of me with Stephen?" I shrieked when she answered her phone. I felt a little unhinged, apoplectic with rage. The sharp edge of a knife hurts most when burrowed between your shoulders. "Are you insane?"

"What are you talking about?"

"The envelope you left on Eli's car with pictures of me at the motel. You've ruined my life!"

"Knock it off, Neve," Bee snapped. "That wasn't me. This is what I was trying to tell you the other day. Someone is messing with us."

But I didn't believe her.

"You have no idea who you're dealing with," I spat. "I will fucking ruin you."

And then I hung up.

But if it wasn't Bailey who put those pictures on Eli's car, who did?

"Do you know the other girl?" Detective Lambert taps the blonde girl in the picture.

I pretend to study the picture. "I can't remember her name. Bee was really popular. She had lots of friends."

"Who took the photo?"

"Honestly, I don't remember for sure, but it was probably Bee's boyfriend. Zac something. His dad was a politician, I think. Zac Hendrix, maybe? I don't know. It's been a while."

She jots this information into a little notebook.

The truth is, I'm not sad that Bailey is dead. If it hadn't been for her, I wouldn't be hiding behind a lifetime of lies now. But I can't shake the sight of her dead body, pale and limp. And the note that was slipped into a book in my house: *There will be consequences.* And now there's this picture with my face scratched out.

It all goes back to that one night. That one decision. I know I can confront the truth or bury it, but right now my only concern is protecting Ash. She's only fifteen years old. She doesn't deserve any of this. Whatever happened, whatever will happen, it's my fault, not hers, and I will do everything I can to keep her safe.

A noise from the other side of the bar grabs my attention. I twist in my seat to look at the source. Near the front of the bar, Detective Casey and his buddies are staring at Detective Lambert. A couple of the guys are laughing. One looks embarrassed. Detective Casey's face is a cross between concern and pity.

"Why are they staring at you?" I ask, nodding toward the group of guys.

"Eh . . ." Detective Lambert tosses back another gulp of whiskey. "They're harmless. That one's my partner; the others are just some guys from the station."

"Your partner"—I lean closer and drop my voice—"he looks like Daddy Pig."

She snort-laughs. "Ha! Yeah, I can see that."

"So why are they staring at you?"

"They think I'm crazy."

"What?" That's the last thing I thought she'd say. "Why do they think that?"

"Craaaaazy with grief." She spins a finger around her ear and widens her eyes, then shrugs, but her body language, her glistening eyes, say she isn't as okay as she's pretending.

"I lost my daughter almost a year ago." She looks down at the amber liquid in her glass, again massaging her leg. "Drunk driver. I was the drunk. I hit a deer."

"Jesus, that's terrible. I'm so sorry."

"We were shopping over in Springfield. I took her out to lunch and decided to have a margarita."

"You were drunk after one margarita?"

"Even one is too much," she snaps. She sighs and continues. "I got called into work. I had to take Isla home to my husband. There was a terrible storm. It was . . . torrential. I thought I was okay, but I guess I wasn't sober enough to avoid hitting the deer that jumped across the road.

"The shitty thing is, I can't get away from it. The worst thing I ever did, and I've not paid at all. There's no . . . justice." She spits the word out. "They never pressed charges against me. By the time they found me, I was so messed up." She gestures at her leg. "I was nearly dead. Isla, she was dead. Nobody took me off to jail. But it's where I should be."

She stares off into space for a long moment. Her resting bitch face has been replaced with something else, something raw, a map of pain and trauma. I know how she feels, the ache of doing something wrong, of wanting to protect your child and that helplessness, the impotence you feel when you fail.

I remember how I froze when the attacker burst into our house. I should've told Ash to hide, should've fought, should've stood my ground instead of running like the coward I am. I don't know what horrible twist of fate took her daughter and left mine.

"How'd you get through it?" I ask quietly.

"I'm not sure I have." She sips her drink. "You know, my mom always said there's a direct link between suffering and sin."

"Only for the good," I counter. "The bad don't suffer no matter what they've done."

She thinks about this. "Sometimes I still see her."

"You see your daughter?"

She laughs, dry and brittle. "I mean, not really, obviously. My shrink says they're called grief hallucinations. They're, uh . . . normal, I guess? Part of the whole grieving process."

I look at her, feeling a kinship with this woman. She's lost something, too. Different than I have, but loss is still loss. And there's something to be said about trauma-bonding. Something about seeing another person for who they are because of what they've lost. And I can suddenly see so clearly who she is now, this broken, fragile, but strong woman who blames herself for what sounds like a horrible, horrible accident.

Maybe you have to lean in a little, have to wear that hair shirt for a while, but at some point, you have to get up and face the world again, and that's what she's doing. I can't help but admire her for it. Maybe it's time for me to start facing the world again, too.

"It must be hard," I say, "being reminded of her. How you lost her."

The detective seems to consider this. "Actually, I guess it's kind of comforting."

"Do you talk to her?"

She snorts. "No, of course not. She's not real. She's *dead*." The detective's lips pinch together, her jaw clenching. She kneads harder at her thigh and gives an angry little laugh. "My colleagues would lock me up for sure if I started talking to dead people."

"You don't believe in ghosts?"

"No. I don't believe in ghosts or bogeymen or apparitions. Just bad people who do bad things." She swirls the last of her drink around her glass. "You?"

"I don't know," I say slowly. "Maybe it isn't the dead who haunt the living but the living who do the haunting. Or maybe we haunt ourselves. Like, we're haunted by our pasts, by our mistakes, the ones that aren't so easily forgiven. But maybe those ghosts don't have to be the only thing that defines us."

"You're saying we're not good or bad. That our mistakes don't define us."

"I guess, yeah."

"But what about choice? My daughter died because of my choice to drink. Actions have consequences. Choices have consequences. What I've done . . . that's a part of me now."

"Yes, but it's just a part, right? It's not all of you. Bad people. Good people. It isn't that simple. None of us is just one or the other. We're both. A collection of the best and worst things we've done. That's what my mom always told me: people are more than the worst things they've done."

"Maybe." Detective Lambert throws back the last of her drink and stares into her empty glass. "But those ghosts will sure as shit come back to haunt you."

I study her. "You should talk to her."

"I already told you. She's dead."

"But you said you still see her. If my daughter died and I had one more chance to talk to her, I'd tell her all the things I didn't get to say when she was alive. That I would've gladly died in her place so she could live. That I'm sorry and I hope she can forgive me. But most of all, I would tell her how much I love her. How much I'll always love her."

Detective Lambert is staring at me. The silence expands between us, and I start to feel a little awkward, like I've said too much.

"But that's just me." I reach for my glass of untouched whiskey but end up sloshing liquid over the side.

"Oh, shoot." I look around for a napkin, but there aren't any.

"Don't worry 'bout it." Detective Lambert waves a hand. "This isn't the kind of place you have to mop up a spill."

I look down at my wet hands. "I'll just go wash this off."

In the bathroom, I lock myself in the last stall and sit on the toilet. I rip off toilet paper in great chunks and wipe my hands dry.

I can't stop thinking of how close I came to losing Ash. How lucky I am. And how my heart breaks for Detective Lambert's loss.

After a minute, I flush the toilet and wash my hands. There are no paper towels, so I wipe my wet hands on my shorts and leave. I'm just coming around the corner when I hear the voice of that other detective talking to Detective Lambert.

". . . body's been found."

I flatten myself against the hallway and lean in, straining to hear what he's saying.

". . . same MO . . . message carved into the tongue."

"Same MO?" Jess slurs.

Detective Will Casey hisses out an exasperated breath, his voice rising in frustration.

"Jesus Christ, Jess, that's what I'm trying to tell you! Another woman has been murdered."

Chapter 27

NEVE

I peer around the corner as Detective Lambert snaps her cane open and limps after Detective Casey. Her bad leg drags more than usual in her drunken state, and I notice a few of the cops nearby exchanging smirks. I feel bad for her, angry on her behalf.

I follow the detectives outside but stop when I see them arguing at the edge of the parking lot. I can't hear what they're saying, but after a few minutes, Detective Casey gets in his car and drives away while Detective Lambert limps down the road in the opposite direction.

I consider going inside and finishing that drink, but in my peripheral vision, I see a flash of long dark hair, flawless porcelain skin.

It can't be.

I turn, my eyes scanning the parking lot.

There, heading across the road in the direction of the beach. For a brief second, the woman is illuminated by a backlit sign standing in front of the little white clapboard church across from the bar.

I stare in stunned surprise.

Bailey.

I hurry after her. She moves out of the light, into the shadows, but I'm catching up to her.

And then I'm right there, almost directly behind her, and I hear her laugh. She has a cell phone pressed to her ear when she steps into the arc of the next streetlight, but her head swivels over her shoulder, as if sensing I'm there. My footsteps falter, and I hover in the shadows because it isn't Bee at all. Just a woman who looks vaguely like her.

The woman tosses an alarmed look at me and hurries away. I stand there in the dark, waiting for my heart to stop beating so hard. Of course she wasn't really there. I was stupid to go running after a stranger like that. Sometimes we want something so much, we imagine it rather than facing the truth.

Why do I keep seeing her? Or keep *thinking* I'm seeing her? She's dead. Although I never saw her body.

I stop in the middle of the street.

I saw *a* body, but I never saw her body. Could this all be a mistake?

No, there's no way. Her husband ID'd her body. The police are certain it was her. Perhaps this is just my dirty conscience coming back to haunt me.

I continue to where the street dead-ends against the lake, the beach stretching along the water. My shoes sink into the sand, which has turned white under the milky moonlight. The water is still, an oily black with a white moon smudged across it.

A little way down the beach is an old playground, a rusted swing set next to a merry-go-round and a slide. I sit on a swing and kick my heels into the ground so I'm rocking gently. Faint music from the bar leaches down to where I sit on the swing, pulsing as the door opens, then closes.

I think of the things I overheard the detectives speaking about. Another body's been found, a message carved into her tongue. The detective said it was the same MO. Is that what happened to Bee?

But who? And why? And what did the message say?

I shiver, fear raking down my spine. Does Bee's murder have any-thing to do with me? For the first time, I wonder if maybe the home invasion wasn't random. Was everything that happened to Ash, to me, my fault?

Guilt claws at me. I should've protected Ash better, should've stopped the attack. Should've fought harder. I feel the emotional walls I've built beginning to crumble like sandcastles on the shoreline, my heart breaking into a million pieces. Because as a mother, all you want is to protect your child.

I scoop sand into my hand, letting it slowly trickle out, like sand slipping through a timer. Being here reminds me of the last time I was on this beach.

That last summer, Bee had become cruel, flippant, even to me, and the way she treated Sandra was appalling. When we were in town, the other kids avoided Bee like she had a disease. But she seemed completely unbothered. So unbothered I wondered whether I was imagining it.

When I asked if everything was okay, she would change the subject or distract me with gossip about the other girls we'd been friends with who weren't around anymore. She started buying me presents—lip gloss and nail polish, bracelets, a new bikini. I wondered if her dad was giving her more money than usual to make up for never being around. But sometimes I felt like she wasn't really present. We still spent every moment we could together, but I could feel Bee slipping away from me. Where once our friendship had been so solid, it now felt balanced on a precipice.

When she told me Sandra was now dating her ex-boyfriend, Zac, had *stolen* him from her, of course I took Bee's side. I didn't want to lose Sandra, but Bee had been my friend most of my life.

So when I received an invitation in the mail to Sandra's birthday party, I told Bee.

"You should go," Bee said.

"Seriously?" I was surprised.

We were lying on the beach in the brand-new bikinis Bee had bought. Fortunately, my dad had gone back to Boston for work. He would've flipped if he saw me showing so much skin.

We were eating ice cream cones we'd bought from the shop where Sandra worked. While we waited in line, Bee had whispered overly loud comments about Sandra into my ear. She'd made fun of Sandra's lisp ("Thandra. My name's Thandra, tho nithe to meet you."), her large forehead ("Football Head"), and her new haircut ("She looks like a page boy from a bad medieval play.").

Now, Bee sat up, licking a drip of cherry chip ice cream rolling down her cone. She stretched out her long, bronzed legs, the coconut oil she'd applied glistening in the sun.

"You should. I mean, this is silly, right?" She shot me a sheepish grin. "I'm the one who dumped Zac. I guess I just thought he'd wait a bit longer. And, you know, not go out with one of my friends." She laughed and rolled her eyes. "But you should totally go. I'll even get her a present. You can take it for me."

"Okay. If you're sure."

Her lips stretched into a smile, something that seemed a little sinister. But I quickly dismissed it. I told myself Bee was coming around. By the end of the summer, we'd all be friends again.

That weekend, I arrived at Sandra's party with two gifts: one from me and one from Bee. I set the presents next to the others, on a table where a cluster of balloons floated, proclaiming BIRTHDAY GIRL! and 17! in bright, bold colors. I poured myself a Coke, then approached Sandra.

"You came! Yay!" Sandra broke away from a crowd of teens I recognized from past summers and threw her arms around me.

Pretty and petite with yellow-blonde hair cut to her jawline, Sandra was one of those girls who was just so sweet, so welcoming, you couldn't help but like her.

"Of course I came." I bent a little to return her hug. I always felt like the giant in "Jack and the Beanstalk" next to Sandra.

"I wouldn't miss your birthday." I touched the tips of her hair. "I love your haircut."

Sandra flushed. "Thanks. I, uh, had to get it cut a couple of months ago."

It felt like there was more to that story, but before I could ask, Zac approached, putting his hand on Sandra's waist in an annoyingly proprietary way. Zac came from Black Lake royalty—a dad who worked in politics, a mom who was a wealthy heiress, a house in one of the nicest neighborhoods, a place at Harvard in September. It was a little surprising he was dating Sandra, to be honest. Even in a town as small as this one, there were some lines you didn't cross.

"Hey, dude! What's up? Haven't seen much of you this summer," Zac said with a grin.

I ignored him. Zac had the self-confidence of a kid who knew he had the whole world laid out at his feet. Handsome, wealthy, the type of boy every mother hopes her daughter would bring home, neatly pressed in chinos and a white polo shirt. He wasn't a bad guy, I guess, just arrogant and entitled. He rubbed me wrong.

Instead, I focused on Sandra, who entwined her fingers through mine and pulled me toward the lake. One of the people from Sandra's church had let them borrow a two-story jungle float.

We swam and played all afternoon, climbing the rope slides and bouncing on the giant floating raft's trampoline until Sandra's mom gathered everybody around to eat. Sandra's dad said a prayer; then he cut the cake while Sandra opened her gifts.

I was chatting with Lorna, a chubby, freckle-faced girl, only half paying attention to Sandra sitting on her other side, when someone passed her the gift from Bailey.

She opened the card and read out loud: "Happy birthday, Sandra. Thanks for letting me borrow this. Passing the torch back to you. You totally changed my life!"

She turned the card over, frowning. "It isn't signed."

I was about to tell her who it was from, but she was already ripping off the glossy pink wrapping paper. Inside was a nondescript box, no markings or brand names. When Sandra lifted the lid, the box was filled with white tissue paper. She thrust her hand inside, the tissue rustling.

I saw it then, the change on her face. Her expression twisted into one of disgust, lips curling.

"What the . . . ?" she murmured.

As if sensing something was about to happen, everybody had gone quiet, watching Sandra expectantly. Sandra withdrew the item from the tissue paper. It was huge, made of what looked to be rubber. A long muscular bit, thick as my forearm, protruded from bulging . . . balls? My hand flew to my mouth as I realized what it was.

A dildo. A giant dildo.

Sandra held the dildo up with two fingers, as if trying to figure out what it was. A blob of white liquid dripped off the end onto her dress. It left a damp splotch in her lap, the color darkening from baby blue to denim.

Next to her, Lorna leaped up, screeching with disgust.

Understanding finally crept in, and Sandra jumped up as well, her face going a shiny, dark puce. She screamed, her hands flapping in front of her, and flung the dildo into the sand at her feet. Zac stepped away from her, disgust etched into his handsome features.

I knew what the right thing to do was. I knew I should tell her the truth: that I'd brought the present for Bee. I should say that I was sorry. But I didn't. I just sat there with a deliberately blank look, watching Sandra's lips tremble, her face go redder and redder.

Her panicked gaze flew to her mother and father, who looked on, completely stunned. Next to them was Sandra's little sister, her small face bright red. She was too young to know what her sister was holding, but she understood Sandra's mortification.

"This isn't mine!" Sandra shouted. "It isn't mine!"

But nobody was paying attention. The boys were howling with laughter, the girls giggling hysterically. And at the back of the crowd, there was Bee, her eyes gleaming as she held a video camera, recording it all.

◆ ◆ ◆

I wish I could undo it, all the things that came next. Especially the last thing, the thing that severed our friendship and defined the person I became. If only we could change our pasts as easily as changing a light bulb.

The truth is, Bee wasn't a nice person. Perhaps a jilted lover or an angry wife or a person she'd wronged came looking for revenge. There must be a million people who'd want her dead.

I can't be the only one she fucked over.

But that picture with my face scratched out makes me uneasy. And the note I found in my house. *There will be consequences.*

The chance that this is all unrelated is receding rapidly. I can't help but feel that whoever killed Bee is coming for me next.

I have to go see Sandra. Because she's the only one I know who would have any reason to do this.

Chapter 28

JESS

"Jess? Are you listening?"

The stifling night air slaps me in the face, making me feel a little sick. I glance over my shoulder at Sammy's, longing for the soothing chill of the air-conditioned bar. I watch as Neve exits and disappears around the corner of the building.

I mentally kick myself. I should've remembered to get her maiden name, birthday, her past address. I had a perfect chance and wasted it.

"We need to do a background check on Neve Maguire," I tell Will.

The canvassers hadn't found anything important, and neither had any of the security cameras in the area so far. But something is bugging me about Neve. I can't put my finger on it, but some sixth sense is telling me something is off about her. I find it hard to believe she doesn't remember posing for that picture. And while I have no proof it is her, I'm certain it is. If the firepit didn't give it away, the look on her face when I suggested it was her, the tightening of her eyes when she couldn't recall the other girl's name, did. She knew more than she was saying.

Is she victim or murderer? Prey or hunter?

That restlessness roars in me, twisting so hard that it's almost painful, my blood buzzy and jittery in my veins. I tap my chin, trying to corral my thoughts. But my brain feels like it's been attached to balloons, floating off into space.

"Did you ever look her up in Boston?" I ask Will.

Will frowns, crossing his arms. "Jess, did you hear what I said? Another body's been found."

But I'm no longer listening, because standing behind Will is Isla.

She's wearing the blue-and-white dress with the Peter Pan collar she died in, her blonde hair messy and falling out of her braids, her Hello Kitty headband askew, pushed a little too far back on her head.

"Why are you here?" I whisper.

"I *told* you." Will's patience is wearing thin. "I just got an email. The details from Bailey Nelson's murder flagged a match in HTS."

I drop my hands and peer up at Will, trying to block out my dead daughter. The pressure in my ears is so intense, I feel like my head will pop off. I swallow, trying to ease it.

"HTS . . ."

Will looks flat-out annoyed now. "The Homicide Tracking System. Whoever killed Bailey Nelson has killed before. The body was found yesterday."

"Mommy . . ." Isla's voice is plaintive. "I saw her. I saw the dead lady."

I lean heavily on my cane, my mind spinning. Isla saw Bailey? What the hell is happening here? Am I losing it? I need to call my shrink or schedule that MRI or . . . something.

"Jess . . . ," Will begins.

"I heard you," I snap. "I'm not that drunk."

But I *am* that drunk, I realize. I barely touched my cheeseburger, the only thing I've eaten today. Other than that, it's just whiskey sloshing in my belly.

It isn't just that, though. I'm exhausted from too many sleepless nights, and it's messing with my mind, with my focus and my concentration. It's getting harder to control these grief hallucinations, to separate my personal life from my professional one.

Will glances over his shoulder again. "Look, I'm worried about you, old girl. Drinking like this. Talking to the damn air . . ."

"I'm not talking to air! I'm talking to Isla!"

Will freezes. "What?"

I exhale. "I know it sounds crazy, but my shrink says it's normal. They're called grief hallucinations."

"Do you really think you see her?"

The question feels like a trap, and I immediately regret telling him the truth. I've worked so hard to claw my way back here, to be lead on a case again. I'm aware of the rumors and snipes, that I'm not ready, that I'm too damaged, that I can't be impartial. I refuse to allow these grief hallucinations to get entangled with my case.

"It isn't a big deal," I say. "Come on, let's go. We gotta talk to the investigators . . ."

"You're not going anywhere except home, Jess." Will's voice is firm, adamant. The good ol' country boy is gone. "I'll contact the investigator on that case in the morning and let you know what they say."

"This is *my* case, Will!" I snap. "I know you want to look like the big man, like you're head honcho or something. But this one's mine. Don't you dare try to steal it."

Hurt rolls over Will's face. "I'm not . . ." But he doesn't finish his sentence. "Go home, Jess. You're gonna get hurt or you'll hurt someone else."

You'll hurt someone else.

I recoil, pain bursting in my heart as the words hit home. Before I can reply, Will is walking away. I watch him go, my body shaking with a sudden, white-hot fury. A minute later, his taillights disappear in the distance.

"Y'all right there, Jess?" a voice calls from behind me. I turn to see Lou heading across the parking lot toward Sammy's. "Coming in for a drink?"

I want a drink, but I know quite suddenly that I shouldn't have any more. Will is trying to take my case, and I sure as hell won't let it go without a fight. And that means being in good shape to talk to our lieutenant tomorrow.

"Just heading home. Night, Lou."

He waves and heads inside.

I walk the three blocks home, my shoes crunching on the gravel scattered over the side of the road. August is the worst time of year, so hot that it's almost melancholy, like grief rising from the soil. It coats my skin, makes me feel limp. I look around for Isla, but once again, I'm alone.

I climb the front steps of my three-bed clapboard, a house I inherited when Mac left, returning to his old job, his old life in New York. As if the life we'd had here hadn't even happened. Maybe a little part of me can't forgive him for that.

The timer kicked on long ago, releasing warm, homey light as I unlock the front door. I head into the kitchen and rummage around in the freezer. I find a solitary Lean Cuisine and throw it in the microwave, noticing, as I do, that I missed a call from my dad. He calls every Wednesday after his poker game like clockwork. I delete the message, too drunk to talk now, and take my food into the living room. I sit in Mac's old armchair, the footrest pulled out to support my leg.

I forgot how gross Lean Cuisines are, the oil already congealing over the pasta. But I need some soakage, so I force myself to eat it, thinking of what Will said.

Another body has been found, the details matching Bailey Nelson's murder, a message carved into the tongue. The carving is the key, I'm sure of it. It's some sort of message. But no matter how much time I've spent brainstorming and googling, the meaning of M1237 hasn't become clear.

I type it once again into Google, scrolling past the links I've already seen. M1237 is a type of armored vehicle, heatproof and bulletproof. It is an item number for a doorknob and a list number for an automotive paint color and the color for a natural leather pillow.

I take my Lean Cuisine container to the kitchen, rinse it, and drop it into the recycling box. As I do, I catch sight of a half-full bottle of tequila on the glass shelf above the cupboard. My mouth waters.

I don't drink tequila often. My poison of choice is whiskey or, when I'm at work, vodka. Tequila brings back memories.

Memories better left locked away in the darkest corners of my mind.

I return to the living room and open a report one of the techs sent this morning. I don't bother turning the lights on, instead working by the light of my laptop. The imprints they took of the shoe print in front of Bailey Nelson's house are for a size nine Adidas tennis shoe. Unisex. Which doesn't help me, other than to exclude Bailey herself.

"The shoes in her bedroom were size six," I say out loud. I find myself talking to myself more when I'm tired, when the edges of my consciousness become blurred with exhaustion. "Angus Nelson's were size ten."

I'm becoming more and more certain that my gut feeling is correct: Angus Nelson is innocent of his wife's murder.

It's past 2:00 a.m. by the time I shut my laptop. Fatigue and the lingering effects of the alcohol are tugging at me, working to pull me under despite my best efforts to keep my eyes open. I feel like I'm dreaming, like everything about the last few days hasn't been real.

I lean my head back in the chair and stare out the window. Moonlight shines like melted butter, landing in pools of silver across my knees. A tree stirs, sending shadows chasing each other in patterns on the floor.

I flinch, the shadows igniting images that I'm suddenly not strong enough to block. Emotions expand inside me like a balloon. I'm filled with such a heavy sense of inertia, I can't seem to get my limbs to move.

And so I don't.

I just sit there thinking about my daughter, not even bothering to push away memories of the day she died.

Chapter 29

JESS

It's funny the games of *if only* you play with yourself when a tragedy occurs. *If only* I hadn't been gone every night that week working. *If only* I hadn't gone for drinks the night before to celebrate finding a solid witness for a case. *If only* I hadn't taken Isla to lunch the next day and run into Sean, one of the other detectives who'd worked the case. *If only* I hadn't accepted that margarita he'd ordered so we could toast finding the witness.

Isla might still be alive. Mac might still be here.

I know there's no one perfect way to be a mother, but one thing you're supposed to do, the one unspoken, immutable rule is that a mother protects her child. And I didn't do that. I didn't protect Isla. I didn't protect her from me, I didn't protect her from that deer, I didn't protect her from that dark and stormy night.

I spent a week in the hospital dipping in and out of consciousness before Mac told me about Isla. I vaguely remembered someone questioning me, but Mac and my dad both put a stop to that. I was a mess. Everything from the days and weeks before and after the accident was—and still is—a blur. And then came being released, learning to walk again, weaning myself off the pain meds.

And then facing my husband after I'd killed our daughter.

I quickly turned to booze, and within six months, Mac had returned to New York. I knew that chronic destructive behavior was usually an attempt to resolve the painful experience that initiated it. My dad was an alcoholic before I was. He's the one who convinced me to go to AA, which is where I learned that I was the type of person who *liked* the pain.

Sometimes, I found, the only way to ease the pain was with a little more pain.

I suddenly want nothing more than to hear Mac's voice. I fumble in my pocket and withdraw my cell phone.

He answers on the first ring, his voice warm and soothing.

"Jess?"

Tears fill my eyes. My throat goes gummy so I can't respond. We sit for a minute just listening to each other breathe.

"You have to stop punishing yourself," Mac finally says.

Mac's a good man. I first met him when he was an idealistic young law student and married him because I knew he would never hurt me. And he never has. But I've hurt him, and that's somehow worse.

"I was drinking," I blurt.

There's a moment of silence. And then his reply: "I know."

This surprises me. Why did he never say? All this time, I've been keeping this secret, it's been eating at me, and he knew?

"I also know you had one drink. One," Mac continues. "And you couldn't have changed that deer crossing the road. You can't continue like this, Jess. This guilt . . . you've gotta find somewhere to put it. Something that matters more."

I rub my thigh where it throbs a brutal tempo and close my eyes. I'm so tired. Tired of feeling shame, tired of feeling guilt. It's an anchor around my neck, but I can't imagine setting it down.

"Please come back to me," Mac says.

"I'm trying," I whisper. And then I gently hang up the phone.

A buzzing noise begins in my head. I feel suddenly dizzy, my brain thudding, that strange pressure in my ears. And then I hear

Isla's laughter, a pulsing crescendo that comes from somewhere down the hall.

It isn't real, I tell myself, out of habit more than anything else.

I grab my cane and follow the sound. Blonde braids disappear around the kitchen corner, a gentle skid of socks against hardwood. I knuckle my leg in frustration, trying to get it to go faster.

What you're seeing isn't real.

But I can smell my daughter's strawberry shampoo. I can hear her laughter, an echo as it disappears up the stairs.

I hesitate at the bottom, looking up at the climb. I haven't been up there since Isla died. At first I was too injured to walk properly, and then after physical therapy started helping, Mac left, and I never felt strong enough to go on my own.

Cool air blows across my cheeks, and all I want to do is cry and scream, to crawl into bed and never wake up. But instead, I start the long, slow climb up the stairs. At the top, I follow the sound of Isla's laughter down the hall. My hand hovers over a doorknob. I hesitate, not sure if I want to see what's behind the door, but my hand is already pushing it open, my legs already moving.

Isla's bedroom is dark, the moonlight turning everything to shimmery shadows. A cold mist crawls over my skin, as if I've been draped in fog. It's only then I realize the window is open, the sheer curtains moving in the summer breeze. Has it been open this whole time?

Nothing in here has been disturbed. Not the books stacked in the corner, the little pile of LEGO, the doll Isla used to bring to bed with her at night. Not even the bed, the pink quilt with its tiny white flowers still rumpled, as if Isla jumped out of bed this morning.

And there, sitting on the edge of the bed, smiling and kicking her heels against the box spring, is Isla.

Isla, quietly, painfully beautiful. My sweet daughter. Forever eight years old. Her blonde braids are coming undone, long strands falling in front of her pink Hello Kitty satin bow headband. Her body, dead inside the car, still wore that headband.

I shut my eyes. My head whirls dizzily. My teeth start chattering, and my breath fogs, the pressure in my ears intensifying, like taking off in an airplane. Am I dreaming? Am I imagining this? Or hell, maybe I'm dead? But the pain in my leg is very real, like lightning, like electricity.

I've never believed in ghosts. Not once. Even when I was young, I was the kid who knew there was no way the tooth fairy could exist. I never believed in Santa Claus. Never believed in God. I always thought the task of these things was to soothe the young and *plámás* the old, to keep them hopeful, to stop their minds from caving into terror.

Science now makes it impossible for any intelligent adult to believe in these things as literally true. I put my faith in science and data. Cause and effect. Action and consequence.

I know better than most that the consequences for some things can't be undone. So I can't explain what I'm seeing right now. I don't understand why Isla is here, in her bedroom, nearly a year after she died.

Which is why I decide I have nothing to lose by trying to talk to her.

I sit on the bed next to Isla, wincing at the pinch in my leg.

"You aren't real," I say.

Isla laughs, and I close my eyes, wanting to capture that sound, to hold it in my heart forever. "That's silly, Mommy. I'm real to you. Isn't that all that matters?"

It's childish logic that somehow makes perfect sense.

"Isla . . ." I take a ragged breath. "Are you okay? Are you . . . hurting?"

Because that's it, isn't it? I'm terrified that Isla is dead but also terrified that she's stuck somewhere, in some in-between place, in pain, because of me.

Isla smiles sweetly. "I'm okay, Mommy. It can't hurt anymore."

"Because . . . you're dead?"

"Yeah. But it doesn't hurt."

I blink at Isla. This is crazy. I must be going crazy. "Are you . . . always here?"

"Sometimes. It's kinda weird. Like a dream, I guess."

"Are you alone?" It breaks my heart to think of my baby all alone wherever she is.

"No, there's lots of us. Sometimes I talk to them, except . . ." Isla's brow puckers. "Except sometimes they don't see me. Sometimes they're stuck."

"Stuck?"

"Yeah, like stuck in between. They're alive but mostly dead. They can't see us because they don't know we're there. And sometimes they don't know they're dead or about to be dead. But we see them. That pretty lady, the one who was killed. She doesn't know."

"Bailey Nelson," I murmur. "Who killed her?"

Isla pins me with her blue gaze. "She doesn't know. You should tell her, Mommy."

"Tell her what?"

"That she's dead. She's so sad, but she won't listen to me. She's still there, in that house. I see her sometimes. I want to help her, but she won't talk to me . . ." Isla's voice cracks, and the tears on her lashes spill over.

"I'm sorry, baby. I'm sorry."

I'm sorry for so many things. For drinking that margarita. For hitting that deer. For driving Isla home instead of having Mac come pick her up. For not cherishing every single second I had with her. But mostly I'm sorry that I couldn't take her place.

The pressure that's been building in my chest detonates then, and my tears overflow. My guilt isn't just a feeling but a living, breathing thing suffocating me, wrapping tentacles around my neck and squeezing.

"I'm sorry, baby," I sob. "I'm so, so sorry. I wish it had been me. I would gladly have died instead of you."

"I know, Mommy. It's okay."

I feel a hand, small and cool, slip into mine. I look down at Isla's fingers laced through mine. And suddenly I feel very, very sober.

Because this is no grief hallucination. Hallucinations aren't real. You can't touch them. You can't feel the smoothness of their skin. They aren't firm and heavy. And yet Isla's hand is reassuringly solid in mine.

I can't explain it, but right now, I don't care. Maybe some things just have no explanation. They just are. Like why we yawn, or why there are so many more right-handed people than left-handed ones, or why the placebo effect, something that is basically just a whole lot of bullshit, is so powerful.

I pull my daughter into my arms, and together we lie down on Isla's bed. I drag the quilt up to Isla's chest, tucking it under her arms, the way I did when she was alive.

"I love you, Isla," I murmur into my daughter's baby-soft hair. "I'll always love you."

"I love you, too, Mommy."

And for the first time in a long time, I fall into a deep, dreamless sleep.

Chapter 30

Awareness came in peculiar chunks.

A rustle of leaves.

The warm caress of a summer breeze.

A bird chirping somewhere far away.

My eyes fluttered open, but all I could see was blackness. My head was clogged with confusion. Shadows stirred. Trees rustled and swayed above me, gnarled limbs shifting in the shadows. How did I get here?

The memory was distant, heavy, sinking rather than floating. I couldn't quite reach it.

A skeletal arm reached toward me and something else, twin red beads of light flashing in the dark.

My heart surged into my throat, so fast that I thought I would vomit. Sweat prickled under my arms. I tried to move, but I was trapped, tangled in something, my whole body swaying.

I was in a hammock. Outside on my porch.

I wrenched myself free, a scream tumbling from my throat. A scuttle of claws. A flash of red fur. The eyes disappeared.

I stood in the dark, sweating, waiting for my brain to defog and my heart to stop pounding so hard.

It was a fox, that was all, out for a nighttime stroll.

I felt sick, feverish, my face damp with perspiration. I staggered upstairs to my bedroom and fumbled with the antibiotics I'd swiped from work earlier. The wound in my belly had started seeping yesterday, and today it was a nasty shade of red. I'd torn the stitches at the lake the other day, and infection had set in.

On the dresser, Tweety hopped about the cat carrier, chirping anxiously. I ignored him and went into the bathroom, swallowing the antibiotics with water straight from the tap; then I splashed cool water over my face. I made my way downstairs on wobbly legs, grasping the wooden banister with hands like claws.

In the kitchen, I made myself a cup of chamomile tea. I could hear movement in the front room but didn't feel well enough to check on her. I splashed orange juice in my tea, then took it up to my room.

Tweety was still upset, his good wing beating against the metal bars of the cat carrier. Outside my bedroom window, leaves rustled in the trees.

The room suddenly seemed strangely cool for a summer's night, a chill wind prickling the bare skin on my arms. A moment ago, I was so warm, and yet now goose bumps stippled the exposed skin at the back of my neck. As if someone was watching me. As if someone was here.

I peered out the window into the dark, my eyes raking across the backyard. I thought I heard an engine rev, but when I leaned out, nothing was there. Just a row of run-down houses with rotting porches, slabs of plywood over windows.

I slammed the window shut.

Across the room, Tweety squawked frantically.

"What's wrong, baby?" I pushed my glossy-leafed plant out of the way and gently extracted him from the cat carrier. His wing was fine, the splint still holding strong. In fact, he calmed as soon as he was in my hand.

"Did you just want a cuddle?" I crooned.

He tilted his head at me, left, then right. After a minute, Tweety had calmed completely. I set him on the bed and went to find a seed cookie in my top dresser drawer.

As I did, my gaze landed on something half-hidden amid the Hanes cotton underwear folded neatly there.

I moved the underwear to the side, exposing the dildo beneath. I held it gingerly in my hand and sat carefully on the bed.

I stared at the dildo. I wasn't sure why I'd kept it.

A memento, maybe. A token. I didn't know.

Maybe I just wanted to remind myself there was more than one way to fuck someone.

Chapter 31

NEVE

Work passes in a blur. I am exhausted and distracted after Ash woke me at 4:00 a.m., screaming for her dad. It's a job just to focus on my patients: a Maine coon called Princess MeowMeow who'd cracked a few ribs when she'd met the bad end of a car; Polly, a pygmy goat who'd broken a leg jumping off a counter; Guppy the chinchilla who is inexplicably unable to keep food down. I sign worming prescriptions and do teeth cleanings, hand out heartworm and flea medicine, take X-rays for an iguana, and look inside the beak of a screaming macaw.

And then there are the farm visits in the unrelenting sun. It's well over one hundred degrees today, and with no breeze, it's just a cruel, oppressive blanket of heat. The landscape is parched, the dirt dry and cracked, the grass brown, long dead.

When I finally get back to Dullahan House, it's late afternoon. My shirt is damp, sweaty patches seeping through. I head straight for the kitchen for a long drink, then take a glass of water and tip it onto Priss's soil, which seems to be bone dry no matter how often I water it.

I stare at Priss mournfully. She's dying, I realize. Her pink pinstripes have faded to white. Chunks of crunchy brown spots freckle her leaves, the edges curling defensively. I feel a horrible panic that I'm killing the last connection to my old life.

I use my phone to google *how to help a pinstripe calathea*. It tells me to avoid direct sunlight. To mist her leaves. It says I may be watering her too much or I'm not watering her enough.

I'm pulling Priss to a shadowy corner in the living room when I hear a knocking sound coming from the kitchen. It comes again, more like someone clomping up the stairs than knuckles on wood. I follow the sound to the basement door.

My mouth dries. My hand moves toward the doorknob. I am sweating, I realize, beads of moisture dripping down my temples. I don't want to go down to the basement, but I can't seem to stop myself: I twist the knob. Slowly. Slowly. Until I can't twist it anymore.

The door is locked.

"Ash?"

She doesn't answer. I call up the stairs. "Ash, are you up there?"

Radio silence.

I climb the stairs to the turret room and knock on the door. There's no answer, so I push it open, but Ash isn't inside. Her room is a riot of jumbled clothes tossed onto the floor. The bed is rumpled and messy, a single sock lying on the pillow. Are all teenagers this slovenly?

I glance at my watch. It's just after 3:00 p.m. I figure she's out for a walk or took a kayak out onto the lake again. I should be grateful she's getting out more, but the first niggling of worry worms at me.

I swoop up clothes and separate them into dirty and clean piles until a thought occurs to me. The washing machine and dryer are in the basement, which I can't go into. The door's still locked.

Even if I could find the key, I wouldn't go down there.

I stuff the dirty clothes in Ash's closet. I will have to find a Laundromat in town.

I know I need to see Sandra. I have so many questions. But I'm so tired, I can barely keep my eyes open. Fatigue runs over me uncontested, eyes burning, ears filled with a distant ring. Clouds fill my head, a strange electric feeling hitting me. Like an impending migraine or an extreme case of vertigo.

I'll just have a nap first. I'll feel better after that.

I go downstairs and lie on the couch, sinking into a sleep so deep, it's like I've been pulled under the waves of the ocean.

I'm not sure how long I sleep, but I come to when I hear a car engine revving.

I'm outside, but I'm confused and disoriented. I can't figure out how I got here; I was just on my living room couch. My stomach hurts, a fierce ache low in my belly, and my head is swimming with a thick exhaustion dragging on my limbs. I sit up, blinking, and look around, trying to get my bearings.

It's dark. I'm on the sidewalk of a run-down neighborhood. A black car is speeding away from me, its brake lights flashing once as it slows and turns a corner.

I stagger to my feet. My heart races, my fingers tingling with adrenaline. Black specks dance at the edges of my vision. I wipe a bead of sweat from my forehead. Even now that the sun has gone down, it is hot. Everything feels sticky and damp. My lips taste salty from the festering heat.

I look around, feeling vague and blurry, the way I used to when I was a kid and would sleepwalk, when I couldn't remember anything, just stray images roaming the cavern of my mind. Fear trickles down my spine, along with something richer, the full, stinging sensation of embarrassment.

In the yellow light of a streetlamp, I see a sign that says BLEEKER STREET in faded black print. Up and down the road is a series of ramshackle houses. Windows punched through and replaced with boards. Sagging porches. Doors with slabs of plywood nailed over the openings. I turn in a circle, spotting one that looks familiar.

I feel shock freeze my body.

Chipped and faded mustard-yellow paint. Once-white shutters now black with mildew. A deep crack creeps up to broken gutters hanging loose against peeling siding. Puckered brown drapes block the windows. There is a weathered flag, slack and listless, hanging above the front porch. A cracked and crumbling path cuts through a tiny front yard with grass so overgrown and sun-dried, it looks like wheat. Above the door are numbers: 6284. The 2 has come undone and lists to the right, leaning on the 8.

6284 Bleeker Street. Somehow, without even realizing it, I've come to Sandra's house.

I bite my lip, realizing what must have happened. I got an Uber. I fell asleep, or maybe blacked out, and am only now properly coming to. Blacking out is a common symptom of PTSD. It seems to be happening more and more. Every time I sleep, it's more like a sudden cessation of existence, a descent into blackness.

I rub my eyes, finally admitting something I haven't thus far been able to: I can't continue like this. I need to find a counselor who specializes in PTSD. Someone we can talk to about the home invasion, the trauma we experienced.

I stare at Sandra's house. In all these years, I've never once visited. I followed her on Facebook, watched from afar, despite the horrible things we'd done to her. I mailed her that photograph of the three of us with a little note, but I never went to see her. I should've; I know that.

I didn't talk to Bailey for a week after the dildo prank. I was mortified but also terrified Sandra would find out I'd been involved, however mistakenly. I stayed in my room and refused to come downstairs when Bailey popped over.

My mom must've known something was wrong because she kept trying to take me shopping and out to lunch. Finally, she offered to let me have a few people over for a bonfire on Friday night, our last night in Black Lake before my dad came to take us home.

I cheered up a bit at that. Maybe I could fix this. Bailey and Sandra didn't have to hate each other forever. We'd been friends for too long to let a stupid boy get in the way.

The thing is, when you're a teenager, you think your friendships will last forever. Best Friends Forever. That's what friendship bracelets and necklaces are all about. You think boys and jobs and life won't get in the way. It's only later you realize the truth: friendship doesn't last forever, but betrayal does, and it will break you like a promise.

I thought I could fix it, so I borrowed my mom's car and drove across town to Sandra's house, where she lived then. I rang the doorbell and gave her mom my biggest, most charming smile.

"Hi, Mrs. Baker. Is Sandra home?"

Sandra's little sister, Robin, came up beside her, slipping an arm around her waist. She had her mother's eyes, a shade of very pale gray, like ice reflecting a stormy sky. Sandra's mom crossed her arms, scowling at me. Had Sandra told her?

Just then, Sandra came downstairs, her fingers twined through Zac's.

He jerked his chin and called, "Yo!" in greeting, while Sandra threw her arms around me in that sweet, exuberant way she had. "Neve!"

She was wearing a pink T-shirt and cut-off shorts, her red-and-white bathing suit strings poking out under her tank top. She smelled like Clinique Happy and nostalgia, hugging me with such unabashed delight that I decided she must not have connected Bee's gift to me.

She told me they were on their way to the beach and asked if I wanted to come. I agreed, waiting in the living room with Zac while she grabbed her beach towel and Hawaiian Tropic suntan oil. I ignored Zac and looked around. I'd never spent much time at Sandra's house; we always hung out at mine or Bee's because our houses were bigger and right on the lake.

I guess her dad didn't make a lot of money as a preacher. Everything looked a little shabby; she shared a room with her little sister; she never had designer clothes; they never went on vacation. When you're a kid, nice things don't matter much. When you're a teenager, they matter too much.

Sandra's house was small and cramped, the interior stuffed with dark wood and oversize, secondhand furniture. One wall had a row of shelves stuffed haphazardly with religious books, cheap knickknacks, chipped vases. Another had glass-encased shelves of what looked like antique guns, the metal dull and brassy.

Zac saw me looking. "They're the shit, right? They're antique revolvers. Sandra said her great-great-grandpa fought in, like, Germany or something in the First World War. He started the collection." He pointed at a silver, needle-nosed gun with a black handle. "That was his."

He was standing too close to me, his breath hot on my neck. I moved away, feeling weird, a little out of my comfort zone without Sandra there to act as a buffer.

"So. You and Sandra," I said.

A smirk curled one corner of his mouth. "Yup."

I shook my head in disgust. "Let me guess. You have a bet with Charlie you can get the town virgin."

"Of course not!" He glanced over his shoulder and lowered his voice. "It's not like you're some paradigm of virtue, hanging out with Bee."

"What's that supposed to mean?"

"Haven't you noticed? Everybody stays away from Bee these days. Even Sandra, and you know how nice she is. Didn't you wonder why Sandra cut her hair? She didn't. Bee took a pair of scissors to Sandra's ponytail at the end of English lit."

My mouth dropped open.

"Bee's like a firework waiting to explode," he continued. "You know there were rumors around school that she was banging our history teacher? They don't call her Easy Naldoni for nothing."

"I don't believe you," I said automatically. I knew something had changed in Bee, but no way did I believe any of what he was telling me.

"Like you'd know," he scoffed. "You're just a summer girl. You don't have a clue what any of us are like the rest of the year. That girl is rotten.

You know someone found a video of her banging Sleazy McShitface earlier this year? He got fired, and she got suspended. Wanna guess who found the video?"

I stared at him.

"His own daughter."

"Who's Sleazy McShitface?"

"Our history teacher. Mark Saunders."

I was too stunned to reply, but Sandra saved me by poking her head in. She was holding up three Mountain Dews. "My mom said I can take these!"

Sandra was grinning like she'd just won the lottery, and it *was* a big win. Her parents rarely allowed her sugar or caffeine; she wasn't allowed to watch TV; and alcohol was considered evil.

"Can I come with you to the beach, Sandra?" Robin pleaded.

Sandra ruffled her sister's hair with a smile. "Not today, Peep. Next time, 'kay?"

Sandra turned to Zac, who pulled her close and kissed her ear. She blushed, glancing over her shoulder to make sure her mom hadn't seen.

I suddenly didn't feel much like being around them. "Actually, I better get my mom's car back. I just came over to invite you to my house Friday night. I'm having a bonfire before I leave Saturday."

"We'd love to come!" Sandra glanced up at Zac for confirmation.

He shrugged. "Sure, why not?"

I didn't exactly want him there, but I figured if it got Sandra there, I could deal. We agreed on a time, and I left, waving as I headed to my car. But as I backed out of their driveway, something caught in my peripheral vision. A curtain had twitched in an upstairs window.

And then a face came into view. It was Sandra's mother, her eyes narrow, her lips pressed flat as she watched me drive away.

Chapter 32

NEVE

I shake the memories away and cross the road to Sandra's house. Sandra's mom stayed in contact with people my mom knew in Black Lake, so I knew when her dad died and when they left town and moved in with their grandfather.

That's how I found out about Zac, too. Karma came after him quicker than it did Bailey or me. But trying to undo the past is like trying to unscramble an egg. All you can do is move on, so that's what I did.

The porch light flickers on, and someone comes out. In the dim light, I can just make out a woman I don't recognize dressed in a nurse's uniform. She's carrying a bag of what might be garbage and disappears around the side of the house. I wait on the sidewalk, giving her a minute to dump the trash. When she doesn't return, I climb the porch steps.

After a minute, I hear two female voices, and when I peer around the edge of the house, I see the silhouette of the woman chatting over the fence with the neighbor.

The woman has left the front door open a few inches; she clearly doesn't expect to be gone long, so I climb the front steps and knock on the door.

"Hello?" I call. "Sandra?"

No one answers.

I peek my head inside and stare into the gloom. Directly in front of me is a long staircase with old-fashioned, peeling floral wallpaper, and beyond that is a hallway with the same hideous wallpaper leading to what looks to be a kitchen. The flooring is a dark hardwood, scuffed and worn. Low-lit sconces throw out pale, anemic light.

Despite the ancient look of the place, it is immaculately clean. Not a hint of dust, just the antiseptic smell of bleach and floor polish.

I push the door open with the toe of my shoe. The hinges make a squealing sound that sends a shiver down my spine. I step inside, calling out again: "Sandra?"

Still no answer.

I move down the hallway to the kitchen. Everything is neat and organized. I pull open a cupboard and see canned food, labeled, everything in straight rows. The crockery is straight out of the seventies, brown and olive green but clean, ordered.

I peek out the back window. The lawn is unkempt, weeds stabbing up from the ground like skyscrapers. A hammock sways gently over a bent and bowing porch.

I step back into the hallway. To my right, there is a door that's open a few inches; I can see the corner of a bed from where I stand.

I'm not a person who scares very easily, but this place gives me the creeps. Every hair on my body is standing on end as I gently, so gently, push the door open and step inside.

The room is spacious, dimly lit, with a thick, shaggy maroon rug covering most of the floor. There is a fireplace with an ornate wooden mantel on the far wall. A ceiling fan wobbles from a cracked coffered ceiling. The blades scoop up hot air, moving the scent of warm urine and cleaning products and illness around the room. A brown couch has been pushed against the far wall under the wide bay window, half disappearing under the dusty brown drapes. Next to it is a wheelchair.

On the far side of the room is a hospital bed, and on it lies a woman in a thin white nightgown. She is hairless, shriveled, her skin hanging loose on a brittle skeleton. She's in the final stages of what looks to be a terrible illness, her body attached to a variety of tubes that snake in and out of her.

"Sandra?" I step closer to the bed.

Her eyes snap open. I barely recognize the girl in this woman, and yet it's her. Her complexion is gray, her skin impossibly thin, translucent. The sweet pastor's daughter with the large forehead and the adorable lisp is gone. What remains is a ghost of the girl I remember.

A pale blue blanket is folded over her waist, her arms crossed over her chest, like she's already dead. Except she isn't. She's close, but not yet. She stares at me blankly for a moment, her eyes watery, the whites a sickly yellow. Recognition dawns slowly.

"Neve?" The word comes out as a wheeze. "Am I dead?"

"I don't think so."

"I can't believe . . . you're here." She sucks in a breath, struggling, and gives a soft little laugh. "I only have to go and die, right?"

"At least you haven't lost your sense of humor." I pull up a brown plastic chair and sit down. "My mom told me where you live." I don't add that this was years ago. That I should've come long before now.

"It's cancer. Nothing to do with that." She nods toward the wheelchair. "If you were wondering." She reaches for another breath, her chest rattling. "Thought I could fight it . . ."

I work my throat, trying to hold back tears.

"Where'd you hear it?"

"What do you mean?"

"Where'd you hear I was dying? Was it Facebook?"

"Uh, no. Not exactly. It's kind of a long story."

"Well, hurry up. I don't have much time." She tries for a smile, but it looks more like a grimace.

When I speak, I realize it isn't such a long story after all. "I wanted to come see you, to tell you . . ." I swallow. "Bee's dead. Someone killed her."

Sandra's eyes close. She's silent for so long, I think she's gone back to sleep. Or died. I lean over to check, but her chest is still moving.

"Sandra?" I put a hand on her arm.

"I'm still here." She shivers as her eyes flutter open. "The fan . . . ?"

I find a remote control on the mantel and press a button. The fan whirs to a stop with a groan.

"Bee . . ." She inhales, a ragged, uneven sound. "What . . . happened?"

I measure my response carefully. Because what I haven't told the detective is I may have been one of the last people to see Bee alive.

I think of driving to Black Lake the day before the home invasion. I parked in front of Bee's office and waited for her to leave. And then I followed.

She went to the post office, the grocery store, then the dry cleaner's. It was so mundane, so stupid.

I don't know what I thought I was going to do. Confront her. Hurt her. Or . . . worse. I was furious; I know that. I thought she'd left those photos on Eli's car. I blamed her for the destruction of my marriage. But when she came out of the dry cleaner's, her hands laden with plastic-wrapped clothes, I remembered what she'd told me about the photos: "That wasn't me . . . Someone is messing with us."

It was possible she'd lied, but why? It just wasn't her style. Bee liked people knowing she had power over them. She lived by a scorched-earth policy: destroy everything as a necessary cost of getting what she wanted, whatever that may be. No apologies, no explanations. If she'd left those pictures on Eli's car, she would've happily admitted it.

"They found her in the lake," I tell Sandra. "She'd been there a few days."

I don't tell her about the message that was carved onto Bee's tongue. There's no sense in scaring her. Not when she's so close to dying anyway. "I thought maybe it was her husband. It's always the husband, you know? This guy, he's not what you'd expect. Short, balding. He's a little flashy, though, which Bailey would've liked. But the detective says he has an alibi. Oh, and then there's the neighbor. I saw her break into Bailey's house right after they found her body. I don't know . . ."

I let my sentence trail off. I don't actually know who else it could've been, and it reminds me how vulnerable Ash and I are. How scary it is living right where a murder has occurred.

"It's crazy . . . I always . . . thought she'd die dramatically," Sandra says with a breathy chuckle. "A plane crash or a boat explosion or maybe a . . . violent home invasion. Something as big and memorable as she was. Not like me. Boring old cancer. How pedestrian, right?"

I startle at her words. *Home invasion.* They feel cold and slippery, like bubbles popping on my skin.

Does Sandra know what happened to me? I scan her face, but when I look at her, I see nothing that would make me think she knows. Only sickness and disease, a future that could be counted in days, perhaps hours.

Of course, that means nothing. I know better than most how well you can hide yourself, the deep corners where you can shove the true versions, like cotton stuffing in a teddy bear. Maybe Sandra *did* know. What if she not only knew but was responsible for it? She could've hired someone. Some sort of hit man. One last deed to tie up, a final bit of revenge before she died.

I shove the thought away, because it's highly unlikely and because that isn't why I'm here. I owe Sandra the truth now. There is no place for lies here in this narrow space between life and death.

"Sandra, that night . . ."

"Stop." Sandra closes her eyes, catching her breath. Her chest rises and falls, uneven, ragged. "I don't blame you . . . I never blamed you . . . for not looking back."

"Is that what you think? I *did* look back. I still do. I just . . ." I shake my head, tears tightening my throat. "I just couldn't go back."

"It's . . . okay . . ."

I hear the front door open, and the nurse who'd exited with the garbage earlier returns. I stand, embarrassed that I didn't wait for her to let me in.

But the woman doesn't come into the living room. Instead she passes straight down the hallway, heading into the kitchen. I hear pots rattle and the slam of a cupboard, then a grating sound as something settles on the stove.

When my gaze returns to Sandra, she has fallen asleep. Her mouth hangs open a little, and I can tell she doesn't have long. I pull the blanket to her chest, tuck it under her arms, the way I did for Ash when she was little, and take her hand in mine.

"I'm sorry, Sandra," I say softly.

I wait another minute, just listening to the jagged, moist rattle of her breathing. But she doesn't wake again.

So I quietly slip out the front door.

I know now I won't find what I'm looking for here. Because it's perfectly clear: there's no killer in this house.

But I can't help feeling more unsettled by this than reassured.

Chapter 33
JESS

I wake in Isla's bed early. Birdsong and pale morning sunlight in shades of blushed pink and creamy cornsilk stream through the open window.

I know before I roll over that Isla isn't there. Next to me, the bed is empty. Last night already feels like a long-forgotten dream, golden and a little hazy.

I swing my legs over the edge of the bed, wincing as pain zips down my leg. My first thought is for a drink, but I push the craving away.

"Not today." I'm going to do better. Be better.

I shower and dress in a tank top and loose yoga pants, slide my feet into flip-flops, then grab my cane and make my way into the kitchen. I brew a strong cup of black coffee. The rich, dark smell fills the kitchen, an anchor to the rhythm and routine of my life.

I stick two slices of bread into the toaster and when it pops up, I slather on peanut butter, then take the coffee and toast to the dining room table. I pull open the blinds, letting in the brilliant morning light. I catch sight of my reflection in the window. For the first time in a long time, I look rested, not tired, not crumpled, not hungover. Despite the pain in my leg, I feel . . . okay.

The sun blooms in the distance, a hot, brilliant flower growing, painting the blue with streaks of yellow. Buttery strips of light fall across the table, where I've left my laptop, various pieces of paper, files, documents.

I stand over the table and scan through what I have, nibbling at a hangnail. We didn't get much from the search at Bailey Nelson's house. A ton of medication in the bathroom, uppers, downers, sleeping pills, but not the chlorpromazine found in her system. Nor did we find anything else that would give us a clue as to why she was murdered.

Which reminds me, I want to find out more about chlorpromazine. I google it, scrolling through various medical sites. Like Dr. Arquette said, it's used as a sedative for behavioral problems and is used to treat psychotic disorders that cause difficulty telling the difference between things that are and aren't real. It's also used in veterinary practices to immobilize aggressive animals.

I ease myself into a chair, pull my notebook toward me, and make a note to ask Lou about it. I then begin listing the other things I want to follow up on today. At the top I write: *Vivienne Jones.*

What Neve told me about Vivienne last night is interesting because nobody breaks into someone's house just moments after their body is found to water their plants. It's suspicious as hell. She must've been desperate. What was in that folder she took from the house? And what was in the white paper bag? Was it the chlorpromazine we've been looking for or just medication for the dog after he ingested algae?

Next on the list, I write: *Neve Maguire.*

She lied about knowing Bailey Nelson, and she lied about that picture. Since it turns out Bailey and she did know each other when they were young, there could be something more there. An old resentment, a grudge, a crime.

Neve said she'd only gotten into town the night before we found Bailey's body, but we have no proof of that. Maybe she came into town earlier. Black Lake isn't big. There's only one main road heading into town, and there's a surveillance camera positioned on the first stoplight. I'll get access to that and have the guys look through the footage, try to see if she arrived when she said she did.

I need to find out exactly where Neve Maguire was the night of Bailey Nelson's murder. Does she have an alibi? I wasn't able to find her in the DMV license records under Maguire, so I would stop by later and ask what her married name was. I need to find out who exactly this woman is, what really brought her to Black Lake, where she came from, and when she really got here.

Finally, at the bottom of my list, I write: *Zac Hendrix*.

Neve said Zac is the one who took the photo, so I'll do a bit of digging on him.

This is the easiest lead to follow right now, so I flip my laptop open. As it boots up, I pull out the 3x5 photo and study it. The three girls standing in front of a bonfire, the lake stretching midnight blue behind them, their arms wrapped around each other, grins plastered on their faces. Bailey is easily identifiable, with her short shorts and her low-cut tank top and her sultry, come-hither eyes, and now I'm pretty sure the girl with her face scratched out is Neve. But who is the blonde girl?

"Maybe Zac Hendrix knows who she is," I say out loud.

I sign in to the department's LexisNexis account and type in *Zac Hendrix*. There are billions of results, so I add *Black Lake* to my search. Still billions of results. I try a number of word combinations, adding in Bailey Nelson, then Bailey Naldoni, then Neve Maguire, then a number of years spanning the nineties. Then I remember Neve said Zac was the son of a politician, so I type that in.

And boom. It's really just that easy.

Zac Hendrix, the son of elected county executive Franklin Hendrix, died around twenty years ago in a drunk-driving accident while a sophomore at Harvard. I blink in dismay at the news.

I scan the article and learn Zac had been cited for underage drinking a number of times in the years before he died. The night of the crash, he was found to have a blood-alcohol level of .10, which isn't that high for someone who drinks a lot, as the article implies he did.

A witness driving behind Zac said there'd been no indication he was drunk when the car he was driving suddenly veered off the road. He plowed into a tree and died two days later. Investigators theorized he'd fallen asleep at the wheel, but that had never been confirmed, and the manner of death on his death certificate had been listed as accidental.

I slump back in my chair, massaging my leg thoughtfully. The car accident isn't listed as suspicious, but I can't help wondering. Especially now that Bailey Nelson is dead, too.

At the bottom of the article is a suggested link, which leads to an opinion piece by a local journalist about whether there is such a thing as safe drinking in teenagers and the problems drunk driving had caused in the local community.

> . . . Hendrix isn't the first local teen to have problems with drunk driving. Two years ago, Zac Hendrix's girlfriend at the time, Sandra Baker, another Black Lake girl, was also involved in a serious car accident after a night spent drinking at a friend's house. That accident led local council members to erect the barrier that now exists at Widow's Bend . . .

I glance at the accompanying photo of a teenage girl, maybe seventeen, with a narrow face and yellow-blonde hair cut into a short, page-boy style. My stomach clenches.

"Holy shit," I whisper.

It's the girl from the photo. Sandra Baker is the blonde girl we weren't able to get a hit on with the department's facial-recognition software. I sit back in my chair, stunned.

I think of what Neve told me, that Zac Hendrix was Bailey's boyfriend. And yet here it says he was Sandra's. An intentional lie? Or did he date both girls?

I open Facebook and type in *Sandra Baker*, but there are too many results to look through. A quick Google search, however, shows she works as a paralegal for a law firm in Boston. I glance at the time on my laptop. It's too early to call, but I jot down the number to call later.

I realize I've forgotten completely about my toast. It's now cold, the peanut butter congealed on top. I shove a massive bite in my mouth and wash it down with a glug of cold coffee as I open my work email.

There haven't been any breakthroughs from either DNA or fingerprint analysis—whoever did this was clever—but one email makes my breath catch with hope. The warrant for Bailey Nelson's personal cell phone records has come through. The network hadn't been able to locate the phone, so they'd instead sent her call log and text messages. We're still waiting for records from Bailey's work phone, but this is a good start.

I print out the pages and start going through every call and text from the last month, line by line. As the minutes tick by and my coffee empties, I get a feel for who the numbers belong to: Bailey's mother and father; her husband, Angus; a few to her neighbor Vivienne; local friends; the gym where she worked out. Two calls to the veterinary clinic and . . .

"Hmm . . . what's this?" I cross-check the number with one I also have on my cell phone. "She called Lou Carter?"

Why had Bailey called the vet? Conceivably, she could've called about the dog when he got sick, but why would Lou lie about it? He'd been adamant he didn't know her. Was it just an honest mistake? I make a note next to Lou's name to ask him about it.

I inch down the list of phone calls and texts. By the end, I have only one number I can't place. It's an incoming number listed as unidentified.

I pick up my phone and dial.

Chapter 34

JESS

"Will!" I hobble past reception and into the bullpen, making a beeline for Will's desk.

I want to talk to him about the unidentified number I'd called. The receptionist who'd answered had told me I'd reached a nursing home in Burlington. Something niggled at the corners of my mind, but it remained unclear, blurry, like looking through glasses smudged with oily fingerprints.

I couldn't figure it out.

Will is on the far side of the room, presiding over two other detectives and one uniform who sit on the desks listening to him. I catch only a few words before I stop.

". . . through the woods to find the body. Formal identification . . ."

What the hell is he doing?

Will catches sight of me and stops speaking. His eyes are flat and wary. He looks like he wants to say something, but before he speaks, Lieutenant Luis Rivero pokes his head out of his office.

"Jess. My office."

"Yes, sir."

I drop my backpack on my desk.

"Don't go anywhere," I call over my shoulder to Will. "I have updates."

I walk into Rivero's office, catching the looks on some of the guys' faces. A few smirks. Some pity. A lot of *sooner you than mes*.

Whatever. I'm a female detective. A *disabled* female detective. I got used to those looks a long time ago. I'm damn good at my job and refuse to let them change who or what I am.

Rivero is standing behind his desk when I enter, his back to me, his hands in his pockets.

"Shut the door."

I comply and sit in the plastic chair in front of his desk, dropping my cane to the floor next to me. He rolls back a little, then forward, balancing on the balls of his feet. That's how I know he's thinking hard about something. It's his tell.

I wait. Scratch my elbow. Massage my thigh. Finally, he sits in his leather chair, steeples his fingers on the desk, and speaks. "The Nelson case: I want you to sit this one out, Jess."

I feel like I've been punched. "Wait. What? You're putting me in the cellblock?"

"Cellblock" is what we call desk duty because being pulled off the streets, stripped of a gun and badge, and kept inside four walls is an awful lot like prison to a detective.

"Not officially, no. This is just temporary modified duty. For now. I moved you to lead too fast, and I apologize."

"No, you didn't. I'm perfectly capable—"

"I'm putting Will on lead."

I stiffen, my teeth grinding together so hard, I hear my molars creak.

"No . . . I . . ."

"Jess. We all know what you've been through. And I've been lenient on what you do outside work hours, but your drinking, it's affecting your work. I need to see you're okay to be back on active duty."

"I'm already in therapy, sir."

"Then check in to AA. For now, I'm sending Will to liaise with the detective on that other body with the matching MO. He'll brief you when he's back."

"This is bullshit!" I leap to my feet. At least I *try* to leap to my feet. But my bad leg won't cooperate and drags the left side of my body down. Without my cane, I'm too unbalanced to right myself. I pitch to the side, only saving myself from crashing face-first to the ground by grabbing a corner of Rivero's desk.

Rivero jumps up to help, but I put up a hand, humiliated.

"I don't need your help!" I say through gritted teeth.

I lean heavily on my right foot, pain stabbing up my left leg. Mortified and furious, I pull myself upright, my cheeks flaming red-hot.

Fucking Will. He's gone and stolen my case from me.

"This is . . ." I trail off. *This is all I have,* I want to say. "This is *my* case. You can't do this!"

Rivero's face darkens. "Tell me again what I can and can't do, Detective."

We glare at each other for a minute, eyes blazing, breath coming rapidly.

Finally, Rivero backs down, visibly working to calm the situation. "Look, like I said, it's just temporary. Get your shit together and . . ." He holds his palms up, like it's all in my hands. Like I can just stop seeing Isla. Can just get over her death. "Otherwise it'll have to turn into something more permanent."

I know I've lost the battle, so I don't say a thing. I carefully scoop my cane up off the floor, aware my leg could give out at any moment, and slowly limp out of the room.

Will is still standing at my desk, his round face pink, shiny with sweat. "Jess, I'm so—"

"Fuck you," I spit.

I was about to tell him about Sandra Baker, but no way am I sharing that information now. Thieving motherfucker. I'm so angry, I could scream.

Will flushes an even deeper shade of pink, his barrel chest puffing up with embarrassment. I don't care that everyone is staring at me. I don't care what they think.

"I'm going out for a coffee."

The hot sun washes over my body as I limp toward the town square where Java Jane is located. By the time I arrive, I'm sweating, my shirt clinging to my damp skin. I massage my aching thigh, pain pulsing up my leg into my back muscles. Not only am I disabled by my fucking leg, I'm disabled by the fact that I've been sidelined on my own case. By my own partner.

Java Jane is busy, the air thick with the scent of roasting beans. The line of people waiting for their morning joe snakes out the door, irritated customers angrily tapping their toes.

When I finally reach the cash register, I order a black coffee and take it to a nearby bench. I pop the lid off, tip half onto the sunbaked brick, then pour in a healthy splash of vodka from the flask I keep in my backpack.

"Heya, Detective."

I jump, vodka sloshing onto my pants. "Oh, hey, Lou."

The old vet looks a little worse for wear. His white hair is stuck to his forehead with a sheen of moisture. Deep pouches stand prominently beneath watery brown eyes.

"Mind making mine Irish, too?" Lou asks, holding out his own coffee cup.

"Uh . . . sure. Sit down."

I pour vodka into his cup, and he takes a long sip, his eyes closed. When he finishes, he leans his back against the bench and stares up at the hot blue sky.

Still not looking at me, he says, "You all right?"

"Could be better. But could be worse, you know? You?"

"Well, this heat wave can just about fuck off."

"Too right. Did you see how low the lake's water is getting?"

"Yup. Worst I've seen in a long time. Some of the ranchers are already selling off livestock due to lack of feed for the winter."

He scrapes a hand down his grizzled cheek, which looks like it hasn't seen a razor in a few days. The cuff of his long-sleeve linen shirt lifts as he touches his jaw, and I catch sight of what looks like a long, crusted claw mark along the inside of his wrist.

I point at the scratches. "One of the cats at the clinic get you?"

Lou tugs the cuff down. "We got this Maine coon with busted ribs. Can't reason with a cat in pain."

"Or a person in pain," I crack.

He laughs, his teeth flashing white against his mahogany skin. "Ain't that the truth."

"Hey, quick question. Do you ever use a drug called chlorpromazine as a vet?"

"Sure. We use it all the time, sometimes as a sedative and sometimes as an antiemetic. Why?"

"Just something I'm working on for a case. You know, the Bailey Nelson one."

"How's it going?"

"Eh." I shrug noncommittally. "You said you didn't know her, right?"

"That's right."

I pause, waiting to see if he'll change his answer. But he doesn't. "I saw your number on her call log, Lou. She called you. Any idea why?"

A drop of sweat slides down his cheek. I watch as it hovers on his chin before dropping onto his sleeve, leaving a dark splotch on the cuff. He snaps his fingers.

"That's right—my receptionist, Joyce, gave her my cell when she brought in that dog. I was at Java Jane grabbing a coffee. I think I mentioned that she was very insistent."

"Yeah, I remember that. How's Joyce working out?"

"Joyce? Yeah, she's good. She's helped out a lot since Simone left."

Simone is Lou's daughter. She worked at the practice until she married and left town with her new husband, looking for better work, better pay.

"How's Simone doing?"

"Good, good." Lou bobs his head, looking into the distance. I get the sense he isn't really telling the truth.

"You worry about her?" I ask.

"Yeah. Her fella . . . I don't know. I just get a feeling." He darts a look at me, something crackling in his eyes. "You'd want to protect your kid, right, Detective? Do anything you could to help her?"

My breath sticks in my throat. *Anything. I would've done anything, if only I'd had the chance.*

And that other little voice inside my head: *Isla deserved better than you. She deserved a mother who could protect her.*

"Yeah, 'course. But sometimes"—I shake my head—"sometimes, Lou, it just isn't our choice."

Lou regards me in silence for a moment. I clear my throat and change the subject. "Glad to hear you're getting more staff to help. And what about Neve, how's she working out?"

"Who?"

"Neve Maguire. Your new vet. Started earlier this week, right?"

Lou's white eyebrows draw tight, and he shakes his head. "Nope, not with me. I don't have any new vets. Truth be told, I'm thinking about closing down, retiring soon. Dorothy needs full-time care these days."

"Yeah, I remember," I murmur.

But my mind is whirling. I thought I'd gotten confused, that Neve had maybe been hired as a receptionist and only said she was a vet. But it turned out she didn't work there at all. And why would Neve lie about working at the clinic unless she had something to hide?

Lou gets to his feet then, lifting his coffee at me. "I best be getting back to work. Thanks for the drink, Detective."

I say goodbye and watch him walk away, my face tight. I pull out my phone and call up the number for Sparks Property. A woman with a voice like silk answers. I explain who I am and ask to speak to someone about Dullahan House, reciting the address when she asks.

"Can you tell me what day Neve Maguire arrived?" I ask.

The woman on the other end pauses, keys clacking as she types on her computer.

"You're talking about Holly Maguire's property?" she confirms.

"Yeah. It's in her name, but her daughter's staying there right now. Neve Maguire."

The woman sucks her teeth. "I'm sorry, we have no record of anybody renting or staying in that property right now."

I hang up the phone without saying goodbye. Another lie from Neve. It's weird as hell. I could dismiss the lie about being a vet as foolish pride or maybe a deep wish to be a vet. But two lies, on top of those about the picture, that's something else altogether. What is she hiding?

I feel my thoughts lurch to a stop, my brain making connections in the background as I sit there, frozen.

Something isn't right. It snags deep in my mind, a prickly, nagging feeling. And then it clicks, a puzzle piece dropping into place. The phone number from Bailey's cell came from an elderly home.

I pull up the number I called this morning.

"Trinity Manor Care Home, this is Doreen, how can I help you?"

"Hi, Doreen, my name's Detective Jessica Lambert from Black Lake Police Department. I'm investigating a homicide that might have a connection to one of your residents."

Doreen chuckles, a thick smoker's laugh rattling in her throat. "Well, I doubt that very much, Detective. Our residents are quite elderly and suffer from Alzheimer's and dementia."

"And is Holly Maguire one of your residents?"

A beat of silence. "I'm not sure I can release that information."

"I'm not asking for personal details. Just confirmation she lives there. Or I can come down with a bunch of cops and a warrant . . ." I let my sentence trail off, the threat implied.

Doreen sighs. "Yes, I can confirm Holly Maguire is a resident, but I assure you, she hasn't left in two years. This is a specialist dementia facility. Holly's barely able to speak anymore, and our facility is very secure."

"Thanks, Doreen," I say sweetly. "I'll let you know if I need anything else."

I punch "End" and toss back a gulp of cooling coffee. I stare across the town square, the fading little plaza with its chipped stone fountain, the art gallery and bookstore and ice cream shop on the far side, the taste of alcohol sharp in my mouth.

Something is connecting, but I don't know what. It's too subtle, too slippery to fully grasp hold of.

Either Holly is an extremely good faker or Neve called Bailey from her mother's care home before Bailey was murdered.

Which raises a flurry of other questions. Why did Neve lie about staying at Dullahan House? And why did she say she was working at Lou's vet practice if she isn't? And most important, how is she really connected to Bailey Nelson?

With no immediate answers, and too afraid of getting assigned to desk duty indefinitely, I head back to the station.

I want to go talk to Neve Maguire. Want to find out what she's hiding. But Rivero tells me to go through the surveillance videos Bailey's neighbors sent in, so I spend the rest of the day hunched over my laptop, trawling through every tedious second.

The minutes pass in an agonizing blur. I find nothing. Even the video from Vivienne's across the street doesn't turn up anything. Someone had angled the camera directly at the ground. The only thing I see is a mouse scuttling across the driveway.

Frustrated and furious, I leave early and pull a bottle of whiskey from the liquor cabinet. I know it's a bad idea to drink when I feel this bad. It goes down too easy; I drink too much, do dumb stuff. But I need to numb the jagged edges of my life.

I figure I'll just have one. But that one turns to two, and two to three, and then I lose count and go all in. I proceed to get absolutely blind drunk, hammered enough to wash away the guilt and shame and fury and sink into an ocean so black, it almost feels like there's no coming back.

It's only as I sink into oblivion that I remember something. Something important. The scratches on Lou's arm weren't fresh. They were crusting over, maybe a week or so old.

And then I have a thought.

According to Lou, chlorpromazine is used by vets as a sedative and an antiemetic.

And he admitted to using it regularly at his practice.

Chapter 35

NEVE

Sandra's house is quite close, so perhaps it's unsurprising that I find myself standing outside the house I shared with Eli. My old home looks different somehow. The grass needs to be mowed. The car needs a good wash. It doesn't look loved, filled the way I remember it.

The lights inside are dim. Out here, the streetlights leave smudges of yellow on the paved suburban sidewalks. Other houses up and down the road are dark as well. Behind the houses on my side, the twisted boughs of the forest lay quiet, a patch of woods mandated by city zoning and confined by fences. The air is dark and heavy, oppressive and full of whispers.

For a second, I feel something unusual, a tingling of a memory, like being haunted, the past clawing its way out of the grave. Somewhere, distantly, I hear a voice shouting. Something whips at my arms. But when I look down, there is nothing there.

Whatever it is evaporates then, like water through fingertips, the essence of the images dissolving, leaving a void, a vague sense of unease in its place.

I let myself inside, feeling like an intruder in my own home. I tsk quietly, wondering why Eli hasn't had an alarm installed yet. Did we discuss it before I left? We must have, but I can't remember.

Inside, the air-conditioning is turned up so high, my hair stands on end. I start to shiver, my teeth chattering. A tremor moves through my entire body. Eli always did like it cold at night. Our sleeping compromise was a window cracked but a thick feather duvet on the bed. I would sleep with one leg wrapped around the edge of the duvet to hold it in place while Eli flopped from side to side, muttering throughout the night. I was a sleepwalker, but Eli was a sleep talker.

The floor creaks under my weight, like gunshots cracking through the silence. I move into the living room, the safety of the thickly carpeted floor, and am greeted by an enthusiastic Molly. Her entire body is wiggling with the force of her wagging tail, a banner of happiness. Her tongue lolls out of the side of her mouth as she gives me a doggy grin. I drop to my knees and wrap my arms around her.

"I've missed you, too, Mol!" She drags her tongue across my cheek.

I hold her wiggling body in the dark until I spot something. I stand and move to the window, on the other side of one of the inbuilt bookcases, and where I used to keep Priss, my pinstripe calathea, is a new pinstripe calathea. Eli has replaced mine with an almost exact replica of Priss.

I feel a flash of irritation, like he's trying to replace me, even though it's just a plant. It isn't even like he's taking very good care of it. The pink pinstripes have faded to white, and the leaves are wilting and freckled with brown spots. I go to the kitchen and fill a glass with water, pouring it around the plant's base.

Molly flops down in her doggy bed, and I let my eyes roam the rest of the room. The fireplace mantel is still covered with family photos; a huge canvas picture of the three of us is mounted on the wall above. On either side are inbuilt bookcases filled with well-loved books. The furniture is arranged how it's always been arranged. Nothing has changed. The soft gray walls, the brushed-silver lamps, the warm oak flooring, all of it speaks of a much-loved home.

This was my first and only true home. As a child, my father made it clear that our house was his home, and I was simply a guest in it. His authority was absolute and never questioned by my mom or me. He had strict ideas about right and wrong, all centering around religion and Hell. He was the fire-and-brimstone type, not the peace-and-love type. He taught me that I was born sinful, and no matter how good I tried to be or how many prayers I prayed, I was ultimately still a sinner, and as a sinner, I deserved death simply for existing.

I still hear him now, his voice thundering about how the world of men is sinful and undeserving, how the only way to be saved is through Christ. My mother and I were partners in calming him, alternatively telling him what he wanted to hear and making ourselves as small as possible so we wouldn't draw his wrath. I never understood why she stayed with him. All those years of feeling like she was worthless. But I suppose our devotion to those we love can wind around us like a vine, twisting us into knots, keeping us in relationships that are no good for us.

When Eli and I first met, I was a young veterinary student with little experience in love and a history of self-flagellation. I flirted with bulimia as a teenager. I still have the scars on the insides of my thighs from my cutting phase. I spent a summer picking up litter by the highway after a night slashing tires up and down my street.

Even though my father was long gone by the time I met Eli, a lifetime of his voice telling me that without God I was nothing and deserved to be nothing, that I needed His forgiveness or I would be destroyed, had internalized in me. I suppose maybe my self-destruction is a reflection of my upbringing.

But loving Eli, being loved by him, by Ash, made me feel like a better person. And for a while, that was enough.

I thought Eli would be a one-night stand, much like all the previous one-night stands. But that night led to the next night and to another, and then we were dating, real dates, like *dress up and put makeup on* dates. And then a spontaneous weekend in New England, followed by more weekends together until suddenly we were married and building a future together. Sometimes I think Eli rescued me from myself.

But one thing I've learned is if you're always looking outside your-self to be rescued, you're going to be waiting an awfully long time. No one can rescue you except you.

A sound from the kitchen startles me, and I nearly jump out of my skin, my heart pounding. I sidle along the living room wall and peer into the kitchen.

I gasp. "Ash?"

But then she flickers, like a hologram, and disappears. Why would Ash be here? *How* would she be here? I rub my eyes, telling myself I was seeing things. I *must've been* seeing things. Because Ash isn't here.

I hear a noise upstairs, and I move toward it. There's light, soft and diffused, coming from under Eli's office door. I gently push the door open, and my heart leaps when I see him.

Eli, my beloved husband, is slumped over his desk, his head buried in his arms. He hasn't shaved in days. He looks beat, undone, and smells as if he hasn't even showered. A half-empty bottle of Jack Daniel's sits on the desk next to a sweating tumbler, the ice melting into a pool at the bottom of the glass. Next to it is Eli's favorite coffee mug: two thumbs up with WHO'S A BADASS ARCHITECT? A skim of milk swirls on the cooled liquid.

Some men when faced with a divorce rally and find their best self. They go to the gym or get plugs or start running marathons or go on a diet. But my husband does not look as if he's tried any of those things. Impending divorce doesn't suit him in the slightest.

Behind him, the window is open, a warm summer breeze ruffling the sheer curtains, colliding with the chilled air and turning Eli's breaths to puffs of fog. Riding the crest of that breeze is the sweet scent of malt and the rank smell of old body odor and something else, Eli's familiar scent, pepper and lemongrass.

The desk lamp is on low, giving everything a sepia glow. It makes me nostalgic, a beautiful ache, and all of a sudden I'm home. *Really* home. I've missed him *so much*. Missed *us* so much. And I'm happy, a feeling that spreads through me like warmth, like magic.

There is a sort of strange inevitability in the disaster I've made of my life. Self-sabotage is a difficult needle to walk away from. But I do love Eli. I love so many things about him. He's brilliant and kind. He's creative and impulsive and fun. But most of all, I love him for giving me a chance at a normal life. I don't know if I've ever told him thank you for that.

I lift my hand, wanting to feel his hair in my palm. But he stirs, his head turning to the side so I can see where his sleeves have pressed wrinkles into the side of his face. Eli mutters something and shifts in his seat, and as he does, his hand flops onto the desk. His fingers open, and something tumbles out, landing on the desk with a dull crack. I pick up the item. It's a little engraved wooden stump we got on one of our first dates, a whirlwind weekend spent at the county fair.

Neve + Eli.

I press the wood to my lips, the spell that's descended over us coating my skin like warm mist.

"Eli . . . ," I murmur.

I run my fingertips gently over his hair, down the prickly stubble along his jaw. Sometimes you have to lose someone to know how much you really love them.

"I miss you," I whisper. "I love you."

At the sound of my voice, Eli rouses, his body rocking forward and then back as he lifts his head. His eyes are open, but I know he doesn't see me. They are blank and filled with sleep. He opens his mouth, as if he'll say something, but then his body relaxes. He folds his arms again and lowers his head on them.

"Neve." My name comes out as a sigh.

I open my mouth to reply, thinking I'll wake him, but then a sound comes from Eli. One that sends chills up and down my spine.

A guttural sob spills from Eli's lips.

The sound breaks whatever spell has been cast over us, and instantly the room loses its magic, the shadows suddenly stark and bleak.

Eli twitches in his sleep, and I catch sight of something under his elbows. My face. And Ash's.

It's a framed picture of our family, but the glass has been smashed, cracks snaking like spiderwebs. I recoil in horror, staggering backward. There is that feeling again, that vertiginous tilt, like my life is spinning out of control.

Why would he do this? Why would he break our family picture? I don't understand. And then, irrational or not, I'm angry. At Eli. At myself. At this entire situation. I fling the wooden stump across the room. It hits the back wall with a thump and clatters to the floor. Eli jumps up, whirling wildly. His eyes fall on the wooden stump, and he bends to pick it up, back to me.

He stares at it for a moment. For a second, I think he will turn and face me, that he'll explain what he's done, and I want him to, but I don't. I stand, frozen, not sure if I'm ready to confront him. But the moment is broken when his phone rings, a sharp staccato bell that pierces the room. I step back, out of the room, as Eli snatches his phone from the desk, and I slip quickly into the shadows of the hallway.

"Hello?" I hear Eli say. There's a beat of silence and then: "I'll be right there."

I flee then, my steps silent on the thickly carpeted stairs. But as I run, I think I hear Eli calling for me, the sound of my name drifting in my wake.

Chapter 36

Killing people was a messy business.

Messy and, I was learning, didn't always go exactly to plan. Which was why I was sweating under my long-sleeve shirt. I needed something to cover the scratches on my arms. The bandage around my belly didn't help. I worried I looked conspicuous, but it was the lesser of two evils, really. At least the antibiotics had kicked the infection. Small victories.

The night was silvery with moonlight when I returned home after my shift. I had an hour before I needed to be somewhere, so I reheated a slice of lasagna and went to check on Tweety. He'd been a bit lethargic the last few days, but his eyes were bright, and he chirped once when he saw me.

I lowered myself onto my bed carefully, mindful of the wound just beginning to heal on my belly. I didn't want to burst the stitches again. I turned on the TV and scrolled through the menu. I eventually decided on a documentary about Greek history while I ate.

I took a number of ancient Greek mythology courses in college. In the traditional Christian ethos we've inherited in our modern society, there were concepts of forgiveness and cancellation of wrongdoing. Like many, I was raised Christian and was more than familiar with the biblical passages that discussed the merits—or lack thereof—of revenge and justice. Let bygones be bygones. Forgive and forget. The past is the past.

But I preferred the Greek ethos of justice and law, rather than mercy or forgiveness. I was Artemis, the goddess who, in her revenge, turned a man into a stag that was then hunted by his own dogs.

The past, I've found, bleeds into the present like a lacerated vein. I will never forgive. I will never forget. This world would be a better place if certain people were not in it.

I pulled out my phone and spent some time reading the local news, then the national news, until the silence caught my attention. Tweety wasn't chirping. I peered inside the cat carrier and saw he was sitting very still. I opened the door and carefully lifted him out. He was okay but just stared up at me with his bright, beady eyes. He didn't struggle in my hand at all.

I wondered if he was bored. Or perhaps he had an infection. Or his wing wasn't healing properly.

I've always loved animals more than people. They didn't betray you; they didn't hate or get suspicious. They didn't lie. All they wanted were the basest things: food, water, a little love. I loved Tweety, and I knew he'd grown to love me, too.

The thought of losing him was suddenly too much to bear. I felt tears gather in my throat. I'd already lost nearly everybody I loved.

"Please be okay, Tweety." I stroked a finger down his back, my voice shaking.

And then tears, big, unexpected tears, began streaking down my face, gathering in salty pools in the hollows of my clavicles. I knew I was redirecting, placing my enormous feelings onto this tiny little bird. But knowing that didn't actually help me feel better.

All of this was triggering my childhood trauma, making me relive my past. Was it worth it?

The thought was fast, the tail of a ghost whipping through my mind. Gone before it had time to settle. Because of course it was worth it.

I thought of the cool, smooth throat, the scalpel in my hand, the beads of blood bubbling under my message. Heat prickled over my skin, a strange desire throbbing deep in my belly. Not lust, no, something else. Something darker.

Just then, Tweety did the most unexpected thing. He tried to fly. I caught him before he fell to the ground and laughed through my tears.

"You want to fly, baby?" Maybe all of us just wanted to be free.

He was due to have the splint off in a few days anyway, so I unwrapped the bandaging and sat him on the edge of my bed. He didn't do anything at first, but I could wait.

In the background, the voice-over on the documentary droned on about the justice of the gods. I sat next to Tweety and opened the news article I'd been reading. The detectives were still no further along in their investigation into Bailey Nelson's murder. They still hadn't made any connection with the other body; as far as I could tell, it hadn't even been found yet, which was good.

I tapped one more name into the browser—my one mistake, I suppose I should call it. It took me a minute, but I eventually found a short article. My eyes scanned it quickly, my heart dropping when I reached the bottom.

The prognosis had been upgraded to good.

I never intended to hurt an innocent, but sometimes in the pursuit of justice, people got hurt. Justice could be a bruising, destructive process, but in the end, it was better than the alternative.

My alarm went off then, shrill and insistent. It was time to go. I could use a day in bed to relax, some time for my body to heal. But right now, I had pressing issues to attend to.

My grandfather always said, if you're gonna do it, do it right. There was no sense half-assing anything.

There was one thing I needed to do, one loose end to tie up.

One last person left to kill.

Chapter 37

NEVE

The night I met Bee at the restaurant in Back Bay, I arrived home late to find Eli waiting in the dark. I threw my keys in the bowl we kept in the entry. It was long past midnight, and Eli and Ash were supposed to be in bed.

I had just kicked off my heels, sending them clattering into a corner, when he spoke. "Hey."

I whirled to see Eli's silhouette outlined against the living room couch. "Eli, you scared the crap out of me! What are you doing hiding there in the dark?"

When he answered, his voice was filled with laughter. "*I'm* definitely not the one hiding."

I froze, my first thoughts darting to where I'd been all night. Did he know? Tendrils of fear trickled down my back, but I pasted on a calm, composed smile.

"I don't know what you mean." I flipped the light switch on and shrugged out of my coat.

Eli was watching me, his fair eyebrows lifted, a small smile playing at the corners of his mouth. He seemed amused more than anything else.

"What's going on?" I asked warily.

"You got a package today."

I tried to remember if I'd ordered anything from Amazon but came up blank. "Look, I've been on my feet all day. I had two euthanasias and an emergency surgery after a dog got hit by a car, and I'm completely exhausted, so do you want to give me the package or not?"

"Sure." Eli lifted a box I hadn't noticed at his feet. It was square, about one foot by one foot. No Amazon logo. He flipped the box around so the label faced me.

Across the front on a massive white label was printed: 3 XXL BIG-ASS DILDOS.

I felt my mouth literally drop open. I grabbed the box and turned it over in my hands. No other markings, just the label with my name and address and the description.

"Care to explain?" Eli said, smirking.

I lifted my eyes to his, disbelieving. "Eli, I didn't order this!"

Eli frowned, suddenly uncertain. "You didn't?"

"What the hell, Eli? Why would I order three dildos? And even if I was going to order one, why would I do it from a business that wrote all over the box for the world to see?"

"Then who did?"

"I don't know." I turned the box over again. "There's no return address. No postage. Eli, someone dropped this off here! At our house!"

"But nobody was here. Ash went to pick it up from Cindy's next door. She said we had one of those missed mail delivery slips."

Cindy was our elderly neighbor, a gossipy old busybody who lived alone and spent most of her time at her living room window watching the goings-on of the neighborhood.

"Oh my God!" I was breathless with mortification. The entire neighborhood was going to hear about this. "It went to *Cindy*?"

Eli nodded.

"And *Ash* collected it?"

Another nod.

My lips parted in horror. What would Ash think of me, her mother, getting a box of dildos? I stared at the offending box. "I don't understand."

"Maybe there's a note inside?"

I grabbed a knife from the kitchen and sliced open the packing tape. Inside were three big-ass dildos, and they were *big*. I fumbled around at the bottom and pulled out a slip of paper.

Don't worry, I'm cuming for you.

Eli took the note from my frozen fingers and read it out loud. "I'm *cuming* for you? What the fuck is that?"

Eli was the least jealous person in the world, so his mind never went to me cheating. Instead, he defended me, confirming again my belief that this man was far too good for me. I didn't deserve him.

He waved the note. "Is it some kind of joke? One of your friends or maybe your colleagues?"

My mind whirled dizzily as I tried to work through the possibilities. There was no way in hell Stephen would've sent this to me. Had his wife found out about us? Who else would've sent it? The same person who'd been sending those texts?

"I think you're right," I said weakly. "It must be a prank. Our receptionist, she's getting married next weekend. I bet she sent them as a joke."

"That is some seriously fucked-up humor."

Eli seemed surprisingly upset, and for a second I worried he would do something stupid, like call the practice or confront my receptionist.

"It's just a prank," I said with a tight smile.

"I guess if you're not upset about it . . . ," Eli said doubtfully.

"Not at all. You know these Gen Z kids. They're totally bonkers. I guess it's kind of funny if you think about it."

I forced a laugh, but Eli didn't look convinced.

I took the box into the kitchen and broke it down. I shoved them into the bottom of the garbage bin except one. For a moment, I just held it in my hand, thinking. I knew women were more sexually open than they used to be, but I'd never owned a dildo in my life. The only time I'd ever even seen one was at Sandra's party . . .

The thought sent me reeling. Would Sandra send me a dildo in retaliation for Bailey's stupid prank all those years ago?

I stared at the note.

I'm cuming for you . . .

Eli came up behind me then. "You okay?"

"Yeah." I dropped the note and dildo into the trash. "Just annoyed about this."

"Come here."

Eli's hands, warm and firm, settled on my shoulders, kneading with a quiet intensity. I closed my eyes, letting myself lean into him, my back pressed against his chest. He tucked my hair behind my ear and pressed his lips to my cheek. I could smell the familiar scent of him, pepper and lemongrass. He nuzzled my neck, his breath warming me.

When I turned in Eli's arms, he was gazing at me with bedroom eyes. My heartbeat kicked up. It had been weeks since we'd made love. I could feel that familiar tug low in my belly. Eli was a handsome man. He'd never looked like a typical architect, stuffy with glasses and a plaid blazer with patches at the elbows. Eli always appeared crisp, a little preppy. Even now, his shirt was unwrinkled, his chinos freshly pressed. He smiled, long and slow.

Everyone liked Eli. He lit up a room. I thought of all the magical moments we'd shared: catching his eyes on me from the other side of a party; sitting side by side at a movie, his hand brushing against mine; the sound of the word *wife* in his mouth when we were first married; the way he held Ash in those first moments after she was born. I got so lucky with him, and somehow that luck had held. But I knew if I didn't stop what I was doing, that luck would run out.

I decided right then to finish with Stephen. Nobody needed to get hurt here.

There have been times in my life when I've gone wildly offtrack. When I looked back and was able to pinpoint the exact moment it happened, the precise choice I made to get to the exact point I'd gotten to. Sometimes one bad decision leads to another and another, and soon you're so lost in the labyrinth of twists and turns that resulted from that one choice.

But everyone made mistakes. Nobody was all good; neither were they all bad. Good was subjective anyway. Maybe all we could do was make the most of the choices we made and right the wrongs we'd done.

My eyes were open now, and I was seeing clearly. Sometimes life changed us. We created different versions of ourselves in order to survive, to weather the bad times, often becoming unrecognizable as we did. But Eli had been my one constant. Eli and Ash.

I couldn't lose them. I wouldn't.

I took Eli by the hand and pulled him upstairs to our bedroom. I undressed slowly, enjoying the feel of my husband's hands on me, the rapturous look in his eyes as he gazed into mine.

I wasn't deluded enough to say Eli's love had redeemed me, but I felt washed clean in it for sure. And for now, that was enough.

Afterward, when Eli was snoring lightly next to me, I crept out of bed and went downstairs to the kitchen. I pulled one of the dildos and the note from the garbage and set them on the island. I flattened the note, the pale glow of the moon lighting the words.

I'm cuming for you . . .

There were two ways to read that note: flirtatious or threatening. And something black and slimy squirmed in my belly, telling me it was more likely the latter.

◆ ◆ ◆

I wake abruptly, feeling like the ground is sliding out from underneath me.

I'm lying on the floor under the window in Ash's room again. I blink, disoriented, and slowly sit up. My body is stiff, sore. It feels like I've been beaten all over. My head is spinning, a vertiginous faintness pulling at the edges of my consciousness. I put a hand to my forehead. Once again, I can't remember how I got here. At least this time, Ash isn't here to see me.

"Ash?" I get to my feet awkwardly, feeling like every joint is creaking.

I look around, and my heartbeat instantly ratchets up, a tempo that feels like it will detonate.

The room is empty.

Not just empty; it's been put back to the way it was when we first arrived.

The bed with its yellow duvet has a dust cover drawn over it. The dresser on the far side of the room is covered as well. The yellow curtains are pulled shut. There are no clothes or crumpled dirty socks thrown carelessly onto the floor, no hairbrush or lotions or nail polish lining the vanity. No brushes or scrunchies or bobby pins or black makeup.

When did this happen? And why hadn't I noticed when I first came in?

I stagger to my feet and rush to the closet, throwing the door open. But there is only darkness inside. Darkness and a few old wire hangers rocking gently on the pole. There are no clothes hanging here. I throw the dust cover off the dresser, yanking out the drawers. But there are no clothes folded inside.

I try to imagine my daughter, my indifferent, apathetic teenager, taking the time to not only pack up her belongings but make the bed and pull the dust sheets over the furniture, but I can't.

I snatch at the curtains and yank them open, peering outside into the dark, dark night. No Ash.

My hands are shaking, my body cold despite the heat. My legs feel like rubber. I run down the twisting turret stairs and move through the rooms one by one, calling Ash's name.

There is no sign of Ash inside. It's as if she was never here.

I throw the kitchen door open and head outside, running down the back steps to the beach, but I don't find her. I keep running, heading for the boathouse, remembering our first day here, how she'd disappeared, a glitch in a computer game. Has that somehow happened again? Am I spacing out, my traumatized brain causing a strange malfunction in my life, but soon she will appear, as if she had never left?

"Ash!" I call as I run, my bare feet flying over the twigs and stones along the path. I don't feel a thing. "Ash!"

But there is no response.

I push through the foliage, feeling myself start to wobble, like I'm losing my grip on reality. I stand for a minute, listening. Breathing. Trying to wrestle back control.

The black space between the trees mocks me with its silence. I must not have relocked the door the last time I was here, because it opens when I twist the knob. But even before I enter, I can tell she hasn't been here.

I start to cry then. Everything that's happened—the home invasion, Bee's murder, Ash disappearing—it all gets on top of me, and for a minute, all I can do is stand there and gasp for breath as tears course down my cheeks.

Neve.

I hear my name, a whisper from far away. I turn, peering into the shadows. A wedge of moonlight falls on the boathouse stairs, a blur of silvery-black stars peeking through the trees. There is a rustle, and a shadow passes to my right.

I whirl and think I see someone. Porcelain skin, long dark hair. It's only a second, a microsecond, really, and then she disappears into the forest shadows.

I blink. It can't be. Bailey is dead. Why do I keep thinking I see her?

It's not that I'm afraid of ghosts or, at least, the idea of ghosts. Honestly, the living have always scared me far more than the dead. It's just that I've never believed in them at all. But now I'm beginning to wonder if perhaps Bee *is* a ghost. Can such a thing exist? But why is she here? And does she have anything to do with Ash going missing?

"Bee?" I say into the darkness. "Is that you?"

Silence.

"Where's Ash?"

Still, no one replies.

I feel dizzy, my entire body shaking. Light and shadow crisscross in front of me, a blur of silvery-black. I sink onto the steps and drop my head in my hands. I think I will black out, but I can't allow that. I have to find my daughter.

I return to Dullahan House, letting myself in through the sliding glass door. I am standing in the kitchen when I feel a presence. It's like an electric shock running over my body. The hairs on my arms stand on end. Sharp prickles tap the back of my neck.

My eyes dart around the kitchen, looking for anything out of place. And then land on the basement door.

It's open.

Confusion and fear hit simultaneously. All this time it's been locked, but now someone has opened it.

"Ash?" My voice comes out as a croak.

My heart is thudding a horrific beat, the sound swelling in my ears. I don't want to go down there, but what if Ash is already there?

I know what I have to do. To kill the past, I must confront it. I walk toward the basement door.

And I begin my descent down the stairs, back to where it all began.

Chapter 38

JESS

Pain floods every one of my senses the second I wake. My head is banging, a throbbing so intense, it is a color. Red. No, purple. No, red. I think my skull is trying to swallow my eyeballs.

I barely have time to make it to the bathroom before I puke. Yellow bile pools like acid at the bottom of the toilet.

It's been a long time since I've puked. I'm a functioning alcoholic, not a sloppy one. The realization that I've gone too far this time surprises me a little. Normally I have my boundaries and I stick to them.

I grab a couple of aspirin from the medicine cabinet and swallow them with water straight from the tap. I force myself into the shower, letting cold water beat down on my aching head.

I dress in jeans, an old T-shirt of Mac's, and ballet flats, then pad into the kitchen and make myself a strong coffee and some toast. When I check my phone, I see I've missed four calls from Will. I groan. I'm way too hungover to deal with him right now.

Outside, soft apricot light is just streaking over the horizon. Great gray clouds gather in the distance, humidity thick in the air. A storm is coming. Finally, something to break this damn heat wave.

I drink my coffee and stare at those clouds, thinking about Mac.

We weren't one of those couples who fought a lot. In general, we negotiated the pathways and diversions of married life with a sanguine cheerfulness. I was a paramedic when we met, and he'd had to deal with the drama of long shifts and late nights. When we moved to Black Lake and I said I wanted to pivot to being a detective, he was my biggest cheerleader. A defense attorney and a cop had all the cards stacked against them, but we made it work.

Mac's biggest complaint was always how easily I'd sectioned myself off: mother, wife, daughter, detective, trickster, martyr, bitch, alcoholic.

Murderer.

But I always saw my ability to compartmentalize as a strength. It allowed me to take a step back, to sort through my emotions in a neat, organized way, locking them into their own separate rooms. It allowed me to survive the traumatizing death of my daughter.

Or had it?

I knew I'd been using alcohol as a crutch, but I'd needed to numb the pain, to compartmentalize. Except now I realize that, while compartmentalizing was useful right after Isla died, if I didn't let those barriers down, I would drown. I'd lose my job, and then I really would have nothing.

I go to the cupboards and grab the bottles of whiskey I keep there and pour all of them down the sink. In the bathroom, I dump out the bottle stashed behind the towels. The bottle in my bedroom closet is next, then every bottle of wine in the wine rack until I've poured out every last drop of alcohol in the house.

When I'm done, I grab my leather jacket and go out to my motorcycle. The engine stutters to life. I give it some gas and ease out the clutch, leaning in as the bike takes off. The deep, hypnotic hum vibrates in me, calming me.

The streets are deserted as I drive toward the station. Inside, I head upstairs to the lab. I quickly stuff the things I need into my backpack, then hurry back down the stairs and outside.

To hell with staying at my desk. I'm going to Bailey Nelson's house.
There's more than one way to work a case.

I limp through Bailey's house, my cane thumping loudly against the
glossy hardwood floor. The house has been cleaned, everything back in
its right place.

"Bailey?" I call.

I feel a little stupid speaking out loud to a dead woman. But Isla
told me Bailey is still here. If I can talk to Isla, who's dead, maybe I can
talk to Bailey, too. I figure I have nothing to lose at this point.

"Bailey?"

Still no answer. Just the thick, bleak silence of an empty house.

I push through the kitchen to the back door and step out onto the
patio. From here, the only place Bailey could've gone is down the stairs.
So I go down. At the bottom, I head up, toward the road. The beach has
been thoroughly swept by the CSIs, so there's no point going that way.

I continue in Bailey's footsteps, trying to see it from her point of
view. I stop on the lawn in front of the house and sweep my eyes up and
down the street. Birds chirp a morning song. A garbage truck is rolling
through the gates. A cat hops onto a fence.

My eyes stop on Vivienne's house.

There's something to the side of the door. I cross the street for a
closer view.

It's a Ring doorbell recorder. The surveillance video was pointing at
the ground, but maybe the doorbell camera caught something.

I think of what Neve told me Wednesday night. That she saw
Vivienne break into Bailey's house, leaving with a white paper bag and
a folder.

Vivienne answers my knock quickly, as if she was already awake. A
fluffy little white dog is barking wildly behind her. Vivienne hushes the
dog and invites me in, tucking her robe tighter around her. She doesn't

look happy about being interviewed so early in the morning, but I rarely care what people think these days.

I follow Vivienne into a lovely, large living room. The room is pale and sleekly minimalist, with numerous plants dotted around. It smells gorgeous, the rose geranium and eucalyptus scents floating obligingly upward.

"Can I get you a drink, Detective?" Vivienne asks, her face tense. "My husband's still sleeping, but I was just having my morning coffee."

"No, thanks."

She sits on the couch across from me, the dog flopping down at her feet. "What can I help you with?"

"We've had a witness state that you broke into Mrs. Nelson's house the day her body was found. Do you want to tell me about that?"

The scowl on Vivienne's face melts away, and her eyes widen. "Who . . . ?"

"Is it true?"

"I . . . yes, but it's not what you think." Vivienne reaches her hands up, scrapes her dark hair into a ponytail. "My dog, Toby, was sick. He got into some algae when Bailey was watching him, and she took him to the vet. His antibiotics were in her house; I saw them when I went looking for her and found Toby. I just wanted to grab them. I didn't think it was a big deal."

"You didn't think it was a big deal to break into a murder victim's house?"

"I didn't break in!" she protests. "Bailey told me where the spare key was. We often went into each other's houses."

I study the other woman. "What was in the folder you took from her house?"

Vivienne's eyes widen. "How do you . . . ?"

I raise my eyebrows.

Vivienne sighs. "Here . . ."

She goes to an elegant rolltop desk and lifts the lid. Inside is a plastic expanding file organizer. She extracts a green folder and hands it to me. Inside is some sort of legal-looking document. I scan the paper quickly. It basically says that Bailey Nelson had loaned Vivienne and her husband, Bill, $100,000.

"My husband has a gambling problem," Vivienne says quietly. "It's been . . . difficult. I only found out about it a few months ago. We were struggling to pay off some bills, and we were going to lose the house. Bailey helped us."

"You stole valuable evidence from a crime scene."

"I'm sorry." Tears have filled Vivienne's dark eyes. "I was embarrassed, and I didn't want you to think we were responsible in any way. I swear, I didn't kill Bailey. She was my friend."

I shift gears. "I noticed you have a Ring doorbell recorder."

"Ye-es?" Vivienne says slowly.

"They're handy little things, aren't they? The camera automatically starts recording when there's motion. You can see all the recordings on your app. Mind if I take a look?"

"S-sure . . ." Vivienne fumbles in her purse for her phone. She opens the Ring app and hands me the phone.

I scroll back to Tuesday, the day Bailey was killed. Despite the distance, the quality is good, and I have a clear view of Bailey's front yard. I fast-play the videos for that day, watching as delivery drivers arrive and leave, neighbors come and go. Bailey goes for a run and comes home.

"Maybe I would like that cup of coffee after all," I say when Vivienne starts fidgeting. "Just black."

She nods and leaves. I can hear her moving around the kitchen, the sound of a kettle boiling, a spoon scraping against a mug.

On the video, evening falls. Movement activates the camera, and Bailey comes into view, her body a silhouette in the street lighting. She walks slowly up the path. Her attention is on the book in her left hand, the key she took from the cupboard in her house in her right hand.

After a second, Bailey heads up the hill, disappearing off camera. And then another second later, a figure clothed in black follows her.

I hit "Pause," my mind whirling.

The figure is wearing a baseball cap pulled low so I can't see their face. He, or she, doesn't have the same body type as Angus, but that isn't what strikes me. What I find most interesting is that both this figure and Bailey are heading up the hill, toward Dullahan House.

"What the hell?" I mutter. "I need to talk to Neve about this."

I grab my cane and head for the front door.

"Neve!" I rap my knuckles against her front door. "Neve? I need to talk to you."

But there's no answer. There's no car in the driveway, and the house has an empty feel about it. The drapes in the windows are pulled tight. The lights are off.

"Nobody's there, Detective," Vivienne calls. She's followed me out to the street. "The only person who's been there in years is the cleaning girl who comes every other week."

"Thanks!" I call.

I pull out my phone and dial Sparks Property. The receptionist doesn't even argue, producing the entry code within minutes of me explaining why I need it. I tap in the numbers, and the dead bolt slides open with a click.

I step inside Dullahan House. Away from the unwavering eye of the sun, the temperature drops noticeably. The air is heavy and stale. Musty. Like the windows haven't been opened in a long time.

I shuffle down the hallway, peering into each room as I go. The living room is embraced by deep shadows, the heavy drapes pulled tight. I sweep my phone's flashlight around: furniture covered in thick dust sheets, a fireplace on one wall, a giant TV above it.

The only sign of life here is a dying plant that's been dragged into a shadowy corner. The soil is bone dry. The stripy leaves have curled at the edges, brown and crumpled.

I feel the hairs on the back of my neck rise, a strange, prickling energy. My hand on my cane has grown damp.

I continue into the kitchen. The drapes are drawn in here, too. On the island is a book. When I pick it up, a folded piece of paper drops out.

In red ink: *I know what you did. Did you ever stop to consider the consequences? Because there will be consequences. There always are. And yours are coming soon enough.*

And then a sound . . .

Creeeaakk.

I whirl, my heart in my throat. It sounded like a door opening.

"Hello?" I call.

But no one answers.

I bounce my flashlight around the kitchen. On the far wall is a door. It's open a crack. Adrenaline zips up my arms, an electric shock. I unstrap my gun and train it on the door. Shit. I can't hold my phone with its flashlight and my cane and my gun.

I slowly, quietly place my cane on the floor. I'm off balance, but no way in hell am I giving up my flashlight or gun.

"Hello?" I call again. "I'm a detective, and I have a gun. Come out with your hands up."

Silence.

I hobble to the door and elbow it open wider. The phone's flashlight illuminates a flight of stairs. I train my gun on it, sweat dripping from my chin. I wipe it away with my forearm.

The wood groans under my weight as I descend, leaning too hard on the banister. At the bottom, I find myself in a completely ordinary, if a bit retro, basement. I flick the switch, and light floods the room. Dust glints in the light. The room is wood-paneled with high, wide, grime-covered windows. Vague strips of light beam through.

There are couches and overstuffed chairs. A chunky wooden coffee table. An ancient, blocky television set. A tatty old green shag rug. The back wall is covered in shelving stuffed with an old stereo system, CDs, DVDs, cassette tapes, Atari games.

Nobody is here, but the room feels off, a strange sensation buzzing along my neck. I circle the room, but it isn't until I'm at the back that my gaze snags on something. The rug under the coffee table is out of place, one corner exposing a clear triangle with no dust on it.

Like it had recently been moved.

I holster my gun and awkwardly drag the coffee table back. I flip the rug up. Nothing. But the naked eye doesn't always pick up blood. That's why I stopped by the station to grab some luminol. Long after blood has been cleaned up or wiped away, traces of hemoglobin remain. If Bailey was killed here, I would find out.

I mix the luminol and carefully pour the ingredients into a spray bottle, giving it a quick shake. I flick the lights off, then return to the space where the rug had been and give it a spray.

The wood floor lights up like a Christmas tree.

"Holy shit," I say out loud. "I think I've found our primary crime scene."

Just under the rug had been a puddle of blood, smeared, as if someone had tried to clean it up. And moving out from the rug are bloody drag marks stretching to the stairs.

I spritz the luminol again. The area around the rug shows tiny splatters dotted like a night sky. I re-create the scene in my mind.

Bailey came over to Neve's house with something in her hand, something small. Perhaps to hide it? She would've flipped the rug back, because I don't see any blood on the fibers. She knelt here, her back to the door, and the figure in black incapacitated her with a blow to the head, followed by the injection.

Was it Neve? Had she arrived at Dullahan House sooner than we thought?

I turn the lights back on and stare at the floor where, just a second ago, blood glowed a fluorescent blue. Now there is just a completely normal wooden floor.

I shake out a pair of latex gloves from my pocket. Slip them on. I bend awkwardly, shining my flashlight along the cracks in the hardwood floor. There's a little notch in the wood. I wiggle my finger into it. The panel comes loose. I set it aside and stick my phone's flashlight into the gap.

There, burrowed under the floorboards, is an old shoebox. I pull it out and lift off the lid. Inside are stacks of SD cards and mini digital tapes, like what you'd use in an old camcorder.

"An SD card," I mutter. It makes so much sense. Small enough to slip in and out of your purse, to hold in the palm of your hand. "This must be what Bailey grabbed from her purse and brought over here."

The light catches on something—a piece of paper?—at the bottom of the shoebox. I reach in, scraping at it with my nail. I finally grasp it between two fingers and pull it out.

It's the photo we found at Bailey's house. The one of her with Sandra and Neve. And wrapped in the photo is a mini digital tape.

NEVE is written in neat black marker.

A shuffling sound comes from behind me. I whirl.

And there, as if I've conjured her just by seeing her name, is Neve.

Chapter 39

NEVE

"Detective Lambert?" My voice is shrill with surprise at seeing her in my basement. "Where's Ash?"

She frowns. "Who?"

"My daughter. Is she down here?"

"No."

She takes a step away from me, her fingers tightening on her gun. She has something gripped in her other hand. It takes me a second to understand: it is the picture of Bailey, Sandra, and me.

"What are you doing?" I glance up the stairs. "How'd you get in? Actually, never mind, it doesn't matter. I'm glad to see you. I think my daughter is missing. Her stuff is all gone, and I can't find her. I need your help."

The detective's eyes on me are sharp, assessing. "Your neighbor says nobody has been staying here. And Sparks Property confirmed; you never arranged with them to stay here. Why are you *really* here, Neve?"

They are Ash's exact words, and they cause something to spasm in my stomach. "I don't have to arrange with anybody to stay here! It's *my* house. My mother's."

"This room is covered in blood."

"What?" I rear back, feeling as if she's reached across the space between us and slapped me. I look around, trying to see what she sees.

She points at a spray bottle on the floor. "Luminol. Shows blood that you can't see with the naked eye. Now, you want to explain to me what's really going on here? Is this where you killed Bailey Nelson?"

I gasp. "What? No, I swear to you, I would never do that! I didn't . . ."

Detective Lambert lifts a mini digital tape and points at a shoebox on the floor. I notice for the first time that the rug has been pulled back and the floorboards have been lifted. Inside the shoebox are stacks of SD cards and mini digital tapes.

"This one's labeled." She lifts it so I can see NEVE written in neat black marker.

A cool, numb sort of adrenaline trickles from my shoulders down my back. My whole body feels as if it is shrouded in an odd, distant buzzing. It's the missing video that Bailey kept. She warned me, and here it was under my floorboards all along.

"Want to tell me what's on it?" The detective's fingers tap the tape restlessly, that agitated, impatient energy coming off her like flies on blood.

I close my eyes. "It was so long ago."

Her fingers tighten again on the gun. "I can always arrest you and take you to the station. We have a nice comfy seat there. You can sit back, kick your feet up. I'll get some popcorn . . ."

Honestly, it's a relief to know I'm finally going to tell somebody. I've wanted to for so long. I had a chance to once a long time ago. After we came home from Dullahan House. I knew I needed to tell my mother what I'd done. It was swallowing me whole, that guilt. Eating me up like darkness and I feared soon, there would be nothing good left in me.

"I did a bad thing, Mom," I told her.

"We all do bad things sometimes, sweetie. But we can fix it."

"Not this, Mom. I don't think it can be fixed."

She looked at me curiously, her hands covered in soap as she washed dishes in the sink. She wiped her hands dry and sat me down at the dining room table and asked me what had happened. I wanted to tell her. That night was the closest I ever came. Instead, I told her soft lies and half-truths. I told her I knew Sandra had been drinking. That I hadn't stopped her from driving.

I meet the detective's eyes now. "I'll tell you everything. The whole truth. But you have to promise you'll help me find Ash. Swear to me you'll help me find my daughter."

She nods. "I'll do my best."

I close my eyes. The choices we made that night have had a domino effect on everything else, each knocking the next one down. I knew it was a mistake; everything that happened that summer was a mistake. But sometimes small mistakes lead to bigger ones.

Relief is like a cool mist washing over me as I tell her everything.

Maybe it's true what they say: the truth will set you free.

Chapter 40

NEVE

Bee was the first to arrive at my going-away party. My mom had gone out to a friend's house to play bridge for the evening, and I was so excited, I was practically vibrating.

When I opened the door, Bee swaggered past, her metallic-pink lip gloss sparkling in the dwindling light. She carried two paper bags of chips and candy to the kitchen, leaving the scent of her Victoria's Secret Pear Glace hand lotion in her wake and calling, "'Sup, girl!" over her shoulder.

"Hey, Bee!" Relief was instant and sweet as honey. I hadn't expected her to come, I realized.

"Look what I got," she said, eyes gleaming. She pulled out the bags of Doritos and Lay's, revealing bottles of vodka, Malibu, and absinthe buried like secrets underneath. "Look, look! You can't have a going-away party without alcohol."

My mouth dropped open. "This must've cost a fortune! Where did you get the money to even buy this?"

Bee laughed. "I have my ways."

We took everything outside, and Bee set the bottles of alcohol next to buckets of soda and ice. We built a bonfire in the sand, piling old cardboard boxes and chunks of dried, broken wood I'd gathered earlier into a massive pile. When we'd finished, Bee pulled something from her back pocket and handed it to me.

"I got you something. You know, to say sorry about the dildo prank. It really was just a joke, but I'm sorry I got it wrong. You're right—we've been friends, like, forever. We should totally celebrate that."

She dropped a slip of material into my outstretched palm. It was a rainbow-colored friendship bracelet intricately braided into an elaborate diamond pattern.

"Oh, Bee, it's so pretty!" I exclaimed. "Did you make it yourself?"

She laughed. "Ha! As if! I bought a pack of them from Claire's."

I smiled. Yeah, that made more sense. I couldn't see Bailey sitting down to make friendship bracelets. That totally wasn't her style at all. "Well, it's *mad* gorgeous. Thank you."

Bailey spooled the bracelet around my wrist, snapping the plastic clasp together.

"I got one for Sandra and one for myself, too." She pulled a matching bracelet from her back pocket and snapped it onto her wrist. "See? Twinsies."

I hugged Bee and exclaimed over the gift, just as I knew she would want me to. She made me a fruity drink with Malibu, and by the time the doorbell rang, I was so giddy from the alcohol that I didn't even remember to be nervous as I pulled Sandra through the house to where Bee was waiting outside.

When Sandra spotted Bee, she looked horrified, but Bailey was smooth as silk. "Hey, Sandra, I got you a pressie."

She handed Sandra the friendship bracelet. Sandra hesitantly accepted the gift, turning it over in her hands and looking a little confused. I wondered if I was the only one who noticed her fingers trembling a little.

"Our friendship is totally so important to me," Bee said, her voice sweet as syrup. "I would never want to lose that. Look, Neve and I have matching bracelets, too." She held her wrist to mine to show them off.

"That's nice of you, thank you," Sandra said politely.

"And I got alcohol! This party's gonna be the bomb!"

Bee handed Sandra a fruity drink. Sandra tried to say no, but Bee persisted. "Oh, come on! Don't be such a buzzkill!"

Nobody said no to Bailey.

"Okay, but my parents can't find out."

A low male voice came from the side of the house. "Yo!"

Sandra bounced over to Zac, who looked particularly preppy in a white polo and khaki shorts. "My parents can't know Zac was here tonight, either," she said. "That's why we drove separately. They'd flip if they knew I was at a party with a boy."

"I'm down with that!" Bee's eyes glowed.

Buzzed on booze and youth, we cheersed and then cheersed again, feeling totally grown-up with the house to ourselves, the warmth of the fire sparking beside us.

"Pictures!" I exclaimed.

I got out the disposable camera my mom had left and handed it to Zac while Sandra, Bee, and I posed on the beach, the glittering lake lit by the setting sun and the sparking bonfire our backdrop. We wrapped our arms around each other, our white teeth flashing against tanned skin, waving the bracelets on our wrists in the air.

I cranked up my mix tape on the boom box. I'd spent hours all week listening to the radio with both fingers hovering above the "Record" and "Play" buttons, just waiting to capture my favorite songs for this party. The Cure and New Order, Depeche Mode and R.E.M., even a little Nirvana, TLC, and Madonna.

I was so happy to see Bee being nice to Sandra, and happier still to see that Sandra seemed to have forgiven her. The alcohol slid cool and refreshing down our throats, and we got drunker and drunker. I was so drunk, I almost didn't notice when Bee grabbed a canvas bag and slipped inside the house.

Almost, but not quite.

We drank under a sunburned sky while planes wrote tracks above us. Sandra found a string along the water's edge, and we played cat's cradle until we realized we couldn't get our fingers to work properly, laughing uproariously as we became entangled in our mistakes. Then we talked about music and movies and our plans for college. At some point, Bee jumped up and twisted the boom box volume all the way up, insisting we all dance. I was so drunk by that point, I didn't even argue. Sandra was even worse, tripping over her own feet and tumbling to the ground in a heap of giggles.

We pulled her back up and kept dancing, Bee and Sandra and I, whirling and grinning and spinning, best friends forever, with the newly formed stars wheeling overhead. Soon moonlight had replaced the sun, and velvety darkness deepened over the lake.

At some point, Bailey's bracelet fell off, and Sandra fell over trying to retrieve it. She knelt and tried to snap it back on Bailey's wrist. "Will you marry me, my lady?" she slurred, giggling uncontrollably.

"Here comes the bride . . . ," Bailey sang, managing to get the clasp to snap back in place.

Sandra announced she had to pee, so I went inside with her and grabbed another bag of ice. Sandra was still in the bathroom, so I headed back outside. As I rounded the corner, I saw Bee sitting next to Zac on the picnic blanket, her arm brushing against his. They shifted apart as I approached, but not before I saw Bee drop something into his hand.

I tried to push aside what I'd seen. Everything was going so well, and I didn't want to ruin it by accusing Bee of anything. And so I kept drinking.

I remember the crackling of the fire as it hissed and spat. I remember the thumping strains of "Rhythm Is a Dancer," our limbs moving to the beat. I remember the scent of suntan lotion and cherry ChapStick and the hot feel of skin on mine. Only later did I remember the strange, satisfied smile on Bee's face, the glint in her eyes as she watched Sandra dance.

And then Bee and I were alone, stretched out on the picnic blanket side by side, staring at the swirling stars above us. The trees spun around me, gyrating silhouettes in the darkening sky. My eyes were so heavy, I could barely keep them open.

"Where's Sandra?" I slurred.

"Who cares?" Bee said indifferently.

Catching my surprised look, she softened. "She probably just went to pee."

I stared up at the whirling stars, the silence expanding between us. The tension felt as thick as the velvet night sky. All I wanted was to regain the chill vibe from before.

"Is your bracelet broken?" I changed the subject, watching as Bailey fiddled with the clasp.

"I think it's just loose. Whatever, I have an extra one from the pack."

"Can you believe next time we see each other, we'll have graduated?"

"Thank God!" she exclaimed. "I can't wait to bounce."

I wanted to ask her why she hated it here so much, but I was too drunk; I couldn't get my words to string together properly.

And then it was too late. There was shouting from the house, and Zac was running down the hill toward us, his eyes wild.

"Help! I don't know what to do!"

Bailey and I ran after him, our feet clattering against the wooden stairs as we ran into the basement. The light was too dim to really understand what I was seeing.

"Oh my God!" My hands flew to my mouth.

Sandra was lying facedown on the floor next to the coffee table, a small pool of black spreading out from her head.

"What happened?" Adrenaline made me suddenly very sober.

"We were . . ." Zac swallowed hard. "Going to, you know, and she, like, I don't know, freaked out, and she tried to run away, and she tripped. I think her head hit the table. Look . . ."

He touched Sandra's head, and his fingers came away covered with blood. Bailey dropped down next to Sandra. She pressed her fingers to Sandra's neck, then raised wide eyes to mine.

"She's dead."

Time seemed to stretch and thin. I stood, frozen, my legs rooted like tree stumps to the floor. I started shivering, my teeth clattering.

"No." I shook my head. "No. Just . . . no."

Zac started crying. "My dad's gonna kill me."

I wanted to punch him. "You're such a selfish prick."

Zac spun to Bee. "This is your fault. What did you give her?"

Bee's eyes flashed. "You're the one who gave it to her!"

I looked between them. My brain couldn't seem to catch up. "I don't understand . . ."

"She drugged her!" Zac shouted, leveling a shaky finger at Bee.

"What the actual fuck, Zac. I just gave you what you asked for."

"It was only supposed to help her relax! It wasn't supposed to hurt her!" Zac wiped a hand over his sweaty face. "Dude, I'm not going down for this. This was all you, Bee."

"Don't be stupid," Bee said coldly. She stormed over to the bookshelves, moved aside a fake cactus, and pulled out a chunky camcorder, its light blinking green.

My mouth dropped. Bee had been recording them? I remembered what Zac had told me about that girl finding a video of Bee having sex with her history teacher. Maybe he hadn't been lying after all.

"Shall we watch what really happened? We all know you can get a bit rough when you're fucking people, Zac. Did she really trip?" Bee had turned accusatory. "Or did you attack her?"

Zac paled. "No, I swear . . . !"

"Bee . . . ," I whispered.

"Shut up, Neve," she snapped.

"We need to get help," I said, panicked. "We need to call 911."

"No." Bee's voice cracked like a whip. "We're underage and we've been drinking. If we call 911, we'll go to jail. She's dead. There's nothing we can do for her."

I shook my head frantically. "No, you're wrong. I'm calling an ambulance."

I moved toward the stairs, but Bee had stepped in front of me. I tried to push past her, but she dug her fingers into my arm and yanked me back.

"Let me go." I struggled against her frantically. Tears fell thick and fast. "Maybe there's still time to help her."

Bee gripped my shoulders, forcing me to look at her. "There isn't. I checked her pulse. She's dead, okay? We can't save her."

"We have to call the police!"

Bee's hand cracked against my cheek, snapping my neck backward. I gasped, shocked, my cheek stinging.

"Knock it off," she said. "We're not calling the police! I'm not going to jail!"

I stared at her, mouth hanging open.

Her mouth twisted into an ugly sneer. "You're not innocent here, either, Neve. The party's at your house. You're underage. What do you think your dad would say about what we've done? Your mom? Their precious little goody-goody throwing a drunken party where a girl ends up dead. At best, you're an accessory to murder."

Fear washed over me. I knew exactly what my dad would do. He would rant at me about the consequences of sin and tell me the horrors that awaited sinners like me. And then he would turn me in to the police himself.

"Stop it." Zac stepped between Bee and me. "We can't be fighting right now. None of us wants to go to jail for murder." He turned to me. "Bee's right. We can't save her, but we can save ourselves."

I pressed my fingertips into my temples, trying to think.

"Give me the tape," I said.

"Hell no!" Bee clasped the camcorder to her chest.

"We have to get rid of it. If anybody finds that—ever—we'll all go down."

Bee hesitated. Finally, she turned, setting the camcorder on the couch. I heard the machine click open; then she slammed the tape into my open palm.

I ripped it open and yanked at the tape, ribbons of shiny black tape unspooling into my hands. I shoved the tape into my pocket to throw in the lake later.

The scent of blood was making me nauseous, and suddenly I couldn't take it anymore. The alcohol rose up my throat and launched out of me, splattering onto the floor at my feet.

"Jesus Christ," Bee said in disgust.

"It was an accident," I whispered. I wiped my mouth with the back of my hand. "What happened to Sandra. We can't leave her here."

"We'll take her somewhere else."

"That's not what I mean. We have to make it *look* like an accident."

Bee and Zac stared at me.

I straightened, swallowing a sob. "I think I have an idea."

We wrapped Sandra in a tarp I found in the boathouse and drove her car to Widow's Bend.

I felt like I was in a dream. A nightmare. I was stuck on a roller coaster that wouldn't stop. All the while, I cried, my body shivering with fear and horror despite the warmth of the summer night. Above us, stars twinkled impassively.

"Get her out of the tarp." Bee's voice was cold, impassive. I'd never seen this side of her before. She was in charge now.

We wrangled Sandra's body out of the car. She fell to the ground with a thump, one pale arm spilling out. Again, I fell to my knees, vomiting into the dust at the side of the road. Sweat dripped from me, even though I was ice-cold and shivering.

"For fuck's sake, pull it together," Bee snapped. "Hurry up. Before anybody drives past."

We unwrapped the tarp. She was completely limp, blood still seeping from her head, streaking down her throat and soaking into her tank top.

It took all three of us to lift Sandra again. Her body was horribly limp, sagging. We finally got her into the driver's seat. Zac bent over her, fumbling with the seat belt. Bee slapped at his hands, trying to get him away, but Zac was stronger. He snapped the seat belt into place.

The car's engine was still on. Bee leaned in the driver's window and put the car in drive.

"Help me push," she whispered.

We ran to the rear of the car and threw our backs against the fender.

I felt like I was out of my own body, somewhere high above, looking down, watching it all happen. The car picked up speed, the slight downhill incline helping it move toward the blind edge that dropped into the water. And then the car was airborne, flying through the air.

Bee, Zac, and I moved to the ledge, the lake stretched before us like some sort of hulking arachnid, and watched as the car crashed nose first into the lake, sinking slowly beneath the still black waters.

And then we went back to Dullahan House and cleaned up Sandra's blood.

Chapter 41

Today I was setting Tweety free.

His wing was healed now. To be perfectly honest, it had been healed for a few days. He'd been practicing flying around my room and was getting stronger every day. I just didn't want to face letting him go. But it was time.

I know Tweety is just a bird, but he'd been more than that to me these last few weeks. He'd been company and friendship and something to make the solitary nights less lonely. There was something comforting about sitting in the dark and knowing you weren't alone.

I took the cat carrier to the park and set it down near a copse of woods. Over by the little pond, a family of ducks waddled past, Mommy, Daddy, and six little ducklings. Family. It's important. And in the short time he'd been with me, Tweety had become my family.

I reached inside the cat carrier, and Tweety hopped onto my fingers.

"Hey, Tweety," I said softly. "It's time for you to go find your bird friends. I'm sure they've been missing you."

He tilted his head at me, and I swear he knew what I was saying. I stroked a finger down his silky back. I was surprised he hadn't flown away already, but maybe he needed this goodbye as much as I did. Letting go could be the hardest thing, even when you knew it was the right thing. Sometimes we held on too tightly, crushing the delicate things we were trying to nurture.

"I loved you while I had you, but it's time to let you go."

A bird called in the distance, something bigger than Tweety. He turned his head. I lifted my arm, and Tweety took flight, soaring into the blue sky.

For a moment, I was blinded by the sun, Tweety just a black smudge, and then he was gone, disappearing into the halo of light.

I waited there under an old oak tree for a long time. I suppose a part of me hoped he would come back, which was ridiculous. He was a bird, not a dog. But hope could be a powerful force, destructive and useful in equal portions. I suppose hope was the thing that kept us going. The thing that made the broken-winged birds fly again.

I'd always felt abandoned by the people I cared for, often through no fault of their own, and I felt that same familiar twist now. It reminded me I had no one but myself. Myself and this plan I'd set in motion.

It was that plan that motivated me to get up. To get going.

It wasn't too long before I was watching from my hiding spot as the detective with the cane crossed the street to Dullahan House. She must be putting the pieces together by now. Not too long and everything would become clear.

I knew eventually the police would find Bailey's little cubbyhole. That's why I put the picture in there. I wanted the police, the town, the world, to know who Bailey really was.

How clever of her to hide everything at Neve's house. She had the keys, after all. But then Bailey was always clever. Just not clever enough.

I slid the binoculars into my backpack and turned to go, moving silently through the trees.

There was just one more thing left to do.

Chapter 42

JESS

"Please, Detective," Neve pleads. "I've told you the truth about what happened with Sandra. Now will you help me find Ash?"

I lift my eyebrows. Could she actually be that clueless? "Seriously? You've just admitted to being an accessory to murder. You know there's no statute of limitations on that, right?"

"Sandra didn't die."

I feel my mouth pop open in surprise. Is she lying? I need to find an old recorder and play the tape I found to get the whole unvarnished truth.

"Sandra was . . ." Neve's mouth turns down. "She was paralyzed from the waist down."

"From the car accident?"

Neve nods.

"That you caused."

"Yes." The word comes out as a whisper.

"All these years and you never told anyone?"

"Bailey had that video of me suggesting we do it. I would've gone to jail. I didn't have a choice!"

"You always have a choice."

"I . . ." Neve puts her hands over her face, pressing her fingertips into her eyes.

I notice her nails again, her smooth pink nails. They are so perfectly pristine, the exact same as they were the first day I met her.

"Nobody asked," Neve finally says. "My dad took us back to Boston the next day. I thought eventually a police officer would come to question me. I was planning on telling them everything then. Days passed, then weeks and months. The police, Sandra's family, everybody thought it was a drunk-driving accident. Nobody ever came. I only found out about . . . what happened later, when my mom told me she'd heard it from a friend."

"But you never told anyone *you* put her in the car? You and Bailey and Zac! She was paralyzed because of *you*!"

"Don't you ever find that some memories are so heavy they just . . . sink?" Neve asks quietly. "I couldn't undo it; you can't just erase your past. And so I let those memories sink rather than float. I forgot about them. I mean, I didn't forget, of course I didn't, I just, I put them in the same place where bad dreams go. I didn't let myself think about it. I couldn't change it, so I shoved it away, and I moved on. But it's haunted me every day of my life. I think some mistakes aren't forgivable. Maybe acceptance and regret are the closest I'll ever get."

I stare at her. Didn't I do exactly that with Isla's death? Store it away, fold it into a tiny box, and put it in the deepest, darkest corner of my mind? I cover what happened with booze and work rather than addressing the pain festering beneath the layers.

"I sent her a get-well card and a copy of that picture." Neve nods at the picture I'm still holding. "I wanted her to know I was thinking about her. But you're right, I never told the truth, and I should have. What we did, she was alive the whole time. It's almost worse than dying, isn't it?"

"Do you think Sandra killed Bailey?" I ask. "She'd certainly have a motive."

Christina McDonald

"I doubt it. I visited her. She's dying of cancer." Neve presses a hand to her head, like she's feeling dizzy. "Look, I just want to find Ash. She's innocent in all this."

I adjust my stance, trying to release some pressure from my leg. "I'll look for your daughter."

"Promise me." Neve grabs my hand. Her fingers are cold, bony. She's squeezing me too tight, bending my fingers in strange ways.

I try to step back, but Neve won't release my hand. Her eyes burn into mine.

"Promise me you'll look for her. Something's wrong." Neve taps her chest. "I feel it."

"I promise I'll look for your daughter. But first you need to tell me what happened with Bailey. The truth, okay? Did you kill her?"

Neve releases my hand. I fight the urge to shake it, to release some of the blood.

"I swear, I didn't kill Bailey."

"Why did you call Bailey from your mother's care home?"

"What do you mean?"

"I checked Bailey Nelson's cell phone call log, and someone called her from the nursing home where your mother lives. I confirmed with reception that your mother is mostly nonverbal. Who else would've called her from there?"

"I have no idea. I visited my mom on Wednesday, but before that, it was months before I'd been there. They have a calling station for residents, but I've never used any of their phones to make a call." Her eyes drop to the shoebox at my feet. "One thing I *do* know. Bailey always liked recording things. It was a . . . hobby, I guess you could call it."

I narrow my eyes. "Explain."

Neve sighs. "It was just this weird thing she did. Maybe it was for power? She liked sleeping with powerful people, and she liked feeling powerful. She liked it when people owed her. When she *owned* them. I don't know, I just . . ." She shrugs and looks away. "I remember her recording people having sex."

The bleat of my cell phone blasts through the quiet room.

"Jess?" Will's voice is low and tense. "Where have you been? Rivero's looking for you. He knows you're out there working the case, and he's pissed."

"Never mind him," I say, my words almost tripping over each other. "I found something at Neve Maguire's house."

There's a thick, heavy silence on the other end of the phone.

"Remember Bailey Nelson's neighbor?" I prompt his memory. "She was one of our witnesses. Anyway, Bailey was the property manager of her house, so she had the keys . . ."

My eyes dart to Neve. I tilt the phone away from the other woman, trying for a little privacy, and lower my voice.

"I found a box of SD cards and video recordings that Bailey hid at Neve's house. Neve says Bailey liked to record herself having sex with powerful people."

"Jess, wait—" Will tries to interrupt, but I'm on a roll.

"We need Tech to go through these videos. There could be something in one of them. Also, can you look up what happened to a woman called Sandra Baker? She used to live in Black Lake. I'll explain more later."

"Whoa, Jess, what do you—"

Will's voice is cut off as someone grabs the phone. "Detective Lambert." It's Rivero, and he sounds pissed.

"Oh, hey, Lieutenant, what's up?" I say, my voice casual. "I've got a lead on—"

"You disobeyed a direct order, Detective." Rivero's voice is edged with ice. "You're officially on desk duty."

"No, wait, Lieutenant, I—"

"I don't want to hear it. I expect to see you back at your desk within the hour or I'll make sure you're filing crime reports for the rest of your career."

"Lieu—"

But he is no longer on the phone.

"Jess?" It's Will, his voice pleading. "Come back to the station. Please. We need to talk."

"I can't." I lower my voice even more. "Not yet. I think I might be about to crack this case. I'll come in once I've finished speaking to Neve."

And then something occurs to me. I press my phone to my chest and turn to Neve. "How did you know Bailey liked recording . . . ," I begin.

But Neve is no longer there.

I stare stupidly at the place she was just standing. I'd been so focused on my phone call, I hadn't even heard her leave.

"Will, I'll call you back in a sec."

I slide my phone back into my pocket. I know I'll never be able to catch Neve, not if she's running, but I have to try. I clutch the shoebox to my chest and hurry up the stairs, hauling my bad leg up each step as fast as I can. I grab my cane from the kitchen and turn to the front door, which is now wide open, spilling bright sunlight across the hallway.

Outside, I look up and down the street. But there is no sign of her. Neve Maguire is gone.

I dial Will.

"I lost her!" I shout, furious. "Neve Maguire was here, and I lost her! I need you to get a patrol car out to Dullahan House. We have to find her!"

"Jess, slow down. What are you talking about?"

"The witness I told you about. She was here. Neve Maguire was the one who told me about Sandra Baker. And what's on the SD cards. I think she might have killed Bailey Nelson."

"Did you say Neve Maguire?"

"Yeah, why?"

"Neve Maguire Bennett?"

"Maybe," I admit, remembering Neve's mother's name is Holly Maguire. "She said she's separated from her husband, so Maguire could be her maiden name. I . . . I should've checked, but she wasn't a suspect."

There's a long pause. "Jess, that other body in Boston, the one with the same MO as Bailey Nelson? It's been identified as Neve Maguire Bennett."

Will's voice has gone impossibly soft, gentle, as if he's talking to a skittish puppy.

Or a woman who's gone stark raving mad.

"But . . . I don't, I don't understand. She was h-here, Will," I stammer as a cold horror washes over me.

"I'm sorry, but that's not possible," Will says. "She couldn't have been there with you, Jess. Neve Maguire's been dead for more than a week."

Chapter 43

NEVE

I'm running and tripping, my legs flying under my body, so fast it almost seems I am floating. And then I am, my body filled with a sensation like helium, my feet somehow hovering, gliding above the ground, which is black and coated with mist beneath me.

Black sky. Air on bare skin. Hissing breath. A scream. Then blood. Always blood.

I'm home, sitting across from Ash in our dining room.

Boom. The sound of the front door splintering.

And then a figure dressed entirely in black is in the dining room doorway.

"Run!" I scream at Ash.

She bolts for the closest door, the door to the garage, as I grab a steak knife. Wooden-handled. Sharp, serrated teeth. I slash it out, like I'm fencing, and it slices through skin and sinew.

I am running, my hands covered in blood.

The only thing on my mind is Ash. I have to protect her.

I follow her, my feet *thud, thudding,* past the neatly trimmed rhododendron bushes to the back steps, where I see Ash's feet disappearing beneath a loose plank under the deck. I follow her, and we crouch in the small space. It smells of mold, the damp dirt tickling my nose. We tremble in each other's arms as dust shakes loose above us. Electric shocks of fear spark in my chest. The stairs creak, footsteps slowly descending. They get closer. And closer.

And then the hooded figure is there, eye level with us, raising what looks like a gun.

Hot panic sears through my veins. I don't stop to think. In a moment of blind panic, I lunge, claws out, teeth bared. No way is this stranger going to hurt my child. I throw the full weight of my body at him, pummel him with my fists, biting, scratching, kicking. He falls back with a grunt but manages to keep the gun in his hand.

I rip at his hood, snagging a corner between my fingers, and get my first full view of his face.

But he isn't a he. He is a she.

Something is jangling in my mind, but I don't have time to acknowledge it, because the woman staggers to her feet, and once again, she is lifting the gun, pointing it at me, an antique, black-handled, needle-nosed gun.

Again, that jangling. I recognize the gun, but from where?

I don't have time to grasp the threads of whatever is nagging at me, because the woman is squeezing the trigger. I close my eyes. There is nowhere to go, nowhere to run. I have lost. I wait for her to pull the trigger. But a strange clicking sound comes from the gun. It's jammed.

With a shriek of fury, the woman slams the gun to the ground and leaps on me. She pulls me down, wrapping her fingers around my throat. I hit the ground with a stunned *oomph*, trying to twist out of her grasp. But she's too strong. Her fingers are like bands of steel pressing on the tender skin at my throat.

My lungs burn. Stars begin to dance across my vision.

I hear Ash screaming my name from across the lawn. We lock eyes. I've never seen someone so terrified. It makes my insides twist and coil. I want to tell her to run. To save herself. But I can't move, my mouth flopping open and closed like a guppy. Light and shadow dance in and out of my vision, one big, distorted blur.

Crack.

The other woman falls to the ground with a grunt. Cool, fresh air gushes into my lungs. I drag in greedy, panicked gulps as I lurch to my feet, trying to get my bearings. Ash is holding a large rock in her hand, but the woman is already rising to her feet, barely fazed by the blow. She slides something open in the gun, swipes at whatever is stuck, and relatches it. She does all this with calm determination, her face expressionless. Her hands aren't even shaking.

With the last bit of breath in my lungs, I scream at Ash: *"Ruuuun!"*

Once again, we're both fleeing, this time for the low retaining wall at the back of the yard that separates our property from the woods beyond. I don't dare look behind me, but I know the woman is coming. And then I hear a deafening crack.

I duck and from my peripheral vision see Ash stumble and fall. But I don't have time to go to her because the other woman has turned the gun on me. I launch myself at the retaining wall, scrambling over and dropping into the woods. I must draw her away from Ash.

My ankle buckles, and I fall hard, crumpling into a ball. Pain shoots up my leg, and tears spring into my eyes, but adrenaline powers me on. I scramble back to my feet and dive into the shadowy forest.

I half run, half limp, my feet crunching over sticks and twigs. My heart is throbbing, my ankle hurting so much that I'm crying as I run, white stars of pain shooting up my leg. All I can hear is the roar of blood pounding in my ears and my own ragged breath. I plow into the undergrowth, searching for a track, somewhere to go that will lead me to safety.

Sticks and stones assault my bare feet, brambles and thorns and sharp twigs slashing at my exposed skin. I push through a copse of bushes, and a low branch I didn't see thwacks me in the head, sending me to my knees. Pain blasts through me, and I cry out, tears pouring from my eyes. But again, I get back up. I keep running, careening, arms out in front of me.

Behind me is a rustling, snapping sound. The woman is close. I can hear her jagged breathing cut through the darkness.

I feel fingers whisper past my hair. I duck, but I catch a root and stumble. And then there is a yank, and pain explodes in my scalp. My neck snaps backward, and I slam into a tree, my temple cracking against its unforgiving trunk with a sickening smack.

I feel my scalp split open, skin peeling away from bone. My teeth bite into the soft flesh of my cheek, and blood gushes into my mouth. The earth rises up to embrace me, dirt and blood filling my mouth. I try to get up, but the woman is there, a swift kick to my stomach laying me flat on my back.

She climbs on top of me, her face warped, misshapen in the dark. Her breath is heavy, her eyes cold and dead. I struggle, but she grabs my shoulders, and I feel my head lift up, up, and then smash down.

There is a horrific crack as my skull slams into something hard, a rock or the root of a tree. My vision goes fuzzy with pain, but I don't stop fighting, my fingers clawing at her arms, great chunks of skin wedging under my fingernails.

Crack.

Another explosion of light and pain as she again slams my head down. This time, everything goes black, and my body sags. Instinct causes me to let go of her forearms, my hands going to my head. Blood, hot and sticky, warms my fingertips.

I stare, stunned, up at the bony limbs of the trees above. Blood trickles from my temple into my hair like tears. She wraps her fingers around my throat, a bony prison. Sweat is pouring from her body, her lips twisted into a sneer, her eyes black with menace.

She bends close to my ear, her breath hot and rancid against my skin. "I know what you did," she hisses. "This is all your fault."

I pluck at her hands, but my head is too thick, my movements too stunted. My vision is blurring, specks of light gathering at the edges of my vision. Her fingers tighten even more around my throat, her eyes burning on mine. I try to claw at her fingers, but she is too strong, my body too starved for oxygen. I can feel my eyelids begin to flutter, my fingertips going numb.

Above me, I see leaves whirling through the air, like birds or butterflies or angels. There is a deafening roaring in my head, the sound of a thousand wings beating, pulsing. I gasp, but no air comes in. My hands have stopped grasping at hers. There seems to be a disconnect between them and my body. A rushing sound fills my ears, and my eyes close. I can't fight it anymore. My body goes still as the cold seeps in.

I'm dying.

Blackness rises in me like a tide, and then I'm spinning, twirling with the leaves, and the ground becomes the sky and the sky becomes the ground and I'm floating, hovering above my body, as if it has been filled with helium, watching as she squeezes the last drop of life from me.

"You had a choice," she whispers. "You chose wrong."

My eyes collide with hers, and suddenly she smiles, the most menacing smile I have ever seen. I stare, transfixed by the fury, the menace there, into those pale ice-gray eyes, and everything clicks into place.

I know exactly who she is.

But it doesn't matter now. It's too late.

White-hot pain is burning me up, turning my words to ash. I'm so tired. All I want to do is go to sleep.

It almost feels like a relief to close my eyes.

Chapter 44

I killed Neve first.

Before I killed Bailey, that is.

Because Neve was my first, she was also the most educational, since absolutely nothing went the way I'd planned.

For one, I didn't expect her to stab me. Fortunately, I had the training, the tools, and the medication necessary to tend the wound. I've always had a high tolerance for pain, but it certainly surprised me.

For another, I never meant to use the gun. I took it from storage, from an old metal box I found it buried in. I didn't even know it was loaded. It was ancient, clearly an antique. How was I to know? I only brought it to threaten Neve, to force her to walk to the place I'd prepared in the forest.

It was never my intention to hurt the girl—she was innocent. Neve's daughter and husband weren't even supposed to be there. Only Neve. And I never meant for the girl to see my face. That was a problem I was going to have to fix.

After Neve, I knew to plan for extenuating circumstances better. You know what they say about the best-laid plans. That's why I brought the drug for Bailey. I swiped it from the medicine cabinet at work. I wanted to make sure she was subdued properly. Honestly, it was a lot more fun to carve my message onto her tongue when she was alive. Neve was already dead by the time I managed to do hers.

I wasn't even sure I should do it. I knew the police would arrive soon, and I had to get her body to the place I'd prepared. But it was important in order to relay my message.

And now the truth was permanently on their tongues.

We are all bad in someone's story, but aren't those who choose to be blind when they should see, who choose to be silent when they should speak, aren't they the real villains?

Bailey was a narcissistic monster who used and extorted and ruined people for fun. And Neve. Practically perfect PTA meeting, stupid husband, nice house, great career *Neve. She spent her life being a fraud. A cheating, traitorous slut who pretended she was a good person.*

I told her I was coming for her. Those dildos were more than just a warning. More than a threat. I wanted her to know I was going to fuck her the way she'd fucked me.

After I killed Neve, I dragged her body through the forest to a tree that had been cleaved in half when it was struck by lightning. The roots were exposed, the stump lifted to a forty-five-degree angle, a three-foot hole hollowed under it. I rolled her inside and poured bear urine around the hole to disguise any decomposing scents. It wouldn't work forever, but it would delay things a bit. That was all I needed.

I was under no illusion that their blood would bring back what was lost. But I did what needed to be done in order to right a lifetime of wrongs.

They should have been honest about what they did. They had a choice. They chose wrong.

And some things can never be forgiven.

Chapter 45

JESS

The phone slips from my fingers, slamming into the pavement with a crack.

Neve Maguire is dead.

Will's words send everything spinning, a great twist of colors and textures and sounds.

"Jess? You there?"

I stare at the phone as my knees give out, and I sink down onto the step, my mind a blur of chaos. I reach for my phone with shaking fingers. I minimize my call with Will, open Google, and search for Neve Maguire Bennett. The results spool onto my phone.

Local Vet Missing After Horrific Home Invasion.

The Search For Neve Bennett Nears Week Mark.

Beloved Vet Found Dead In Woods.

The proof is right here. Neve Maguire is dead. I stare at her smiling picture, her face already familiar. It's the same woman I interviewed the day we found Bailey Nelson's body. The same woman I was talking to at Sammy's only a few nights ago. The same woman inside Dullahan House just now who told me what happened to Sandra Baker.

Neve Maguire.

"If she's dead, who the hell have I been talking to, then?" I ask out loud.

And the thing I don't say out loud: *Am I losing my mind?*

"Jess. Are you there?" Will's voice comes from very far away.

My heart is throbbing, a thudding pulse of adrenaline. Across the street, Vivienne stands on her front lawn, watching me, a look of concern on her face.

I dig my fingers into my temples. Around me, whispers ride the hot summer breeze, speaking of their sorrows and losses, their births and deaths, their trials and tribulations.

"This can't be happening," I mutter.

"Jess? Are you okay?" Will's voice cuts through the whispers. "Where are you?"

But I can't answer. The whispers are rising like butterflies ascending into the air. I'm too stunned to do anything but listen.

"Stay there!"

And then the line goes dead.

The whispers turn into a cacophony of sound. And then I hear the sound of a child laughing. Or maybe crying. It's too far away, too faint for me to be sure.

"You can still save her."

My head jerks up. Isla is standing in front of me, the satin bow on her pink Hello Kitty headband waving in the breeze. I struggle to stand, leaning heavily on my cane. I reach out a hand to touch Isla, but the harder I reach, the farther away Isla moves, as if a giant vacuum is behind her, sucking her away.

"Isla. Baby." I'm crying now, tears streaking down my hot cheeks. I don't understand what's happening, what's wrong with me. "Are you dead? Am I going crazy?"

Isla smiles, but it's a sad smile, a smile that holds all the memories of our life together, mother and daughter, joy and pain, sorrow and love. I try to touch her, but again Isla seems to drift farther away.

"I want . . . I want . . ." I can't stop crying, the sobs hitching in my chest. I'm having a breakdown right here in public, and there's nothing I can do about it.

"I love you, Mommy," Isla says. "But you can't save me now. You can only save her."

"Who?"

"The girl who lived."

"I don't understand." I turn to look over my shoulder, trying to see if Isla sees something I don't.

But when I turn around again, Isla is gone.

"Isla!" I wail, a single note of sadness and anger and pain, everything I've holed up inside me.

I fall to my knees on the ground, my forehead touching the gravel as I weep. Sharp bits of rock press into my skin, my hands, my face, ripping at my jeans. The air is hot, heavy with humidity. My T-shirt clings to my skin, my forehead damp with moisture. A great darkness pulls at me.

Soft arms surround me, the scent of lavender and coffee swirling around me.

"Oh, honey, come here. It's gonna be okay." Vivienne pulls me close, but I can't accept what she's offering.

"The bar," I murmur. "The bar."

I sound like a lunatic. Or maybe just an alcoholic, which I am, but that isn't why I need to go to the bar right now.

I want to tell Vivienne that, but I can't seem to get my thoughts to coalesce, can't verbalize what I want or need in the wake of this shock. I pull away and struggle to my feet. My whole body pulses with tension and fear, a dark swirl starting deep in my core.

"I'm sorry." The words come out in a hollow, gasping whoosh, tasting dry on my tongue.

My head is spinning. Whatever I do now, whatever I don't do, everybody will know that Jessica Lambert isn't right in the head.

I back away, stumbling across the lawn. I feel like I'm losing my grasp on reality. I have to get to the bar. Have to look at that security footage.

There has to be a reasonable explanation. An evil twin or someone who looked a lot like Neve Maguire. I wasn't just talking to the air. I couldn't be.

I climb on my motorcycle. The roar of the engine grounds me. I pop the clutch and take off. The wind rushing over my skin feels good. Soothing. I turn out of the gates and gun it, pushing the bike even faster. I slow for Widow's Bend, remembering what Neve told me, but there's no evidence here, only the solid wall delineating the past.

I arrive at Sammy's within minutes. The bar isn't open at this time in the morning, so I climb the rickety wooden stairs that hug the side of the building and hammer my fist against his upstairs apartment.

Sammy yanks the door open, his face barely registering surprise at seeing a haggard, crazed woman on his doorstep. He leans against the doorframe, holding a large mug that says KEEP CALM AND DRINK GREEN TEA. He's wearing tight spandex pants and a breathable mesh tank, his wild gray hair tied back in a neat ponytail. I can see a yoga video playing on the TV in the background.

"You have security cameras in the bar downstairs, right?" I skip the pleasantries.

Sammy nods. "Yeah, of course."

"I need to see Wednesday night's. Do you still have it?"

"Sure."

Sammy doesn't even ask for a reason. He seems to understand it's important. He leads me downstairs and unlocks the bar, then we move through the dim room to the office at the back of the kitchen. I follow, body vibrating with tension. He powers up the ancient old brick of a computer, and we wait in silence while it boots up. I want to scream. Why isn't it turning on?

Sammy logs in and navigates to the security cameras from Wednesday. He motions for me to sit down. The chair gives a rusty squeak, protesting against my weight.

Sammy offers coffee, but I decline, too keyed up to add caffeine to the mix. He disappears into the kitchen anyway as I fast-forward through the footage.

I watch as the day moves on high speed, customers coming and going, Sammy serving food, people talking and laughing.

And then there it is.

I watch myself limp through the bar's doors at 9:47 p.m. The camera is positioned over the front door and trained on the bar, but I'm clearly in frame. I order at the bar and sit at my usual booth in the back. Sammy brings me my drink and a burger. I pick at it. Keep drinking by myself for another half hour.

At 10:19 p.m., my body language changes. I watch on the screen as I lean forward slightly, my mouth moving, as if I'm talking to someone. I can see my colleagues, who are sitting near the front of the bar, watching me. They're whispering to each other, darting furtive looks at me.

Mei approaches, and I speak to her. I remember I ordered two drinks. Mei's gaze moves to the empty spot across from me, a confused expression on her face. After a minute, she returns with both drinks, placing them in the center of the table. On-screen Jess takes a swig, then pulls a 3x5 photo from the inside of her leather jacket and passes it across the table.

But no one is there to grab it.

Because no one had been there at all.

I watch as the photo flutters like a broken feather onto the table. I can practically hear Neve's voice in my ear, that soft, whispery lilt.

"You don't believe in ghosts?" Neve asked.

"No. I don't believe in ghosts or bogeymen or apparitions. Just bad people who do bad things. You?"

"I don't know. Maybe it isn't the dead who haunt the living but the living who do the haunting. Or maybe we haunt ourselves. Like, we're haunted by our pasts, by our mistakes, the ones that aren't so easily forgiven."

And that's when I know. I feel it in my gut, like a sixth sense or a preternatural ability to know something before it happens.

These aren't just grief hallucinations.

I'm seeing the ghosts of people who once walked the earth and died needlessly, senselessly, too soon.

My eyes have gone hot and dry. I want to cry, but the tears are jammed in my throat, too hard and too big.

The chair squeals in protest when I stand, launching myself out the back door into the alley. I only just manage to make it outside in time to fall to my knees and spew yellow bile onto the hot black asphalt. The world wobbles and tips, and I puke again and again until I'm spent and light-headed.

Isla. Neve. The dead want something. They want something from *me*.

But why? I'd never even met Neve Maguire. Bennett. Whatever. What did she want from me?

I sit with my back against the building, staring at the grimy alley. I pull out my phone and look up the date Neve went missing. I calculate back to the first day I met her, when Bailey Nelson's body was found. Neve was already dead then.

I rub my forehead, my eyes on the little white clapboard church down the narrow alley and across the road. Something snags in my mind, my eyes coming to rest on the large white sign standing at the front of the church.

"COME TO ME . . . AND I WILL GIVE YOU REST. –MATTHEW 11.28."

Something is stirring, a thought that's growing.

Matthew 11:28.

I navigate to my email and open one of the photos from Bailey Nelson's autopsy. There, carved onto her tongue: M1237.

My mind is whirling. The thought grows, pulling at the edge of my mind, becoming solid and taking shape.

What if M1237 is Matthew 12:37?

I google the passage.

"For by thy words thou shalt be justified, and by thy words thou shalt be condemned."

I exhale, stunned.

There's a *whoop, whoop*, and a police car turns in to the parking lot with a squeal of brakes. I hear the crunch of shoes against gravel and then Will calling my name.

I think about hiding. How can I face him?

Neve Maguire had been dead for over a week, and I've been having conversations with her. With a dead woman. There's no way he'll believe me. He'll think I've lost the plot.

He comes around the corner then, his pink face shiny with sweat. He hesitates when he sees me on the ground, a puddle of puke next to me.

"You all right, old girl?"

I look up at him, dazed. "I'm seeing ghosts."

Will raises his eyebrows but doesn't reply. Just sits on my other side—the side with no puke.

"Neve Maguire was there, at Dullahan House," I tell him. "She *grabbed my hand*. I felt her skin."

"But she's dead."

"I know! I can't explain it, Will. It makes no sense. Maybe something shook loose in my head after the accident or, or, or I have a tumor. I've made an appointment for an MRI. I don't know! But I *do* see Isla, and I *do* see Neve. I know I sound crazy, but I see them. Please believe me. They're real, and they're telling me something."

I tell him about my nights with Isla, about holding her and tucking her into bed only a few nights ago, and about Neve telling me what happened when she and Bailey and Sandra were teenagers.

"There's no way I would know these things unless somebody told me."

Will takes in everything in silence.

"Go ahead, say it!" I cry. "Tell me I'm insane. Or that they're just grief hallucinations, like my shrink keeps saying. Tell me I need to go on meds."

But Will just shakes his head. "I know you've been through a lot, but I don't think you're crazy."

"Do you think I'm seeing ghosts?" I drag an arm across my hot, damp eyes.

"I mean, how the hell do I know what's possible or not? Just because I haven't seen something doesn't mean it doesn't exist. And maybe, Jess, maybe you're seeing Neve because you *need* to see her. Maybe the accident, the trauma, it's opened you up to her. A way to . . . I don't know, make up for what happened. But only you can know what exactly that is."

"I need to see where Neve Maguire was killed," I say. "Maybe there's something there . . . something she wants me to see."

"Uh-uh, no way." Will shakes his head fiercely. "Rivero will kill you. You're already on desk duty. You wanna get fired?"

"I have to. Please, Will. Neve doesn't know she's dead, but I bet she knows the person who killed her. I bet it's the same person who killed Bailey Nelson. You said it was the same MO. Did Neve have something carved into her tongue, too?"

Will hesitates, but I can see the truth in his eyes. I read the Bible verse on my phone out loud for him.

"*For by thy words thou shalt be justified, and by thy words thou shalt be condemned.* Matthew 12:37. I think it's M1237. Bailey Nelson and Neve Maguire must've said something. Something to do with what happened to that other girl, Sandra. *That's* why they were killed. *That's* why the killer left that message."

Will looks thoughtful. He takes his glasses off, polishes them on his shirt, then puts them back on. "Or didn't say something."

"What?"

"Maybe they didn't say something. Maybe they kept the secret about what happened to Sandra when they shouldn't have. Maybe nobody ever found out what really happened to Sandra, and that's why they were condemned."

The truth of what he's saying leaves me momentarily breathless. "Will, you're a goddamn genius. Bailey and Neve, they didn't speak up. That's why they were murdered. The killer must be someone connected to Sandra. Her mother or maybe her father. We need to find out more about them. Come on—we can find their killer. We can finish this. Just let me help."

Will hesitates, mopping a hand over his sweaty brow.

My shoulders drop. "You don't believe me."

The sun dips behind a bank of clouds, a sudden coolness trickling into the air and drying the sweat on my skin. I shiver.

Will holds my gaze. After a moment, he releases a long breath. He nods, like he's made a decision. "I do believe you. Whatever's going on, you know something, and we can use that to help us find this killer. I'll take you to Neve Maguire's crime scene."

Will gets up, offers me a hand. "Come on. I'll drive."

I hesitate. I haven't been in a car since the accident. I take my motorcycle or walk. The thought of getting in Will's car terrifies me. Will catches my hesitation.

"I'll take you, Jess, but we're doing this my way. I'm trusting you; now you gotta trust me. You have to get in the car."

I know if I go with Will to the crime scene, there's a very good chance it's the end of my career. Rivero might fire me. Maybe he'll even fire Will. But I can't just sit here and do nothing.

It doesn't take me long to decide.

I get in the car. And as Will speeds out of the neighborhood, lights flashing, siren blaring, I don't look back.

Chapter 46

NEVE

Two years ago, a friend of Ash's died after a short illness. Ash struggled with it for a while. We even put her into counseling. One particularly sad day, I tried talking to her about her feelings, using all the trite words you say when you want to comfort someone you love, like "appreciate the moments you had" and "it's better to have loved and lost."

When I'd finished, she said, "Would you rather know the date of your death or the cause of your death?"

I thought about it for a moment. "I suppose the cause, so I could do whatever I could to avoid it."

"So you wouldn't want to die."

"No," I said quietly. "No, I wouldn't."

"Neither did Shay."

There was nothing really to say after that, so I just laced my fingers through hers and held her hand in silence for a very long time.

I'm thinking about that as I awaken.

The world around me is dark, like my eyes are shut even though they are wide open. And I am floating. It's like being in a sensory-deprivation tank. No sight. No sound. No senses. I know I am somewhere in between.

There is a ripple in the darkness, and it begins to lighten, showing a thick mist all around me. The mist tickles my ankles like feathers, cool and startling, little beads of moisture popping up on my skin.

I glance at my watch, wondering what time it is, but the hands are no longer moving.

"Hello?" I call out, but nobody is there.

My heart rushes with terror, but with that terror comes the sensation that my feet are again touching solid ground.

"Do you see now?"

I whirl at the sound of the voice. Behind me, half-obscured in the fog, is the girl I've been seeing. She has messy blonde braids and a pink Hello Kitty headband with a floppy satin bow. She has a high forehead, a heart-shaped face. Her blue eyes are sad.

A raw, soul-crunching pain, physical in its force, hits me, along with the sudden understanding.

"I'm dead," I whisper. The words feel like stones I'm trying to dislodge from my throat.

"I tried to tell you." The girl speaks quietly, matter-of-factly.

I bend at the waist, clasping my fingers to my knees as I take shallow breaths, my mind reeling. Because no one wants to wake up dead.

Those abrupt awakenings in strange places; arriving out of nowhere at Sandra's house; seeing Bailey, a woman who was already dead; waking on the floor in Ash's bedroom. And Ash's disappearances, how she sometimes looked like a glitch in a computer game. The way the sun never seemed to burn her skin. That sense that I was only half there, disconnected from everything.

It all makes a perfect, horrible sense now. The only ones who can see me are animals, the dead, or the dying.

"I didn't know," I whisper.

A discordant clang is sounding somewhere far away in the back of my brain.

But why? Why am I here? I never believed in ghosts or goblins or fairies. I never believed in heaven or hell, in purgatory or any of the fire and brimstone my dad used to thunder down on us. I cannot explain this. But there must be some reason I'm here.

Everything that happened the night of the home invasion comes rushing back then. I'd been suppressing it, my mind unable or unwilling to accept the truth. I wanted to pretend everything was going to be okay, denying every clue, every sign that would've pointed me to what I didn't want to see.

Denialitis, Ash called it.

Ash.

Suddenly, that discordant clang grows louder. A fist of panic slams hard and fast into my solar plexus. I whirl in the churning mist, searching for the girl.

"Where's Ash?" I cry out. "Is she okay?"

But the little girl is gone, and I'm alone again, the dark, whirling fog my only company. Fear is sharp on my tongue.

I have to find Ash. I need to make sure she's safe.

The thick fog is evaporating, sucking away into nothingness. There is a rushing sound in my ears, and I am running, sprinting as fast as I can. I don't know where I'm going, only that I need to find my daughter.

"Ash!" I scream. "Ash!"

But my voice is lost in the dense fog.

And then I can feel my shoes sinking into the grass at the back of the house, and there is Eli standing on the deck, elbows leaning on the wooden panels, his BADASS ARCHITECT mug of coffee in hand. He is staring out at the woods with such a look of despair on his face that I want to go to him, to take him in my arms and tell him everything will be okay.

I have this strange sense that I'm here and yet I'm not. Like I'm transcendent, disembodied. I'm in an alternate world that exists like an overlay draped around me, the way you feel when you wake from a dream that still clings to the edges of your soul.

I take a step toward Eli and then another one, quicker, as he starts to fade and recede. I feel like I'm moving back, away from him, or the lawn is stretching out farther in front of me. I start to run again, but my feet are so heavy now, like they're mired in cement. The faster I try to run, the farther away he moves. I need to reach Eli. I need to tell him where I am, to find Ash. To make sure she's safe. If I can just grab his hand, maybe everything will be okay. Everything will make sense. Maybe I will be able to drag myself out of this strange in-between and back into Eli's world, where I can . . .

My feet tangle beneath me, the world colliding and spinning, a dizzying array of colors twirling in the mist. I reach for the ground as it rushes up to greet me, trying to find something to grab on to.

It takes me a minute to reorient. I'm on my hands and knees in front of a hospital. Above, the sky is a gathering storm, clouds huddled like broken memories I cannot outrun. People are whirling past, traffic buzzing, horns honking, sirens wailing, wheelchairs zipping.

Eli is walking toward me. He's disheveled, wearing sweats and a wrinkled T-shirt. His shoulders hunch forward, his chin dropping almost to his chest. He looks like he's been crying, his eyes red-rimmed and swollen. He appears ten years older than the last time I saw him.

I scramble to my feet. "Eli!" I shout.

But he doesn't acknowledge me at all. He walks right past.

Tears prick my eyes. Of course he doesn't see me. I'm not here. But I'm here. It makes no sense.

I don't know what else to do except follow him.

The hospital is busy, a swirl of humanity: sick patients, worried family members, busy doctors, caring nurses. We walk through the waiting room, down a corridor, through a set of swinging doors, and up the stairs. Eli speaks quietly to a nurse sitting behind a mammoth desk with a panel of lights blinking and sparking behind her. She nods, and he steps around her, moving down the hall until he disappears into a room.

I follow slowly, not sure I want to see what's on the other side of the door.

When I enter, Eli is sitting on a chair next to a hospital bed. His head is bowed as though in prayer. There are beeping monitors and the whoosh of a ventilator. Various tubes and blinking machines. An EKG monitor displays a rapid but steady heartbeat. The ventilator wheezes as I step deeper into the room.

Eli is holding someone's hand, his head bent over theirs. He is speaking, low and urgent murmurs I cannot quite make out. I move hesitantly, afraid of what is coming, until I'm there, next to the bed.

I close my eyes because I don't want to see, I don't want to acknowledge what's right here in front of me. And yet I must. Because on that bed is Ash, my beautiful baby, her eyes closed, her head swathed in bandages. A tube runs down her throat, a needle in her wrist. A machine is breathing for her. She is impossibly skinny, her skin so pale, it's almost translucent.

I gasp, something so heavy and hot pressing on my chest, I can't breathe. "Ash."

"Hi, Mom."

I whirl, and there she is standing behind me, her back against the wall, one leg up. Ash is grinning, a hand on her hip in a way that is just so Ash.

"What . . . ?" I hurl myself across the room, throwing my arms around my daughter. I am shaking all over with relief.

"Oh, thank God! But how . . . ?" My gaze darts between Ash in the bed and Ash standing here next to me. I drop my voice to a whisper. "I don't understand."

"You don't have to lower your voice, Mom. No one can hear us."

I cross to the Ash lying quietly on the bed, surrounded by tubes and beeping machines. I run a hand over the soft fluff of her dark hair, feeling the shape of her beautiful head as I fight back a powerful rush of pain and heartbreak.

"How is this possible?"

"I don't know," Ash admits. "I'm not dead, but I'm not alive. I'm not really here, but I am. It makes no sense."

"This is why you said you don't have two weeks, isn't it?"

Ash nods. "It was the first day I came back here. I heard the doctor telling Dad I might not make it. He said all they could do was wait to see what happened when they tried to wake me up. I'm in an induced coma, I guess. To help my brain heal. But if it doesn't heal . . ."

"You might not wake up."

"Right, only . . ."

"Mr. Bennett?" The voice that interrupts is a smooth baritone. Ash and I turn to see a doctor in a white coat standing in the door. He's a stern-looking, straight-backed, elderly gentleman, completely bald, his head shaped like an egg. He has a stethoscope draped around his neck, and he's holding a file in his hand.

He looks at Eli expectantly. "Do you have a minute to step into my office?"

Eli brushes a hand over exhausted eyes but follows the doctor out of the room.

"I bet he has my tests," Ash tells me. "They took me for an MRI and CAT scan earlier."

"Can you feel . . . anything?"

Ash's forehead puckers. "I'm not in pain, if that's what you mean."

"Will you be okay?" I ask anxiously.

"Who knows?"

"How did this happen? How are you here?"

"At first, everything was a little fuzzy. Like a dream I couldn't quite remember, you know? The first thing I really remember clearly is being at Dullahan House. With you. I thought I'd just dreamed being in the hospital. But then we were swimming, remember? And for, like, a few seconds I wasn't there; I was here. I could hear the machines beeping, and Dad was talking to me. I knew I was in the hospital. But then it was like I blinked and I wasn't there anymore; I was in the lake again."

"That's terrifying."

"It was. I thought maybe it was stress. You'd talked about PTSD, so I thought I was freaking out about the home invasion. But then I started coming back here more, and things started getting clearer, less . . . dreamy, if that makes any sense. I think I started waking up more. I could feel Dad's hand, and I was almost able to squeeze it. I just . . . I don't know, Mom. I don't get it."

But I do. Every time Ash gets closer to death, she comes to me. When she is waking up, stepping closer to life, she returns here, to Eli. To her body.

"Who did this, Mom?" Ash asks. "Who did this to us? And why?"

I stare at her, images flickering through my mind. She doesn't remember. But I do.

And suddenly, I understand exactly why I'm still here.

To make sure Ash stays alive. I'm here to save my daughter.

Because I remember one thing with absolute clarity. Ash saw the face of our attacker. When Ash wakes up—and I can only allow myself to say *when*, not *if*—she will come back to finish the job. She will kill my daughter.

And somehow I have to stop her.

Chapter 47

JESS

Flashing lights and four hundred horsepower sure can get you places. We make it to Neve Maguire's house, located in an affluent suburb of Boston, in half the normal time.

It's a safe neighborhood. Pretty houses with rhododendrons. A cherry tree–lined street. Patches of green lawns, some with picket fences. The house we stop in front of is a navy clapboard with white shutters and a manicured yard, sandwiched between woodland and city. Crime-scene tape flutters out front.

The air is heavy, the sort of motionless, sluggish heat you feel on a late-August day when you're trapped inside a basement. Or a cell. But the weather is starting to change, gray clouds gathering, little rumbles of thunder releasing in the distance. Summer is breathing its last breath.

There are still a number of CSIs milling around the house.

"The body was found in the greenbelt behind the house just two days ago," Will murmurs. "Had been there over a week, they're estimating."

I follow him toward the backyard, ducking under the crime tape. A uniformed officer puts a hand up to stop us. We show our badges. He nods, and we slip past, down a side gate that's been propped open with a large rock. At the back of the yard is a low retaining wall that drops into the forest.

"Come on," Will says, jumping down and holding out his arms.

My face burns, but I let him help me over. It's not like I have a choice. It's too far for me to jump on my own.

We follow a narrow, trampled path that leads deep into the woodland. Someone came crashing through here. Footprints score the hardened dirt. Broken sticks and twigs and crumpled leaves lay scattered and bent, all pointing in the direction moving away from the house.

She was running away. Trying to escape? Or trying to draw the killer away from her daughter and husband?

"Greenbelt's about a mile deep," Will says. "A few miles wide. Woodland and walking trails. Not much else."

We walk about ten minutes or so. It might've taken less, but my limp slows us down. Will doesn't say a thing, his eyes just scanning, scanning.

The woods release that thick, warm smell of rotting vegetation and organic debris decomposing in the summer. The wind rustles in the trees above, giant gray clouds darkening the sky and bringing a welcome thread of coolness to the air. Thunder cracks, closer now. By the time we reach the crime scene, fat drops have started to fall, dashing between the leaves and thudding against the dry earth.

Finally, we burst through the thick overgrowth and reach what we've been looking for. Shredded police tape still flaps from little flags that were stabbed into the hard earth.

"They found her in there." Will points at a massive tree that had once upon a time been struck by lightning.

I use my phone's flashlight to get a better look at the tree. The smoky beam of light illuminates a trunk and roots that have been ripped right out of the ground. The roots hang in the air at a forty-five-degree angle, a narrow, three-foot-deep hole hollowed into the ground beneath.

"It isn't far from the house," I say. "How'd they miss her?"

"Nobody saw her body there when the first search party came through. It took a few days before they could send the cadaver dogs out, but even then, the dogs missed her, too. One of the CSIs said bear urine had been dumped around the area, which probably threw the dogs off the scent. They found her the second time they sent the dogs out. I reckon the bear urine had faded by then."

Sweat gathers in my armpits. The air is thick and humid.

"They found nearly a dozen threatening text messages on her phone."

"What'd they say?"

He takes out a notepad from his pocket and reads.

I know what you did. But what goes around comes around. There will be consequences.

You won't get away with it.

You're going to rot in hell, Neve.

"All in that same vein."

I pace the area, moving between disturbed shrubs and trees, trying to make each piece fit into the puzzle I'm constructing in my head. But it's like someone has combined a dozen puzzles and shaken them together. I can't make sense of anything.

Something darts in my peripheral vision, a form or a shadow. Or maybe it's just the wind, the strange way it's blowing, hot and cold at the same time. Whatever it is slips away into the trees, there and then gone.

"Someone called Bailey from Neve's mother's care home last month," I murmur.

"Maybe it was Neve?" Will says.

"She said it wasn't."

"Neve's mother?"

"She's nonverbal. Alzheimer's."

"There must be a connection. Maybe the killer lives there, too, but that doesn't make sense if it's a home for Alzheimer's patients."

I snap my fingers as something connects. "Maybe the killer *works* there. That would give her access to the drug. I'm not a doctor, but I'd bet some dementia patients are given sedatives."

"It makes sense," Will admits. "But why care for the mother of the person you want to kill?"

I shake my head. I don't know.

There it is again, that shadow. I turn, the light from my phone glinting like fire, darting between the branches of the trees.

"Hello? Neve?"

Something flickers over Will's face. Worry? Or fear? I don't allow myself to dwell on it for long.

"Neve?" I say again.

I don't know how this works, so I hold still, calling for Neve in my mind. The trees are rushing around us now, a storm of tattered leaves and hurling wind. I stand still, letting the scent of rotting vegetation fill my nose, the wind ripple over my bare arms. A raindrop pings off my hot skin. Thunder rumbles.

But nothing happens.

In frustration, I stomp a dead leaf with my cane. The clock is ticking; I can feel it. I just don't know what exactly it's ticking down to. Something niggles at the back of my mind, a fingernail scraping away at the corners of my subconscious.

Where is Neve? I feel strangely disappointed she hasn't arrived. What did I expect? That Neve would just show up and tell me who the murderer is? She didn't even know she was dead. She didn't even know where her daughter was.

I turn to Will, my eyes widening.

"Neve told me her daughter is missing," I say slowly.

Will frowns. "That can't be right. She has one daughter, Ashley Bennett, fifteen. She's at Massachusetts General. The husband, Eli, found Ashley outside in the backyard. She'd taken a bullet to the head. He stayed with her, waiting for the ambulance, instead of going after the shooter. She's been in a coma since, but yesterday she started showing signs of regaining consciousness."

Chills scatter up and down my spine as Isla's words float back to me. "The girl who lived," I say.

You can still save her.

"What?"

I turn to Will, speaking fast. "Isla told me there's a girl who lived. Ashley isn't missing; she's the girl who lived. You say she's in a coma. She's stuck somehow, in that space between life and death. She's in danger."

"Danger from who?"

There is that shadow again, and this time I catch a glimpse of Isla flitting through the wet trees, blonde braids streaming behind her. I let the sadness hold me for a minute, cradle me in its arms, comforting as an electric blanket.

I think of Will's words. *Maybe you're seeing Neve because you* need *to see her. Maybe the accident . . . it's opened you up to her.*

There's a reason I can see Neve. I've lost my daughter, and the guilt is a wrecking ball that's demolished my life. That guilt has opened me up to Neve, to her fear that her own daughter will die and she won't be able to do anything to stop it.

That's why I'm here. I couldn't save my daughter, but I can save hers.

"We have to get to the hospital," I say, already moving back up the dirt path in the direction of the house. "Whoever killed Neve and Bailey is going to kill Ashley next."

Chapter 48

I always loved hospitals.

I loved the sterile scent of disinfectant and cleanliness. I loved the atmosphere, fast-paced but peaceful. Hospitals were a place of miracles, of inspiration and endless possibilities. They were where I always felt safest. Where else could you be surrounded by people who could quite literally save your life at any moment?

Hospitals were where they saved lives.

It seemed only natural to go into health care after spending so much of my childhood there.

I couldn't afford to become a doctor, so I got my nursing degree. When my grandfather died, I inherited the house, and it was a blessing not to have that financial burden on top of all the others.

I never stopped loving hospitals. In fact, I once worked in the very hospital I stood in now. That was more than a year ago, before I knew anything about Bailey or Neve.

And here I was again, surrounded by the soothing bleeps and calming shushes. I took the stethoscope from my neck and folded it into the pocket of my white lab coat as I stared down at the girl in the hospital bed before me.

"Hello, Ash," I said quietly.

I held a pillow to my chest, watching the girl in the bed. Her eyes flickered under her eyelids. Every once in a while, her face moved, a slight grimace.

"I never wanted to hurt you," I told her. "It was only your mother I was after."

My gaze drifted up to the window. There was a fly trying desperately to escape, its small body making tiny little thudding noises as it bashed itself against the glass. Flies would do that until they died, so intent on their one goal that they would kill themselves in their effort to succeed.

"I've always believed in looking forward. It does no good looking back, wallowing in what you've lost." I laughed, a small, mirthless sound. "And trust me, there is much I could sulk over. It took me a long time, but I was patient."

What I lacked in charm and beauty and charisma I made up for in patience. I was crafty. Clever. I couldn't have made it through my medical studies without traits like that.

"I found them. Found out everything about them. Bailey, she was easy. She broadcast her whereabouts everywhere. It was more difficult to find your mother. She didn't use social media, and I didn't know where she was."

But one night, I got a break. I was going through the paperwork in Bailey's real-estate office and noticed she was the property manager for Dullahan House, your grandmother's old home. Her most recent address was listed at a care home, so I visited.

"Getting the job at your grandmother's care home was a stroke of luck," I told Ash. "I heard the receptionist on the phone talking about a nursing job that was available. I applied and got the job. I called Neve with a phony story about needing to send paperwork to her most recent address."

Neve hadn't even recognized my voice. But why would she? She'd clearly moved on with her life, going to college, getting married, having a child.

"I won't lie. I was going to kill your grandmother," I admitted. "The job was the perfect cover, and it would've been ridiculously easy. But as I waited for an opportunity, I found I quite liked Holly. I decided that killing her wasn't what was needed for redemption."

That would've made me as bad as Neve. Instead, I used Holly to find out more about Neve. Where she went to college, where she worked, who she married, and who her daughter was. Holly told me everything about her wonder child. This was last year, before she'd progressed so rapidly into the latter stage of Alzheimer's.

Holly told me Eli and Neve were having troubles, but she always assumed it was Eli's fault. Of course, she ended up being wrong. Neve was the cheater, not Eli.

I suppose it is unsurprising how blind she was to her daughter's flaws. Isn't every mother ignorant, deliberately or not, to the weaknesses of their offspring?

I followed Neve and Bailey for months and learned the rhythms of their lives, a plan forming in my mind all the while. And then I found the video.

Bailey had a little cubbyhole in Dullahan House, handy, since she managed the property. Like I've said before, Bailey was always clever, but keeping incriminating sex videos of powerful men in somebody else's house certainly took the cake. She didn't even make the videos for money, just for the thrill of having power over another human being. Bailey was a fucked-up girl who became an even more fucked-up woman.

Her stash of videos went back decades, to one that answered every question I'd ever had.

Once I saw that video, I knew what needed to be done.

I heard a sound on the other side of Ash's door and reached for my stethoscope, my body on alert. I was wearing the pink scrubs I used to wear when I worked here before. Nobody had questioned me yet, but if they did, I would tell them this girl was my patient.

The voices came closer, then faded. I waited a minute before I lifted the pillow and placed it over Ash's face, gently at first and then more firmly.

I did feel bad; I really did. Like I said, I loved hospitals. Killing someone in a place meant for saving lives felt a little like murdering someone in a church. But I couldn't change what had happened. All I could do was resolve it. And to do that, I had to act.

It was time to finish what I'd started.

Chapter 49

JESS

Will pulls up in front of the hospital's pediatric wing with a squeal of brakes. I thump hard against the seat at the sudden stop, my leg throbbing at the impact.

I shove at the cruiser's door and snap my cane open. The air is thick with moisture. The sky is the color of bruised fruit, a strange apocalyptic yellowy-purple. A tremor shakes up my palms, and I sway on my feet, my head pounding, a queasy, shivery feeling in my gut. My body is crying out for a drink. When was the last time I went this long without alcohol?

"Coming?" Will shouts over the rising wind.

I nod and take a deep breath, steadying myself. I follow him through the sliding doors, out of the murky heat, into the hospital's chilly, recycled air. Will's pink face is set in a look of steady concentration.

Maybe because of the booze or maybe just my own unyielding demons, I've somehow missed that Will is a fine cop. A fine partner. I'm lucky I've had him the last few weeks.

Will flashes his badge at the receptionist, who immediately gives us Ashley Bennett's room number. We ride the elevator to the fourth floor, the doors pinging open just as a tall, Scandinavian-looking man with a week's worth of stubble mashes at the button. He looks distracted and barely notices when Will speaks to him.

"Mr. Bennett?"

Eli Bennett looks up at the sound of his name. His skin is waxy, his eyes clouded. I recognize the effects of trauma and grief and chronic lack of sleep.

"Yes. I'm Eli."

"Eli. I'm Detective Will Casey, and this is my partner, Detective Jess Lambert. Have you seen your daughter today? We have information about a possible threat to her safety."

Eli rubs the back of his neck. His nails have been bitten to the quick, flecks of dried blood around the cuticles. When he speaks, his voice is thin, hushed. "My daughter's in a coma."

"Could we just see her?" I cut in. I feel impatience vibrating in me, that familiar restlessness dialed up to one hundred. It's like an electric tension starting in my skull and working its way through my body, like a tuning fork stuck into a socket.

Eli turns his head slowly to me. Raw grief glows in his eyes. Grief, I've found, has a particular smell, like lightning strikes and burned paper. I can smell it rising off him now, like steam off a shower.

"We need to see your daughter," Will says urgently. "We believe there's a person here in the hospital who could be a danger to her."

The words hang in the air, bright and fluttering. A thousand emotions cross Eli's face: confusion, agony, grief, fear. Finally, he seems to shake himself awake.

"Come with me," he says. "She's just back here. Room 443."

We follow him down the hall, but as we move to open the door, I notice something. I shoot a hand out and grab Will's arm, stopping him before he enters. I tilt my head toward the door, a silent message. There's a shadow there, someone standing on the other side of the frosted glass window. I release my cane with a clatter and pull my gun as Will throws the door open.

A nurse is pressing a pillow over the girl's face.

The woman is wearing pink scrubs. She has thin, mud-brown hair and eyes the flat gray of dirty icicles. She is big-boned, as big as some men. I flash back to the masked intruder on the surveillance video. We thought it was Angus, a smallish man, but it could've just as easily been a biggish woman.

"Drop the pillow!" I'm off-balance without my cane, but my gun stays level with her chest.

Startled, the woman takes a tiny step back, the pillow sliding away from Ash's face. But she recovers quickly and twists her body toward one of the machines next to the bed, her hand hovering over a button. I have no idea what the button does, but I'm not taking any chances.

"My name's Detective Jess Lambert. And this here's my partner, Detective Will Casey. We're here to talk. We want to help you."

Her finger twitches, too damn close to that button.

"You don't want to hurt her." I speak with a calm confidence I don't feel. "She's just a girl. You've got two cops with guns on you. Step away from her, and no one gets hurt."

The woman contemplates what I just said but doesn't step away from the machine.

Suddenly, the pressure in the room drops, a subtle shift that happens between my ears. Ice-cold air washes over me, like the air-conditioning had been left on too long. A shadow moves in my peripheral vision. Adrenaline leaps. I swing my gun left, then right.

My gun hand tremors. Just a tiny shudder, from my elbow to my hand, but I feel it. I know it's there. The woman looks at me intently, a frown prickling her brow—can she sense my weakness?—but she doesn't move.

And then a chill skates over my arms. A tense sort of stillness, my nerves stretching and pulling as light shifts, shadows writing over the linoleum floor. I turn, and there she is, Neve, her face bleached as a dried-out shell.

Her arm is wrapped tightly around a slip of a girl, pale and terrified, who looks to be maybe fifteen or sixteen. She has green eyes and short blue-black hair, one side completely shorn, a red scar at her temple. It's Ash, the girl lying unconscious in the bed.

"Neve," I say out loud without thinking. "What're you doing here?"

I'm acutely aware of Eli's confusion behind me. Will turns to give him a reassuring look.

"You're the only one who can see me, aren't you?" Neve says sadly.

I glance over my shoulder at Eli, who's staring at me like I'm a crazy woman.

I nod.

Neve closes her eyes, understanding washing over her face. "She's going to kill Ash because of me. Because of what I did. Please, you have to stop her. Tell her I'm sorry for what we did to Sandra. I'm sorry. But Ash is innocent. Please don't make Ash pay for the things I did."

I keep my gun trained on the woman. "Who is she?"

"Her name's Robin, but Sandra called her Peep. She's Sandra's sister."

Her *sister*. I turn to face the woman as everything falls into place, every clue dropping like embers of a fire.

"You're Sandra's sister," I breathe. "Robin."

The other woman stares back at me, cool, calculating. Emotionless. I need to unbalance her. I lower my gun, readjust to ease some of my weight from my bad leg.

"Sandra called you Peep."

Robin tilts her head at me, her eyes narrowing. "How did you know that?"

"Neve told me. She's here. You think you killed her, but she's here. She says she's sorry for what she did to Sandra."

Robin's thick eyebrows flicker. "I don't believe you."

"That's okay. You don't always have to see things to believe them." I wipe the inside of my elbow across my forehead, where beads of sweat have popped up. "Why don't you step away from the girl, Robin? We wouldn't want anyone to get hurt."

"You won't shoot me." Robin's voice is soft, the soothing hum you'd want from your nurse if you were sick. It jangles discordantly with the woman who is prepared to kill an innocent teenage girl.

"I will if I have to," I reply.

"No you won't. You could miss; the bullet could bounce off any of this equipment or destroy the equipment and kill this girl." Robin smiles, the smile of a crocodile who knows its prey has nowhere to go.

"Trust me. I won't miss."

"You don't have what it takes to kill someone."

"But you do, don't you, Robin?" My voice is cool, calm. "You have what it takes. You killed Neve Maguire, and you killed Bailey Nelson."

"They deserved it."

The icy delivery, as much as the words themselves, slide down my spine, settle in my stomach like fire.

"They *deserved* it?" My lips curl in disgust. "They deserved to have their tongues carved open, chased down like dogs, their lives cut short?"

"For by thy words thou shalt be justified, and by thy words thou shalt be condemned."

"Matthew 12:37."

Robin quirks an eyebrow. "I'm impressed you figured it out."

"So you think what you did is justified? You think quoting scripture means it's okay, that you get to be judge and jury?"

"You don't know what they did."

"I do, actually. Neve told me everything, all about putting Sandra in a car and pushing it over a cliff. But this"—I wave at Ash—"won't undo what happened then."

"You wouldn't understand."

"Then make me," I say, trying not to betray the urgency I'm feeling. I need to get a grip on this situation, need to get on top of it fast. "Make me understand what happened, why this girl needs to die."

The only sound is the whooshing of the hospital machines between us. Then Robin opens her mouth and begins to speak.

Chapter 50

ROBIN

I fingered the friendship bracelet on my wrist as I assessed the two detectives standing in front of me.

Not Bailey's bracelet. Not Neve's bracelet.

Sandra's.

My sister's.

All those years I spent blaming myself for not convincing Sandra to stay home that night, blaming my parents for letting her go out, blaming God for letting it happen. Only later did I realize I was blaming the wrong people. It wasn't my fault or my parents'. I needed to be blaming those responsible. But of course, I didn't know who was responsible until later.

Much later.

I didn't need to break into Bailey's house to steal her bracelet. Just like I didn't need to leave the box of dildos at Neve's house. I wanted them to know I was coming for them. I'd lived under the weight of "the incident" my entire life, and nothing was ever the same afterward. Only once they realized I was coming for them would I kill them.

You see, I'm the one who found Sandra that morning.

I knew the moment I woke that something was wrong. Pale morning light was just starting to filter through the blinds, spilling across my sister's bed on the other side of the room. But she wasn't there. I could hear my mom downstairs on the phone speaking in hushed, anxious tones.

Sandra, it turned out, had not come home the night before. My parents were freaking out, calling around to all her friends. But no one had seen her.

My mom and I went out to look for her while my dad waited at home in case Sandra showed up.

I don't know how long we drove around. Minutes or hours could have passed before we reached Widow's Bend. Something gleamed in the lake in my peripheral vision, and I knew.

"Stop!" I screamed.

My mom slammed on the brakes and pulled onto the shoulder. I shoved the door open and ran to the edge. The drop wasn't far, maybe six feet. Sandra's car had gone over the edge, landing nose down in the water, which reached halfway up the door.

"She's here! Mom, she's here!"

I didn't wait for her reply. I scrambled down the rocky ledge and threw myself into the water. The driver's-side window was open, and Sandra was facedown against the steering wheel, dried blood crusted in her hair and smeared down her face.

"Sandra," I whispered.

It took all my strength to open the door, pulling against the weight of the water. Water gushed in, swirling higher up Sandra's legs. The movement had caused the car to shift. It groaned and slid another inch deeper into the silt at the bottom of the lake.

I had to get her out. I stretched across her, grasping for the seat belt. There was something there, something between the seat and the inner console. I plucked it up. It was a rainbow friendship bracelet, exactly like one Sandra was wearing on her left wrist.

I remember vaguely thinking it was odd, wondering where they'd come from. But I didn't have time to focus on it. I had to get Sandra out of there before the car slid farther into the water.

I shoved the bracelet into my pocket and shook Sandra.

"Sandra, wake up," I said and then again, louder, "wake up!"

She didn't answer. I thought she was dead; I really did. I started screaming. And then she moaned. "Help . . . me . . ."

It was only last year, when I was packing up some of Sandra's belongings, that I found an old, unopened letter from Neve. Inside was a picture of the three of them standing in front of the bonfire that night. They were all wearing those rainbow friendship bracelets. The same one Sandra had been wearing when I found her. The same one I'd found between the seat and the inner console.

I always thought it was odd there were two bracelets in the car, but I had no idea who the other one belonged to until I saw that picture. I told myself perhaps the bracelet had fallen into the car before that night. I even let myself wonder . . . it's stupid . . . I wondered if Sandra had gotten the extra one for me. But when I found that picture, I knew. The extra one belonged to Bailey or Neve.

I couldn't believe I hadn't put it together before. I'd trusted the police when they'd ruled it a drunk-driving accident. Sandra had, in fact, been drinking, after all.

Sandra never remembered a thing about any of it. A perfect black hole. And so it was up to me to find out what happened. They were always going to have to pay; I just didn't know how yet.

And then I found the video.

That's when I knew that some things could never be forgiven.

"They took my life as I knew it," I told Detective Lambert. "My mother, my father, both dead within a few years. Everything taken by two women who lived like perfect privileged princesses in their perfect polished houses. Maybe I could have forgiven them one day—maybe—if it had truly been an accident. But they put her in that car. They pushed it into the water. And then they never spoke of it again. All those years and none of them took any responsibility for the devastation they caused."

"Them?"

"Zac, Bailey, and Neve."

I truly lamented the fact that Zac had died years ago in college. He deserved a far worse death for what he did to Sandra. Bailey supplied the drugs that led to the tragedy. She was the whip inciting them on. But the plan to cover it up was Neve's.

They all had to be punished.

"What happened after they pushed Sandra over that cliff?" Detective Lambert asked.

"Sandra was paralyzed," I said simply. "After that, everything fell apart. The stress of it all was too much for my father; he died of a heart attack within a year. My mom and sister and I moved in with our grandfather, a hateful old man who loathed having to share his house with us. We put all of my father's things into storage, his books and bibles and teachings on the word of God."

"And your mother?"

"She held on for a few years. The death certificate said stroke, but really it was a broken heart. Losing my father and then caring for Sandra, it was too much for her. Sandra needed specialized care. She was paralyzed, but we also had to contend with the results of her brain injury. She was never the same person again. Her personality changed. She had a facial tic. Depression. Blood pressure that was dangerously out of control. She was never again the sister I remembered."

Outside the hospital window, a fork of lightning cracked through the darkening sky. Trees swirled and swayed in the rising wind. Hail clattered against the glass. And then thunder exploded.

"Do you actually think killing this young girl will make any of this better?" Detective Lambert asked. She seemed to be doing all the talking, brash and bold. Like Bailey. She was beginning to irritate me.

Anger snapped inside me. "I wanted them to pay! I wanted justice! They got to move on like life was completely normal, and what did I get? A dead mother, a dead father, a paralyzed sister. My life was ruined!"

I looked down at the girl on the hospital bed next to me, then back at the detective.

"You don't have a fucking clue. Some people deserve what they get."

Chapter 51

JESS

I stare at the other woman. Anger twines in my gut, so fierce that I don't know if it's anger or withdrawal symptoms that are making my hands shake.

"You're sick!" The words blast up my throat before I can stop them, slamming against my teeth. "Nobody deserves to have their life taken from them. You can't go around playing God like you're the one who gets to decide who lives and dies."

To my left, Will nudges closer. He's trying to get my attention, but I ignore him, my gaze fixed on Robin. She doesn't move. Her eyes are filled with so much menace that it should terrify me, but it doesn't. It only makes me angrier.

"You *stole* their future! And now everybody who loves them will never get to see them again. And it's your fault. How can you live with yourself?"

The injustice of it takes my breath away. That's when I realize the words are for myself as much as for Robin.

The dark fog of my grief and guilt swirls up inside me. It's been looming there, under my skin, ever since Isla died, and now it's made its way to the surface, bursting out so it's no longer contained, spilling into the ice-cold hospital room.

How can I live with myself?

My grief and guilt took my willpower, wiped away my focus, drove me to booze. And now all that's left is a woman who wants more than anything in the world to wrap her hands around Robin's throat and squeeze until she passes out. I want to teach her what it must've felt like, what Neve and Bailey went through in their last moments, what Isla went through . . .

The other woman's body shifts, and with the movement, I glimpse something—the flash of an old-fashioned, black-handled silver gun in her hand.

Time compresses, folding in on itself. How long do I have before Robin begins shooting? A minute? Less?

No. I won't let another kid die. Not when this time, I can stop it. Rage fills me, so hot and fierce that I feel myself leaning forward.

My finger twitches on my gun.

"Detective Lambert."

Something solid lands on my shoulder.

I want to punch whoever it is, to flail and scream and rake my nails over their skin.

Until I realize it's Will. He's closed the gap between us and is now standing by my elbow.

"Robin here is pretty certain they deserved it." Will's eyes dart to Robin's hand. He's spotted the gun, too. His eyes scream at me to pull it together, to deescalate the situation before more people die. "Why don't we listen to what she has to say?"

I gawk uselessly at him, my breath coming hard and fast. I've never felt like this before, never wanted to reach for violence instead of logic. Behind him, I can see Eli, his eyes wide and stunned, and behind him, two hospital guards have arrived. Their weapons are drawn, ready. I'm certain backup has been called; police will be here soon.

"Why don't I have a chat with the lady?" Will suggests.

My head thuds fiercely, like my brain is pushing out against my skull. Robin doesn't move, still completely emotionless.

"Sure. Yeah," I say.

Will takes a tentative step forward. He lowers his gun and makes a big deal about holstering it while giving Robin his most charming smile. My fingers curl around my gun in response, tightening.

"Talk to me, Robin," Will says. "Do you mind if I call you Robin?"

"If you like." Robin's voice is empty.

"Why don't you put the gun down?" Will says. "It looks pretty old. An antique, you said? You sure it even shoots?"

"There's only one way to find out."

"Where'd you get it?"

She lifts the black-handled gun, examines it coolly. "I found it in storage, with my father's things. He used to collect antique guns."

"Well, it doesn't seem fair, does it? I've put my gun away, but you still have your gun."

"Surely you know life isn't fair, Detective."

"Right. Okay, well, you said you found a video. Want to tell us what was on it? Or where you found it?"

"Bailey was a depraved, despicable woman. Her vile little hobby was recording herself having sex with powerful men. Not for money. Just for power. It all started when she was a teenager. She recorded everything that happened that night, and she kept it, used it as collateral."

Outside, the wind gusts against the hospital walls. Trees bend and sway. A branch rips free and whirls past. Thunder booms.

"What's on that video?" Will asks.

Robin's eyes glow with a sheen of angry tears. "Zac forced himself on Sandra. She resisted. She tried to run away, but she tripped and hit her head on the corner of the coffee table. It turned out Bailey had drugged her. They planned it all: she sold Zac the drugs and got Sandra drunk so he could fuck her, and Bailey got to record it."

I can feel the pieces falling into place, like marbles dropping into holes. The video I found under the floor at Neve's house. This is what was on it.

Will shakes his head, confusion etched on his face. "What does Neve have to do with any of this? Or Ash?"

There's a heavy silence before Robin answers. Outside the hospital window, the sky has gone dark, too dark for midafternoon.

When I look at Neve, she's still standing at the back of the room, one arm clasping her daughter tightly, her face pale with shock.

"It was all my idea," Neve whispers.

"It was her idea," I say to Robin.

A spasm flickers across her brow. "How did . . . ? Yes, it was Neve's idea. Neve told them to put Sandra in the car and push it off Widow's Bend to cover it up. They thought Sandra was dead, that they could make it look like an accident. But she was just unconscious."

Robin's voice has gone flat again. I know a cold, calm anger can be deadlier than passionate rage. I tense, tightening my grip on my gun. Beads of sweat gather above my lip.

"If Neve hadn't made them do it," she snarls, "Sandra never would've been paralyzed. Her life would've been completely normal. She would still be alive today. It's Neve's fault her daughter is lying in this hospital bed. If Neve hadn't hurt my sister, I wouldn't have hurt her daughter."

A sound comes from the doorway, something between a sob and a cry of denial. "You're a liar!" Eli shouts.

"Mr. Maguire, please," Will says firmly. "We need to find out what else Robin has to say."

One of the security guards grabs Eli's arm, begins dragging him from the room. Tears are running down his cheeks.

"No! Let go of me!" Eli struggles in his grasp.

"Leave him," I say sharply to the security guard. This man has every right to know why his wife was killed. Even if he has to hear the bad with the good.

"Where is Sandra now?" Will asks, his voice soft and soothing. Good cop in action. "Does she think it's fair to kill an innocent girl for something her mother did?"

Robin's face crumples, her features collapsing like melting snow. A raw, guttural sob escapes her throat. "Sandra's dead. She died two days ago. From cancer. It was a side effect of one of the blood-pressure medications she'd been on since the accident."

She dashes at the tears, her expression morphing into rage. It radiates off her skin like electricity. "*That's* why they deserved it." Her voice is again calm, ice-cold, but her eyes are shiny with suppressed emotion. "Sandra didn't get a say in what I did because she was dying, *and it was all Neve and Bailey's fault!*"

"So you shot Ash as, what, retribution?" Will asks Robin.

"No!" Robin shakes her head. "You've got it all wrong. I didn't mean to hurt her. She wasn't supposed to even be there. She saw my face. The day I broke into Neve's house. When I found out she was coming out of the coma, I knew she would talk. I wanted to stop her before she could."

Outside the hospital window, lightning forks the sky, a jagged tongue of white licking the black clouds.

"Did you feel better afterward?" Will asks quietly. "After you killed them? After you snapped those friendship bracelets on their wrists and carved your message onto their tongues, did it help?"

"Fuck you." Robin's eyes flash, bright and wild. They swing between Will and me. "Fuck you both to hell! It isn't fair if bad people get away with things just because someone can't remember it. What happened to Sandra ruined our lives. They needed to be punished. They needed to be responsible for their actions."

"You're right," Will says. "It isn't fair what happened to Sandra. It isn't fair what happened to your family. It's not right, and I'm sorry. I give you my word I'll make sure the truth comes out. But this girl . . ." He points at Ash lying pronely in the hospital bed. "She did nothing wrong. Why don't you just step away from her now?"

Robin's body coils tight, her gun moving a sliver closer to Ash's head.

I feel a breath of cold air whispering over my skin and then Neve's voice speaking urgently from beside me. "Detective, please . . ."

I lift one hand, placating, and take a tiny step forward. "You don't have to kill Ash. That's a choice you still have time to make. You need to find a way to let go." I inhale, a short, sharp breath. Because I know about things that shape you, that change you from the inside out. I know what it feels like to lose someone you love so much, the loss takes your breath away every single day.

"You have to find a way to let go," I say again, for myself as much as Robin. "Let go or lose yourself. Because some things you can't fix. You just gotta live with it."

"They deserved to feel the same pain I feel."

"No." I shake my head. The words don't hurt the way they did before, because now I see they simply aren't true. "No one deserves that. Trust me."

Robin stares down at Ash, her eyes flat, the emotion, the humanity again sapped out of her. I wonder how someone could live their whole life colored by hate, the taste of it eating away all the good that could've been.

Is that what happens when guilt turns inward?

Maybe that's what I've been doing, too, my own self-hatred taking a wrecking ball to a life that had possibility.

Finally, Robin speaks: "We all make our choices, but they are not without consequences. Not for us and not for those around us."

And then she raises her gun.

Chapter 52

ROBIN

It's true what they say, time slows when you're about to die.

I've heard this from numerous patients who'd survived falls, car crashes, drownings, gunshots, etcetera. They all said the same thing: "It felt like the world was moving in slow motion."

Most people think it's because our brains go into a type of turbo mode, processing everything at higher-than-normal speed. But that isn't true at all. It's actually about memory and our capacity to notice more when we are in high-stress situations.

And so it was for me. Every smell, every sound, every movement and memory and picture stood still for me.

I saw Neve's husband's eyes widen, his mouth framing the word no. *A security guard shoved past him. Detective Casey reached for his holstered gun, too slow because Detective Lambert was already raising hers. There was no hesitation there.*

And then, floating in between each of these people, walking as if her feet didn't touch the ground, was Sandra.

"Oh, Peep," she said. Her face was so sad. She was disappointed in me.

Choices. We make them every day, both knowingly and unknowingly. The only inescapable thing is the inevitability of choice. I said at the start of my journey that the wicked would be punished. That was my choice, and I didn't regret it. We all have our different versions of redemption.

Anyway, it was too late to rectify what was about to happen, because my hand with its gun was moving up, up, up before I really had a chance to make any sort of decision at all. Perhaps, then, free will, choice, was an assumption, a case of neurons firing, an unbroken chain of things happening based on conscious and unconscious thought.

This gun was not loaded, of course. The one bullet that was left in it had gone into Ash's head. And so it was no surprise when nothing happened. Neither was it a surprise when Detective Lambert's gun fired, an explosive ringing that ripped through the hospital room.

What surprised me was that it didn't kill me.

Pain exploded in my shoulder, and my body slammed into the wall with a sickening smack. I sank to the floor, my numb fingers releasing my gun. Detective Casey kicked it away while Detective Lambert held her gun on me. When I looked down, blood was seeping from a great gaping hole in my shoulder.

"You fucking bitch," I slurred. "You were supposed to kill me."

Detective Lambert's smile landed somewhere between smug and sad.

"Nope," she said, holstering her gun. "I've been responsible for someone's death before, and trust me, that shit'll tear you up."

"Joke's on . . . you." Blood filled my throat, tasting of iron and despair. I coughed, and it splattered my chest. "I'm going to . . . die anyway."

"Fortunately, you're somewhere they can save you pretty quick. You'll have a long time to think about what you've done."

She shouted for a doctor, and within seconds, someone was ripping at my pink scrubs and stemming the blood flowing out of me.

I slumped onto the cold floor and stared up at the gray tiles on the ceiling. A shadow fell over me. I blinked, struggling to understand what I was seeing.

Green eyes glowed against alabaster skin. Long dark hair. Tall, willowy frame. A front tooth just slightly crooked. A woman I never thought I'd see again.

"Neve?" I gasped.

It couldn't be. I killed her.

I was shaking with terror as Neve knelt next to me. She reached out a finger. Her touch was cold, a torrent of frost cascading through my body, the horrible, icy pull of darkness. And then Neve smiled. It was a soft smile, a sad smile. And I knew then that she would haunt me for the rest of my life.

Chapter 53

NEVE

When I was a little girl, I loved fairy tales. My mother would read them to me as I sat on her lap in the old rocking chair in my bedroom. "Snow White," "Cinderella," "Sleeping Beauty," "The Little Mermaid." Anything that ended with " . . . and they lived happily ever after."

Of course, I dismissed all the terrifying parts—wolves with flashing teeth, poisonous fruit, creepy forced marriages, gruesome tales of child-eating—in anticipation of that happily ever after. But in real life, there are no happily ever afters. There's just *after*. And I am heading there now; I feel it.

I turn to Ash and draw her close. "I love you, Ash. I'm so sorry for everything."

What happened with Sandra was my decision, but who is paying the price now? That's the thing about choices. They never affect just us. Our choices are not free of consequence, for us or for others they may impact.

I made the wrong decision all those years ago. I've known that for a long time. I thought by not speaking up, I just wasn't making a choice, but not making a choice is still a choice. And when you decide something, you also end something. *Cide* means "to kill" in Latin, after all.

"I've made so many mistakes, Ash, but you're the one thing I got right."

"Mom, no." Ash can feel me leaving, too. Her eyes are welling up, her face a mask of panic. I've always hated seeing her cry.

"Shhh . . . it's going to be okay."

I look at my daughter's beautiful face. I always thought she looked more like Eli than me, but now I see parts of myself in her, in the shape of her eyes if not the color, the smattering of freckles on her cheeks, her pointed chin and the arch of her eyebrows.

"I'd do it all again, Ashley Rose," I tell her. "Every bit of it, if it meant I got to have you. I would rather leave this earth right now and know I've spent this time being your mom than ever having lived a moment without you. Being your mom has been a gift. I have no regrets. I love you so much."

Through the hospital bedroom window, silver-laced clouds are huddled, like gathered promises. Light has broken through the gray, a pale yellow ray shining onto the tiled floor. I step toward it, knowing what I need to do now. Ash grabs my arm, pulling me back.

"I want to go with you."

"No, Ash, you have so much to look forward to. I don't want to keep haunting you like this. I want you to have a full life. A wonderful life. And that won't happen if I stay here."

I touch my thumbs to her eyes, gently wiping away her tears. "But I want you to know, if I'm not here and you don't see me around, it's not because I don't want to be. It's just sometimes . . . you have to move on, you know? But it's not your time yet. You hear me? It's not your time. Besides, your dad needs you."

We both turn to look at Eli, who has physically put himself between Ash's bed and the bloody drama playing out with Robin. And suddenly, I'm not here in this hospital ward but am instead sitting on the couch in our living room the first Christmas after we moved in. Ash is just two, her thighs chubby, her shrieks of glee filling the room. Eli is on the floor, helping her open a present, and I watch them, my family, and I am suffocated with longing for them, with such an overwhelming need to feel them in my arms that I stand and cross the room, scooping them both into my arms. And they fill the space that was there, the aching, desperate sadness, and they make me whole. They give my life meaning.

And I realize then that maybe life isn't defined by the moment you die but by all the moments you spent living. By the people and the memories and the good deeds you fill it with. I am more than just my greatest mistake. Everyone has darkness in their life, but that doesn't mean we can't move into the light.

"Tell him I love him," I say. My voice is so faint, I'm barely sure she can hear me.

I pull Ash tight against my chest.

"I love you both."

I close my eyes, and a kaleidoscope of memories plays across my mind. I think of Ash's birth, holding her in my arms in those first moments, her face squishy and red as she mewled weakly, entirely dependent on me to provide for her. Watching Eli fall asleep with her on his chest when we first brought her home. Her first steps and words and the pain of those first teeth. That day when she was eighteen months old and she got hold of a bowl of blackberries I'd left on the counter and ate every single one of them. I'd come in to find her little body streaked in purple.

Watching her walk into her first day of kindergarten, that first terrifying moment of letting go, releasing her tiny hand so she could step into a new world away from me. Teaching her to ride her bike, dropping her off at her first slumber party, watching her drive away for her first driver's ed class. Maybe that's all parenting is, a succession of moments where we let go and then let go again and again.

I think of all the layers of Ash, her past, her present, and her future. Who she will be at eighteen, graduating from high school, and twenty-two, leaving college for her first grown-up job. Or maybe she won't get a grown-up job. Maybe she'll travel the world or join the air force. Right now, her future is unwritten. And I'm so angry I will miss it. So angry I won't get to be there or watch her get married or see my grandchildren be born.

I feel like I was just cradling her as a newborn, walking her down that darkened hallway and tucking her into her crib, and now here she is as a teenager, a fully formed human. I can see the woman she is becoming. How swiftly time has moved. And although I don't feel like I've wasted any of our time, it still isn't enough. A mother can never have enough time.

"I'm scared, Mom." Ash's tears are hot on my neck.

"You've got this. You are the bravest person I know."

We are both crying, and Ash clings to me as tight as I cling to her, and I let the moment go on and on until I feel a tugging in my soul, a loosening, a release, and I know I have to let go, because love lets go. And I love my daughter so much.

And so I let go and step into the light.

I'm moving away from her now, the light and warmth and color of my body slipping away into a billion particles, like stardust or rainbow mist or the light scattered from a crystal.

"Do you still feel my hand in yours, Ash?" I say. My voice is very far away now, faint as a wind chime carried on the breeze as I slip into the light.

"Mom!" Ash is crying, but I can't go to her now. I couldn't even if I wanted to.

"It's always there," I say.

I see it on her face: understanding.

Over Ash's shoulder, Eli turns around, his eyes searching, perhaps sensing something in the air, an electrical current, a pressure, a chill. For the briefest second, his eyes find mine, and in that moment, he sees me.

I love you. My lips form the words, even though no sound comes out.

And then I am glowing light, sharp and beaming, slipping through the gaps in our world to the next, where I become dreams and memories and soft words and gentle tears tied to the hearts of those I loved and who loved me in return.

Chapter 54

JESS

I step out of the glass doors of Bracknell Rehab Center into a beautifully crisp fall day. The air is clear and brisk. The sun cheerfully climbs a cerulean sky. I haven't had a drop of booze in two months, and I feel pretty damn good.

I don't think I actually realized how much it was impacting every part of my life. My personal life. My job. My relationships. I wasn't okay, and pretending I was just hurt the people around me.

I snap open my cane and make my way down the stairs to where Will is leaning against one of the giant maple trees that lines the street. The leaves are now yellow and crimson, the ground covered in a riot of color. I've always found it funny how beautiful fall is when everything is basically dying. All this death in the cycle of life.

Will's glasses glint in the sun as he grins at me. "Well, look at you all fresh and sprightly."

"Fresh, maybe. I don't know about sprightly," I reply wryly.

Will pulls me in for a great bear hug. He smells of burned coffee and old ink and faintly, just faintly, of woodsmoke. He hands me a Tupperware container. "Fresh chocolate-chip cookies. Shelby made them for you. A congrats gift, she says. For making it through rehab. She's been there, done that and knows how it feels, she says."

"That's really sweet of her. Please tell her thanks for me."

I follow him to the cruiser and thank him for picking me up.

"You got it." He shoots me a smile as he starts the engine. "Partner."

I smile. I was put on extended leave the day we found Robin at the hospital. It was that or quit, and since I already knew I needed to go into rehab, I took the leave. But "partner" is still nice to hear.

"You ever get those MRI results back?" Will asks.

I nod. They came back the day before I went into rehab, the same day I heard Ash had woken from the coma. "Clear. No abnormalities. No lesions. Nothing. Nothing to explain . . ."

I let the sentence trail off. Nothing that could explain the things I'd seen. Sometimes I still think about why I was able to see Neve and, briefly, Ash. Why no one else could except me.

I'd watched Neve speak, laugh, walk, flutter her hands, and cry with emotion. She told me things no one else could possibly know. I smile to myself, remembering how she'd called Will "Daddy Pig." She was as real to me as Will is right now. And I had no way to explain it.

But something drew us together. The universe. Kismet. God. Whatever you want to call it. We needed each other.

I think Will was right: I was open to seeing Neve because of my own experience. Maybe saving Ash will help me take the first step forward into a new world without Isla.

"Maybe some things don't need or even want to be explained," Will says quietly. "They just are. And maybe after a while, they'll disappear, or maybe they'll change. Maybe you don't need to explain it."

Will drops me off at home, giving me a long, hard hug. "I'm sorry," he says.

"What for?"

"For everything you've been through. I wish I could make it easier for you."

"I appreciate it. I do," I say.

We say our goodbyes, and I go inside. I walk the old floorboards, my cane clattering loudly against the hardwood. I go upstairs and stop outside Isla's room, but I don't go in. Not this time.

Instead, I go downstairs to my bedroom and pack a bag. I lock up the house and go outside. I climb on my motorcycle. The engine roars to life, comforting, reassuring. I feel it then, the energy of my life and my daughter's and all the other lives around me, connected by energy and time.

And I take off.

It's dark when I park in front of the house, a cat's claw moon glowing in the night sky. It's a beautifully updated colonial farmhouse, blue with white trim and white shutters and a wraparound front porch with a hammock hanging on one side. It's obvious someone has done a lot of work to the place.

I cut the engine and get off the bike. I unsnap my helmet and drape it over the handlebars. The crickets are chirping, their cry for a mate elevating at this time of the year. The night is clear and cool around me, a visible strip of stars pressing into the velvet sky. Low-hanging mist fingers its way through the tall farmland grass.

A light gleams inside, casting a warm, welcoming glow out toward the driveway. I stare at the soft circle of light, feeling like maybe it's illuminating a path forward. I can feel my life expanding, dividing, branching off into hundreds of different directions. All of them, these choices, are available to me now, if only I will take that next step.

The farmhouse's living room blinds are wide open. A man is standing on a ladder, a paintbrush in one hand, his bare arms muscled and tan. A tool belt is draped around his waist. He's dressed in a white T-shirt stained with flecks of paint. His jeans hang low on a waist now slimmer than it was before. His blond hair is shorter as well. He's grown a beard, and a single splotch of white paint has dried along his stubbled jaw.

The urge to brush it away, to feel the warmth of my husband's skin, surprises me, even now.

I take a step toward that soft light, the moon shining like liquid silver above me. I'm one step closer to Mac when I hear something. I stop. Cock my head.

It's the familiar sweet sound of Isla's laughter.

I turn, catch a flash of pink somewhere down the quiet street. My eyes scan the dark as the wind kicks up, rushing from the shaggy valley in the distance, over the mist-cloaked hills, and through the farmland meadow and trees the house is nestled between.

A flurry of leaves kicks up, whirling like a mini tornado. When they finally die down, there is Isla, standing in the middle of the gravel drive. Her blonde hair is falling out of her braids, her pink Hello Kitty satin bow headband just slightly askew. She's waving at me, smiling her gap-toothed smile.

I step behind the trunk of an apple tree in the front yard. Its fruit lies bloated and rotting on the grass. My gaze moves between the warm circle of light where Mac is remodeling the old farmhouse and the dark driveway where Isla is waving.

Maybe, like Neve said, the dead cling to the living as much as the living cling to the dead. Maybe we are all haunted by our ghosts.

I close my eyes. Saving Neve's daughter doesn't absolve me of what happened to Isla. Maybe nothing ever will.

I feel something break inside me then. Will I ever be the Jess I used to be: mother, wife, detective? Because there is something dark and cold living inside me now.

But I'm hopeful. Maybe someday. Someday I'll be ready to go back to Mac. I'll feel like I can be a whole and complete person. Someone who deserves his love, who can hand to heart say she deserved the family she had.

And just like that, I have the clarity I need. I know who I want to be. Who I *need* to be. One day.

When I open my eyes, Isla is walking away, moving toward a scrim of mist that creeps with delicate fingers over the road. And in my pocket, my phone is ringing. It's the lieutenant, calling with a new case, a new chance to help the dead.

Maybe it's why I was left here after all.

I glance again at that warm circle of light, at my husband standing on a ladder, a paintbrush in hand. And then at Isla, who has nearly disappeared into the mist.

I turn my back on that circle of light. Away from the warmth of my husband's arms. And I get back on my motorcycle and follow right behind Isla.

Maybe some ghosts are easier to exorcise than others. But not this one. Not Isla.

She isn't done with me yet.

ACKNOWLEDGMENTS

I'm always so grateful to everyone who supports my books, but especially this one, as it's been a pretty wild ride getting here. Thank you to Sharon Pelletier for believing in me, even when I didn't. This book wouldn't be here without your energy and enthusiasm.

Thank you also to the amazing team at Thomas & Mercer. If authors write stories, publishers create books, and I'm grateful to be working with this team. To Jessica Tribble Wells for your phenomenal vision and for loving this book as much as I do, and to Charlotte Herscher for pushing me to dig deeper and write better, and for every single edit that made this book into what it is today.

Authors are truly the best, and I'm so lucky to call a number of authors friends. Thank you to Hannah Mary McKinnon, Kimberly Belle, Jess Lourey, Heather Gudenkauf, Robyn Harding, Hank Phillippi Ryan, Layne Fargo, Amber Cowie, Catherine McKenzie, Samantha Bailey, Megan Collins, Liz Fenton, Lisa Steinke, Daniela Petrova, Danielle Girard, and Rea Frey for cheering me on, believing in me, and inspiring me.

If you're reading these acknowledgments, you're the reason I write. I have the most generous, loyal, amazing readers, and I am grateful for you every day. To everybody who's read, reviewed, posted pictures, blogged about, purchased, and shared your love of my books, you've made my biggest dream a reality. Thank you.

My friends Danika, Aimee, Natalie, Ningthi, Joyce, Malinee, Andrea: thank you for sticking with me, even when I disappear into my writing, and especially to Joyce for giving me a major plot thread in this book. You're an absolute legend.

For my boys, Adam and Aidan, I'm in awe of you every day. Thank you for giving me so much to write about. Thank you for showing me a whole other realm of love. You are my world.

And, as always, to my husband, Richard, my rock, my warmth and strength and steadiness, the light that breaks any darkness. There are a lot of ups and downs in writing (and publishing!) a novel, and you've stuck with me, cheered me on, and lifted me up through every one of them. Thank you.

ABOUT THE AUTHOR

Christina McDonald is the *USA Today* bestselling author of *Do No Harm*, *Behind Every Lie*, and *The Night Olivia Fell*, which has been optioned for television by a major Hollywood studio. Originally from Seattle, Washington, she now lives in London, England, with her husband, her two sons, and their dog, Tango. For more information, visit www.christina-mcdonald.com.